# EMP RETALIATION
## Dark New World: Book 6

## JJ HOLDEN
## &
## HENRY GENE FOSTER

ISBN: 1548929298
ISBN-13: 978-1548929299

# EMP RETALIATION

# - 1 -

1100 HOURS - ZERO DAY +334

THE WAR WAS finally over, for now at least, and Cassy stood in her kitchen mixing drinks while Frank and the Clan Council—Ethan, Choony, Grandma Mandy, Michael, and Joe —filled the limited seating in her tiny living room. Construction was underway on a larger room off the east side, but it wasn't done yet.

It was a damn good thing she had finally persuaded Frank to take over as the Clan leader, Cassy decided, and she had been trying to get him to for almost a year. After forming the Confederation, an alliance of nearby survivor communities, staying on as Clan leader would have created a conflict of interest as far as she was concerned, and managing both jobs would have been an impossible task.

"Thanks for making us lemonade, Chancellor," Michael said, his grin belying the grand tone he always used when saying her new title. It had been almost three months since she had officially become Chancellor of the Confederation, but he liked to occasionally tease her about it.

Cassy saw that Michael wore his Medal of Generator, which he had earned during the recent war with the Empire

—their name for the Midwest Republic, which had been a growing power based out of Fort Wayne, Indiana before their defeat at the hands of the Confederation. As the Clan's military leader, Michael rarely took it off because he felt it was a good visual reminder of his qualifications to be the military leader of both the Clan and the Confederation as a whole.

Cassy brought a tray of drinks out and handed the first one to Frank. His rank as Clan leader entitled him to it, not that she was a stickler for silly protocols.

Cassy noticed Frank's new forearm tattoo. She had gotten a facial tattoo a couple months earlier, a mix of tribal-style patterns and a crescent moon, done in blacks and blues. It swept from above her eyebrow, past her eye, continued down her cheek, and ended just below her mouth. The moon portion was formed of simple Celtic knots. She thought it looked pretty good, and the smaller children were less frightened of her tattoo than they had been of her scars—the price she had paid to survive since the EMPs had destroyed the America she had known.

For Frank and the rest of the Clan, their tattoos—referred to as "clanmarks"—were vitally important. Since the Clan functioned as a tribe, the tattoo—now worn by nearly every adult, generally on their forearms—had a unifying effect, not to mention the convenience of easily and quickly identifying Clanners.

Cassy said, "Your tattoo is healing up nicely."

Frank moved his hand to touch it, but stopped himself.

Grandma Mandy, Cassy's mother, said, "I don't know why you all have those silly things. Cassy may have covered her scars with something she feels is more attractive, but the rest of you are just followers in my opinion."

There was an awkward silence, during which Cassy finished passing out drinks. She recalled her last exhausting talk with her mother and how Mandy didn't agree with her tattoo. She had complained that rather than covering her scars with makeup and being "normal," Cassy was yet again thumbing her nose at adversity, a fact that Cassy took great pride in. But now wasn't the time to have a repeat of that talk...

Cassy leaned against the kitchen island facing the rest and changed the subject. "Just so we're clear, I may have passed Clan leadership to Frank, and I may now be the Confederation's leader, but Clanholme is my home. Always will be. Hell, I built it."

"We didn't doubt it, honey," Grandma Mandy said, now smiling again. "This is home to all of us. I'm sure the new Clanholds will soon be all marked up with their own silly tattoos, as well."

Ethan said, "Some already are getting inked. It's that Founder's Effect I told you about. In a generation, you won't be a Clanner if you don't have the mark. You'll be an outsider. It's already starting, really."

"A sad day," Mandy said, though she smiled as she said it. "But if even our resident geek hacker says the clanmark is the future, it's probably true."

"Speaking of Clanholds," Michael said, "all twelve of them have logged their numbers with us, and I've equipped them as best I can with enough weapons and ammo to get by for now. We keep most of the ammo here so we can distribute it where needed, but it also keeps them from getting any brave ideas."

Mandy shook her head at him. "You know very well no one in these parts would challenge the Clan. It's invincible, or so they say as far away as Carlisle and Reading. Plus the Clanhold leaders are all from here, long-time Clanners, so the holds are loyal as a Labrador."

Cassy cut in before that old argument got even older. "Of

course they're loyal, and of course we should take steps to cement that loyalty." That seemed to mollify both Mandy and Michael. To add a lighter note, Cassy continued, "Can you believe it? Twelve new holds in three months."

Ethan said, "Well, the Taj Mahal was started long before the others. And thank goodness Cassy took pity on them when they were just refugees—they're damn fine people, and as loyal as we are."

Frank cut in. "Yeah, but Taj Mahal is a lot bigger now. The Indians who first settled it might retain leadership, but they have people now who aren't Indian."

Ethan nodded. "Two or three hundred people in each Clanhold, all within a few miles of Clanholme itself. And it's starting to seem like every freehold within fifty miles wants to join the Confederation as soon as they're solid enough."

Michael nodded and said, "Good thing, too. The 'vaders aren't gone, and neither is the Empire. Then there's the other threat."

Cassy didn't want to think about that right now. She changed the subject. "Where are our 'dirty dozen' Clanhold leaders?"

Ethan pursed his lips and shook his head. "Why not just be honest and call them your Jarls?"

Cassy's jaw dropped.

Michael interrupted before she could respond. "Because we're the Clan, not the Vikings? And we have no slaves, if that's what you're implying."

Ethan looked up toward the ceiling and held out one finger, then another, as he said, "Well, you have Jarls, the holdleaders. And you have thanes, the Clanners who joined other holds to get them established, or who earned a spot by fighting with us in the Empire War. And frankly, the Indentured might as well be the Viking slaves."

"So you finally arrive at your point. But the Indentured

can leave at any time," Choony said, speaking up for the first time since the conversation started, "so they aren't the slaves you consider them to be. I doubt any of us would ever agree to slavery."

Ethan usually looked cheerful or mischievous, but now his expression was grave. He held his hands up, palms toward Choony, in the universal no-threat gesture. "Whoa, slow your roll. Of course they can leave. But the point is, they won't. They'll work themselves to death for two years to earn their Clanner status and get into the next hold we set up, before they'd ever leave us. They'd be cut off, forced out with whatever gear they arrived with. Usually, that's almost nothing. If the choice is work or die, then it's slavery. And no mistake about it, that is the choice, at least in practice."

Cassy let out a long breath. "Ethan, the anarchist. It's an old argument. They made the choice, it's voluntary, and they're better off for it."

Frank nodded and hastily added, "The Indentured have the same legal protections that Clanners do, and anyway, they're only doing work they'd have to do to survive on their own."

Mandy smiled and said, "For most of them, it's their first experience farming, so it's like boarding school or university more than like being indentured. People can call it what they wish."

"Alright, that's enough of that conversation." Cassy took a long swig of lemonade. It was really refreshing on a devilishly hot day like today, when even her home's passive cooling system only got the inside temperature down to about seventy-eight degrees. "Make sure we have lots of refilled water bottles on hand when the Fourth of July festivities begin. We don't want anyone dropping because they're dehydrated. Not even the Indentured," she said, shooting a glance at Ethan.

Choony nodded, water supplies being his main duty for the day.

Out of the blue, Joe Ellings spoke up. "My money's on the *Claninator*."

Cassy smiled. Joe's outrageous southern drawl hadn't lightened up since he had joined the Clan after being among the White Stag army that conquered them early on, but that was another story.

Michael laughed at him. "Probably. The car from Liz Town—*the Lizzy Borden*—has a small block engine, I hear. It's fuel-efficient, but not as much horsepower as ours, especially with the woodgas they use now. Either way, though, a tractor pull between two battlecars is good fun for everyone."

After that, the conversation devolved into idle chatter and rumor-mongering, a favorite pastime with no TV available. Yes, Cassy mused, life had become as "normal" as it could be since the Empire War ended.

Cassy joined in the chatter, smiling and enjoying the company. These were her family, more so than had been any blood relative except her own mom and kids. Her mind wandered to the delicious watermelons growing outside, now perfect for harvesting. She'd have to fight to get a slice before the kids ate them all, of course.

\* \* \*

After lunch, Ethan went into Cassy's house. He left through the secret tunnel under the stairwell, which led to a bunker located well away from the house. It was huge, for a bunker, but most of it was either full of supplies and ammunition or set aside for emergency living space. Ethan had taken over a small portion of the main living compartment and set it up as a shielded command center, from which he monitored the

Clan's precious radios and securely housed the few working computers that Cassy had stashed there, shielded against EMP attacks, back when she was only a hobbyist "prepper." The bunker had proved its worth many times during the chaos preceding the Empire War, as well as during the war itself.

Ethan normally used encrypted messaging to communicate with Watcher One, whom he decided was an agent of the 20s—General Houle's shadowy private Intelligence arm. That bastard Houle could rot in hell, as far as Ethan was concerned. But the 20s hadn't contacted him in weeks, which was just the way Ethan liked it. He knew it was too good to last, especially after the Confederation had demolished the Empire's army—the Empire was Houle's lapdog. How much control Houle actually had over them was up for debate, but it was probably quite a lot.

Ethan clicked on the laptop and radios—he had decided the best idea was to check the radios and whatnot right away, rather than the usual later time in the day, because tonight would have the best fireworks display he had ever seen. With no laws to stop them, Clanners had been competing to outdo each other in making the biggest, baddest, loudest fireworks mortars and rockets they could. Ethan had joked that if someone didn't blow themselves up tonight, it would only be due to sheer dumb luck. He sure didn't want to miss the display.

As his laptop came back online, he noticed that he finally had a new message waiting in the strange little chatbox utility the 20s had planted in his computer system. The message timestamp was from twenty minutes ago. He sighed. Then he loaded up his "virtual machine," a sandbox in which he could open strange files from mysterious hacker groups without endangering his actual computer. Even if they hacked through his defenses, the virtual machine ensured they would only see what Ethan wanted them to see. It was a fake computer image, essentially. Once that was set up, he opened the attachment.

```
To: Dark Ryder, AKA D.Ryder
From: Watcher One, AKA Watcher1
Date: Today, 13:12
Subject: Mission Parameters
```

Dear D.Ryder,

It has come to our attention that the residents at your location have established certain technologies that threaten to complicate the plans of the Commander-in-Chief of the U.S.A.

Inasmuch as you have trusted-level access to the residents and their equipment, structures, technologies, and other facets enabling their continued operations, you are hereby issued the following commands. These are to be considered Top Secret, and you are reminded to limit access to those with a need to know. Authorization under P1776 Cypher: A9832BS59L.

1. Regarding the local creation of generators that enable production of electricity in sufficient quantities to restore lighting and the operation of powered devices such as water pumps, kitchen appliances, etc., you are commanded to alter said generators sufficiently to limit or eliminate their usability in the immediate future, for a term of at least four months.

2. Regarding the operation of modified civilian vehicles equipped to run from the fuel known as "woodgas," you are commanded to alter said

vehicles as follows: First, capacity to operate under woodgas power is to be eliminated. Second, capacity to function correctly upon restoration of woodgas power is to be eliminated. Both items to be accomplished in a manner that prevents operation for a term of at least four months.

Agent is to accomplish the above goals in such fashion that his or her involvement remains unknown, as high priority is placed upon the continued operations of the agent in his or her current environment.

Thank you for your cooperation. Please see attached.

[Redacted]

Ethan stared at the screen for quite a while. Did they really think "Dark Ryder" would obey those orders? He wasn't actually in the 20s, being only an asset, and what about the events of the last few months made them think that there was even a remote chance he would follow these orders? The timeline caught his attention even more. What was going to happen in four months? Unless...

What if Watcher One—his handler and a free agent like Ethan—hadn't reported to the 20s what Ethan had done during the Empire War and previously? The Empire was the lapdog of the 20s' master, General Houle in the mountains of Colorado, so Watcher One should have reported everything he knew. Which was quite a lot, actually. But the only way they'd bother issuing orders to their asset, Dark Ryder, was if they believed he might obey, or to provide him with misinformation. This definitely was food for thought.

A beeping noise made Ethan jump, startled. He looked his computer, but it took him a moment to realize that the message had self-destructed. That made the ".txt" file actually a disguised executable file... and it had zapped his entire computer along with it.

Or it would have, had he not loaded it into the VM. With a smirk, he closed his now-destroyed VM sandbox and spent a few minutes setting up a new one. That was a complicated bit of custom programming, and had just shown why he wouldn't leave the home network without a running VM.

Then he wondered at the self-destruct feature they'd used. It was possible that they didn't expect to have to contact him again, which implied that they felt they wouldn't need him after he completed that mission, but he didn't think they would do that prior to confirming it had been done. More likely, they knew he had a VM running and wanted to remove all trace of both the message and the coding they'd used.

Ethan sighed. Well, it was time to go find Cassy. Scratch that—it was time to find Frank. The Clan leader. Whoever. He left the bunker thinking hard about how much of this new information he should share with them.

* * *

General Ree surveyed what was left of his once-glorious dream. The Great Leader's dream, really, but his own will was in alignment with the Great Leader's. What a dream it was—bring America to its knees, and teach the Americans what every North Korean child knew. True glory came only from the people sharing the will of the Great Leader, and striving to achieve his goals. His goals must be the people's goals. His will, the people's will. Unity of mind and purpose brought glory to the State and its Great Leader, and thus to all the people.

Americans just didn't understand self-sacrifice. It wasn't

in their culture. He had once hoped that if their strength and their distractions were removed—which the EMP attack accomplished—then Americans would be more malleable. Trainable.

Instead, the American military, like cockroaches, refused to die. The Americans themselves fought against ridiculous odds, often to the death, like wolverines. Even the civilians! And they often won, too. It was most distressing.

To top it off, even after Ree had punished the American elite, their rich and their celebrities, stringing them up on lampposts to rot for all to see... Even then, the damned Americans didn't bow down to the Great Leader's authority as they should. It was almost as though they weren't the weak, decadent sloths the Great Leader had said they were. But of course, that was impossible. The Great Leader could not be wrong. There must be another explanation for the fierce resistance, the American pathological aversion to accepting the legitimate authority of those appointed over them.

The invasion had seemed like such a good idea at the time. Now, Ree suspected that even if the Americans hadn't retaliated with their own EMP strikes around the globe, they'd still be fighting just as hard.

Clearly, the Great Leader's agents in America had failed in their duty to report accurately. If his agents had given him good information, the Great Leader would not have committed this blunder. That was the only explanation. Sycophants reporting what they thought their superiors wanted to hear. Disgusting.

The whole invasion debacle was a compelling lesson in the need for unity of purpose with the Great Leader's will. Ree was confident, however, that his actions during this invasion were in unity.

Motion below, outside the walls of his north New York

City compound, caught his eye. He squinted to see better, and recognized it as a "Ratter," as the people called them— Ree's talented and loyal agents who were charged with rooting out American disloyal acts and thoughts. He didn't know if they were called ratters because they "ratted out" people, like in the American cinema gangster movies, or because they went into the warrens of the City like the rat hunters of old. Ratters were feared and hated by the liberated peoples of the City, which was a very good thing. They could often succeed without having to damage a useful worker with torture, just through the American fear of them.

Since Ree's temporary loss to General Taggart, his American nemesis, things had been relatively quiet within his own territory. While he and Taggart had fought savagely over the remnants of New Jersey, in the end, the American had built up his army by plundering Ree's agriculture depots, his People's Worker Army, and his supply centers. As every enemy win strengthened them and weakened him, Ree had been forced to retreat to this stronghold on the island of Manhattan, and now had only a sliver of land in New Jersey where he once had solidly held half the state.

Then Ree smiled to himself and thought of his newest program's success. He had split half of his holdings among his highest officers, and had them do likewise for their underlings. This created a feudal structure that made it easier to manage the whole territory.

An unforeseen benefit of that arrangement had been that the only way subordinate officers could expand their own holdings was at Taggart's expense. This quite effectively motivated them to push outward, because although the land they took technically would belong to Ree, he "generously" gave it to the officer who took that land. They were as loyal to Ree as to their superiors, who were Ree's subordinate colonels.

Since then, Ree had hardly had to deal with Taggart directly at all, and with only half the territory to police himself, it was much easier to suppress the vile individuality found among his remaining civilians.

Ree's gaze shifted toward the Central Park greenery. It had been transformed into a strange, mixed forest-and-farmland patchwork by using the bizarre techniques and philosophies he had learned from capturing some of Taggart's civilian farmers. Apparently, they had learned a way—a path called "Permaculture"—that was ideal for this post-EMP, tractorless world. No power, no transportation network to bring petroleum-based fertilizers and pesticides, no way to distribute food far from where it had been harvested. Permaculture needed none of those things, solved those problems, and was already proving to be as productive as the finest mechanized normal farms he had ever heard of. It took far more manpower to begin and to harvest, by an order of magnitude, but that was not a problem. Manpower, he had in abundance.

Yes, seizing some of Taggart's territory swiftly enough to capture the bastard's agriculture advisors had been a stroke of luck, and he was happy to allow his subordinates to consider their capture to be his own stroke of genius.

The larger invasion was failing, it was true, but things were going well indeed for the smaller enclave Ree still controlled. When a junior Korean officer brought in tea, Ree was wearing a satisfied smile.

# - 2 -

1015 HOURS - ZERO DAY +336

CARL GOT OUT of the truck and leaned against the hood while he waited for the meeting's other party to arrive. Four other vehicles—two big flatbed trucks loaded with supplies and two Liz Town battlecars—idled nearby on either side of his car, and he took a moment to admire them.

Battlecars had been the Clan's term for these monsters, and it fit. Thick steel plates, wire mesh over windows, guns up top... and of course Liz Town's cars were garishly painted in vivid colors.

As the Timber Wolves' Alpha, his people had tried to talk him out of coming to this drop, but Carl liked to stay visible in these things. It reminded his people who was in charge, and showed that their leader gave a damn about them. As a political statement, it killed two birds with one stone.

One of the Timber Wolf guards came up to Carl and leaned against the truck's hood beside him. He took out a pack of Camel cigarettes and removed the wrapping, then said companionably, "Want a cigarette, Alpha?"

Carl shook his head faintly. "Nasty habit. I quit months

ago. Tobacco isn't getting any fresher, either."

"Soon they won't be smokeable at all," the guard said, lighting up and taking a long drag. "Can I ask you something?"

Carl looked over at the guard. He was maybe nineteen, thin like everyone these days, yet he had a well-toned, wiry build. And he looked jittery—again, like everyone was these days... "Sure, man. What's on your mind?"

"Just wondering why we keep giving food and supplies to these Empire jerkoffs. Three months ago, they were trying to take over and those assholes killed my pa."

Carl smiled wanly and put a hand on the guard's shoulder. He understood the boy's hostility toward them. No, not a boy... a young man. There weren't many old men left. Carl, in his mid-twenties, was about average for a present-day adult survivor.

Well, there was no harm in breaking things down for the young man. "These people probably weren't the soldiers who invaded us. Most of the Empire's people are slaves, not fighters. And most of the soldiers we did fight were only there because they had to be. If they fought, their family got enough to eat and the Empire's protection. If they refused, the family starved while they got enslaved elsewhere. Or just cast out entirely. For those people, it was a no-brainer. They had no real choice."

The young guard frowned, and Carl could see his gears turning in thought. "Yeah, I guess that makes some sense. Liz Town would rather die before submitting to slavers."

Carl didn't reply to that. Of course every free person in Liz Town thought that way. The warrior's path was already deeply ingrained in the developing culture. Actually, it was kind of amazing how fast new culture and new traditions sprang up these days. But if they were put to the test, Carl believed that most people were simply people—they'd survive if they could, any way they could. Lizzies were no different, though they liked to think so.

When Carl didn't reply, the young guard continued, "It still doesn't explain why we're helping them. Why not send these supplies to Falconry to trade for outside stuff we don't make? Or give surplus to the Confederation to distribute?"

They were good questions even if they were above the man's pay grade, as Michael would have said. But Carl wasn't like the last Timber Wolf Alpha, and he made it a point to communicate everything he could to his packmates unless there was a damn good reason not to.

"It's actually pretty simple. See, we supply some of the eastern Empire zones so that we have fewer refugees to deal with. By doing that, we also make those zones friendly to our cause and to the Confederation. These supplies undercut loyalty to the so-called Midwest Republic so that when push comes to shove—"

"The Empire," the other man interrupted, and he stood taller as he said it.

Carl resisted the urge to smile at the bravado and chest-puffing of the proud young man. Let them be brave, he told himself. It might help them find courage in the next battle. "Yes, the Empire. What we're doing here today will destabilize the Empire at the edges, and maybe it'll spread inward to their neighbors. This could cut down on refugees, and that would be good. We're trying to get some of their outer zones to rebel, making a buffer state between us and the rest of the Empire."

"Yeah, but we could use those supplies. We've given away enough to start a whole new Band, reclaim some more of the people camped out in the wildlands."

The wildlands were the areas of Elizabethtown that hadn't been walled up with rubble and claimed by Liz Town and her several Bands. Carl was close to several wildlands groups, including Sunshine's group—they'd become the Sewer Rats Band after the Empire War ended.

Carl replied, "True, but it's a matter of priorities and politics. Trust our Speaker to know what's best for all of Liz Town. She deals with stuff above both our pay grades, and she trusts us to support her."

That simple statement let the young man know just where Carl stood, and what he expected from his packmates.

"Of course, Alpha. I do, we all do." He cocked his head suddenly and added, "I think they're coming."

Carl looked up from the conversation and saw a swarm of mountain bike-riding Empire civilians coming over the hill. "Show time," he said, turning to face his men. "Everyone get in position," he called out, and watched as the other twenty Timber Wolves took up positions with their weapons, either behind the cover of the vehicles or up in the battlecars' armored "turrets."

Carl didn't envy the people on turret duty. The fire that kept each truck's gasifier primed also made the assignment uncomfortably hot. Naturally, everyone called it "the hot seat," a totally different meaning than it'd had a year ago, before the world ended.

He steeled himself for what was to come and, head high and shoulders squared, approached the oncoming horde of Empire goons. Civvies, he corrected himself. He looked far braver than he felt, being so heavily outnumbered. It was a good thing he was there to give them those supplies at such favorable terms, rather than to trade fairly, or they might have been a lot more of a threat. Although the trade was strikingly unfair to Liz Town, Carl knew that the seeds he was planting sent a strong message back with the refugees: things could be better for them than they were already. Hope was a powerful weapon against the Empire.

As the refugees drew closer, Carl could see they had

sporting guns to trade, which were cheap since so many people had already died. They also had some weird, no-electricity gizmos—he'd have to ask his oldest farmer friends what they were for.

When they came within earshot, Carl smiled. With a boom in his voice, he said, "Welcome to the Confederation."

* * *

Nestor stood a half-mile back from the exchange, watching them through binoculars. A wiry man stood next to him with a notepad and a pen. He fidgeted endlessly, which drove Nestor nuts, but Ratbone was too useful to get rid of in spite of his deviant ways. Nestor often daydreamed of a time when he could let his self-control slip, let the *Other* out to play and rid the word of that hyperactive, scrawny whackjob, but as long as he could focus Ratbone's deviance onto the enemy, he was allowed to live. Sometimes one had to be pragmatic in times of war.

These days, Nestor found it easy to control the Other—his internal, more violent alternate self, who used to step out and dominate Nestor so he could commit heinous acts of unforgivable violence. Nowadays, though, there was plenty of combat to go around. They were opportunities for his homicidal, sociopathic alter-ego to come out and dance to the music of combat and killing. For weeks after a kill, the Other was easy to dominate, leaving plain old Nestor in charge of their shared meatsuit. Nestor felt like the body was indeed a suit, something he wore rather than being something he was. After all, he had to share that body with a guy who might just be the Devil.

Bah. There would be time enough for such thoughts later. Nestor said, "Write this down, Ratbone. Five trucks. Half a ton of supplies each, for two-point-five tons. Mix of food, ammunition, light arms, and swag." Swag was useless but desirable stuff like mini flashlights that worked, batteries, and so on. Not vital for survival, but worth their weight in food, and especially useful as bribes or rewards.

Ratbone said, "Got it."

"This load will feed my unit for a month, easy, and top off our ammo."

"Too bad Altoona isn't getting the supplies. It might have let them break away."

Nestor shrugged, and looked through his binoculars again. "They'll break away anyway, once we finish killing off the raiders out of Shitsburgh. Altoona only joined the Empire for protection, and the Empire delivered it by killing most of Pittsburgh's survivors. Nasty bastards anyway. Good riddance."

"Pfft. Plague was already doing that."

Nestor agreed with a slightly mumbled, "Yeah," then asked, "What's our headcount today?"

"Two less than yesterday, boss. We're still hovering around five-hundred fighters, plus camp followers."

Nestor took the binoculars from his eyes, then nodded. For the Confederation, the Empire War ended almost three months ago. For him and Ratbone, it had never ended. He may have lost a company of guerrillas to that ambush at the derelict train yard, but recruiting was easy within the Empire itself. Just about everyone who had to live in the Empire hated it. Nobody wanted to be a slave. Survivor enclaves voted to join or were slaughtered, often in brutal ways. Those who joined usually did so on the promise of help, safety, and food.

But the Empire rarely delivered on any of their hollow promises. Or if they did, it was only at the same time they moved troops through the town. Naturally, the locals had to feed the Empire's troops as they moved uninvited through their territory, so the effect was like holding a cheesecake out to a starving man, handing it to him, then making him give it back so you could eat it in front of him. There were a dozen other dodges the Empire used to avoid actually meeting the terms of their agreements, and everyone knew it. When the alternative was to be slaughtered, though, people were highly motivated to suspend their disbelief, and once they'd joined, it was too late to have second thoughts.

At least, it had been, until Nestor and his Night Ghosts moved into the area. The result was that recruiting was easy. Feeding and supplying them was the hard part, but this little gimmick he'd cooked up with Liz Town's leaders solved that problem. Sure, Liz Town could say the supplies were for the citizens, intended to reduce refugees. Most of the Lizzies even believed it, too.

But the Speaker of Liz Town and a few Band leaders... they damned well knew better. Those supplies would never reach the refugees, being put to better use with Nestor and his units. It sucked for the displaced locals, but they had to look at the long view. Those refugees climbed over each other to join Nestor's army when his recruiters came around, largely because they were hungry and scared, and Nestor had the food and guns. He worked with stable local communities and the Confederation, building up a buffer state between the Confederation and the Empire. That was a lot more useful in the long run than feeding some refugees who hadn't had the good sense to starve to death yet. Harsh, but reality.

These days, if you weren't in a stable community and you were still alive, then people assumed you were a potential cannibal raider. So screw the refugees, they didn't deserve the supplies anyway. Or was that the Other's thoughts bleeding through? It could be hard to tell sometimes.

"Ratbone," Nestor called. The little man appeared at his side again. "Figure out how many man-trips we'll need to make to retrieve all this. Keep in mind we need one quarter of us to guard the stockpile. We've got to get the supplies either to our base outside Carlisle or to the one outside Duncannon."

"Sure. But I think Duncannon may be kinda small for this much stuff."

Duncannon, a direct river crossing, was important locally despite its small size. The river doubled as a minor transportation route to towns downstream, and also a fine defensive barrier.

"True. But if we can get them to break away from the Empire, they'll be able to cut or steal all the Empire supplies going to Harrisburg and Hershey."

"Freeing up Liz Town troops?"

"Yes, and it would eliminate the usefulness of the Empire's westerly puppets. Maybe even force them to join the rebellion."

"Also true," Ratbone replied. "You're the boss for a reason. Give me twenty minutes and I'll figure out the logistics. Oh, are we still hitting those assholes in Boiling Springs this week? That'll factor in."

Nestor nodded. "Absolutely. That's almost as high a priority as this. Damn, two hundred people control the food production for thousands, and they're Empire groupies. Rotten luck for us. Our presence will be rotten luck for them, however."

"The Boiling Spring leaders had said they'd burn the fields and stocks if Carlisle tried to take any of 'their' territory, even while they gouged Carlisle for three times what the food ought to cost."

Nestor grinned, "We're going to surprise the hell out of 'em and let them know it isn't the fields that will burn."

Ratbone hummed happily. No doubt he was thinking of the joy he'd take in torching the village, Nestor mused. Well, that was despicable, of course, but useful. They were in a war, after all. Nestor assumed he'd have to let the Other out to take control while the burning was going on, since the bastard wasn't bothered by such things. Terrible and tragic things seemed to feed the Other, but then he'd sleep awhile afterward, leaving Nestor in peace.

* * *

A small crowd of a dozen Lititz people arrived shortly after lunch and had been escorted to the "Complex," the area where most of the Clan's tiny earthbag houses were built into a small fortress-like walled circle. The Lititz people brought a man with them, bound and gagged.

Frank recognized the bound man as one of the refugees who had passed through the day before, a few of whom he had allowed to camp outside the north food forest with instructions to leave quickly. He gave them 48 hours to trade and rest, and had generously refilled their water bottles and added more to the group's meager stockpile. Water bottle trash could be found by the thousands almost everywhere, so that had cost the Clan nothing.

Cassy had approved of Frank's decisions, but of course, that was probably why she'd made him the next Clan leader. That, and just to irritate him. He glanced at Cassy, who arrived right before he had, but she seemed content to let him deal with it. Appropriate, since it showed everyone that the transition of his leadership was real, and amiable.

Frank approached the incoming group as they exited "the Jungle." They were led by a Clanner for safety, to avoid the many boobytraps scattered throughout the intensive gardening grow beds. The Jungle's grow beds were fecund enough to provide the reason for the area's name.

"What's going on?" Frank demanded with a scowl. "Who

are you, and why is this man tied up?"

One of the Lititz dozen, a plain-looking brunette woman in her late twenties, said, "I'm Marice, and this piece of garbage killed someone in Lititz arguing over a trade. The bastard ran, but we rode him down and captured him. Instead of stringing him up like we would any of our own, we figured you'd want to know. And I hope it shows you what your stupid generosity to refugees has brought us." She spat on the ground. "You let them in. With all due respect, Frank, you're responsible for the damages he caused."

"Why bring him here, Marice? I hope not just to rub something in my face. You could have resolved this in Lititz without disturbing our work routine. If he'd committed some hanging offense here, we wouldn't have brought him to Lititz to deal with him."

"You gave him and his group shelter. We didn't want to string him up without you knowing about it. Plus, we thought maybe stringing him up could upset some apple cart for you, so we decided to bring him here to make sure it was okay to hang him. It's a courtesy. Rubbing your nose in it is just a cherry on top."

"But again—why bring him personally when you could have sent a messenger?" Frank felt a mixture of concern, irritation, and bemusement.

"We figured since Lititz expects damages, you'd want a chance to question him before deciding whether to make payment arrangements up front or make a counter-offer."

"What exactly are you asking for in terms of reparations?"

Marice shrugged. "What's due. We're asking for a total of ten thousand man-hours of work over the next ten to twelve years. It's what he cost us."

That caught Cassy's attention, Frank noted. Super. So now this would be a test as well as a challenge...

"That's twenty hours weekly, basically forever. Ten years is a long time, these days."

Cassy muttered something about being glad she didn't have to deal with conflict resolution anymore. Right now, Frank kind of envied her.

"You're kidding." Frank didn't sound amused, and his jaw was clenched. "How on Earth can you ask us for that much? Clanners didn't kill your man."

"True, but you did bring those people in and let them stay awhile."

"We don't know anything about the victim. Maybe he wasn't worth such an extreme number of hours. He may have been in ill health. And there's no guarantee that he would live that long. Not these days."

"No guarantee he wouldn't have." Marice shrugged indifferently.

"Your claim is absurd. Or do you really simply want to provoke Clanholme? A test, maybe?" Frank found himself having to concentrate to keep his hands from clenching into fists.

Marice looked relaxed, seemingly heedless of his obvious tension, and he decided that had just been a first offer. Haggling had returned to the world in the absence of currency and global supply networks.

She said, "I figured you'd say that. I have been instructed to let you know that we can go as low as eight-thousand man hours of labor. Or if you prefer, an equivalent amount of production, presuming we agree to the items, of course."

That confirmed his suspicion, and Frank let his shoulders slump. The tension went out of his jaw, and he forced his whole posture to relax.

"That your man died in a dispute with this person is truly tragic, and I'm sure the details will only be more so."

"Thank you for saying so."

Frank nodded. "But with that said, I must tell you that the Clan can't accept either personal or collective responsibility for the actions of a non-Clan member, engaged in non-Clan activities, and outside of Clan territory."

"Even though they were only here to commit this murder because you sanctioned them to stay?" She eyed Frank warily, then, and looked uncertain for the first time since her arrival.

"We'd be worse than foolish to accept such responsibility when it isn't ours to take. Of course, we'll be happy to escort the refugees you rejected out of the Confederation when their allotted time is up."

Marice raised her eyebrow. Hesitantly, she said, "You'd need to take them east to the Confederation-New America border and ensure none of them stay behind."

Frank nodded and smiled. "Oh, absolutely. We were saddled with that responsibility when they approached the Clan instead of some other group. That should serve your need to ensure this doesn't happen again with anyone from this group."

And, Frank thought, it would make sure the hotheads in Lititz didn't let a vengeful mob string up all three-dozen refugees. Those poor people had come from the fracturing Empire, fleeing a low-intensity guerrilla war throughout the eastern region that bordered Confed territory. The quality of life in the Confederation had inspired many to try to throw off the Empire's yoke, or flee to greener pastures in the Confederation, and a vengeful lynch mob could have derailed that encouraging trend, just as it had begun to gather momentum.

Marice slowly nodded as though considering the offer, then said, "We'll be wanting that too, of course. But the Clan's decision to host those Empire bastards led to this. And ten-thousand hours is what your decision has cost Lititz.

What do you propose?"

Frank allowed his features to shift into a sad, tired expression. "I'm so sorry to disagree, but I think that man's decision to kill someone, and your own lax security, are what cost Lititz a man. The Clan isn't responsible for either of those things."

Marice smiled. Frank eyed her carefully, trying to see whether it was genuine, but she didn't give him any tell-tale signs. She said, "I thought that would be your position. And, since we have no real laws or anything to govern disputes between Confederation members, we're in untested waters. So make a counter offer."

Frank froze for half a second. He sensed he'd fallen into a trap of some sort. He knew maybe there was still a way to resolve this problem before it became a real schism between the two groups. "It's simple. We appeal to the Confed Chancellor to hear our dispute and resolve it."

Cassy winced at that but remained silent, and Frank suppressed a grin at her expression.

"Look, Marice," Frank said, "this isn't going to be the last time a dispute crops up between Confed members. The Clan likes Lititz. But this is an important issue. We can get a process laid out now, when the stakes are low, so that down the road we'll have a clear way to resolve our differences quickly. What do you think?"

"Well," Marice said, "If the Chancellor is willing, I can take the offer back to the Lititz Council to see what they think."

"Fine, let's appeal to the Chancellor to figure this out." Frank turned toward Cassy and raised an eyebrow.

Cassy said, "I could appoint a panel or resolution court or something to deal with disputes, if everyone agrees to abide by the Confederation's decision."

"If our leaders agree," Marice said, "then yes, we'd agree

to be bound by their decision. Maybe it's even appropriate that the Clan and Lititz—the two Confed founding members —should be the ones to take the lead in resolving these issues."

Marice looked thrilled, and Frank wondered if he'd been manipulated into volunteering to give up jurisdiction in resolving the problem, but what he'd said was true. The Confederation needed a precedent. Not every dispute would be as clear-cut as this one.

"Very well," Cassy said. "The Confederation Chancellor agrees to act as arbiter of this dispute between Lititz and the Clan. Frank, Marice—let's go and talk about how to handle this."

# - **3** -

1030 HOURS - ZERO DAY +338

FRANK STOOD WITH his back straight, up against one post, and gazed southeast out to the next post fifty yards away. Another fifty yards beyond that stood one of the teens with a thin pole. Frank tapped the air horn once, telling the teen to move to his right a bit. When the three poles lined up, Frank gave the air horn one long blast, and his teen assistant replaced the pole with a posthole digger, and began to dig the hole.

Frank turned to the kid next to him, who looked to be perhaps fourteen. "That's all there is to it. Line them up like that so they run straight. Go two hundred yards out, turn ninety degrees to the right, and go another two hundred yards. Repeat. When you're done, we'll have the key posts set for the wattle-and-daub crews to finish out the new paddock."

The kid nodded, radiating excitement at having such an important responsibility assigned to him, and by the Clan leader himself no less. Frank played along, gravely reminding the boy of the importance of a precise alignment.

In reality, it hardly mattered so long as the wall was

roughly straight. Once the wattle fencing was up, and daubed, they'd have a walled-in paddock for grazing some cows coming in soon from the Gap. The hilltop pens currently in use were woefully inadequate, now, so they planned to turn that space over entirely to the pigs, ten more of which were also due in from the Gap.

Having delegated laying out the initial key posts, Frank headed in toward the HQ. On the way there to meet up with Cassy, he thought about Michael's desire to make the paddock walls from earthbags. Frank had vetoed that, as it would have taken too much labor and been too hard to add gates later, too hard to move as events dictated. Wattle and daub together made sturdy walls from easily sourced materials—sticks and mud—and it wasn't nearly as labor-intensive. The teens could lay the sticks, and they and the younger children could daub the walls.

Tasks like that gave the younger Clanners something useful to do besides pestering their parents, now that planting was done. There was little else to do beyond feeding animals and gathering early crops from the coldframes and lightweight greenhouses.

The latter were made of PVC and clear plastic sheeting, built with two sections, one for plants and one for chickens. The chicken droppings went through the flooring into a dug trench, where droppings and spent nesting straw were turned into worm castings. Those in turn were added to the plants in the greenhouse's other half. The carbon dioxide from the chickens made for healthy plants, and the chickens ate the pests that went for succulent greens. Everything at Clanholme was interconnected, adding to the farm's productivity in more than one way.

When Frank reached Cassy's house, he glanced at the digital clock. It was one of those huge supermarket clocks, visible for quite some distance. Ethan had rigged it with a

Raspberry Pi module to record the time at Solar noon each day, and that night it adjusted its time based on that. Every day, the time was set to actual noon, ignoring obsolete timezones. It also made it easy for everyone's biological clocks to tune in to natural rhythms. Without trains and planes, timezones were irrelevant to the flow of life now. It was no longer "a small world."

The clock was a nice touch, though he knew Ethan had only put it together out of boredom one afternoon. Frank had made a big deal of it though, both to excite the Clanners and to give Ethan the "gold star" he seemed to need from time to time to stay motivated. Managing people was as much about knowing how to inspire individuals as it was about organizing tasks. Frank took some pride in his reputation as a master at the art of keeping it all ticking along.

He reached her door and knocked. Cassy called out for him to enter, and he stepped inside after wiping his feet. His foot, rather—he sometimes forgot he only had one foot now. Frank spared a moment to curse the memory of that psycho, Peter, who had chopped his foot off as nothing more than a warning to the Clan.

As Frank entered the house, he saw Cassy on her customary recliner, a laptop on her lap. She looked up and smiled.

"Howdy, Cassy. Plotting evil destruction?"

She grinned. "No, just ordering a pizza from Blackjack's."

"I wish." Frank had forgotten what pizza tasted like, which bothered him more than it should. "The new paddock fencing is underway. Should be set up within the week, though I don't know how long the kiddies will take to cover it with mud." Dropping into portentous Obi-Wan Kenobi tones, he added, "The mudfight potential is great in those ones."

"Daub," Cassy corrected. "It's daub."

"Dobbie has no master. Dobbie is a free elf..." Frank said, grinning.

Cassy grinned, too. "Fine, jerkface. Mud then. Anyway, what's up? Need something?"

Frank motioned toward the couch with one eyebrow raised, and Cassy nodded. He sat down, parked his crutch, and felt relief to be off his foot. "Ahhh. That's the ticket."

He tilted his head back and let out a deep sigh. Then he said, "First, I wanted to let you know that Lititz is happy with your handling of the trial for that incident with the refugee killing one of their people. They would have liked to get more than one quarter of what they had asked for, but it turns out they hadn't expected you and your Tribunal to rule against the Clan at all."

"Panel. And we had to set an example of fairness. You did allow the refugees to stay camped out for a couple days, so you did share the responsibility. Sort of. Lititz took it as your stamp of approval, anyway. I know that part's pretty debatable. And for the record, I would have let them stay, too."

"I know. I won't argue the point anymore. I think that having those refugees work off the hours themselves was brilliant. Not only will they fulfill all those hours in just a month, those refugees get food and protection while they do it. It's humanitarian, and also practical."

Cassy nodded, smiling at the compliment. She set down her laptop and said, "That was a big part of the reason for the ruling, and Lititz knew it. It also had the effect of getting the refugees to police themselves better. Have you heard how well behaved the troublemakers have been for the last few days?"

"Well, I sure heard about the black eyes and busted lips on a couple of them. A nice unintended consequence."

Cassy grinned. "Who said it was unintended? If they're

going to be in Lititz for a month, I can't have them being unruly to their hosts. But get this—we're seeing way too many refugees from the Empire flowing our way lately. I've been considering how to address it, and I'm thinking of setting up more Clanholds."

Frank thought about that for a moment, then nodded. He considered the ramifications. Despite the risk of enemy agents infiltrating, that could hardly be stopped with or without Cassy's plan going into effect. "It would indeed solve multiple problems."

"Since my permaculture methods mean labor is only intensive during sowing and reaping, we Clanners have plenty of man-hours available to help settle new groups in, handle Hold leader duties, and so on. Especially after the summer fruits were gathered."

She was right, but shop talk wasn't the real reason for his visit. Best get to it. Frank said, "So, I've taken other steps to deal with the increasing refugee crisis."

Cassy tilted her head and said, "Crisis? Is it really that bad?"

Frank nodded, pursing his lips. "Yeah. There are more every day, and they're taking up our resources despite our efforts. They don't contribute much—they don't know how—and that's another reason I liked your ruling on the Lititz thing. In the meantime, however, these other refugees are everyone's problem, and we don't have enough surplus to keep supporting them all." He fidgeted with his crutch, which he had leaned against the couch next to him. "Anyway, this solution stacks functions," he said, using Cassy's permaculture term.

"Okay. Stop beating around the bush. What's your grand plan?"

"I've negotiated with some of their leaders, and we've made a deal you should know about."

Cassy didn't reply for a second, then asked, slowly, "What sort of deal...?"

Frank grinned. "We supply them—and I'd like that to be a Confederation responsibility, not just the Clan's, but that is up to you—and then send them back into the Empire. They go guerrilla, destabilizing things and attacking loyalist communities."

Cassy's jaw dropped. "What... Are you serious? That's something you should have cleared with me first," she said, voice rising a little.

"Do you know how hard you've been to get time with lately? We're heading off an immediate crisis. Preparations are already well underway, yet I'm only now getting a minute of your time."

Cassy took a deep breath and let it out slowly. "Fine, yes. You're right about all of that. But I had something different in mind. I meant that what you're proposing affects the precarious situation with the Empire. That makes it a Confederation issue. You can't just go unilaterally making decisions on the side. If the Empire attacks again, it affects us all."

Frank kept his voice level, despite the anxiety he felt in challenging Cassy. He was habituated to her being in charge, and deep habits died hard. "I'm not making a Clan decision that affects the Confederation. These are Empire citizens, not Clanners, and it's their decision. It's not on us what they do, and that's what we'll tell the Empire if they ask."

"It is on us when we supply them, Frank. The Empire leaders aren't the most legalistic people, you know. The fact that it's the Empire's own people attacking them won't matter much once they realize those people are using Clan supplies. We can't keep that secret—they're going to find out, and it won't take them long."

Frank shrugged. "I get what you're saying, but this is an

unavoidable necessity. We simply can't feed them all, and I don't want to just push them along to become New America's problem, or shove them south into the barrens. They'd die out there. And I did consult with Carl over in Liz Town, and he talked to their Speaker, Mary Ann. They agree with the plan, and they're coordinating with us to do the same on their end."

Cassy's head bobbed slowly, nodding. "Okay... So what exactly is the plan, then?"

"Well, the refugees told us that there's an active guerrilla war going on in the eastern Empire. Apparently, some outsider showed up and rallied a small group through sheer personality, and it grew from there."

"Do we know who those outsiders are?"

Frank shook his head. "Nope. Whoever it is, the refs think he has experience with guerrilla fighting. He's effective."

Cassy nodded. "So we're sending many of the refugees back to the Empire, all geared up to join that resistance. When the Empire's eastern holdings break away, the Clan will reward them by setting them up with Clanholds, or creating new Bands in Liz Town. Is that about right?"

"Yes. Or we'll consult with the refugees on setting up shop independently, if they want to settle in the breakaway Empire provinces. We'll teach them your permaculture methods and so forth."

Cassy said, "If they make it, eventually maybe they'll become allies or even Confed members. And the more people who know how to farm with permaculture principles, the better off everyone is."

Frank shrugged. "Meanwhile, they're off our backs and they're causing more grief to the Empire than to us."

"Elegant solution, Frank. I can strategize with the other Confederation leaders and see if they have more ideas on ways to capitalize on this arrangement. I think we can turn this into a major opportunity, both for the Confederation and the Clan itself."

Frank grinned. He knew his plan's scope covered both long-term and short-term results and goals. By creating pressure points the Empire would have to deal with, they would be distracted from their dreams of conquering everything in sight. Not only that, it would relieve the pressure on the Clan from dealing with so many refugees. It was a much better long-term solution than just feeding them forever. No one had enough food to save everyone—the Dying Time was ending, but he knew it wasn't over.

* * *

In the bunker below Cassy's house, Ethan closed out a conversation with "Pink Toes," one of his radiohead friends. Pink was originally from Florida, but apparently had fled the balkanization going on there and was now in Georgia. Things were only a little better there, as the Russians and their allies still had small enclaves in the Gulf Coast and southern East Coast areas. At least, that's what Pink Toes had told him. Ethan had no way to verify anything Pink told him, unfortunately, but it was good to have the information, even if it wasn't verified.

Ethan checked his computer compulsively, and found that a message had just come in. He opened the message, but instead of the usual writing, there was a hyperlink. He was already in his Virtual Machine, his safe computer sandbox, so he clicked it. The green-and-black chatbox popped open. Oh goody... He wondered why they didn't just open it remotely, as they had in the past.

After the utility beeped five times, trying to alert whoever was on the other end, there was a ding that announced someone entering the chatroom. It was Watcher One, dammit. Of course.

Ethan let out a sigh and hunkered down for whatever bullshit was expected of him now. He hadn't followed the 20s' instructions to destroy the Clan's gasifiers, generators, battlecars and so on, and he wasn't looking forward to having to explain himself to this jerkoff.

> **Watcher1** >> *Hello, Dark Ryder. I need an update on ur mission status.*

> **D.Ryder** >> *I destroyed the Clan's cars and generators. How's ur week?*

> **Watcher1** >> *Vry funny. Srsly—I need an update. Proceed, Dark Ryder.*

Crap. Well, he didn't think that would fly, but it had been worth a try. Watcher One's terse response told Ethan he needed to get serious. He clenched his jaw and felt rising frustration. After clenching and unclenching his hands a few times while he gathered his thoughts, he decided on the approach he'd take to deal with this. Something simple, so he could remember what he said if it came up again later.

> **D.Ryder** >> *Status: I have not had the opportunity. I am trying to arrange a window of time when I can go do it, but it has not yet worked. Each time I try, those things remain guarded.*

> **Watcher1** >> *I see. So, what you need is to make a distraction? Something to get people away from the cars and the generator?*

**D.Ryder** >> *Aff. I'm waiting for the chance. It'll come eventually.*

**Watcher1** >> *Oh. 10-4, I understand. Please expect assistance from the 20s shortly. You'll know the distraction when you see it—then you'll have the chance to follow orders and accomplish your mission. Be ready. TTYL, Ryder.*

*<<End Transmission>>*

What the hell did that mean? Ethan frowned. It didn't sound like anything good, whatever they had in mind. He sure would be ready, but not for their reasons. He'd be looking for the chance to thwart whatever plan the 20s had for him. Experience had shown him that when it came to the 20s, their assistance usually cost a lot more than it was worth. Whatever their plan, this was trouble. He decided that he had better tell Frank and Cassy about the odd exchange, pronto.

* * *

General Ree sat behind the desk in his office, his feet set heels together and his spine ramrod straight. "Thank you, Corporal," he said to the soldier who had delivered the reports. Ree waved him away, a bit irritated. Only once the door had closed behind the departing soldier did Ree allow himself to relax again. Appearances were vitally important to the rank-and-file soldiers, Ree believed, and he only maintained his own position by exuding confidence. Here in America, showing weakness could be fatal. Not much different than back home, actually...

He rifled through the reports and frowned. His new

vassals—his colonels, to whom he had given land and workers—had taken in more people than they could feed from what they grew themselves and from their shares of Central Park's bounty. This was partly because the bulk of the food wouldn't be ready for harvest for another month or two, but mostly it was due to their greed and mismanagement.

Major Pak Kim, who sat silently opposite Ree, narrowed his eyes as he searched Ree's face. It almost made Ree smile, because of course, he only showed Kim what he wanted the man to see. This was basically a choreographed conversation with Ree as director and lead actor, but Kim didn't know that. Kim's concern was genuine when he said, "Excuse me, Great Leader, but you seem troubled. Is there something I can assist you with?"

Ree allowed his frown to fade and slowly nodded, then ripped his gaze from the reports to look Kim in the eyes. "Perhaps, little brother," Ree said, gracing Kim with the honorable-yet-subordinate title. They weren't actually related. "It seems my colonels have mismanaged their Worker Army citizens and now have too many mouths to feed. They request increased allotments from the Central Park production. Have you an opinion on this matter?"

He did actually value Kim's input. Kim was methodical and effective, but unimaginative. Ree already knew what Kim would say, but it was important that he was allowed to say it, and that Ree make it a factor in his decision. And occasionally, Kim connected dots Ree had missed.

"My general, of course you can't give them more. It would leave your own people wanting. Your first responsibility is to manage your people and care for your workers, because this helps them to align their will with yours. Let those who mismanage their people suffer their own consequences, rather than putting them off onto their leader to resolve for them."

Ree nodded slowly, wearing an expression of deep contemplation. Finally, he placed a faint smile on his face. "Your advice is invaluable as always, little brother. Perhaps soon you too will be one of my colonels." Dangle the hope in front of him. "However, I think there may be another way to approach this."

Major Kim leaned forward, listening intently. "Yes, my leader? Will you share your thinking with me, so that I may learn from you?"

Ree smiled and nodded. "Of course. What if I were to respond by telling them that I will take all the people they currently have but cannot feed. My colonels will take one-tenth less in their allotments, to help me feed the people they send. Also, because of their mismanagement, they may accept no new Americans unless they come as a result of securing new territory. You recall that such territory is mine to keep or distribute as I see fit, but they already know that I tend to give it back to those who took it. They are hungry, my colonels, and will be motivated to expand our territory."

Kim's jaw dropped, but he quickly regained his composure. Ree didn't show his disgust at the spontaneous display of emotion, though Kim's impressed response was gratifying, too.

Kim said, "General, your idea is brilliant. Of course that is what we should do. But what of the civilians we take from your colonels? They already don't have enough to feed the Americans they'll send to you, so your ten percent will achieve nothing, and so it still will put you behind. It only moves the shortage from their shoulders to your own, which I must advise against. And taking more territory will give them more desperate mouths to feed."

Ree allowed a smile to cross his face, but this time it was genuine. "This is a simple matter. I will not consider the people they send to be part of the People's Worker Army. They are only refugees. I will place them on half-rations and then use them to finish my many planned walls. Those who survive that ordeal, if any, will be placed into my Worker Army units at full rations and full citizen rights."

Kim's lips curved up faintly at the corners. "Ah, yes. That is a wonderful plan, my leader. You stabilize the colonels' situation to ensure their loyalty. And since the people they send will be worked to death for the good of the People, you gain much food production from the colonels at no cost to yourself—and they will thank you for it."

"Such is my thinking."

Kim smiled again. "Only Hoboken will be an issue, sir. No one has seen Colonel Kang since the night before last. To whom shall I direct your orders in the Hoboken Territory?"

Ree placed a concerned look upon his face, and slowly shook his head. It was true that no one knew what had happened to that treacherous snake, Colonel Kang—no one but Ree. "It saddens me to think he may have abandoned his post. Perhaps he has decided to risk the journey to Alaska, and thus be homeward bound. I am told his personal bodyguard squads left with him, wherever he may have gone."

Kim nodded, and took a deep breath. "I have heard that as well. If true, it seems a desperate plan, but who knows the mind of another?"

Ree stared at Kim for a long moment, until the man looked ready to squirm beneath that gaze. Then Ree said, "Perhaps I will need a new colonel to take that position. Someone I trust, who will take their duties seriously. Obviously, it will need to be someone capable of dealing forcefully with any rival claimants that Kang may have left behind."

Kim, looking grave, said, "There is only one way to deal

with division, my leader, and that is to cut it out. Like surgery, it hurts, but it leaves greater wellness in its wake."

Inside, Ree chuckled. That was Kim letting Ree know that he was capable of dealing with the situation the way Ree would expect him to. He was throwing his hat into the ring for the promotion. "You are correct, of course. Provide me a list of candidates, please, so I can consider my options. I trust your name will also be on that list."

Kim was practically bouncing as he saluted and left Ree's office. It would be burdensome to be without Kim, but Ree needed someone utterly loyal in control of Hoboken, as it in turn controlled access to the City. He had no doubt that Kim, as a colonel, would be utterly efficient and analytical in deciding who to keep and who to cull, which parts of the territory to defend, what to conquer, and what parts would be best let go wild. Ree decided he would push the decision off for as long as possible, however. Perhaps one of Kang's ambitious majors would be a better choice than Kim. Time would tell.

Thinking of Kang, Ree felt a growing irritation. The man had been a fool to try to gouge Ree with "tolls" for supplies and troops crossing through his territory. Ree smiled as he looked forward to playing with Kang after lunch. Ree didn't do it for information, since Kang had none. It was just entertainment, and Karma. Ree would probably end the games today, and was already bored with Kang's weak-minded crying and howling in pain. An officer of Korea should have more discipline than that, which made the torture process so much more gratifying.

* * *

Nestor looked up over the trees all around him, taking a moment to enjoy the view of Dillsburg's outskirts. The residents were either too few or too stupid to post sentries along the creek his guide called Dogwood Run, east of town. It ran downhill from the village.

"Ratbone, I don't need to tell you how important this one is, do I?"

The bespectacled man beside him shifted from foot to foot with nervous energy and smiled as he replied, "No, boss. Dillsburg didn't get sprayed by the 'vaders, so the farms all around it are still good. And they're Empire all the way, so we get to do our 'thing' on them."

Nestor kept his face neutral. Ratbone only looked forward to exercising his deviant desires on someone. Would he skin someone alive this time, or start by cutting off toes one by one? Someday, Nestor would let the Other deal with the little psycho, but Ratbone was still too useful. There were times when those in command needed a subordinate with a taste for getting their hands dirty.

Nestor returned his attention to the path ahead. The creek was said to run pretty much right up to Highway 15, bordering the north end of Dillsburg. It was only lightly inhabited because it had few homes there, being mostly light industrial and warehousing before the war. Now, with dusk racing by, most of the workers should have left for home. Fewer people would mean easier pickings.

"Listen up, people," Nestor said loudly. This would be his last chance to give instructions before the attack, so he wanted to cover the basic plan yet again. He didn't want any screw-ups. "The top of this creek sits between a big lumber yard and a strip mall. If there's going to be people there, they'll be in the strip mall. Third Platoon, you're in the lead, and I want you to secure that whole area as quietly as possible. Don't let the rest of 'em hear us coming."

Nestor looked at the third platoon's commander, who nodded, then continued, "We then cross the highway, moving straight across. That's southeast. It'll take us to an orchard with a thick, tall privacy hedge to the south to screen our movements. We group there into squads and move east. Hopefully we'll have complete surprise, if third squad pulls off their part without noise. Remember, people, this place is full of loyalists. They made their choice—they're the damn enemy."

Ratbone spoke up then, asking, "Will we have you for our commander during this op, or that...Other guy?"

It was a reasonable question. The answer would tell his men and women what sort of tempo this op would have far more effectively than any speech he could give. Nestor grimaced, clenching his jaw. "You will be under the command of the Other this time. Dillsburg gets attacked *his way*, and they deserve it. We need to make this as messy and dirty as possible. This op will send a message to all the loyalists out there—the Empire can't protect you bastards, and if you support them then you will get what Dillsburg got."

Ratbone frowned, but nodded. Weird... Nestor wondered why he didn't seem happy to hear the Other was coming out to play. Ratbone was usually eager for that, but then again, Nestor's guerrilla army usually fought actual troops and militias, not civilians who were clearly noncombatants. Ah, so that was the problem. If even Ratbone had an issue with it, how must the rest feel? Nestor's guerrillas were merely people doing what they had to in order to survive, not monsters like him.

"Let me address one thing, people," Nestor said. "I don't like what we have to do here today, but we're Americans and Dillsburg isn't. They're with the Empire. They're traitors to America, and the people who enslaved your families. Maybe they didn't pull the trigger on your families. Maybe they didn't personally steal your food and leave you to starve. But they support the people who did. They believe in the man who gave those orders. They are guilty of the war crimes you suffered from. This is justice."

Nestor scanned the group of men and woman and saw some of them nodding, grim looks of determination forming on their faces as they prepared themselves for the carnage that was about to fall on Dillsburg. He continued, "They are not human, they're animals. Rabid animals who right now are threatening your kids. It's us or the Empire, and it starts here and now. Let's move out!"

As his force of nearly three hundred fighters mobbed their way into motion, Nestor took a deep breath and prepared himself. He could already feel the Other pushing hard at the edges of his mind, ready to take over the meatsuit they shared. That vile, disgusting personality surged with joy and power at the thought of the coming slaughter.

*Hurry the hell up, bitch. Have you ever bitten off someone's ear? You should try it. I think I'll do that, today. Suck it up, you prissy little uptight—*

"Shut the hell up," Nestor shouted, interrupting his alternate personality. "You get to come out soon enough, asshole."

The fighters nearby knew his strange behavior well enough that they didn't even slow down to look at him. Speaking of rabid animals, the Other had come out an awful lot lately. Sooner or later, Nestor reflected, rabid animals like him needed to be put down. But not today.

# - 4 -

0900 HOURS - ZERO DAY +341

GENERAL TAGGART STOOD behind a large curtained area in the back of Taylor Gymnasium, Lehigh University, midway between Allentown and Easton. The campaign to liberate south Pennsylvania had dragged on for months at low intensity, but the last week or so had seen the end-game flare up and things had gotten downright nasty for both sides. In the end, however, the invader-held towns had been freed and the raider towns were under heel. For the first time since the EMPs nearly a year before, the area stretching along I-78 southward from Reading in the west to Newark in the east was under American control. Previously, it had been a patchwork quilt of raiders, survivors, invaders, petty warlords, and worse before Taggart "pacified" it.

The ceremony about to be held here in the gymnasium would celebrate the region's unification into New America. The resurgent nation now covered almost everything in Pennsylvania and New Jersey, from just south of Scranton and just east of Harrisburg to the coast. At least, it did if he included the Confederation, which of course he did. The Confederation had joined in spirit if not officially, at least, but they did seem to be taking on the coloration of a regional power in their own right.

Staff Sgt. Eagan, ever at Taggart's side, nudged him. "You got fifteen minutes until the speech, sir. You sure you got it down? Can I get you some water? Wipe your brow?"

Taggart glanced at the curtain. "Yes, I have it down. I think. This is a rah-rah about how America is rising from the ashes here, today, beginning with them, and their duty to lead America's bright new future. Shit, are you sure you couldn't find some cheerleaders to form a pyramid in front of spark geysers in the background, with a flag overhead? Maybe with *Flight of the Valkyries* playing in the background?"

Eagan snorted. "I'm pretty sure I couldn't, sir. I think the junior officers stole the cheerleaders I had."

Taggart sighed, maybe too dramatically. He was irritated, though. "I mean, this whole assembly and speech is kind of like that, you know. A pointless display. I could be leading the fighting outside of Scranton, but here I am talking to these survivors—most of whom were cannibals and raiders pretty damn recently. But I suppose we need to let them put that messy chapter behind them. They want something to look forward to and need something to motivate them through the hard times ahead."

"I totally agree, sir."

Taggart nodded. "I imagine there have been other presidents who had to make similar choices. At least I'm in good company. I'd rather it was one of them making this silly speech, though."

"The choice of whether to punish or unify? Yeah. Washington and Lincoln, for example. Because you're totally on their level. Really, sir."

"You're such a shitbird, Eagan. Lincoln got shot."

Taggart's sidekick smirked, but then changed the subject.

"Have you decided what to do about the Philly metro area, sir?"

"We haven't liberated Philly. They've made it clear they'll fight us rather than let outsiders call the shots for them, because they've seen how well that worked out before."

"Yeah. Are we going to call the shots anyway, do you think, or..."

"No. They aren't with us, and they sure don't have the resources to make it worth the effort and losses to force them to join up. Not when we can fight actual invaders instead of other Americans. We'll continue to focus on the Scranton campaign, and just cordon off Philadelphia."

"Good," Eagan said, though he looked sad.

Both men knew the recovering American forces couldn't afford to fight voluntary-breakaway areas into submission and then have to feed all those empty mouths. Most of those breakaway urban areas wouldn't contribute anything back, so New America was still too close to the subsistence level to force the issue. Maybe next year.

"They may join later, when most have died off," Eagan added, somewhat mirroring Taggart's thoughts, but he didn't sound like he particularly hoped it would happen.

Taggart didn't reply. What could he add to what Eagan had said? It was accurate. Taggart didn't want to deal with places like Philly any more than Eagan did.

Taggart pulled his uniform jacket to straighten it out, preparing for his speech. What a crock. How the hell did he get roped into pretending to be the President of the United States? He didn't control all of one state, much less several united ones. Oh well, these were strange times.

He glanced at his watch. Five minutes until he had to step out to the podium. "I guess I better get used to this crap."

* * *

It was a bit early for lunch, but Carl had half a dozen appointments later in the day and he had promised Sunshine they'd eat together. He had sent a messenger to let her know of the schedule change. Actually, he had tried to meet with the leader of the Sewer Rats for lunch or dinner every day for the last four days, but things kept coming up to make it impossible. It was damn frustrating, but today, he had vowed, nothing would stand in the way.

Carl started his motorized bicycle and headed through Liz Town, aiming toward Orange Street. It ran through the center of Timber Wolf territory, and Sunshine was supposed to meet him at the food truck that parked at Orange and Hanover. It was one of their favorite eating joints. What those cooks could do with chicken on a simple rocket stove was magical, though he doubted it was really chicken meat.

At Spruce Street, a block from his destination, his radio crackled. He only carried a little civilian half-mile radio with three channels, nothing fancy, but it worked for non-secure comms while he was out and about. "My Alpha, your office reports that you have an urgent unscheduled meeting with the leader of the Puma Band, ETA twenty minutes."

The voice dripped with disdain when he named the Band. Carl tended to agree, but then, no one liked Puma. General consensus was that the whole lot of them were nothing but little two-faced shits. Nonetheless, they were Lizzies, and he could hardly deny an urgent meeting request from another Band's leader.

It was odd for Puma to request such a meeting, though, since they tended to keep to themselves whenever possible. Carl wondered what they wanted. Probably more ammo again, as if they even needed it. They were safely to the south of the college in peaceful territory. In contrast, the Timber

Wolves had the turf facing the wildlands outside the walls, and all the threats that came with that. More ammo for Puma could only come out of stockpiles the Timber Wolves drew from, so if they had the nerve to ask for that, it would be a contentious meeting.

Or maybe he *could* blow them off. Carl keyed up his radio, then said, "What does the Puma leader want now, anyway? I have plans today."

"Sir, not the Puma's interim leader. The meeting is with their minority leader. Apparently, she'll throw her support behind a stronger alliance and trade treaty with Timber Wolf if you'll support her campaign to become Puma's Matriarch. If we send supplies to them, she feels she can buy off some of their interim's followers. In return for our help, they'll also pay a higher tax to Liz Town, on top of offering favorable trade terms with our Band."

Damn. There was no way he could dodge this meeting, then. This felt like the break he had been looking for—he had been trying to get this sort of deal with the Puma opposition leader for weeks. Damn them, why now?

Carl acknowledged the meeting, got the location, and then continued on toward the food truck. He'd have to apologize to Sunshine, blow her off yet again. They got along so well and had so much in common. He reminded himself that it wasn't as though they were dating, or anything, yet if he was honest with himself, he had already decided that he'd like to be with her. She certainly had always made it clear she wanted to be with him, and he'd long thought about it. Now they were finally in a position where he could be sure he wasn't taking advantage of her situation. This should be easy, so why was it proving impossible to get together for a simple meal?

Pulling up near the food truck, he dismounted and laid his bike down, then headed toward the picnic tables set up nearby on the sidewalk. Sunshine sat at one, but the table was empty, so she hadn't yet ordered for them. She was waiting for him, but he'd have to disappoint her yet again.

He forced himself to smile at her as he got to the table, and said, "Hello there, Sunshine. Thanks for meeting me."

He slid onto the bench opposite her, moving rather carefully to avoid getting a splinter somewhere embarrassing. The aging, peeling pine benches were notorious for that, and no one had bothered to sand them down and repaint them.

Sunshine smiled back warmly. "About time you actually showed up. This is, what, the third time we're trying to have a bite together? A girl might start to think you're ditching her."

"Fourth time." Ouch, that didn't help his cause. "And no way I'm ditching. You lead a Band. You know how it is. Time is in shorter supply than bullets."

She took her hands off the table and moved them to her lap. "I know what my priorities are," she said, staring into his eyes. She still wore a faint smile, but her eyes showed wariness. Maybe she expected him to bail out again.

Well, this was going to suck. "Sunny, you *are* my priority. It's just that our duties outweigh our personal priorities."

"Duties like meeting with Empire goons and giving them our food and guns?" Her eyes narrowed slightly. His arrangement with the Empire's secessionist guerrillas had been an ongoing point of contention between them.

"We've been through that talk before. You know my position—"

Sunshine snapped at him, interrupting, "Which is that destabilizing the Empire is more important than helping Lizzies."

"Wildlanders," he corrected her. "If the Empire comes back, who do you think suffers first? Wildlanders. If they cut off the wandering merchants, who suffers most? Wildlanders. The people outside our gates get by right now, but they won't if the Empire comes back again with even more troops. We barely survived the last invasion."

Sunshine's lips pressed together tightly, but she broke eye contact and looked down at the table. "I understand your position. But it's so *practical*. What about human decency? You used to do a lot for the wildlanders, but now?"

"I can't help the wildlanders more than I already do. I've always helped however I could, and not only because it was strategically sound policy. But I remind you that you aren't a wildlander anymore. You have a real Band. You aren't outside the walls—you're in Liz Town, here with me."

"You still haven't made any kind of move on me, Carl. I practically threw myself at you, back when I was a wildlander and you were just using us as a resource. I figured you never 'made a move on me' because I was a wildlander."

"Sunny, you being a wildlander was never the issue. I really did like you, even then. I still do. But at the time, I never knew if you were coming onto me because I could give you more food and supplies, or if it was because I'm a Lizzie and I could have taken you away from a rough life as a wildlander. I didn't want to abuse my upper hand, or take advantage of you."

Her eyes flared. "Well I wanted you to! And yet you *still* spend less time with me now than you did when you had to sneak the hell out of Liz Town just to see me."

"But you have to—"

"Back when it was all business, you made the time. It's called *priorities*, Carl."

"Back then, the politics in Liz Town were more complicated, more divided. Murderous, even. Timber Wolves needed to court wildlanders in case they ever needed to call on them for help inside the wall, and that saved my life, remember? But things are different now under Kodiak leadership. The new Speaker, Mary Ann, has everyone's support except Diamondback, and they're too busy infighting for who's really going to be their next Alpha, ever since their quisling was executed with that traitorous snake Pamela."

"What the hell does that have to do with right now? God, Carl. If you don't want me, say so and I'll move on. So?"

"So, I don't spend a lot of time outside the wall talking to wildlanders anymore. It's not a fair comparison. I mean, we still send out supplies on the sly just like we used to. I like to help them as I can, but—"

"And when are you going to help me and you?"

Carl felt irritation rising into anger. "What 'us'? We aren't technically anything more than friends."

"You do realize that's your fault, not mine, right?"

Carl felt his anger drain away a bit. He realized it was frustration, and he really had no reason to be angry with her. At himself, yes, but not at her. Knowing it didn't stop him from feeling irritated, though. "Sunshine, you just have to realize that I have duties I can't ignore. This leader crap is the reason I turned down the Alpha spot and being the Liz Town Speaker's right-hand man, the last time around. I agreed this time, under Mary Ann as Speaker, because I saw how it turned out when I walked away from my duty. Shit went really bad, if you remember. I'm doing what I can to keep it from going bad again."

Sunshine stared into his eyes for a long moment, and Carl got the distinct feeling she was evaluating the truth of his words. She was making some sort of decision, and apprehension replaced his irritation.

She said, "Fine. Then come with me right now."

"I really can't. I have a meeting in ten minutes that could change Timber Wolf fortunes for the better, bring Puma into the fold, and eliminate a tough personal enemy." Carl's fists clenched slightly when he thought of the interim Puma leader, a stone-cold bastard who had it in for him. "Most importantly," he continued, "it could finish unifying Liz Town. We need that unity to survive the challenges we know are coming, and if I just shine it on, this chance will be gone. My beta just told me the Puma opposition is ready to throw in with us. You can't ask me to let that chance go. It's too important for my Band, and for Liz Town."

Sunshine closed her eyes and said, "I guess you should get going then, Carl. You don't want to miss your important meeting. I get it—you have duties. I'll be fine." She smiled at him wanly.

Carl eyed her warily. Her change of tone was too abrupt, and he felt alarm bells going off in his mind. "You sure you're going to be okay? Is there anything I can do for you later, maybe? Some way I can make this up to you."

Sunshine slowly shook her head. "No, but thanks. I know your schedule is packed for the rest of the day. I'll see you later."

Blinking rapidly, she got up and spun on her heels. Then she walked away, her back straight and stiff, and didn't look back.

Carl felt his heart drop, leaving something empty in its place. His mind raced. He hated having to disappoint her so deeply, yes, but he was stuck in the real world and really did have duties to take care of. Things that were more important, more urgent than his own desires. She would just have to understand that. They could get through it, though. He'd make it up to her later. There was always a later, right? There just had to be.

\* \* \*

Cassy watched her front door close as the last of her visitors left. She intended to spend the rest of her day on the computer or on the radio, compiling information and communicating with outlying areas. She also had to be available to Taggart's lieutenants to answer questions about permaculture responses to specific problems their communities were having. It was tedious and exhausting.

There was another knock at her door, and Cassy groaned. She straightened her blouse, ran fingers through her hair, and hollered for whoever was outside to enter. She was surprised to see Frank, and she couldn't resist smiling at him. "You're a welcome sight for my exhausted eyes."

Frank gave her a half-smile. "I know, I'm sexy as hell. You're welcome."

"Have a seat," she said. "How can I help you?"

He nodded in thanks, and sat down on the small couch. "I'll cut to the chase. I'm getting a lot of complaints from Clanners."

"About what?" Cassy suspected it had to do with her, or Frank wouldn't bring it to her attention.

"The complaints are about the traffic you get here. It's disruptive to our daily chores, training routines, the works. These strangers traipsing in and out aren't Clanners, and half of them trample plants they think are weeds, they get in the way of people on errands, they always want to chatter while we're trying to move cows to another paddock or transplant seedlings. They're just underfoot."

She hadn't considered that before, but it made sense. Her house, the original little Clanholme retreat she had built long before the EMPs, was now dead center in all the Clan's bustling daily activities. "I can't really move my house away from where it is, unless you know a way. Got any suggestions for how to resolve this?"

"I do, actually." Frank smiled at her mischievously. "We want to banish you from your house."

"Say what?" Cassy tilted her head and eyed him warily.

Maybe this was a prank, payback for some earlier shenanigans on her part.

"You heard me. Kick you out. The idea is to make you go meet these outsiders somewhere else, instead of at HQ. It'll get them out of our hair if you aren't here."

Cassy grinned. "I knew you'd think of something to get rid of me, eventually."

"I know, right? I'm a genius that way. But seriously, I'd like you to think about setting up shop somewhere outside of Clanholme."

Cassy thought about what she'd need for that to happen. "Maybe out on the edge, somewhere along the main path in. Michael will probably know a good, defensible place to put a meeting room. A visitor center? Whatever."

Frank nodded. "Maybe an easy walk from home, but far enough out of the way so people who come to meet with you won't mosey over here out of boredom, not without something particular in mind to do."

Cassy decided it was actually a smart idea. Not only would it reduce the distractions for the Clanners, it would also reduce her own distractions *from* the Clanners, who liked to stop by and chatter a lot. That was great, but it often got in the way of her work. "How about that old fireworks stand by the turnpike? It's close enough to walk to, but far enough away to keep visitors out of the Clan's hair."

"Interesting. It's pretty big for a Tuff-Shed, and we could easily remodel it, spruce it up, fit in a storage pit or something for coffee and such, where the kids won't loot it."

Cassy nodded. "We could have that up and running by the anniversary of the first EMP."

Frank smiled. "Why, so you can hide out and avoid the celebration?"

"Now why would I want to do that?" she asked, feigning shock.

"Because the one-year anniversary of the EMPs will be a sad day for us all. We've decided to celebrate being alive instead of mourning America's death, and people are already planning to come here from all over the Confed for the event. And I know you hate crowds."

"True," she said. "But no, I intend to show up. All the Clanholds are coming, and it's going to be wild. I wouldn't miss it for the world. Besides, as Chancellor, I gotta emerge sometimes to meet my constituents."

Frank laughed aloud and then said, "Oh please. You don't have to worry about elections—it's your job until you step down or the Confed leaders all decide you should go. I don't see that happening. Anyway, with Mary gone, I could use the company to help keep me celebrating life. Care to join me, since you'll be there anyway?"

Cassy knew it was no idle jest on Frank's part, and her concern for him made it easy to decide she should attend. "I'd be glad to have your company, Frank. Sure, I'll join you. We can see who throws rocks the furthest."

Frank smirked. "The word is 'farthest,' and it's not a rock. It's a shot put. And you're on, wimp. Be ready to get your ass whupped."

Cassy grinned and started on the mindless busywork, like stuffing papers into folders and the like, while the two of them chatted about the upcoming Anniversary Festival.

\* \* \*

The Other tried not to smirk at Nestor's feeble attempts to push him back down, and at the fact that these two Empire guards would soon be dead. Hopefully at his own hands. He had prepared himself well for this night. Sure, the guards had found four of the Other's knives, but two were meant to be obvious and two were only meant to appear hidden so they would think those were the last. They hadn't found the fifth blade. Even if they had found it, though, he wouldn't have needed it to finish this job. Cashin' checks and snappin' necks, hells yeah.

After disarming him, the two guards led him through the deepening twilight toward a torch-lit building, once a farmhouse, now usually empty. The Emperor used it for clandestine meetings like the one they thought this would be. It was far away from prying eyes and ears, but also from any ambushers the Emperor thought Nestor could have hidden out in the surrounding country. The building stood in the middle of a large field and had no cover at all for about a quarter-mile. While no rebels could approach it, the building did come fully stocked with extras for the set. Empire soldiers, or as they preferred to call themselves, "the honor guard of the President of the Midwest Republic."

As they led him through the entrance, it took a moment for his eyes to adjust to the bright interior lighting. Torches burned cheerfully every two feet along the walls, which was awesome because they created the perfect mood for this scene. The house was empty of furniture except for two chairs in the so-called great room. The Other didn't think it was so great. It was horribly outdated, with tongue-in-groove faux hardwood flooring and—disgustingly—a flowered wallpaper. It radiated stupid, like everything else about these fools, and detracted from the scene's ambiance. But one made do with the set one had, not the set one wished for.

One of the two chairs was a simple metal folding chair. That would be for him, naturally. The other chair was a huge, fluffy recliner that looked like it cost more than the shack. The Emperor was seated in that one, because rank had its privileges.

The Other felt revulsion at the sight of him. Fat, when everyone else still alive in the world looked half starved, and he wore a burdensome amount of fine jewelry, probably worth millions if people still used money or gave a shit about jewelry. The fat guy had on some designer sleeveless black tee shirt with a white printed logo, and it would probably have cost fifty bucks before the war. His belly wobbled over distressed-but-new jeans, also expensive. And of course, he wore 5.11 combat boots. They were amazing boots, but this dumbshit didn't deserve them.

"So," said the Emperor in a surprisingly high-pitched voice. Not as squeaky-comical as a certain famous ex-heavyweight champion's voice, but close. "I've granted you this audience. You've proven your loyalty by taking out my enemies whenever asked. Yet, it concerns me that you disappear for weeks at a time between missions, Mr. Lostracco. Tell me again what news you bring." He yawned, seeming bored. A bored, fat schmuck.

The Other smiled. "Yes, Mr. President. I'm honored to be in your great presence—"

"Yes, yes. Continue, dammit. I don't have all night."

The Other forced his smile to stay painted on his face. Yep, the Emperor's fat ass was a great presence, truly. Second only to that wobbly belly. "Well, during my between-mission excursions, I managed to get in tight with one of the resistance leaders. I've got him convinced it's time to switch sides. He's in a perfect position to ambush some even higher-ranking resistance leaders, and he can lead about a third of all the actual resistance fighters back into your fold." Lying to this schmuck was fun.

He relaxed his legs, and the precautionary leg irons slid down a bit. Then a bit more. They had been put on rather loosely. Since Nestor was a trusted minion, security was lax.

The Emperor yawned again, this time melodramatically. Nestor cringed at the terrible over-acting. Then His Fatness said, "I'd defeat them eventually anyway. I hold all the cards, because I control the food. Plus, why do I want traitors to join me? There are some trust issues with that, you know."

The Other nodded somberly. "Yes, of course. But something about the news must have interested you or you wouldn't have agreed to meet with me." He slowly lifted his feet, allowing the loose shackles to slide off.

"An astute observation, Mr. Lostracco."

The Other fought the urge to cringe at the asshole's stupidity. This guy was *such a tool*. He fidgeted with his wrist shackles as his gaze darted around the room. His role demanded that he look nervous. "Thank you."

"I came to see how real the offer was. I can read in your face that you like the traitor's deal, not that your opinion is important. Still, these people voted to join me. They *voted*, dammit. They can't just un-vote their membership. I suppose I'll take the fighters back, since they just follow their leaders, as is proper. That's the job of floor workers, right? Follow instructions from their mid-level managers? But those managers... They're to be fired. With prejudice."

"So, you want them dead, of course." The Other smiled. This was so delicious. The Emperor was everything he had expected him to be, and more. Killing him would be a delight. Sublime, even. *Click...* his wrist shackles loosened by several notches. It would be plenty.

"Yes, Mr. Lostracco. I'll take care of that part, if you can just get them to meet with my representatives. To continue the allegory, we'll work out a new contract, they'll sign it, and it'll be notarized. Then my people will fire them, keeping the labor pool under my own personnel. When can my hiring reps meet with these leaders and their troops?"

The Other grinned. "Right now, Mr. President." He stood slowly and took one step forward as his wrist and ankle shackles fell away, clanking loudly on the floor.

The Emperor looked confused. Oh, this was so delicious.

He shouted, "Detain that man!"

Nestor felt hands on his shoulders, the two goons who had led him in. He smiled, then sharply nodded one time.

*Bang. Bang.* Two shots rang out from behind the Emperor, and the Other's captors fell to the ground, one silently and one whimpering. The Other pulled his fifth blade from the small of his back and stopped the wounded man's stupid noise. That was definitely not that man's line. He was supposed to say something like, "Gah!" or "Oohhh!" when the guns let them know it was time for their lines. Amateurs.

The Emperor spun on his heels, head sweeping back and forth among the four guards in the room. All was silent. "Who did that? You'll hang for it. Guards," he shouted at the top of his lungs to summon his other half-dozen goons.

The Other, still smiling, mentally counted to three. No guards had responded. Right on three, right on cue, the Emperor said his line perfectly—"What is the meaning of this?"

The Other was certain this was one of his finest productions, just because of the A-list actor in the scene, and the Emperor was as A-list as it got. He said, "Mr. Lostracco isn't here. He lacked the directorial experience to make this scene flow as it should, to capture its essence. I, on the other hand, am an old hand at this sort of performance. You'll notice the shiny new M4 rifles your fellow actors carry?"

The Emperor froze, obviously noticing the new rifles for the first time. "Those aren't Remingtons."

"Cut," the Other shouted, irritated. "That's not your line. I'll explain it so your tiny, talentless brain can understand this. In this scene, my people have bribed your guards. Guns, your stupid gold coins, food, and the promise of land of their own."

"But... but why?"

"After your studio's last production flopped—*Conquest of*

*the Confederation* went way over budget and was widely panned by the critics—they felt that it was time to consider alternative employment."

"What the hell are you talking about, freak? This isn't a movie. These are my guards. It's not my fault the Confederation got lucky—"

"Shut your mouth. You divas, all alike. Impossible to work with."

"What—"

"Backstory for the scene, you failed to conquer the Confederation. And Michigan. And your western campaign flopped just as badly. Many of your employees have left to start their own companies to the east of the Republic. Your house of cards is falling, and they know it. And, action!"

The Emperor shook with fury. Face red, he shouted, "Guards, kill this impudent psycho." No one moved. Even louder, he shrieked, "I'm the goddamn president! Obey me, or I'll have your kids flayed alive and use their skins to make my lampshades. I'll—"

The Other suddenly moved forward, speed-walking deliberately at the Emperor with knife in hand. The Emperor growled and pulled out a pistol, pointed it at the Other and pulled the trigger, all in one fluid motion.

Click. Click. Nothing happened.

The Other's pace didn't slow. He said, "A good director checks his gear. Here, look at mine."

With those words, his knife slid into the Emperor's abdomen over his liver. It would be an absolutely fatal wound, and it would take an amusing amount of time for him to die. The blood flowed, spattering over the Other's hand and knife handle.

The warm, slick feeling was about the best thing in the world. Way better than shooting someone. "Oops. Did I do that? How clumsy of me."

The Emperor, face painted in shock and pain, gripped the Other's hand with both of his and tried to pull the blade out. The Other let him, smiling the whole time. As the blade drew free, more blood gushed, faster, running down his shirt, down his pants, and dripping everywhere on the floor. Much of the gore was black, not red.

As a look of understanding crossed the Emperor's face, the Other raised his eyebrows. "Oh, you noticed the liver juice? That's not the medical term, of course, but I find it captures the prop's essence perfectly."

The Emperor's legs started to buckle, and he fell forward onto the Other, then slowly slid down while looking into his eyes. "Impossible..."

The Other only grinned. "Not impossible. Turning this boring scene into something entertaining took a lot of prep and effort, but I think this production might become a classic. The results are worth it, wouldn't you agree? I do love the special effects."

The Emperor fell to the ground and lay still. He never answered the Other's question.

"And, cut! That's a wrap."

The Other heard someone mutter, *freak*, and smiled. He knew better. Ordinary people were freaks. The truly creative, the *avant garde*, weren't freaks. They were *eccentric*. He didn't expect the bourgeois to know that, of course, so he took no offense.

He turned and walked out the front door, heading back toward camp for the after party.

# - 5 -

0845 HOURS - ZERO DAY +344

ETHAN FINISHED EATING a breakfast of eggs and pancakes, then left to finish his farm tasks for the day. Ethan's chores usually were the sort that were left to the younger Clan members, simply because he couldn't be spared from his computer and radio duties. They would scamper throughout the Jungle, avoiding the tell-tale signs of boobytraps, and picked whatever plants were ready for harvest. They had been taught to leave about a quarter of them for seeds later and for critters to eat.

That day he was to pick blueberries and blackberries, of which there were more than the Clan would ever use. They were almost all ripening and would continue throughout the next several weeks, along with many vegetables. More fruits would also begin to ripen in the next couple of days and weeks, stretching through September. Until then, it was all hands on deck gathering and preparing the staggered harvests for long-term storage. There would also be more pies than he had ever wanted to eat. What wasn't used or preserved would be fed to the pigs and other farm animals, or left for the wildlife.

With Cassy's farming methods, everything pretty much grew together far more densely than any normal farm, but she had no large areas planted with only a single crop. Each type of bush, tree, perennial, and flower was spread throughout the Jungle, completely intermixed. Even without pesticides, pests didn't ravage her crops because only a few plants would get overwhelmed before predators consumed them. Cassy *wanted* the animals and bugs that most people considered pests, as long as they were in balance. With no "monocrop planting," they were almost always more or less in balance now.

Likewise, disease couldn't wipe out a whole crop since few were close enough together for it to spread. Her method was smart, efficient, and required no chemicals. The one downside was that sowing and harvesting couldn't be done by machine with so many plants intermixed. Not that there were many machines working these days anyway.

Ethan was assigned to work with a girl, about fourteen, whom he had seen around Clanholme a few times but had never really spoken to. She treated Ethan like a rockstar, following him around asking questions, even pointless ones, which gave her an excuse to hang out with him. Ethan, hacker extraordinaire, one of *the original* Clan members. Ethan sighed. Maybe her name was Beth? Betsy? Some "B" name? The girl had been chattering at him for the last half hour, and it was both annoying and cute. Her ponytail bobbed as she spoke.

He humored her, not wanting to be mean to a kid or dampen her spirits. Spirits were damp enough around here from the sense that enemies hid in almost every direction.

The girl, still giddy, asked, "Why does it matter that everything is all mixed together?"

Ethan smiled at her and said, " Everything connects together. For example, the dense plants and fish used to attract muskrats, who moved into the two fish ponds and made a good mess of things. But a week later, hawks moved into the food forests and took care of the muskrats for us. And the birds' droppings fertilized the forest."

"So when are you and das Mommenfuhrer getting married?" the girl asked abruptly.

Ethan was stopped in his tracks. "Das... what?"

"Mommenfuhrer. You know," she said, rolling her eyes, "Amber."

"Mommenfuhrer?"

"Well, yeah. We rarely see Amber except for big events. She's always in a bunker but doesn't officially live there. And we only hear her on the radio mostly when she's telling us what to do. And everyone does what she says." The girl grinned at her own wit.

Ethan laughed heartily. That was hilarious. Where did the kids come up with this stuff? After he regained his breath, he wiped his eyes and said, "She's going to get such a kick out of that nickname. Thanks. Did you come up with it?"

Obviously pleased, the girl said, "No, I think Brianna came up with it. Want to know what the kids usually call you when you—"

Ethan was abruptly shaken like a ragdoll. He felt like a giant hammer had struck him. When he opened his eyes, he found himself looking up at the sky. His body wouldn't quite respond to his mental commands, not just yet. Smoke filled the air. As he lay there, through ringing ears he faintly heard the sound of the Clan's alarm siren. Had he been hit by a mortar?

Finally, Ethan was able to partly roll over and got his arms underneath him. He counted to three and then shoved up, struggling into a sitting position, butt on the ground and legs out in front of him.

The ringing in his ears began to fade. In its place, he now

heard panicked, shouting voices getting closer. He became aware of an intense heat on his back and, still dazed, he turned his head to see what caused it. The Jungle nearest him was burning. He tried to move away, but found that his body was still totally uncoordinated. He tried to rise once, but fell. He decided to just sit there for a moment to collect his wits. What the fuck had just happened?

Ethan felt hands on his arms that lifted him to his feet and held him steady. He saw there were Clanners holding him up. They had been doing guard duty, no doubt, and so they were the closest. He saw that Frank was hobbling toward him as fast as he could, his crutch a blur of movement. Ethan thought it looked funny, and realized he wasn't thinking straight. Every thought moved through his mind at a snail's pace, all cloudy. It felt like he was swimming through some sort of mental mud.

When Frank arrived, he shouted, "Ethan, are you all right? Guard, get the medic. Ethan?—lower him down gently —you got a nasty gash. Did you hit a trap? Where's the girl you were with?" Frank's expression was pale and concerned. His questions came fast as a bullet train.

Ethan struggled to keep up. He sure was dizzy... The guard lowered him to the ground, for which Ethan was thankful. His head didn't spin so much now that he was sitting again. "No, I don't think so," he said, looking around in confusion. Was that the right answer?

He saw a lump. He froze. Dawning horror washed over him. His eyes focused and he saw that the lump, lying among smoldering berry bushes, looked like the pulverized bottom half of a person. A young person. "Oh, Lord no..."

Frank turned to follow Ethan's gaze and froze as well. "Jesus Christ."

What else was there to say? What could they do? Nothing. But that couldn't have done by a Clan boobytrap. Their shotgun shell traps didn't dismember people so violently, deadly as they were. "Frank, is that the kid I was working with?"

Frank's stillness and silence were answer enough.

Then Ethan heard a whirring noise as the din quieted around him. He reflexively looked for the source, as did Frank and the others who had arrived to help. Artificial noises stood out like a sore thumb, these days.

He saw a black and white drone, gracefully soaring above them on six whirring blades evenly spaced around the thin, flat edge of a central disk. Beneath the assembly was what looked like a rotary cannon with four wide barrels. One barrel still smoked. The drone approached and rotated. Ethan saw that it had a camera, which now faced him. Then it rotated again. When the camera assembly pointed at Frank, the drone stopped moving and hovered. Then it slowly approached Frank. It oozed menace.

Ethan said, "Frank, don't move. It's got rockets or something."

Frank nodded stiffly. "Yes, I see that." Then he shouted, "Everyone, move away from me."

As they began to move away, the drone emitted a faint continual beeping noise, which began to rise in volume and pitch. Ethan thought the effect was the most damn ominous thing he had ever heard. "Frank, it's gonna shoot. Run."

"Yeah, right." Frank didn't move.

Oh yeah, Frank was missing a foot. Not that anyone on foot could outrun an aerial drone anyway.

From beside him, Ethan heard a deep *boom* that rattled his ears, and the drone seemed to practically disintegrate. When it hit the ground in a rain of fragments, Frank backed away as fast as his one foot would allow.

Ethan turned and saw Michael standing behind him, holding a 12-gauge shotgun. He racked it to load another round in the chamber and put the stock back up to his shoulder.

Ethan said frantically, "No, don't! It has rockets. You could set them off."

Michael froze and didn't fire, then seemed to relax as he lowered the shotgun.

Whew, that was close...

Michael said, "Where did it come from? Ethan, what's the control range on those things?"

Ethan shook his head to clear his mind. He still had three tons of mud rattling around his brain bucket. "Maybe a twenty minute flight time with that heavy loadout. More like fifteen. Range is a couple hundred yards at best."

Michael turned to the guard who had been helping Ethan and said, "You, go get a team together. Lock down the Complex, and dammit, lock down the refugee camp. No one in or out or you shoot the hell out of them. I'll get another team to sweep the area with me."

The guard nodded and sprinted away. Michael gave Ethan a nod, then he too sprinted toward the Complex to gather troops.

Ethan suddenly felt his thoughts clear up, and then realized what Michael had in mind. With so short a range on this style of drone, it had to be operated from someone nearby. The operator had to be either a Clanner, a refugee, or a spy. Michael had realized that in an instant.

Ethan rose to his feet and staggered toward the girl's ravaged corpse, or what was left of it. Frank soon joined him, and together they stared at her for a long moment. So young, and Ethan didn't even know her name. She deserved better.

He said to Frank, "Can you find out her name and let me know? She deserves to be remembered. This wasn't her fault."

Frank nodded. They continued standing in silence for a

few seconds, then Frank said, "Not her fault. Was it yours?"

Ethan felt a chill run down his spine. It probably was his fault. Maybe a warning from the 20s, or Houle, their master. He looked at Frank but couldn't tell from his body language what the man might be thinking. "I couldn't say for sure until I examine the drone's wreckage. Odds seem good this was the work of the 20s, though. Why they'd do this, I don't know with any certainty."

Frank let out a long breath. "I'll find out her name and let you know. Meanwhile, you find out if this is a 20s drone. And Ethan, I want a report from you in council tonight about why the 20s might have done this. It seems like a warning, and if you know something, or even just *suspect* something, I want to hear about it."

Ethan nodded slowly. "Of course, Frank. I'll get it done." He wasn't looking forward to that presentation.

The Jungle brush rustled and Lance Corporal Sturm emerged. Ethan was grateful for her arrival. The conversation with Frank had started getting awkward, and Ethan needed time to collect his thoughts before getting grilled further. Plus, he was bleeding from a scalp wound and those things bled a lot more than they should.

Sturm carried her field medic kit with her, and he didn't resist when she led him toward a large stone. He sat on it and then she began to work on him. She made a *tsk, tsk* noise with her tongue and brought out her sutures kit, but Ethan only cringed a little. She was never gentle when she worked, being efficient instead, but he felt like he deserved that at the moment.

\* \* \*

Carl walked briskly toward Sewer Rat territory, just southwest of his own Timber Wolf turf. The Rats and the

Wolves were on great terms, and he didn't expect any problems getting in. Still, he carried five loose rounds of 5.56 ammunition in his pocket, just in case he had to motivate the gate guards to let him in. In his left hand, he carried an ornate bag with a card in it. Inside the bag, wrapped in thin white tissue, was a fine glass fantasy figurine of an armed and armored rat, about six inches tall, carrying sword and shield. Sunshine would appreciate such a gift, he felt. She was a rough-around-the-edges woman and appreciated the thought more than the gift, but this had the added advantage of being both thoughtful and pretty awesome.

Carl stopped at the gate and glanced at his watch. He had fifteen minutes to kill, so he chatted with the Rat guards, asking about their families and how they were getting along now that they were inside the Liz Town walls instead of out in the wildlands. The usual small talk. Such chatter could only improve relations with the Rats, even though they were pretty close already.

When he glanced at his watch and saw he had five minutes until showtime, he broke off his conversation politely, and they let him in without asking for any bribes. Small talk could have a big effect.

He made his way deeper into their territory, eyes roving, checking out how well the Sewer Rats had done in cleaning up their area. The walls were even taking good shape, and ought to be finished soon at the rate they were working.

As he walked, he waved and smiled at the many Rats he already knew from his days sneaking into the wildlands with supplies for them. Those who knew him remembered his help fondly, of course, and most waved back with happy smiles. It made Carl feel good about what he had done to help them before they became a Band.

It took only a couple minutes to get to the meeting point, a small garden someone had taken superb care of before the war, and which had survived untended until the Rats took over this area. The Rats looked after it carefully and well, for whatever reason. Maybe just to have something beautiful to look at in a dingy, gray landscape.

Three cement benches were scattered throughout the small park, and Carl spotted Sunshine sitting on the middle one. He walked even faster until he got to the bench, then sat down and handed her the gift bag with a grin.

"What's this?" she asked, but she only wore a faint smile. She began to rummage through the white tissues.

"A cool icon for your desk, maybe. It made me think of you, so I salvaged it. Hope you like it."

Sunshine finally got through the tissue to the glass statue. She held it up, examining it in the sunlight with that same half-smile. "Thanks, Carl. I love it."

He grinned again at her.

Sunshine gently put the glass rat back in the decorative bag, then leaned against the bench's backrest. She closed her eyes for a moment as the sunlight washed over her face. She looked stunning, lit up like that. A natural beauty.

Carl said, "I'm so glad I finally got the time to make one of these meet-ups with you." He let a sharp breath out through his nose. "If at first you don't succeed..."

Sunshine nodded, then opened her eyes. She looked sad, Carl thought, but he couldn't think of any reason why she might be. She wasn't crying, wasn't shying away from him. No body language to say she was upset, just a vibe. A feeling.

Carl let the seconds stretch in silence, then said, "Sunny, is everything okay? If something's on your mind, you know you can tell me. I'm here for you, if you need someone to lean on. You know that."

Sunshine turned her head to look at him, but still didn't smile. Then she looked away. "Carl, that's just the thing. You really aren't here for me to lean on. I'm not sure I can keep doing this, when you just don't have time for me."

"That's not true—"

She interrupted him, snapping, "Yes it is." She took a deep breath and continued, "It's okay, though, really. It's not like you're obligated to be with me or anything. Like you said, we aren't an item, and I have no right to feel bad about this. But I do feel bad."

"Sunny, there's nothing to feel bad—"

She held up her hand abruptly, again cutting him off. "Please, I just need to say this."

Carl felt his heart drop. This was turning into "the speech," he could already tell. A breakup of a relationship that didn't exist except in both their wishes.

"I just thought, or maybe just hoped, that you and I might be more than friends someday. I like you, Carl. You're a great person and a good friend. But I need to face reality."

A hundred thoughts sped through Carl's mind. Finally, he said, "I want us to be more, Sunshine. We can figure this out."

Sunshine wiped her eyes with the heels of her hands. "No Carl, we can't. I thought a lot about what you said the other day and you are right. You have an important role that entails serious responsibilities and I get that. I really do. A lot of people depend on you."

Carl's heart beat faster, and his palms began to sweat.

She stood abruptly, then turned to face him and continued, "So that leaves very little time for us. I can't always be chasing minutes to spend with you, and I can't be the one who distracts you when you have lives in your hands."

Carl's throat tightened. "But—"

"I just think it's best if we both move on."

With that, she spun on her heels and walked away, her pace quick, as if she couldn't stand to be near him anymore.

Carl stared after her, but she never did look back, never gave him his chance at rebuttal. He glanced at the bench where she had been sitting and saw the gift bag. She had left his gift behind, just as she had left him.

* * *

Cassy left one of the earthbag houses to wander the farm, checking to make sure all was in order. Harvesting was still going full swing and the outdoor kitchen was packed with people going all-out to get the abundance preserved. Minus what was set aside for kimchi, meals, pies, and wines, of course. Her mouth watered at the thought of the blackberry wine being prepared right now. In a few months, it'd be drinkable by her standards. She smiled.

Turning a corner, she nearly walked right into Ethan. She stopped abruptly with her face only inches from his, startled. Cassy grinned awkwardly. "Oh, Ethan. You scared me."

Ethan, however, didn't smile.

Cassy noticed his bandages then, and felt a trickle of alarm. "What the hell happened to you? Are you okay?"

Ethan took a step back moving to a more comfortable distance. "Cassy. I've been trying to contact you. Where's your damn radio?"

Cassy looked down at her hip, where the radio sat holstered. The red "on" light was dark. She took it out of its enclosure and checked the volume/power dial, but it hadn't accidentally been turned off. "I guess the battery died. What's going on? What happened to you?"

Ethan looked irritated. "First, Lebanon reports their northern areas are getting pressed hard by 'vader troops from the North Pennsylvania cantonment. Whats-his-name, General Park's people."

Cassy frowned. "Damn. I thought they learned their lesson when they tried to move in at Brickerville last year. Is it a raid or an invasion?"

Ethan shrugged. "I got a bunch of troop data from Lebanon. It's too big for a raid. Maybe not big enough for a full invasion."

Cassy closed her eyes for a moment. "Alright. Maybe it's a diversion. Maybe it's a recon-in-force that went awry—"

"Michael says there's no such thing. Recon-in-force is code for intentionally getting stuck in combat and requiring reinforcements, so a real battle can happen despite orders to the contrary."

"Whatever. All I know is that it's likely to escalate if they bring reinforcements. Okay, we got what, twelve battlecars running now? Let's get them ready and... No, wait. Tell Frank that the Confederation requests the Clan send its battlecars to assist Lebanon."

"You got it. Should I ask him to mount up some troops as well?"

"Yes, a company's worth ought to do it for now. So are you going to tell me what the hell happened to you?"

"You didn't hear the commotion?"

"No," she said. "It must have been when I was in an earthbag house—those things are virtually sound-proof."

Ethan shook his head. "No time to explain. Right now, we have a situation to deal with. Two of them, but I'll tell you the rest when there's time."

Cassy eyed his bandages and let out a frustrated breath. "Well, I hope Frank is at least handling it, if you won't tell me."

"He's the Clanleader now, Cassy."

"Yeah, I got that. Fine—I'm going to head down to the bunker to radio Lebanon directly while you work with Frank to get this circus organized."

Ethan nodded and strode away, pulling out his handheld radio. Cassy had no doubt he'd handle it efficiently.

She returned to her house and went down into the bunker, where she sat at Ethan's Comms Station. It was a desk with a bunch of handheld and shortwave radios on it. She keyed into Lebanon's direct channel on a HAM unit. "Lebanon, Lebanon, come in. This is the chancellor."

A couple of seconds later, the HAM radio crackled to life. "This is Lebanon. Welcome home, Chancellor. Did Charlie Two advise you of our situation?"

"Affirm. I'm requesting the Clan send their battlecars and a company of mounted troops to assist. How are you guys holding up?" She was relieved that the person on the other end sounded calm. It was a good sign.

"So far, we're holding fine and the fighting isn't that intense. We have our own two battlecars on standby, not in the field yet, but the damn 'vader numbers are increasing. It's like they drift randomly into the region and are just walking up to the battle to join in. It's weird."

Cassy frowned. "Actually, that's how they did it before, too, when they attacked Brickerville. It must serve some purpose, but even Michael doesn't know what. I had almost forgotten that asshole Park's cantonment was still out there somewhere."

"If even the Confed's general doesn't know why they trickle in like that..."

"Yeah, copy that," Cassy said. It was just a mystery. "So if the Clan agrees to send troops, the battlecars will arrive shortly and the riders, whenever they can get there. It shouldn't be long."

"Copy that, Chancellor. Thank you. Lebanon out."

Cassy set the mic down and waited for Ethan to return a few minutes later, and then told him of her conversation with Lebanon.

Ethan nodded. "Good. Frank agreed to send the cars and the company, with Michael going in a battlecar. The mobility will keep him safer, and Frank can't be spared for a raid right now."

Cassy knew Frank was a good fighter, but Michael was a scary-ass warrior of doom. "I'm glad to see that he's not making the same mistakes I did. It has to be tempting, though. The urge to keep your eyes on your people when you send them to fight, it's pretty strong."

"Frank's a good leader, and so are you, but everyone has their blind spots. Frank included. They're just different than yours are." He glanced at his monitor—which was blank—and then said, "Why don't you hang out with me and listen in on the battle through Michael."

"Thanks. I appreciate that you try to make me still feel like I'm involved here, with my own people."

Which was true. Cassy often felt left out, which sucked even if she knew perfectly well why it had to be that way.

Ethan nodded, his expression grim. "You are always involved, Cassy."

# - 6 -

0445 HOURS - ZERO DAY +349

CARL SAT IN his dune buggy-like battlecar, the *Lizzie Borden*. His bucket seat's five-point harness held him snugly, uncomfortably so. If he crashed, he'd be glad for the harness, but until then it was rough on the ol' twig-and-berries, and made his broad shoulders ache. Of course, if he did crash, the gunner standing upright at the machine gun mounted on top would be toast.

Carl glanced at the clock and saw there was only fifteen minutes until showtime. In the cold morning air, his goggles should have fogged up, but the Fog-X he had applied was holding up wonderfully. How cool was it that Rain-X was now free and in virtually unlimited supply? He figured it was best to look at the bright side of armageddon.

He looked through the windshield, which was now only a thick wire mesh without the glass, and in the distance saw the outskirts of Liz Town's hated enemy, Harrisburg. Since the Empire enclave in Carlisle had broken away to join the Free Republic—thanks in large part to the supplies the Confederation had given to the refugees—Empire shipments to Harrisburg had stopped almost entirely. Their once mortal enemy was on its last legs.

Carl saw that their wall was pathetic, and felt disgust at the uneven, haphazard, half-finished line of rubble. But then again, Harrisburg hadn't ever expected to get invaded from this side of the river. They once had far too many people to feel threatened by the likes of Liz Town, but with the advent of spring, Carl had begun to hear rumors of illness sweeping through the town. Apparently, when the squirrels and rats started coming out again with warmer spring temperatures, populations blossoming, the little varmints brought Harrisburg a gift of their own... Plague.

Interestingly, Carl had expected the unburied dead to lead to a second epidemic, but that hadn't happened. He had asked a Timber Wolf doctor about it last month and had been told that it was a myth and rotting bodies created no new diseases. The plague remained the only threat. Carl asked if the rotting bodies themselves could make people sick, but the doctor had said one would need to eat over twenty grams of a corpse's rotting flesh to get ill. So long as their water supply remained uncontaminated, the bodies were smelly but not dangerous.

Liz Town had waited patiently for the plague to run its course, which had taken only a couple of months. His spies now reported there had been no new victims in a week. He learned that the Harrisburgers had taken to separating each household from the others as far as possible, spreading among the many vacant houses throughout the city, and had burned every house where an occupant had fallen ill. It stopped the epidemic, but not before half of Harrisburg's population had died horribly. Without antibiotics, bubonic plague was a deadly, implacable killer.

The Lizzies were bouncing off the walls in their eagerness to get revenge, in typical Liz Town fashion. The preparations for the upcoming attack had turned into something of a party, with barbeques and beer everywhere. Many of the warriors made bets with each other on who would die first, and who would get the most kills. Carl loved the way Lizzies approached life.

He glanced to his left and saw the Kodiak Band's lead vehicle, which was painted in a brown-based cammo pattern. To his right was the Sewer Rats' battlecar, painted entirely in an almost neon putrescent green. Boy did the Rats' color stand out... It was the Band's only battlecar, so Carl had assigned it to his own group. Bless the Clan for thinking up these Mad Max cars! They were perfect for the Lizzie mentality.

Behind him, Carl heard the foot troops' hushed conversations, nearly a thousand of them. He knew that Diamondback had only sent half the troops that Mary Ann had demanded of them for this operation. Apparently, Diamondback would rather give up fines—a *lot* of their food stores and crafted goods—than risk their necks. Typical...

Tic, toc, the dashboard clock arms swept inexorably toward 5:00 a.m. At the ten-second mark, Carl began to count down with the clock, mouthing the words silently. And then it was showtime.

His heart leapt, and his face lit into a savage snarl. Now he only had to get inside, get through their walls. The gate would be his real target, and the real challenge. Since it had never been completed, Harrisburg had set up two 40' cargo containers standing on end, in the space where the gate should be, filled with rubble for stability and sturdiness. They no doubt each weighed tons. If Liz Town attacked those directly, the cavalry or foot soldiers would have to do so under heavy fire, which didn't sound like fun, they now had some battlecars of their own, each with more horsepower than all their horses combined.

He stepped on the gas pedal and the car surged forward.

His unshielded engine's beefy roar drowned out the war cries of the fighters behind him. He led the battlecar wing toward the haphazard gate.

At first, there was no visible reaction from those on the walls. Once Carl was about halfway to the gate, however, the defenders fired their first shots. Their muzzle flashes were starkly visible in the faint light of the dawning day, and he heard his gunner returning fire.

Because of the way the wall ran between the river and the gate, an S-shaped arc blocked his view of the gate itself. That peninsula of wall was where the defenders began to congregate, judging by the increasing flashes he saw. He led his wing in a lazy arc. They approached the tip of the peninsula, which was beginning to light up like Christmas from all the muzzle flashes. He heard the distinctive *tink, tink* of bullets striking his car's armor plating, but he ignored them. Unless they hit him with a fifty-cal, the rounds would never penetrate his thick armor. His gunner just had to take his chances, though.

To his left, the wall peninsula seemed to loom larger as he continued to close the distance. He figured that he'd pass maybe fifty yards from the wall at the closest point.

A blinding flare appeared up at the top. Had someone hit it with a grenade? No—that was backblast. A rocket grenade? Carl swerved right, hoping not to be where the shooter had intended in case his car was the target. As he jinked to the right in response to the rocket, the entire battlegroup followed suit. Then there was an explosion, and a pickup truck two cars away flew ass-over-end and landed upside down, aflame. It had been a Wolverine car.

The battlecar gunners poured streams of rounds into the rocket launcher's position, and no further rockets came their way. Then they passed the outcropping and the wall seemed to sweep away back toward the gate.

Now beyond the outcropping of wall, Carl veered left to head straight at the cargo containers. Because the containers were full of rubble, blowing them up wouldn't likely open up access to the ripe pearl of Harrisburg beyond, so they had to be brought down another way. Spies had reported that the temporary gate didn't have a lot in the way of attachment points, which presented a problem, but Lizzie engineers had built him a solution that was crude but hopefully effective. Puma's two battlecars stopped abruptly in front of the gate, back ends mere feet away from the cargo containers.

The rest of the wing concentrated heavy automatic fire at the top of the wall to keep its defenders occupied. The idea was to create multiple threats so the defenders had to further split their forces. But the longer this took, the more town defenders would awaken, grab a rifle and get their butts up on the wall. This part of the operation had to go quickly.

Carl spared a glance at the Puma crews by the cargo containers. He saw one man drop, but the others kept busy. Two used pickaxes to punch holes in both sides of one container. Two more, with massive hooks made of rebar, slid the hook points into the new holes. The crews sprinted toward their vehicles.

Carl had to turn right to avoid the opposite wall, which took the Puma crews out of view again. Movement farther to his right caught his attention—a Wolverine car barreled straight at him. Carl veered left and the city wall loomed in front of him. He veered right again, and he heard a crash behind him.

His gunner shouted down, "Driver got shot. We're good, they're not."

Damn, that was close. Carl tried to regulate his breathing, willing his heartbeat to slow. It didn't obey, at least not right away. He continued to circle back, ready to make another pass, when he saw a glorious sight. The cargo container had been hooked, and the hooks were chained to the Puma cars. With their huge V8 engines, the cars strained against the chains.

Those containers, thought Carl, were where Harrisburg screwed up. They were full of rubble and were top-heavy. Once they tilted even a little, their center of gravity crossed a threshold and physics took over.

The chained tower creaked and moaned, and as it began to topple, the bottom edge buckled, speeding the process. A moment later, that huge metal-and-rubble monster crashed into the ground with enough force that Carl felt the ground shake through his steering wheel. He let out a low whistle, then glanced back and saw a flood of Lizzie fighters on foot streaming around the wall outcropping, sprinting toward the newly made gap.

Carl grinned. The real fighting was about to begin.

\* \* \*

Ethan balanced his orange plastic food tray precariously, travel mug of juice on top, as he punched in the bunker door code. When it popped open, he almost dropped his whole breakfast, but his reflexes were fast enough to salvage it without losing more than a couple small bits of egg and a splosh of juice. He'd have to clean all that up, of course. He let out a long, frustrated breath.

Setting his tray down, Ethan got a rag and cleaned up his mess. Then he slid into his usual office chair, now super-comfy and molded perfectly to his own butt, and dug into the chow while his computers booted up. It still amazed him how much better this tasted than the supermarket food back in the day. Before the EMPs came, he didn't know the difference, but now he wouldn't have gone back to food raised the old way even if it were an option.

As he finished his breakfast, he wondered where Amber was. She often joined him for breakfast down in the bunker because it was one of the few times each day when they could be alone. No kids, no Clanners underfoot. She was supposed to meet him today after she finished her morning chores, so he figured she'd come down whenever she was done, but wondered what had delayed her.

As he sipped at the last of his juice, he watched his main laptop finish up its load routines. As soon as it was done, however, the green ASCII chat box popped up and Ethan growled. This morning was one damn frustration after another. The chat box meant that bastard Watcher One was finally back online. Good.

Ethan clicked the waiting message that said Watcher One was asking to chat. He noticed that his hands were shaking, he was so angry. "Calm down," he told himself. "Nothing good will come of losing my temper now, only bad things. But how I hate this sonovabitch."

*Watcher1* >> *Hello D.Ryder It has been awile Lets chat*

*D.Ryder* >> *I feel like u said whats on ur mind already. A few days ago.*

*Watcher1* >> *I wasnt the driver for that package delivery. But the driver is missing. Have u seen him, he might still b in ur neighborhood. Also, we might have another package for you, not sure. It's in ur delivery zone but it could get cancelled, dunno.*

Ethan paused to think. It appeared the 20s didn't know for sure that Michael had captured the drone pilot who had been fleeing east, but Ethan considered the possibility that they might have a third one nearby.

Why had Watcher mentioned that he wasn't the driver? And could Ethan take the chance of believing Watcher One when he said he hadn't been responsible for the deadly drone attack? Too risky.

While he considered how to respond, Ethan ran a tracer routine to check Watcher One's IP address. The software automatically compared that to previous ones, and it took only a second for the IP to pop up. It was shaded red—it didn't match any previously used IPs on file. Most of Watcher One's chats came from one of three IP addresses, but this one was new. Interesting, but not very informative by itself.

> **D.Ryder** >> *The last package got sent 2 the wrong person. A kid. She wasn't old enough to sign, but they left it with her anyway.*

> **Watcher1** >> *That's 2 bad. I did warn u it was coming, tho. You've been a naughty little elf.*

> **D.Ryder** >> *U said another 1 is coming?*

> **Watcher1** >> *Probly. Last 1 might have been a warning. Next 1 probly won't b.*

> **D.Ryder** >> *I thot the manufacturer needed me to 4ward other packages for em.*

> **Watcher1** >> *The market is weak. Company is downsizing. Seems like they r shutting the northeast regional office. Too expensive, not enuf R.O.I. from u.*

> **D.Ryder** >> *I should get a severance package, not a*

*pinkslip. I've been useful.*

**Watcher1** >> *Like I said, sales are down too much. Can't afford a severance package.*

**D.Ryder** >> *Maybe they wud allow me 2 just retire. Then there is no conflict of interest.*

**Watcher1** >> *You wud leave ur office? W/out a pinkslip? Maybe they would go 4 that. Cheaper than pinkslip, with all the deliveries and expenses, u know.*

**D.Ryder** >> *Yup. I signed an NDA, remember? That's valid whether I retire or get fired*

**Watcher1** >> *U would have 2 leave ur office without complaining, tho. It would b a requirement.*

**D.Ryder** >> *Yup, I got that*

**Watcher1** >> *I will see what they say and let u know either way. If they still want 2 send u a pinkslip I will let u know when u should expect it tho, so u can get ur office in order b4 u get it.*

*<<Session terminated>>*

Ethan's mind, prone to seeing conspiracies, definitely saw one now, and he cursed out loud. So the 20s, working for General Houle, had murdered the fourteen-year-old girl Ethan had been working with just to deliver a warning. And another drone attack might be imminent. But Watcher One was going to see whether Houle would spare the Clan from another such attack if Ethan would walk away from the Clan and everything else. Why would Watcher One help him like that? He suspected that Watcher hadn't been involved in the attack, and had only been told about it after the fact. Why else would he hint that he might forewarn Ethan if another drone attack was coming? That assumed Watcher One would know about the next one, though. It was all so confusing.

Ethan decided he would need to stay in the bunker from then on, at least until the situation was resolved. If Houle sent another drone, it might kill more people, but if Houle accepted his offer to retire, he'd have to leave the Clan forever.

He glanced at his bugout bag, sitting in the corner as always, and wasn't sure whether he hoped to retire or not. If Houle agreed to let him go into exile, the consequences if he backed out on the deal would be severe, for him and for the Clan. Something big enough to demolish a lot of Clanholme and kill many Clanners. That, Ethan couldn't abide. He had already decided he would leave the Confederation if Houle would let him. Maybe he'd head east and join up with Taggart's forces. Bringing a radio would buy his admission if he could make it there alive, possibly by stealing a battlecar. It was only a thing, an object, and Ethan would rather the Clan lose it than lose lives.

"I won't allow the Clan to pay for my mistakes," he said aloud, suddenly very certain.

"What mistakes would those be?"

Ethan jumped at the woman's voice behind him. Startled, he spun around, but saw that it was only Amber. She had finally made it down. He smiled at her. "Oh, just 20s business. Nothing big."

How had she gotten in without him hearing the locks disengage? Then he recalled that he hadn't locked the bunker door, hands being full at the time. A damn foolish mistake, given how tight security was supposed to be surrounding the bunker's very existence.

Amber put her hands to her hips, jaw set. "Yeah? Why are you worried about the Clan 'paying' for it, then?"

Why'd she have to be so smart? Ethan forced himself to smile casually, trying to be nonchalant. "If I don't give them some information they want, they'll zap my computer remotely."

Amber's eyes narrowed and she said, "The Clan needs that computer."

"The easy fix is to just email the file, though. No worries." Until he was certain which way Houle would decide, he sure didn't want to tell her he might have to die or leave. If he had to leave, he wouldn't tell her anyway—he'd leave a note so she had closure, but to tell her would invite either her insistence on coming with him or begging for him to stay. Nope. He cared for her too much to put her through that ordeal needlessly.

Amber examined him closely for a minute, but he kept his expression steady. Finally, she gave him a nod and smiled. "Cool. I came down to grab your tray. Figured you'd forget. Sorry I missed our breakfast time. I had a chore that ran long."

Her smiles were the prettiest ones he had ever seen, and she was just so beautiful like that... He felt a growing urge, but she had only come down for his tray. He tried to think of unsexy things.

He needn't have bothered because it turned out that his tray wasn't the only thing she wanted from him that morning. The next half hour was almost enough to take his mind off his chat with Watcher One.

* * *

Carl was grateful for the cheap, open-walled pavilion that

blocked out some of the brutal afternoon sun. He sent out two more runners to deliver orders to platoon commanders where they were still fighting the Harrisburg survivors deeper in the city. The battle's tempo had slowed and he had spent the last hour getting the medical bays supplied with freshly recovered wounded fighters for triage and treatment. Some of those wounded had to wait in the field for over two hours before they could be recovered. For some of the dead now coming in, it had been too late.

Thankfully, with the fighting winding down all over the city there would be fewer casualties coming back. The troops he had diverted to find and retrieve the wounded were staying out a bit longer before returning, or so it felt. Every Band had fought, even Diamondback, and they all had their share of casualties, although the numbers overall had not been that bad.

As Speaker Mary Ann's right hand, Carl didn't have the luxury of focusing on his own Timber Wolves bandmates, but he had made sure to keep a couple of runners for his own use so he could stay updated on his own wounded. Rank had its privileges.

One of his runners was sprinting toward him, panting, and came to a halt in front of him. "Alpha... We have a prisoner you'll want to see," he managed to say in between gasps for air.

"I can't leave this post. Bring them here."

Carl watched as the runner jogged away, head down, shoulders high up and tense. That man was about to drop, yet he kept going. A good Liz Town fighter.

Carl went back to the map of the city and his many notes. The reports coming in made it clear that the Harrisburg defenses all over the city were crumbling, and they had begun to fall back toward the I-81 bridge over the Susquehanna River. Harrisburg may have lost the vast railroad and shipping depots just east of the bridge, but they still had a beachhead on this side of the Susquehanna. Everything from North 6th Street westward still belonged to Harrisburg's defenders, and all those retreating units were linking up in that small zone. It allowed their defenses to stiffen considerably as their troop densities increased in the area.

"Runner. Take this order to the battalion commander at the rail depot. I need them to stop pressing the attack. They need to just keep the enemy hemmed up until we can figure out something suitably nasty to do to them. We're going to take unacceptable casualties if we try to push them across the river in a frontal assault. Tell him I want to keep the enemy engaged so they can't regroup and counterattack, but he must not assault their positions."

The runner nodded, took the paper, and sprinted away.

A commotion caught Carl's attention. Turning his head, he saw four fighters manhandling two Harrisburg men, herding them toward him. Those would be the ones the first runner had told him about. The prisoners wore civilian clothes, nothing special, so what was important about them?

When they came close, one of the Lizzie guards said, "Alpha, these two aren't Harrisburg, and they aren't Empire. Guess who."

"I don't have the time to play guessing games. What did you find?" Carl raised an eyebrow at them.

"They're from the Mountain. We found them in a hidden room at the back of what used to be a grocery store. A grenade took out part of a wall that hid their back room."

"What else you got? Any intel?"

"Yes, a lot. We found maps, copies of orders, and a stack of files. They had a cache of tradable goods, as well as a shortwave radio. The unit had a weird box, which we think encrypted their speech into some pattern language."

"Why do you think that?" Carl asked, genuinely curious about the box.

"They received a transmission while we were getting them ziptied. We heard a lot of bleeps and bloops from the radio, and a robotic voice came out the box half a second later. Like, text-to-speech."

Carl looked again at the two prisoners. Both men looked ordinary in *almost* every way. Maybe more fit than most, but the one thing that really stood out was that both men were clean shaven. Shaving had become less common in general, and to see two shaved men in Harrisburg was odd.

Actually, once he looked more closely, he saw that their hair—now growing out, but still short—was a lot longer on top than on the sides, and the transition between the two lengths was abrupt. It was possible they had once worn their hair in a fade or high-and-tight, and that it had had grown out. That showed the two men *could* have been in the military.

And then he saw their boots. Those were *Belleville*'s "Tactical Research" line of combat boots. U.S. Army-approved, Army-issue. The distinctive "ribbing" pattern down the sides meant they were the real deal, not a knockoff. Michael had taught him that during a conversation in Carl's time as the Liz Town envoy to Clanholme. Carl had asked about Michael's boots and then got more of an earful than he cared to about the subject of military footwear.

Carl looked at his four fighters, who stood by patiently. "I've seen enough. Nicely done. I expect a report from everyone involved, okay? In the meantime, secure these two men and keep them separated. I want them held under continual guard. Also, we need to get everything from that room you found them in and take it to the HQ in Liz Town so we can get this all figured out. Dismissed."

Those two prisoners would require *special* interrogation.

Questioning of the sort Michael did well and didn't talk about. Carl realized he'd have to arrange for the Mountain's agents to be delivered to Clanholme along with the intel they had captured.

The presence of agents from NORAD gave Carl a lot to think about. For one thing, the Empire had stopped sending supplies to Harrisburg via the river. He had heard the Mountain supported the Empire, but Harrisburg never joined the Empire officially. They had taken to accommodating the Empire's every demand, however, so they might as well have been members.

But if Harrisburg had joined the Empire, it would explain why the Mountain had agents here as well, despite the town's being so close to the Confederation. Or maybe *because* it was so close. How long had those two been stationed there? Long enough to be set up in a secret room with radios and other gear. They hadn't just arrived yesterday, that was certain.

"Alpha," said a voice behind Carl, interrupting his internal debate.

He turned and saw a Timber Wolf fighter, who looked flushed and was breathing heavily. A runner, then. "Yes, what is it?"

"Sir, a report from the company commander at the front, near the bridge." The messenger held out a note, folded in half and then half again, and sealed with wax.

Carl took the note, carefully cracked the wax seal, and opened it. He quickly read the report of troop movement on the far side of the bridge. The report was clear: hundreds of armed fighters amassing quietly.

"Runners," he shouted as he continued to read. "Go to your assigned officers and advise them that the enemy has reinforcements gathering on the far side of the river. They need to brace themselves at the bridge and get ready to receive an assault, once the two enemy groups join together. Our battalion at the rail yard needs to be on standby to deploy, reinforcing wherever they're needed. Dismissed."

Carl watched the runners sprint away and clenched his jaw. The mass of new troops could only be from the Empire finally coming to Harrisburg's rescue. The intel reports Carl had heard said there weren't a lot of Empire goons available to go on the offensive, but apparently they felt Harrisburg was more urgent than keeping a tight grip on their own civilians. The Empire might have some uprisings if they weren't quick about this, Carl mused with a faint smile. That would be nice. Too bad it meant a new army for his people to fight.

He turned to his duty officer, the woman who would replace him in the command chain if he bit the big one. "You have command until you hear from me. I need to get eyes on the situation."

She nodded, and Carl grabbed his binoculars off the table then headed toward the nearby water tower. He had posted a sniper up there because it gave a good view of everything between the command post and the river, but it was a long way up to the tower's top.

By the time Carl reached the top, he was breathing heavily. The binoculars around his neck had made it twice as difficult, banging against rungs and getting wrapped around the occasional hook or other jutting bits of metal. But he had made it. He scooted on his butt along the catwalk until he had a good view of the bridge.

He put the binoculars to his eyes and began a slow, methodical search of the entire area and both ends of the bridge, looking for anything unusual that might indicate the gathering enemy force's current location. It only took a minute to find them. They hid behind dead cars that had been pushed off the road long ago. They hid behind bushes.

They hid on the back side of the few buildings, and under the bridge on the far side. He counted for a while, but there were too many. He lost track at about one hundred, and there looked to be about twice that in total from what he had seen. It was a big force. Liz Town could contain two hundred more enemy troops, but it would be costly.

Carl considered the options. He could retreat quickly and in good order right now, saving his numbers, or he could order a push through the weaker defenders on this side, taking heavy casualties, and then engage the other force when they crossed that bridge. Cassy, perhaps, would have retreated, but that wasn't his way. He had no intention of getting pushed out of Harrisburg, only to have to attack it again later. He pulled out his radio, a tiny one good only for a very short range. "HQ, this is Alpha."

"Copy, Alpha. Standing by for orders," said the woman he had left in charge down there.

Carl noted with satisfaction that her voice was steady and confident on the radio. That would be useful. "Urgent, urgent. All units—repeat, all units—are to assault the bridgehead. Push them back, but do not cross. Just secure the bridgehead. How do you copy?"

"Good copy, Alpha. Doing it now." Carl heard no tension in the woman's voice, or maybe it just always sounded tight.

Ten minutes later, he heard Lizzie unit commander whistles from afar, shrill and very faint, signaling the assault. Then a quick *pop, pop* here and there, which quickly became the sound of a full-fledged battle.

That's when he saw the Empire goons surging across the bridge from the far side. Damn, it was too soon. They must have realized the danger, and were moving in right away instead of waiting to be fully assembled. Liz Town would still win this fight, albeit with terrible casualties. If he ordered a retreat, now that the goons were joining the battle too soon, casualties would be just as high yet would leave the enemy in control of the city, so retreat wasn't even an option anymore. It was a rock and a hard place, but Carl had faith that his wild, wily Liz Town veteran fighters would win.

Surprisingly, he saw the Empire troops begin to fire when they were only halfway across the bridge. Terrible fire discipline—they'd burn through their ammunition quickly, which was good...

Amazingly, they kept up a heavy fire. That made no sense. They couldn't possibly even see more than a few of the Liz Town defenders from there. He scanned the Harrisburg line to see how they were reacting to sudden reinforcements. No doubt they would get suddenly brave.

Through his binoculars, however, what he saw was far different from what he expected. The Harrisburg troops went prone in droves, while most of the others turned around, getting ready to make a break for safety on the far side of the bridge. Why would they do that?

No, wait... they were firing toward the bridge's far end. Carl was confused, but then it hit him—the goons were firing at the Harrisburg fighters, striking hard in their rear, and the defenders were firing back at them. He was still trying to make sense of what he saw when his own forces began vaulting over their makeshift defenses around the bridgehead. They engaged the totally disorganized Harrisburg forces at close range, some even in hand-to-hand combat.

Carl scrambled down the tower as fast as he could, heedless of the binoculars around his neck that bounced off rungs and smacked him in the ribs. He'd have bruises later, but he reached the ground in record time.

Then he sprinted toward the HQ. His motorbike was there in case he had to bug out. Instead, he was going to use it to get down into the action. He kicked it into life and then revved the engine, racing down street after street, weaving around dead cars. In minutes, he was at the front.

Except there was no front. It had utterly collapsed, and all that remained was to mop up a few remaining knots of resistance. Ahead, he saw Empire goons and Liz Town fighters... mingling and shaking hands. What the hell was going on?

When he got close enough, he dumped the motorbike and strode forward like a tornado. "Who's in command?" he bellowed at the nearest Liz Town trooper.

To his left, a woman standing among a knot of Liz Town fighters raised her head, spotted him and shouted back, "I'm the C.O. Name's Major Breen. And you are?"

Carl nodded. "I'm the Alpha in command, Liz Town. Care to explain this? I'm confused."

Breen smiled. "I'm sure you are, sir. But let me just say that the Free Republic sends its greetings. We'd like to come to an arrangement with the Confederation and figured, what better way to get on good terms than by delivering Harrisburg? You beat us to the punch, but I'm glad we could help. Between the two of us, we cut them down too fast for them to do much harm to either of our forces."

That was a total surprise. Carl's jaw almost dropped. The Free Republic? Clearly, the Confederation's schemes had worked. The Empire was breaking apart. "We welcome the Free Republic. Your help was indeed timely, and you saved us a lot of casualties."

Breen nodded, and sucked her front teeth, making a *tsk* noise. "Yep, that's the size of it. But we've hated these Harrisburg bastards for a long time now. Before the Middies brought them into the fold with us, we suffered their raids just as much as you did."

"Middies, huh? We call the Midwest Republic 'the Empire.' Okay, whoever your envoy is going to be, I'll give them a ride to Clanholme. The chancellor is going to want to talk to them."

The woman nodded and turned to one of her fighters, who then jogged away toward the bridge to get whoever Breen had in mind. "One envoy, coming right up."

Carl grinned and took stock of the major. She was tough, he could tell, and had that look of confidence soldiers got after surviving a few battles. Her troops seemed to respect her. Yes, so far he liked this new Free Republic unit commander. "I can't wait to meet them."

# - 7 -

2115 HOURS - ZERO DAY +349

FRANK HOBBLED TOWARD the Complex and randomly stopped people to ask whether they had seen Ethan. None had. He wondered if Ethan might be in the bunker, though he had already checked there once.

Frank spotted Michael heading toward the outdoor kitchen, where mounds of snacks were being prepared as a treat for that evening. Frank shouted Michael's name and his head whipped toward the sound, searching for the shouter.

When Michael saw him, his face lit into a smile. Michael came to him and said, "Quite the party starting tonight for no reason, eh?"

Frank returned the smile. "It seems to turn into a party any time we make snacks. Maybe it's the sugar in the Brittle Bits," he said, referring to Grandma Mandy's homemade candy recipe, modified for the ingredients they had available.

"Or maybe," Michael's face turned overly-dramatic, "it's the hard cider that seems to come out any time we make snacks. Woo woo, it's a mystery."

"You're terrible at making ghost noises, Michael."

"Hurtful."

Frank chuckled, then asked, "Have you seen Ethan?"

Michael pointed to the earthbag circle that ran from dome to dome around the Complex. "He's sitting on the wall, on the east end somewhere. He's with Amber."

"Thanks," Frank said with a smile and headed toward the Complex's far side.

In a couple of minutes, he found Ethan and Amber, along with her daughter. Kaitlyn was adorable, and had recently turned eight years old. It brought a good, healthy feeling to Frank's heart to see Kaitlyn sitting on Ethan's knee, grinning and playing with him, happy once again. She hadn't been very happy since her dad, Jed, had died almost a year prior. Frank had known Kaitlyn since he'd met her dad, back when she was almost still a baby. She had even called him "Uncle Frank."

He hated to interrupt Ethan's time with them, but in a way this was the best time to ask him what needed asking. As the festivities grew louder, the mood was upbeat, and Ethan was finally out of the bunker where he couldn't easily make excuses to run away from the conversation. Frank shook his head, clearing that last uncharitable thought. Ethan was a good man, he just wasn't one who liked conflict. Frank hobbled up toward them and when he got closer, Ethan spotted him and waved. Frank closed the distance.

"Hey Ethan. Amber." Frank sat next to Ethan on the wall and let out a contented sigh, thankful to be off his one foot. It usually ached terribly from overuse.

Amber smiled in greeting. "Frank-o. How's the foot?"

"Good enough to find Ethan up here. It would be nice to have two, though."

"Kaitlyn and I were about to go get snacks. Want anything?"

When Frank shook his head, she walked toward the outdoor kitchen hand-in-hand with her girl, leaving Ethan and Frank as alone as they could be with a rising party going on all around them.

Ethan said, "You know they weren't planning on going to go get snacks, right?"

Frank shrugged. "I figured they were just trying to be polite. I've been looking for you for a little while now."

"What can I do for you, my friend?" Ethan asked. "Glad to see you joining the fun. It started with the snacks, as always."

Ethan's words echoed Frank's earlier thoughts. Frank chuckled and said, "Yeah. Well, someone's gotta drink all that hard cider. And if there's any more drones around, let them get a good look at how the Clan parties, right? Psychological warfare at its finest—the best revenge is a good life, they say."

Ethan snorted. "I hope those bastards really miss the drone Michael shot down."

Frank noticed that Ethan made no mention of the poor girl who had died right in front of him when the drone attacked, nor of the fact that the drone had proved there was a nearby agent at the time. Frank knew from other conversations that Ethan was still shaken up about the teen girl's death, and he had no intention of ruining Ethan's night.

Frank sat in silence for half a minute, enjoying the view of people having a good time. Finally, he decided it was time to get to the real point of this conversation. He let out a long breath, as though it could blow the tension right out of him, then said, "Speaking of that drone, what did you learn about it? Tell me everything."

Ethan looked irritated—this was a spontaneous party, after all—but instead of arguing, he said, "Definitely from the Mountain. It's one of the 20s drones. I confirmed that easily enough by virtue of it having a small Gatling-gun rocket system. Who else would have something like that? No one that we've seen. And the parts are labeled in English."

Frank felt a flash of anger at General Houle and the 20s for murdering that sweet young girl. He also felt a flash of fear. "Give me the truth. Do you think they might send another drone after us?"

"Well," Ethan said tentatively, "I think drones are irreplaceable. NORAD has a big stockpile of them, no doubt, but they'll still be hoarded for just the critical missions. I think it's more likely that they would send a Predator loaded with Hellfires. I'm sure they have more missiles than drones, and they can get the Predator back, unlike the smaller drones."

Frank shuddered as an image of a Predator drone strike crossed his mind. He would have to ask Michael later about the operational range of a Predator drone. Could one go all the way from Colorado to Pennsylvania, or would they need to be launched from a bomber much closer? But that was curiosity, not really relevant, and he had a more urgent curiosity to satisfy. "Why'd they send those drones then, Ethan? It seems like it must have taken a lot of effort to get two little drones all the way out here."

Frank peered at Ethan intently, observing his body language. Ethan looked tense.

"As I said before, it was a retaliation. A warning to me."

"Ethan, you're a smart guy, and I know you must have put a lot of thought into this. You've already said they wanted you to sabotage us, and you didn't follow their orders. I get that. Not a person here is blaming you for being loyal to the Clan. And we paid the consequences of your decision, but it was still the right choice."

When Ethan nodded, he looked a bit more relaxed and Frank continued, "What I meant to ask is, why did they send a fatal warning? It must be very important to them to take out our gear, but why do you think they'd waste so many resources on warning you? It was a rather elaborate show of strength, which puzzles me."

Ethan looked like he was thinking hard about how to answer, then finally replied, "They're on a timeline. I think that must be it."

Frank felt his heart rate speeding up. He couldn't think of one scenario that ended well for the Clan if there was a timeline involved. "What the hell for? If you know something, you had better spill it."

"At first, I thought it was just a sort of guideline on just how disabled they wanted things, so I didn't mention it while I tried to figure things out."

Frank let out a long, frustrated breath. Typical Ethan—he would view it as an intellectual challenge, a mystery, not thinking to say anything until he had cracked it open.

Frank said, "I'm giving you a direct order now so there can be no confusion later. If you talk to the 20s, I want a full report on what was said. That very day, no matter the time of day. You need to do this every single time they contact you. Do you understand me? I can't make informed decisions when my Intelligence Chief isn't being intelligent."

Ethan nodded. Frank was Ethan's friend, and the poor guy had very few of those. He was a loner by nature. Ass-chewing him must have felt like a kick in the teeth.

Frank put his hand on Ethan's shoulder and then said, "Good."

"I'm sorry, Frank. I swear it won't happen again."

"I know. We're square, okay? I'm off to get some grub."

"Okay," Ethan said.

Frank hopped up, and Ethan handed him his crutch. He waved with his other hand and then hobbled toward the outdoor kitchen for snacks and regular ol' apple cider. He had a lot to think about, so he'd be leaving the hard cider alone tonight.

\* \* \*

0530 HOURS - ZERO DAY +350

Carl felt the engine rumble through the steering wheel as the *Lizzie Borden* raced along, and nine other battlecars from several Bands trailed behind him. They streaked along I-76 westbound, heading toward the mountains. The Empire had pushed the rebel Free Republic forces out of the pass, threatening to spill out into the lowlands. That would put Carlisle in jeopardy, and the rebellion had passed word that they needed help. If Carlisle fell, the Empire would again threaten Harrisburg, forcing the Confederation to divert much-needed forces.

Carl shuddered to think of what Mary Ann had done to the enemy survivors in Harrisburg when the town fell. Those bastards had raided, killed, raped, and pillaged almost since the first month after the EMPs, and so they were Liz Town's most hated enemies. Harrisburg had never offered mercy on their raids, and they could expect none from Mary Ann. The battle he was racing toward was good timing, as far as Carl was concerned—he'd much rather go into battle than deal with the gruesome aftermath of the victory at Harrisburg.

On the horizon, he saw a bright flash of light in the dim predawn. It had come from a mortar, probably, though of course, he couldn't tell which side's. Probably the Empire's, since mortars were heavy and the rebels were falling back almost as fast as they could run. The thought of enemy mortars was sobering, yet it made him grin. Taking out mortar crews behind the main fighting lines was a perfect use for his mobile, armored battlecars.

He wiped a bit of grime off his goggles, then put his foot into the gas pedal and felt the buggy-like *Lizzie Borden* surge forward. He'd be fighting again in only a couple minutes, and his heart began to race in anticipation. If all went well, he'd soon have the rebels rallying and the Empire fleeing for their lives back over the pass. It was enough to make any good Lizzie's heart sing.

* * *

General Ree nodded to the messenger, who bowed low before leaving. Ree knelt upon a pillow, hands on his knees. He felt serene as he reached down to the wax-sealed note, picked it up and opened it. The note was from one of his officers—now vassals—reporting great success in liberating supplies from one of Taggart's nearby defensive stations. The officer had seized the supplies and withdrawn to safety with only minimal casualties.

Ree smiled faintly. Nearly two weeks ago, he had cut rations to his vassals. The last time one had seized new territory, Ree had given it to the man's neighbor. Those two events combined to achieve the result he wanted, and now he was seeing his plan bear fruit. Why take territory, with all those hassles, when Ree might just give it to your nearest rival? But when they seized only supplies, Ree only took a cut and left the spoils with the victor. The colonels were beginning to aggressively hit into Taggart's territory, seizing everything of value and retreating. Every troop Taggart used in response to reinforce his front lines was a trooper unavailable elsewhere. Besides, it disrupted Taggart's operations in general, which was "all good," as the Americans said.

Except that everything else wasn't all good. Production had slowed down all over the city. Not just in gathering, processing, and distribution of food, but also among the textiles workers who sewed and repaired clothing. And the munitions section, making homemade mortars, mortar rounds, and reloading spent small arms shells. And the fishing people. Just about everything, in fact, had slowed noticeably.

Maddeningly, it wasn't caused by anything he could put his finger on. Unfortunately, it wasn't just slow workers. That, he could fix. It was small, simple things that added up. Straps and belts were giving out three times more often than they had only a month ago. Tools somehow broke or disappeared, in between shifts. Wagon wheels that had been securely bolted were mysteriously falling off. Important supplies vanished overnight, or even in broad daylight. When mundane goods were moved from station to station, or to warehousing, the shipments came in missing an item or two.

No one thing was huge, but it all added up to a noticeable slowdown and was beginning to affect his operations. If this went unchecked, it could grow into something terminal. A cancer. Ree knew he'd have to cut that cancer out before it spread too far, but where to begin? All the problems couldn't be traced to any one person or cause. They just... happened.

The only solution he saw was to increase the guards on most of those things, and put spies to watch everything as best they could. If he could capture one responsible person, he might get more names out of them. His ISNA interrogators were excellent. As far as Ree was concerned, torture was the only thing the sand-eaters were actually good for. He amended that—they were also good as cover. They caught bullets in battle so his own Koreans were hit less often.

Ree raised one finger on his right hand, and his servant shuffled forward, head bowed. Ree didn't look at him, but closed his eyes and said, "Fetch Major Kim. He and I must discuss operations."

The servant shuffled backwards through the exit, and Ree smiled at the thought of the delicious tea his servant would bring for him to share with Kim. Delighting Kim with his generosity and exquisite teas pleased Ree for some reason. The Americans had lots of wonderful teas from every corner of the globe, and Ree felt that he was becoming quite an accomplished connoisseur of fine teas and their qualities. He loved the fine teas. The death of the old electronic world didn't mean he must recede into barbarism with it, did it?

He would leave the barbarism to his disgusting sand-eaters. Arabs would only waste good tea by getting their unseemly facial hair in it. Hah, the image amused him. Those ISNA were worse than Americans when it came to having far too much ugly facial hair. Unlike Yankees, however, his ISNA animals knew their place in the grand scheme of things—at the bottom rung, along with everyone else who wasn't North Korean.

* * *

Frank sat atop his horse, fitted with a special saddle. His left foot stump had been strapped into the custom stirrup, and now he awaited the inbound Liz Town messengers. He had grown used to the strange stirrup, and it no longer chafed the stub where his left foot had been removed.

Why had the Lizzies asked to meet him at Clanholme's north food forest instead of simply riding into the settlement? It was odd.

He tried not to feel irritated at the inconvenient process of getting to his horse, strapping in, and riding down there. The damn straps meant that even though Michael had been in the fields, he beat Frank to the rendezvous point.

Right after Frank trotted up beside Michael, the Liz Town messengers rode into view. The narrow gravel and dirt road, which ran from the main road all the way into Clanholme proper, doglegged within the food forest to prevent anyone seeing in from the outside. It had been one of Cassy's pre-war privacy decisions that had turned out to be useful now. One of many such preparations she had made.

Frank looked them over and saw that the lead messenger's head was lightly bandaged. Her companion had no shirt beneath his Timber Wolf-painted war jacket, and his ribs were wrapped tightly. They must be coming from the battle at Harrisburg, where Liz Town had assaulted the residents to put an end to their threat once and for all. Frank peered at the messengers' faces and saw their expressions were pained and tired, but surprisingly cheerful. That was promising.

"Welcome to Clanholme. I'm Frank Conzet, leader of the Clan. I hope all is well in Liz Town?"

The riders stopped their horses and smiled. The woman dismounted and said, "I'm Reject, of the Timber Wolf Band. Nice to meet you, Mr. Conzet."

Frank realized she had used his proper name to show that she knew of him, and he felt amused. Before he had taken over as the Clan leader, few people knew his last name. "Do you need some water, Reject?"

She nodded and her companion shook his head. Michael motioned to one of the Clan outriders, who gave Reject a water bottle. She guzzled it greedily, wiped her face on her sleeve, and handed the empty bottle back. Water was one of the few things it was polite to accept as a guest, since it was plentiful.

"Much obliged," Reject said with a relieved expression. "My Alpha didn't want this broadcasted over the radio, so he sent me directly. We've taken Harrisburg, first of all."

Frank felt a grin forming. "Good. I hope those bastards got all the mercy they deserve."

Reject nodded, eyes glinting merrily. "Oh yes. So that's the first thing."

Michael cocked his head to the side. "There's more?"

She nodded. "Yes, sir. At the end of the battle, the remaining Hairyburgers had fallen back to positions on just this side of the bridge. We were preparing to launch the final assault on Harrisburg and expected high casualties, but then another force streamed across the bridge. We figured it was the Empire, come to save their allies."

Michael said, "I take it they weren't?"

"No, sir," Reject replied, and then she laughed. "They were *once* Empire, but now they're independent. The Free Republic, they call themselves. It turns out those Confed supply runs to the guerrillas worked better than we had hoped. Practically the Empire's whole eastern territory has broken away, dealt with their loyalist traitors however they chose"—she curled her upper lip into a snarl as she said that —"and then came to help us deal with the enemy in their rear. They hate Harrisburg as much as we do, and when Harrisburg joined the Empire, it didn't sit well with their former victims who were then supposed to welcome them with open arms. I guess it was the final straw for many people."

Frank nodded slowly. He knew that it was fantastic news since they wouldn't have to deal with the Empire directly any more, now that the Free Republic was between the Mountain and the Confederation. "I'll let the Chancellor know right away. We'll want to send Confed envoys."

"Yes, sir. But there's one more thing."

Frank raised an eyebrow expectantly. Reject dug into her saddlebags and withdrew a small box and a long cardboard tube. She handed them to him and said, "These are maps, documents, and other trinkets we captured from a hidden radio room in Harrisburg."

"Oh? Hidden, you say." Frank felt a childlike desire to know what was in the tube and box.

"They're from the King Under the Mountain. It seems NORAD had an outpost in Harrisburg."

Frank's jaw dropped. Analyzing the documents would be of the highest priority... "Michael, get those. You and Ethan have them analyzed, would you?"

"You got it." Michael waved to the Outrider, took the items, and turned his mount to ride off toward the HQ.

Once Michael had left, Frank said, "Very well done. We are always grateful for the Liz Town contributions to the Confederation and to all our safety. With the fall of Harrisburg, the loss of a Mountain outpost, and the developments in the Empire, today is a damn good day for the Good Guys."

"You bet," Reject said. "We'll have a funeral for our people tomorrow, if you want to send someone."

Frank nodded, shifting in his saddle to get comfortable. "Yes, we'll definitely send someone. Please let Carl know that we'd like an update on Lizzie casualties so we can bring something appropriate to the funeral."

Reject eyed Frank for a moment. Maybe his response had surprised her. Then she nodded and threw a sloppy salute-and-grin combination at Frank before she, her companion, and the Clan outriders turned their mounts and galloped away, heading back the way they had come.

Frank was left with both joy at the news and a nagging fear about what the Mountain's involvement at Harrisburg meant for the future. His conversation with Ethan—four months, Ethan had said—came back to him. Surely this was connected.

Frank decided it was time to let the Clan Council know the details and get their advice. He'd also have to inform Cassy. He turned his horse back toward the lower stable, near the HQ. Definitely a good day. So long, Harrisburg... They would not be missed.

# - 8 -

1200 HOURS - ZERO DAY +365

ETHAN GRINNED AND clicked "save as" on the computer, thus completing version 1.0 of his latest magnificent programming gem. He copied the program to an external hard drive and a USB token, just in case—one couldn't be too careful or have too many backups, these days. "How ironic," he muttered.

Amber sat across from him on the loveseat as she munched on her lunch. "What's that?" she said over a mouthful of food, raising her hand to cover her mouth.

Ethan snorted. Amber was not the most delicate flower out there, but she was everything he had wanted in a woman. Smart, funny with a biting wit, a bit tomboyish, and as happy in sweatpants and a tee shirt as she was in a dress. She didn't have a pretentious bone in her amazing body.

She smirked as Ethan stared at her. "I said, what's ironic?"

Ha. Of course she would demolish him with a smirk. And he loved it. "It's ironic that, on today of all days, I'm finishing this program. It's a worm and trojan horse one-two punch to hack into Watcher One's systems."

Amber shrugged, then set her scraped-clean plate down. "What's so important about today?"

"Are you kidding? The lights went out one year ago today. About eight hours ago, actually." Ethan felt a weird mix of excitement and sadness. Although when he thought about it, he realized that his mixed feelings weren't that odd. Many people had died, but he had not. Sad and happy.

She shrugged. "All that means to me is that sixty to seventy percent of Americans are now dead. Fewer in the country, more in the cities. What's to celebrate?"

It was Ethan's turn to shrug. "It means the Dying Time is nearly over and we beat the odds. We made it. The Clan, you, me, all of us."

"For now," she replied. Then Amber tucked her feet underneath herself on the loveseat, which served as a couch in the confined Bunker. "Still ten percent to go, according to the estimate."

"As much as ten percent," Ethan corrected her, "but it could be less. Whatever happens, we're golden. We got our community."

\* \* \*

Taggart ate his sandwich—the bread people made these days blew the doors off the supermarket bread he had grown up on—and nodded at Eagan. "Yes, for the tenth time, we're having a memorial and celebration. Quit nagging at me, shitbird."

"If I was still King of New York, you wouldn't talk to me like that," Eagan replied, grinning. "Sir," he added hastily, and with much emphasis.

"Kingly titles, eh? Easy come, easy go," Taggart replied. He set the crust down and grabbed a pickle. He had already finished the chips, if they could be called chips. Homemade potato chips did *not* compare to supermarket chips. One of the many things he missed. "I've got a whole work detail set up to get things ready."

"So we're going to have a mass memorial for all the people who've died, probably close to two-hundred million. Then we're going to get drunk and mingle with the local ladies. Right?"

"You are. I'm not getting drunk."

"Such a party pooper, sir. Whatever shall I do with you."

Taggart chuckled. "Salute, mostly. But with Ree's people raiding heavily, we can't get too comfortable."

"Are you still going to have a third of our men and women on guard duty tonight?" Eagan didn't look happy about that.

"Yes. Tonight would be a great time for Ree to raid deep. He has to know this is the anniversary of the invasion. It won't have the same deep meaning to him that it has to Americans. If he celebrates, it won't be because he's alive, but because over half of all Americans are dead. Bastard."

"Why do you have to talk about that," Eagan replied glumly. "For one day, I want to forget there's a war going on."

"The war won't forget us, numbnuts. Try not to get that little Italian girl pregnant tonight, okay?"

Eagan laughed, his face brightening again. "Forget that, sir. I'm going to do my best to get Sophia knocked up. Tonight's the night to celebrate life. Maybe start a new one."

Taggart nodded. He understood the feeling. Life goes on, even amidst a war and the end of civilization. "I'm surprised she's not already pregnant. You two seem pretty serious."

"Maybe we are. I think so. I haven't asked, but I feel like it's serious. She introduced me to her parents last week. And her three brothers... Scary-big, those guidos."

"Yep. But they kept Sophia alive and got their entire

family out of Brooklyn even before we broke out out the City ourselves. That's a tough family. She's gotta be tough, too, I imagine."

"She must be, to put up with my ass."

"You have no idea how right you are," Taggart said, chuckling. "Gonna marry her?"

"I'm thinking about it. I don't feel like that really matters anymore, but she and her family are the opposite. They think that social values and family bonds matter more now than ever. Maybe they're right, I don't know."

Huh. Taggart pondered that for a moment. It was an interesting thought. People these days went one of two ways —wild out, or retreating into traditions and conservative values. Both reactions had their pros and cons from a survival-of-the-species point of view. "How do they feel about you being so... white? Painfully white. Like, salt cracker white. Whiter than White-out. SPF-nine-hundred white. More white than—"

"Sir!" Eagan interrupted. "You hurt my feelings. I'm Irish, not white. In Europe, that makes me black, like you." He said it with a straight face.

Taggart burst into laughter. Leave it to Eagan to say something stupid like that just to be funny. "Half black. The good half, in my opinion."

"Fair enough," Eagan said, grinning. "They're fine with my pasty complexion, though. My family's from Catholic Ireland, not going-to-Hell Ireland. That's how my mom always put it." He paused. "Or, used to."

Taggart nodded. Eagan's family was lost in the City, and he had never been able to find them. Taggart knew it was a sore spot. "There's still hope. And today's a celebration of life, so celebrate yours, and the chance they are alive."

Eagan nodded but remained silent.

Taggart put down the nub of pickle, having eaten the

rest. "How is our strategy working out for dealing with Ree's increased raiding? He was becoming a serious thorn in our side. Now I know how he felt when we were the thorn."

"So far, so good. By moving extra troops into the areas just interior to our front lines, creating a defense in depth, they aren't raiding as deep into our turf anymore—"

"Territory."

"Into our *territory* anymore. And they've depleted the supplies in the area around the front lines, having scrounged it out already. That gives them less incentive to raid. It's helped a lot."

"Good. Things have hit some sort of point-of-stability, I can feel it."

"Me too. I think this is going to be our new status quo hereabouts. To the west, our border is the Confederation, so we're good there, too. Our front lines to the south with General Yi, between Allentown and Philly, are still mighty fluid—troop densities on both sides have become low."

"The meat-grinder worked on them as much as on us, at least. Thank goodness."

"Yes, sir. And the I-80 corridor between Scranton and State College has stabilized as the front lines against General Park's invading forces, though Scranton has remained stubbornly out of our grasp. Fighting there has slowed, as well. We may just have to accept Scranton is enemy territory for the time being."

Taggart said, "Thanks for the rough update. You're off duty tonight, got it? After fourteen-hundred hours, you're free to go play boyfriend."

Eagan nodded. "I appreciate that. Sophia and I are going on a picnic with her parents and her brothers, before tonight's real celebrating begins. Then me and her—"

"She and I."

"—me and her are going off on our own to check out the

displays, and that 'Food From Around the World' thing."

Taggart grinned. "I don't know how authentic it'll be without fresh imported spices and so on, but I'm damn sure going to try it out myself. I hear there's going to be some fantastic German cuisine."

"There ought to be. Those Amish, or Mennonites, or whichever groups they're from, they all speak German. So I'm hoping to have some honest-to-god fresh frankfurters."

Taggart let out a sigh. Frankfurters... "Who would have thought that fresh hot dogs would become the special treat everyone's talking about?"

"It's a strange world we live in, sir. Your AgSec, Cassy, calls it a 'dark new world,' but I think it's a lot brighter than the old world in a lot of ways. More dying, but a whole lot more really living, too."

"Maybe... But don't go getting all philosophical on me, shitbird. Save those big words for Sophia—you don't know enough of them to waste on me."

"Sir, I appreciate your confidence."

"No problem, Eagan. I'm always here for you," Taggart replied with an impish smile. And the truth was, he always would be there for Eagan. The young man—he no longer thought of Eagan as a kid—had become as much his son as his right-hand-man. "By the way, and this is just a thought... Tonight would be a pretty damn good time to propose. If you want to look through the jewelry stockpiles, take your pick."

Eagan's jaw dropped. Taggart had never before given anyone permission to "requisition" personal items like jewelry, and probably wouldn't ever again, so Taggart was glad Eagan recognized its significance.

"Thank you, sir. I... Perhaps I will. This is a good time to declare that life goes on. What better way to say it than with a ring? It's a big step, though."

"True, kid. But she's pretty and kind, funny and smart.

She won't be on the market long. If she loves you, and you love her, this world no longer gives us the assurance that we can always decide later. Tomorrow isn't promised us."

Eagan nodded, pursing his lips. "No, it sure isn't. I'm gonna go, sir. I have some thinking to do before I go meet up with Sophia and her family."

Taggart waved him off and watched as the young man left. His advice to Eagan wasn't bad advice, all around. Taggart thought about that and decided that he should make the time to at least consider finding a better half for himself. He had put that thought off for a year now, because of the war. Fighting and planning had taken all his time, and until a couple months ago, every day had been a crapshoot on survival. Now things were settling down. Perhaps he should, too? Life went on, after all.

\* \* \*

2000 HOURS - ZERO DAY +365

Cassy lit the fuse, then watched as her firework shot into the air and exploded over the west fish pond. Cheering erupted at that official commencement of *Blackout Night*, the name that had just sort of stuck for this memorial and celebration.

All throughout the day, people had held ad-hoc memorials for lost loved ones and family. They had taken turns saying what they had been doing when it dawned on them that the lights were out for good. Many of the stories were sad or scary, and tears had flowed.

Tonight was for the flip side of that coin, the celebration of life for those who remained. No doubt similar events were going off all across America, Cassy mused. In nine months, there would likely be a slew of new babies in the Clan, judging by the raucous mood of the crowd. The existing children would be herded to bed in an hour or so, and Cassy would probably join them as they tried in vain to sleep amidst the noise of celebration.

She brushed her hands on her pants and then wandered around through the party, being seen and greeting everyone she could. She shared a short story here, listened to an anecdote there. It was fun to see the Clan so alive and happy. Everywhere, people drank freely of the hard apple cider for which the Clan was so rightly famous. A barrel of regular cider had been brought out for the kids, unless they snuck a cup of the hard cider. More than a few of the teens would likely be dragging ass in the morning, Cassy knew, and she grinned. Mostly, the adults turned a blind eye tonight, and she would too.

Along the way, she ran across Grandma Mandy and stopped to say hello. "How's it going, Mom?"

Mandy looked cheerful, and replied, "It's good, sweetie. This was a great idea. Not the hard cider, of course, but the celebration."

Cassy tried not to roll her eyes. Her mom didn't drink, didn't approve of drinking in general, but she wasn't a hardliner about it. Cassy replied, "They're blowing off a year's worth of steam, that's all."

"Indeed. They're welcome to it. Old ladies like me do better with regular cider, though."

"Especially with your diabetes? Water might be best."

"True. Juice isn't great for me either, but I have to have my little vices. They make life worth it."

"Juice makes life worth living, huh?" Cassy grinned.

"Also, steaks."

Cassy laughed out loud. They shares pleasantries for a moment, then Cassy continued her rounds.

With everyone drinking the lightly-alcoholic cider, and given that booze wasn't readily available anymore otherwise, only a few adults were likely to get truly drunk. Thankfully, there was double security for the night, and people had been exchanging work chits frantically right up to the celebration's very start. It had been fun to listen to some of the horse trading going on as people tried to offload their work chits on others.

Let them have their fun... Things had been going rather well lately, and she knew it couldn't last forever, but for tonight, all was well in the world.

* * *

Jaz wandered among the crowds of people, cup in hand and feeling slightly off balance. It was a good feeling—not drunk, but not sober. Perfect, in other words. Her cares and concerns melted away, at least for now. But where was Choony? She had been looking for him for what felt like a half an hour, but she didn't wear a watch.

Every time she wrapped up one brief, friendly conversation, someone else waved at her to come over. From one conversation to the next, she found herself slowly drifting away from the Complex and out into the Jungle's maze of verdant overgrowth. Another conversation. And another. Hi, how are you? How's Choony? When are you two leaving again? How did your last trip go... The usual catching up that people did during events such as this.

Jaz sat on a large, dark stone for a moment to rest her legs. She had been standing for quite a while. Finishing her cup, she set it on the mulch beside the stone, leaned back with her arms behind her for support, and looked up at the stars. With no ambient light, they shone brighter and more crisply than she had ever thought possible before the EMPs came. The silence washed over her as she found herself alone at last, and she let out a deep, contented sigh.

A noise to her left caught her attention, and she opened one eye. It was another reveler, one of the newer Clan members. John, maybe? She couldn't remember his name for sure. He waved.

She didn't feel like shifting position enough to wave back, so she just said, "How's it going?"

"Good. I'm Jack. You're Jaz, right? The envoy." He smiled politely.

"Yeah. So how have you liked being in the Clan, Jack?" she asked, opening her other eye as well.

He stepped up beside her rock. There wasn't room for two to sit on it, so he stayed standing. "It's interesting, for sure. So much to learn about how things are done, but I dig the traditions you guys are building up, here."

"Thanks." It was good that he could appreciate the details and how things were done. Many people didn't get it, at least not for a long while. She gave up leaning back and sat up, folding her hands in her lap. "Traditions build themselves, really. There's not much reason to keep most of the old ones, so new ones take their place."

"Yeah." Jack nodded. "Did you know... the ISNA invaders have a tradition? If they find a woman out alone, they figure she's a harlot. Their word, not mine. They have their own tradition, which is that women have to be with a male relative if they're outside the house."

"How barbaric," Jaz replied. "I couldn't live in a place like that."

"No, probably not," he grinned. "They also figure that if you're wearing short shorts and a tank top, like yours, then you're... available. You know, for rent."

Pinpricks shot up her spine and her scalp tingled. This was a totally weird conversation to be having with a stranger late at night in the middle of the Jungle. She stood up. "Yeah, they're weird," Jaz said, "but I need a refill. Thanks for the chat, Jack. I'm sure I'll see you around."

Jaz felt a hand on her arm, iron-hard like a vice, and Jack spun her around to face him. He wore a good-natured smile, but his grip didn't feel so good-natured. He said, "Hey, don't go just yet. I was hoping to ask you some questions about being an Envoy."

"Sure, but not right now, Jack. It's Blackout Night, and I totes need a refill. Gotta bounce. T.T.Y.L.," Jaz said, spelling out the acronym for 'talk to you later.'

His grip didn't lessen. "Aw, c'mon. I'm not asking you to do anything you don't want to do. Just hang out a bit more. I want to kick it with you for a while."

Jaz's alarms were going off full-bore even before he said that, and now she felt a rising panic. This had happened before. She knew the signs. Maybe he didn't mean anything by it, but in her experience, when dudes didn't want to let her go, they had something else in mind. Something that would very quickly be completely out of her control.

Adrenaline surging, she said more loudly than she realized, "No, Jack, let me go. I need to get back to the party."

Jack's eyes changed, then. They narrowed, pupils wide. His breathing was suddenly shallow and fast. "The party could be right here, Jaz," he said. His voice sounded husky.

Jaz glanced Jack up and down. He was probably twice her weight, all muscle. A fit young man. She decided she couldn't overpower him. Old Jaz would have gone inside herself and waited until it was all over, but New Jaz didn't like that idea. Maybe with one well-placed kick, she could escape...

Behind her, another voice. "Hi, Jaz. Hey, Jack. How you two doing? Say, Jaz, could you show me where the cider is being hidden? I'm parched." It was Choony! He looked at Jack, gaze direct and unwavering. "You don't mind, do you, Jack?"

Jaz felt Jack's grip loosen and then fall away. Jack smiled at Choony, that good-natured smile he had worn earlier. "Hi, Choony. Sure, she's all yours. I had some questions about being an Envoy, but they can wait. No rush..."

Jaz didn't like his tone when he said that.

"I thank you," Choony said. He stepped up and took Jaz's hand in his own, shaking it. Then he turned to Jaz. "Shall we? The cider awaits, and the night is young."

Jaz made herself smile and laugh. Inside, her adrenaline still pounded. She still felt trapped like an animal, and visions of gutting Jack with her knife now flooded through her mind. "Yes, of course. The cider is just this way." She led Choony away from the isolated spot in the Jungle, toward people and fires and cider and food. When they were safely away from Jack, she whispered, "Thanks. Your timing was great."

Choony lightly squeezed her hand in his own, reassuring her. "Of course. That didn't look like a comfortable scene. I am glad I found you when I did. My Karma and yours made sure I found you tonight."

Jaz nodded and clenched her jaw. Yeah. Uncomfortable was not the word she'd have used for that scene. "I was looking for you earlier, and just stopped to rest my feet. That's when Jack stumbled onto me out there."

Choony waved at someone going the opposite direction, then said, "I will talk to Frank about Jack's failure in his probation period. You won't have to worry about him again."

Jaz rested her head on Choony's shoulder as they slowly walked toward the party. Part of her thought that exiling Jack was harsh for a guy who hadn't done anything, but the bigger part of her was convinced that Choony's arrival was the only reason. She loved the feeling of having Choony beside her. Sure, he was non-violent, but she felt safe with him in a way she hadn't felt with with anyone else before. He used his mind to keep her safe. And once, at an event they never discussed anymore, he had used force to save her life.

She had no doubts about the depth of his connection to her, and realized that his unwavering support was half of what had let her come out of her shell, becoming "New Jaz." Jack's unexpected advances had surprised her, and she had reacted in the ways that had been beaten into her for most of her life. That weak reaction disgusted her. She didn't want to feel disgusted with herself. Maybe she should have gutted Jack anyway. She had thought about it...

"Choony," she said, "let's get something to drink, and then maybe you can get me away from this crowd. I'm just not feeling it tonight."

"Feeling okay?" Choony asked. When she nodded, head still on his shoulder, he smiled down at her. "Of course we can. You just need a breather, some quiet time to collect yourself."

Choony led her to the lines for cider and they each got two cups of the fermented stuff. Then he led her east, around the guard tower and the east fish pond, into the small network of tents that housed anyone for whom there wasn't an earthbag dome yet. She and Choony refused a dome, despite being among the first ones to be eligible. They spent so much time on the road that it felt wasteful. There would be domes for them eventually, but in the meantime their spots went to full-time residents.

The tent they shared was a heavy, military-style bivouac, meant for six people. It fit fine on the wagon, where they spent more of their time than they did at Clanholme, and they had set it up more permanently than it would have been on the road. They shared the tent on the road, and they shared it here as well.

Choony held the door flap open for her, and Jaz smiled as she ducked inside. Within the tent, their queen-sized inflatable air bed occupied the back left corner, leaving the front half and part of the rear empty. There, they stored their bugout bags, toiletries, and other necessities.

Jaz looked wistfully at the air bed. How many nights had they slept together, often with his arm over her for warmth? Her knight in shining armor.

She didn't need such a knight—not this new, stronger Jaz —but it was such a blessing to have one anyway. Choony was her rock when she felt herself spinning out of control, like now. The encounter with Jack had shaken her, brought back memories, causing her body to react on its own however much she wished otherwise. It was a PTSD-related response, she had once been told. Understanding what was happening to her didn't make it any easier to go through, but she could handle it.

She set her empty cup on a simple wooden crate, which they used as a nightstand when it wasn't packed full of toiletries in the wagon. One big gulp downed half of her other cup, and she set that down as well. "Choony," she said as she sat down on the air bed, "thanks for coming when you did."

Choony smiled and took a sip of his own hard cider. He didn't drink often, she knew, nor did he drink a lot on those rare occasions. He said, "I didn't rescue you. If he had tried anything else, you would have dealt with him quite effectively. I saw your posture change from victim to predator, and he had no idea. I saved him, not you. You're stronger than you give yourself credit for, and more skilled as well."

The compliment brought a smile to her lips. The room spun a little, just a slow veering to the right. She was drunker than she had intended to get, she realized, but not the drunkest she had ever been. Not by a mile.

She let out a giggle when he said "skilled." The confused

look on his face was even funnier. "Oh, Choony. You have no idea what 'skills' I have. I'm totally awesome at a few things." She wiggled her eyebrows at him.

Choony chuckled. She realized that he had taken it as a joke. He said, "I have no doubt about that. I think you're amazing at everything you do. Hey, are you feeling well? You look a little pale."

Jaz nodded, but she really wasn't feeling that well. The room was definitely spinning faster now, and veered more sharply. Ugh. She looked up at Choony, her gaze roaming over him from toes to top. He stood with the doorway behind him, the faint moonlight highlighting his high cheekbones, his pronounced chin. And she had seen him naked before. It would have been impossible to avoid, given their time together on the road.

Yes, she had the liquid courage now. If he turned her down that night, with any luck she wouldn't remember it in the morning. But if she hoped to do anything, she'd have to move quickly, she realized. She felt as though she could pass out soon.

"Choony, come sit next to me. I need you to lean on, tonight."

Choony nodded and moved away from the door, sitting gingerly next to her on the airbed. "I'm always here to lean on, Jaz. Tonight or any night."

Jaz leaned her head on his shoulder. Reaching for his hand, she slid her fingers between his own and rested it on his lap. She tilted her head to look up at him, her lips slightly parted. "Choony..."

He looked down into her eyes, his face mere inches from hers. "Yes?" he asked, voice steady and calm. His gaze didn't waver.

Jaz felt herself melt into those soft, brown eyes. Where they held hands, she felt like she could almost crawl into his skin. She willed her desires to flow through her, out her hand, and into Choony. Her mind spun, trying to think of something to say, some way of telling him what she wanted without risking hurt feels if he rejected her.

But screw it. No words came to mind. She decided to let her body speak for her. She moved her mouth to his. Room spinning, she almost missed, but then felt their lips connect. It was amazing, soft, hot to the touch. She watched to see his reaction.

Choony smiled, but slowly pulled his hand from hers. His other hand brushed her hair away from her face, where it had cascaded down, and then kissed her forehead. He stood up, and Jaz felt her heart drop to the floor. She fought a tear from welling in her eye. Why was he rejecting her?

"Choony, I'm sorry—"

Choony interrupted her, voice low and soft, "Jaz, don't apologize. You know my feelings for you, without ever hearing me say it. Tonight, you found yourself in a bad situation. I helped you. I think right now, you may be confusing things. And the cider hasn't helped."

"But Choony, don't you want me? Why do only the bad guys want me, and you don't?"

Standing before her, he reached up and again brushed her hair with his fingertips. It was gentle, and loving. "What is there not to want? You're beautiful, Jaz. You need to learn that your truest beauty is on the inside. What's outside, as gorgeous as that is, it's a mirror of the beauty within you."

"So, why not?" Jaz looked up into his eyes, longing to be in his arms. Was she confused, like he had said? She didn't feel confused.

"Tonight, you're drinking. I would never want to think it was only because of the cider, or that you had to force a smile onto your face in the morning. That would kill me." He turned toward the door flap.

"Stay with me," she said plainly.

But instead of walking outside, as she had expected, he pulled the canvas door flap shut and tied it closed, then sat on the bed beside her. He put one arm around her shoulders and laid back onto the bed, his head on the pillow, and pulled her down with him. She ended up half laying on him, her head resting on his chest, one arm over him. She felt him stroking her hair, and his lips briefly on her forehead again. He said nothing, and she relished that soft, tender moment.

She closed her eyes and let the alcohol take her into oblivion, feeling like she had never closer to another person. Most of the time, Jaz was a warrior, a fighter. She could channel the darkness inside her to stand strong in the world, to fight the good fight. Good enough for both of them.

But being able to let that hard, warrior part of herself go for just a little while, to feel open and relaxed without her masks... That was something she relished about that moment. She was glad he had turned her confused advances down, now.

Those thoughts rolled around in her mind for a few minutes until, all at once, a heavy sleep overcame her.

# - 9 -

0600 HOURS - ZERO DAY +366

FROM THE BLUFF, overlooking Uniontown, Pennsylvania, Nestor looked down upon the farthest bastion of the rebellious Free Republic. He had helped make that possible. Everything east of the Monongahela River, south of Pittsburgh, and the Allegheny River north of it were consolidating rapidly, with only a few Empire-loyalist survivor groups remaining.

The rebellion had simmered for quite a while, courtesy of the Empire's lies and draconian policies that had made the people little better than slaves. But once the simmering burst into the open, the open rebellion had exploded, seemingly spontaneous, and had raced east almost as fast as Nestor's units had.

He and his four hundred troops had only been camped outside of Uniontown for a few days, and had caught the tail end of the "civil war" going on inside. The fighting here, as elsewhere, had been brutal, with no quarter given between the rebel and loyalist sides. Now, the losers were finally buried—the winners had given the enemy dead that much consideration, at least in part because Nestor had suggested that treating their dead well might help speed the healing from that rift, and it would clearly show off the difference between the Free Republic and the old Empire.

The small town below resounded with the noises of rebuilding, clearing rubble, and the chaos of establishing a new government under the umbrella of the Free Republic. He heard the voices of criers in town wafting faintly up to him and his encampment.

"They sure are busy beavers," Ratbone said. He sat at a folding card table beside Nestor. "More enthusiasm than skill, but it's a good start."

"I agree. They'll make it now that they're unified in purpose. At least I think they will. If any of the towns we've freed will make it, these guys will. They're just so... happy to be free. It's been a long time since I've seen happy."

Nestor heard horses fast approaching from the west. Two of his riders were coming in, horses running full speed. Most of his people used bicycles, but he had horses for the scouts. They were faster than bikes in the short term, only losing to the cyclists after a day or two in the field. The scouts didn't spend that long apart from the unit, so horses were more effective for this use.

Nestor stood and awaited them. When they arrived, the two men slid from their horses almost before they had stopped. "Boss, we have a big problem," blurted one.

The other spoke rapidly as he reported, "There's a big unit to the southwest, coming up fast. And boss? They got vehicles. Small tanks, APCs, humvees. Who the hell are they?"

Shock and fear slithered into his brain like tentacles of some mind-control monster, and he froze for a second before he stammered, "What? I don't... Were the vehicles marked?"

"Yeah. They got the American star on them. Their infantry are all in cammies, half carrying mil-grade rifles and the other half with civilian weapons. At least six hundred of them, but that's a guess. We bugged out before they saw us."

Ratbone shouted, "Shit, boss, we gotta pack it up. We need to fade out. *Right now.*"

Nestor was inclined to agree. It sounded as though he was outnumbered, and they had vehicles—real ones, with real big guns. "Two choices, boys. Slide into town and bolster them, or head back the way we came. Thoughts?"

Ratbone said, "Run and hide. It's the Highlander Way."

One of the outriders gave Ratbone a dirty look, then said, "The Free Rep's got six hundred fighters in town, we think. With us, that's a thousand. Against six hundred. If we get pushed back from Uniontown, there's nothing to rally around until Johnstown, nearly halfway back to Harrisburg."

Nestor's mind raced. Running was their way, as Ratbone had so eloquently put it quoting a movie line. But the rider was right, too. If he fled now, they'd be forced marching for up to sixty miles, and there was no guarantee that this new enemy unit couldn't catch up to them with their vehicles en route, when his own forces were stretched out on the move.

"Strike the camp, and we're going into town. You two riders, go alert our friends in Uniontown. Ratbone, send bike messengers to Johnstown and Harrisburg. We have to warn them."

Nestor hoped the approaching unit wasn't hostile, but it seemed rather unlikely. He knew the Empire had been the puppets of the Mountain General, and the only explanation for a new unit with tanks and more was that the Free Republic had just kicked over a hornet's nest.

At the very least, a stand in Uniontown would buy the rest of the Free Republic time to rally. He hoped it would be enough.

\* \* \*

0700 HOURS - ZERO DAY +367

Frank looked at Michael, his eyes as bleary as his friend's. They had been up for two days evaluating the intel they'd received from Harrisburg, and it didn't look good. They had read through a veritable mountain of papers, and had a mountain still to go, but the overall situation was clear.

"Houle is coming," Michael said, finally putting voice to what they had clearly both been thinking.

Frank nodded. "Seems that way. We know where his forces are and where his strongholds are. Colorado is his—we figured that. But we couldn't have imagined that he claims everything between NORAD and Kansas City, Oklahoma City, and El Paso."

"From the reports we've read now, Houle's system of forts stretch from that border all the way out to the Mississippi River. It's just... genius. Historically, that was called 'encastellation,' and it's effective. It's how the English finally brought the Welsh under heel, you know."

Frank paused to think, when an idea struck him. "On the other hand, that means he can't be sending a huge army right now. His core territory is just too far away from here, right? These troops have to be compiled from his forts, whatever they could spare from several different ones. They had to move up the Mississippi to St. Louis, his northern frontier, because they'd have had to come a long way impossibly fast if they had just headed east on I-64, don't you think?"

"That seems likely. We have no idea how many units he could send, but we know he's sending them. When they'll arrive is anyone's guess, but they could easily upset the tenuous balance of things between us and the Empire."

"I guess we had better have Ethan let the rest of the Confederation and Taggart know. Thank goodness we still have those two battalions Taggart loaned us from New America."

"I suspect those are more or less permanently stationed with us. Soon they'll be married into our people and so on. But Frank, these soldiers don't have tanks. Very few mines. A handful of anti-tank weapons, which we've been holding onto to crack heavy fortifications such as our own earthbag construction. Nothing we have is powerful enough to stop a mechanized unit, trust me on that."

Frank frowned. He rubbed burning, tired eyes. "I need sleep or more coffee. This is too much to process in my condition."

Michael said, "I'm for sleep. We'll pass the word to Ethan and then get some rack time. We're no good to anyone if we're too tired to think straight. Besides, we'll get little enough sleep once the fighting starts."

He and Michael then carefully organized the paperwork stacks that dominated Cassy's kitchen counter, then headed down to the bunker to tell Ethan. Frank figured they could get sleep down there, too. There wasn't any noise or daylight to disturb them, down in the hole.

Once they got down below, as Frank punched in the bunker door's security code, he said "I hope we have enough time to prepare. We're going to need it."

\* \* \*

1000 HOURS - ZERO DAY +367

Cassy saw Choony and Jaz sitting together in the chow hall, that massive military tent the Clan had repurposed. No one else was inside at this time of day, being busy with working the farm and building more earthbag domes for people, or other important projects. "Hello, you two. How's life treating you, sitting idle in Clanholme?"

Jaz smiled and waved. "We're totally good. Bored,

though. I'm so used to living life on the road that sitting here for so long is, like, driving me bonkers."

"Well that's fortunate," Cassy said with a wry grin, "because I have a new mission for you. But only if you're up for it."

Choony set his cup down. Clearly, she had his attention. He said, "Yes, do tell."

"So here's the deal. Instead of sending you south again, I need you to head west into the Free Republic. Wander around making contacts, just like you always have, but instead of finding people worth joining the Confederation, you'll be doing two things."

With a straight face, Jaz said, "Are you sure we can handle two things? That's totally more than one thing."

Cassy ignored the jest. "Spy out Free Republic strengths and weaknesses, and keep a journal of it for when you get back. That's the first thing."

"And the second thing?" Choony asked. "Assuming we can keep track of two things."

Cassy smiled. "Try to set up trade relations between them and the Confederation. Especially aim for trade deals with the Clan, since you are Clanners, but deals for the Confederation, too, will strengthen the whole alliance that keeps us all safe."

Jaz nodded. "Awesome. We're much less likely to get shot at on this trip, since they're mostly friendly to us anyway. I'm down with that. Getting shot at sucks."

Cassy knew very well how badly getting shot at 'sucked.' She said, "Other than the ever-present threat of bandits, however, or one of the few remaining Empire loyalist guerrillas, you don't have anything to worry about."

Jaz nodded, though whether in agreement or just acceptance, Cassy couldn't tell. Jaz said, "I don't think Empire guerrillas will bother us too much. Their hatred is saved up for the Free Republic. We just need to stay out of their way is all."

"So when do we leave?" Choony said, rolling his head around, stretching his neck. "Sleeping on a bed is giving me cricks in my neck."

Cassy grinned. "I'd like you to leave in an hour. Your wagon is getting packed and restocked even as we speak. If you don't see Frank and them before you go, I'll tell them you said goodbye, but I want you to leave quickly. You need to get well past Harrisburg before dusk. They weren't truly part of the Empire before they fell, but you know our history with them."

"Too bad Liz Town spared some of them. Those Harrisburg peeps deserve to be rockstars."

Cassy didn't know what that meant, but Jaz's tone seemed opposite to what the word meant to Cassy. "Yes... rockstars. Absolutely."

Jaz let out a short giggle and smirked. "You don't know what that means, do you?"

Cassy's face lit into a friendly grin. "Nope, no idea. But whatever it means, you still need to be moving shortly. And watch out for invaders. We've had a couple skirmishes with them, but mostly up north around Lebanon. Just be careful."

"We will, Mom," Jaz said.

Choony elbowed Jaz lightly. "We will be delighted to get moving again, Cassy. Thanks for giving us this mission. I know you have a lot of people you could have chosen."

Cassy nodded. "Yeah, but I wanted my best out there. I need people I trust implicitly. That would be you two dweebs."

Jaz's expression became completely neutral, and in a monotone voice, she said, "No one says 'dweeb' anymore, Cassy. That's almost as old as, like, 'poindexter'."

Cassy smiled and said, "Just be safe." She turned to walk

out. As she reached the door, she turned and added, "Oh, by the way, you'll be happy to know that, in addition to the usual pemmican, we loaded you up with jerky, some saltpork, more flour, even a bottle of dried yeast. And salt, pepper, and a ton of dried herbs. At least your pemmican can be spruced up a bit, this time."

Choony looked at Jaz and groaned. "Fat and powdered meat. Yum."

* * *

1800 HOURS - ZERO DAY +367

Frank awoke in the deep darkness of the underground bunker's closed-off, unlit barracks wing. "Hrmph," he grunted. Sitting up, he smacked his forehead on the bars of the bunk above him. Grimacing, he called out Michael's name, but there was only silence. That man slept light as a feather, so if he had been in there, he would have responded. Frank figured he must have already gotten up and left.

Slowly, Frank felt his way toward the hanging curtain that served as a room divider, faintly lit around the edges by the LED bulbs in the main chamber. At least Ethan was up. Frank made it to the curtain and drew it aside, squinting against the light. His throat felt as dry as toast. "Ethan," he croaked, "got anything to drink? Where's Michael?"

"Over here," said Michael's voice from the bunker's couch. "Good morning, sleeping beauty."

Ethan got up and poured a cup of water, then handed it to Frank, who drank it eagerly.

He felt the scum of sleeping too long wash away. His throat hurt a little as the water hit it, then felt much better. "Ahh. Thanks, Ethan. Michael, have you filled him in yet?"

Michael nodded. "Yeah, the basics. He just got done

radioing Liz Town and the other radio-equipped groups."

"Good," Frank replied. "We don't know when those new troops will arrive, but it'll be soon. We have a couple weeks at most, I imagine, before we start getting reports from the Free Republic about Houle's forces attacking."

Michael said, "I believe it'll be mixed troops, Houle's and the Empire's. He'll use his people and theirs to crack open the defenders, and the Empire's people to garrison what he's taken. By the time he gets to the Confederation—assuming the Free Republic doesn't stop him first—he'll be without most or all of his Empire goons."

Frank took another gulp of water, then said, "Maybe. We can't count on that, though."

The door hissed open, and Frank turned to look. Cassy stepped through the door and closed it behind her.

"Morning, Cassy," Frank said.

She smiled and waved at each in turn. "Good evening, actually. It's six o'clock now. They're serving chow, but I figured you two would be sleeping off your marathon session. Find anything out?"

Michael said, "We did. General Houle intends to send units into the Empire's rebelling regions, using both goons and his troops to bring them back under the Empire's heel. Then Houle will advance through Harrisburg and into the Confederation. We got a glimpse at the size of Houle's territory while we went through the liberated intel out of Harrisburg. It's impressive."

Cassy's jaw dropped. "What? When will they be here?"

"A couple weeks."

"Dammit, Frank. Why didn't you tell me that earlier?"

Frank frowned. "Excuse me? Why would I? You'd find out in tonight's council meeting, which you sit in on. Houle's soldiers aren't going to be rampaging through Clanholme tomorrow, or anything. And I needed sleep, first."

Cassy closed her eyes, clenching her jaw. She took two deep breaths, and when she spoke again, Frank thought she sounded calmer. "I'm sorry for yelling. You had no way of knowing."

"Knowing what?" Frank asked, voice rising in pitch a little. This didn't bode well...

"Frank, I sent Choony and Jaz west on a Confed mission into the Free Republic. They left before lunch."

Frank turned to Ethan. "Get Liz Town on the radio. Tell them to turn Jaz and Choony back. We can't let them be in the middle of what's coming."

Ethan nodded once and turned toward the radio. Frank heard him relay the message. Then he heard their reply: "Sorry, Charlie Two. They passed through a couple hours ago."

Frank clenched his fist. "Shit. Ask them to send out riders to find them, dammit!"

Ethan did, and after a long pause, Liz Town came back on the radio. "Riders sent. I don't know if we'll find them, but we'll do our best, Clanholme. Liz Town out."

The radio turned silent. Frank looked around the room, but it was as silent as the radio.

* * *

1130 HOURS - ZERO DAY +369

Carl walked along the wall's catwalk with Sunshine walking in front of him. As they went, they made notes on the condition of the walls bordering Sewer Rat territory, and exchanged ideas for improvements.

It was awkward being near her again. They hadn't really spoken since she had walked away from him, days ago that seemed like months. Between writing notes for the wall, his mind churned trying to think of things to say that might open her up to him again. He had been thinking about her far more than he ought to have been, given their circumstances. Nothing had come to mind, however, and she still seemed stiff and cold toward him. Maybe the timing would be better later.

"So we have two weeks, at minimum?" Sunshine asked over her shoulder as they walked.

"Yes. Probably more. The intel Clanholme sent us suggests the Mountain will work with the Empire in recovering rebellious Free Republic territories before they get around to attacking the Confederation."

There was a long silence, and the walked on together another dozen yards before Sunshine said, "Did the riders ever catch up to the Clan scouts that came through the day before yesterday?"

Carl smiled wanly. "How did you hear about that?"

"Carl, did they ever find them?" Her voice was stern.

"No, nor could we keep riding all over Free Republic territory forever. The searchers returned this morning empty handed."

Sunshine shook her head.

Carl continued, "But the scouts did report disturbing news. They heard rumors in the Free Republic about waves of people heading their way from out west. Refugees. I guess the Mountain is moving forward with their plans already, but just haven't reached us yet. The report said there is fighting near Springfield, Illinois—the wackos that the Empire couldn't crush on their own, before—and near Uniontown, Pennsylvania."

Sunshine whistled. "That's fast. Uniontown is the Free Republic's only real stronghold in the entire southwest of their territory, right? If that falls..."

"When it falls," Carl corrected, "then the only serious

opposition between Uniontown and Harrisburg is Johnstown and maybe Chambersburg. Rumor has it the Free Rep is moving as many units toward Johnstown as they can spare. Uniontown was left on its own, but they're buying everyone else time to prepare. They're Liz Town brave, those Uniontown people."

"God help them. It could have fallen by now for all we know. That news has to be two days old at the least."

Yeah, Carl thought, God help them. They'd need it. And God help the Confederation, when their turn came. He didn't think for a minute that the Free Republic was organized well enough yet to stop the Mountain's forces. "Pray for the Clanholme scouts too, Jaz and Choony. I know them both from my time as envoy to the Clan. They're good people, and they're out there alone somewhere."

"I guess we'd better also get ready to deal with refugees. They'll be coming. Some we can arm and use. But most, we'll have to turn away at the bridge."

"Cold, and true." Carl knew she was right, but didn't have to like it. They couldn't handle a tsunami of refugees, some of whom could be sympathizers. The ones they turned away at the bridge would probably stay there, praying for a miracle but finding only Mountain bullets when Houle's forces arrived behind them.

Oh well, Carl thought coldly, at least we had a nice vacation from all this crap. Now back to the cold realities of survival. Would that ever end? He doubted it. Not in his lifetime.

# - **10** -

0515 HOURS - ZERO DAY +374

MULTIPLE EXPLOSIONS SOUNDED, instantly waking Cassy. She jumped out of bed and bolted down the stairs, grabbing the rifle she left leaning against the wall next to the door, and rushed outside. Others were already emerging as well. Abruptly, the guard tower's air raid siren went off, deafening her. She saw Michael emerge from his earthbag dome with his M4 rifle in hand, rubbing his eyes before he sprinted toward the guard tower.

Cassy watched as Michael climbed the tower ladder in record time. He spoke briefly with the guard, then slid down the ladder without bothering to use the wooden rungs, his feet gliding down the outside bars to control his speed.

Cassy ran toward him, and was there when he landed.

Michael's eyes went wide when he spotted her and he shouted over the air horn, "Sabotage. Guard says two fireballs east of the pond."

A flood of rage washed over her. On the other side of the eastern fish pond, two of the battlecars had been stored under camouflage netting. Those would be the two easiest to find. "Two fireballs? The cars!"

Cassy and Michael ran east, bypassed the pond, and once they got to the other side, the shore foliage no longer blocked their view. The faint glow of the explosions' aftermath clearly marked where the two cars once were hidden.

Just then, the air raid siren went silent, thankfully. Cassy knew everyone was in defensive positions or getting into place now. The Clan's response to the sirens was drilled into every member, and each person had a post to get to. In this case, the threat was probably long gone already, though.

Cassy started to walk toward the nearest glowing car, but Michael blocked her with his arm. "Wait for reinforcements, Chancellor," he said.

Cassy didn't want to wait, but he was right. If the attackers were nearby, she'd have made a delicious, easy target. During a minute that seemed infinitely long, five Clanners gathered with her and Michael. "Now we can go," Michael said.

They approached the first car slowly, cautiously, with two Clanners in front, she and Michael in the middle, a Clanner to either side, and two in the rear. Cassy felt her heart beating in her ears.

When they arrived at the battlecar, an up-armored Ford F250 and a beast of a vehicle, she stopped and stared, grinding her teeth. The frame wasn't a total loss, but the tires were on fire. They threw short, bright orange flames and billowed thick, noxious smoke. The wire screening that replaced the windshields were shredded by the blast, but the worst damage was to the gasinator assembly in back. It was a heap of glowing twisted metal.

"The other will be the same," Michael said, his voice monotone from tension.

Cassy let out a long breath. "That leaves us only ten, including the flatbeds. But it could have been much worse."

Michael grunted. "Still bad. It'll take us weeks at least to rebuild those battlecars. Maybe longer. We're down to eighty percent of our battlecar force without firing a shot. It's a big blow."

Cassy only nodded. They approached the car to get a better look. A Clanner nudged past her with a fire extinguisher—the Clan kept them in abundance all over the farm—and sprayed down the tires, starting at the base and moving up. Then he sprayed down the gasinator, though the damage was already done. Maybe they could salvage some of the components. Whoever had done this, they weren't Clan. Everyone in the Clan probably knew the location of a couple other vehicles besides these two, if not more.

Michael said, "I don't see tracks. They covered them up." He picked up a small bit of wreckage from the truck bed and peered at it in the dim, dawning light.

"What is it?" Cassy asked, eyes narrowed as she looked at it the way she might a copperhead snake.

"Radio detonator, I think. They used small, easily shapecharged explosives and radio detonators. They moved in and out without being seen by the guard in the tower, who have night vision goggles. And they left no tracks."

"What are you saying, Michael?"

He shrugged. "Odds are good these were SpecOps." When Cassy looked at him blankly, he explained, "Special Operations. Special forces."

A Clanner beside her let out a low whistle. "Should we be afraid?"

"Yes," Michael said with emphasis. "Cassy, find Frank and let him know what's going on."

"What are you going to do?" Cassy didn't like the feeling she had about all this.

"I'm gathering some Marines and soldiers with experience like mine, and we're going hunting. We can't just leave snakes in the sleeping bag, right? I need to dig them out and kill them."

Michael turned and jogged away, leaving Cassy feeling very nervous.

"Okay, troops. You're with me," Cassy said, then turned around to go find Frank. For the moment, she didn't give the guard tower the all-clear, feeling better with her people in place and ready.

Breakfast would be late, today.

\* \* \*

Choony awoke from a light sleep with the first rays of sun just starting to hit the tarp lean-to as it rose over the crest of the small hill adjacent to camp. Jaz was stirring as well. It had been a long night as the two of them had been woken up repeatedly throughout the night by the sounds of movement on the nearby road.

He stepped out of the lean-to and stretched his back, which felt tight and ached. He saw a few sporadic people on the road, heading east. They all seemed to be loaded like mules, carrying all they could. "What the heck?" he muttered.

Jaz stepped up beside him, groggily rubbing the sleep from her eyes. "What's going on?" she said, the words half-jumbled.

"I'm not sure. But I guess we know what kept waking us up last night. I'm going to go talk to one of them. You get the rifle and stay back, just in case. I don't think they'll be a problem, though."

Choony took a deep breath and steeled himself, then strode toward the road. He intercepted a man and a woman walking together. "Good morning. I'm just a traveler, but since last night people have been walking down this road, like you two. What happened?"

The man looked at Choony with eyes red-rimmed from fatigue. "You must be from back east," he said. "The Mountain King and the Midwest Republic are taking issue with our new freedom."

The woman chimed in then, saying "They got cars that work. Some light tanks. The Mountain troops have lots of gear. It's a bloodbath."

The man nodded, his expression somber. "We're hoping to find refuge back east. Maybe Liz Town. Maybe a new Clanhold. The Mountain King isn't showing a lot of mercy. You'd best head back east as well."

"Thanks for the advice, mister. Uniontown? How are they?"

The woman replied, "They fell at about three o'clock this morning. Everyone's falling back."

Choony frowned, but quickly reminded himself that things were as they were. Deal with what is. "What about Donegal?"

The man grunted. "I don't imagine Donegal will hold. We're headed to Lawson Heights. That's the Free Republic's main westerly base now, so we'll go through there before moving on to head farther east. It's about a day's hard walk north of here."

The couple trudged away without looking back. Choony was left to stand in the road, wondering what to do. After a moment, he turned around and headed back to camp to tell Jaz what he had learned.

* * *

Ethan's system chirped with the distinctive high-pitched alarm that indicated an unauthorized access attempt. A new window popped up on his screen: "Authorize file deletion?" He moved to click "cancel," but it was too late. The hourglass popped as files vanished. Another dialogue box popped up.

Fine. Asshole. From his USB drive, Ethan launched two programs—one to essentially "target lock" the intruder, and the other to backtrace. They ran on the toggle, not in his virtual machine that was being hacked. Hopefully, the split second the two connected to get the target lock wouldn't be enough for the hacker to realize what was going on and hack the USB drive, too, but Ethan had a spare one just in case.

While the tracer ran its routine, he focused on saving his virtual machine. He turned off file sharing, but it wouldn't do any good—whoever was in his system had admin-level access. He went into his customized control panel, into Admin Rights, and clicked "remove access" and then "all other users." For three seconds, his system was blissfully without activity. Then more files popped up with a deletion query. These were system files, he saw. If he didn't stop this attack, his whole VM might crash.

He couldn't cut the connection physically yet, either, as that would neuter his tracer programs if cut before they installed somewhere else. Instead, he spent the next ten minutes frantically trying to counter the hacker's moves. If this had been his main system, he might have had a chance, but this was his virtual machine. It wasn't set up as well or as securely. At almost exactly the ten minute mark, his VM crashed. It was still running, but it had become a barren wasteland without applications or data. Shit.

A moment later, he got the alert that his tracking program had found a server along the hacker's path. It installed itself there and continued to track. Ethan was frustrated that he, Dark Ryder, had been hacked, but he had kept his system alive long enough for his counter-attack to install elsewhere—probably only seconds before he crashed. With a sigh, Ethan manually turned off his internet connection and went through the process of safely destroying his virtual machine. The faux computer-on-a-computer closed with finality.

Now he had nothing to do but get a new virtual machine set up again, figure out how he had been hacked and how to close that barn door, and then wait for his bloodhound to sniff out the hacker's actual location. That could take minutes or hours, if it succeeded at all. He was confident it would, though. He had coded that program himself, so it wasn't yet out "in the wild" on the internet. With the way antivirus software worked, the chances of any system noticing it, much less stopping it, were remote.

He leaned back in his chair. Was this a real attack, or had it been only a warning? He had no doubt that Watcher One was his attacker, but had no idea why he'd attack like that. It was so obvious, so blatant. Anyone who could monitor Watcher One's system remotely would have seen the brutal hack, as it lacked any finesse.

Or maybe that was the point? Did Watcher One know he was burning down a virtual machine, and not Ethan's real system? In that case, it would have been both a real attack and a warning. Why Watcher One would warn him, he didn't know. And what was the warning? Obviously, he'd have to mask his internet activities much better in the future, whether it was a warning or the real deal.

The worst part was that he couldn't bore a hidden connection to Watcher One and sound him out about it—if it had been an earnest attack, that would alert him that Ethan was still up and running.

Dammit, Ethan hated this cloak-and-dagger bullshit.

* * *

Nestor careened through the streets of Uniontown driving a liberated Humvee as his gunner eliminated random U.S.

soldiers who came into view. He had to get the fuck out of town and rejoin his troops, who were even now fleeing north. The town's defenders were giving the Mountain invaders hell, but most of it had already fallen. It was only a matter of time before the rest fell, too, and he didn't intend to be there when that happened.

"I feel for the defenders," Ratbone said, sitting in the passenger seat with his rifle, scanning ahead for threats. "Brave."

"Yup." What else could Nestor say about it? The Uniontown defenders were indeed brave. Soon they'd be dead or captured, though—courage meant little against armored vehicles when all you had were rifles and a couple of stickybombs. Nestor's people had taken out two Bradleys with those stickybombs by destroying the tracks. They weren't dead units, but with the battle lines flowing quickly, immobile was just as good as dead. That had happened several minutes ago, and of the squad who had accompanied him, only Ratbone and his gunner remained.

Ratbone said, "So now what?"

Nestor glanced at Ratbone and saw his jaw was clenched tightly, muscles standing out. Nestor said, "We'll head north, link up with our survivors and head toward our fallback area in Lawson Heights. Hopefully we have the gas to make it."

Nestor saw he had half a tank. It should be enough, but he couldn't be sure what the miles-per-gallon was on a Humvee, nor how many gallons it held. What's half of "X gallons"? He didn't know.

Ahead, three U.S. soldiers stepped into the road. They spotted him coming toward them and when he didn't slow down, they opened fire. So did Nestor's gunner. The Humvee's ass end bounced high into the air as they drove over the corpse of a bullet-riddled soldier. Ha! The suspensions on these things really were amazing...

Ratbone nudged him as the vehicle shot down the road and out of town, leaving the carnage behind them. "Lost our gunner, boss."

Nestor glanced back and saw that the gunner position wasn't empty, but wouldn't be in use again until they got a new, living gunner. The old one had a gaping hole where one eye had been. "At least he died quickly."

Ratbone grunted in agreement, but neither spoke again for many miles. Nestor knew he wouldn't be the last casualty of this war, and resigned himself to the task ahead.

* * *

1400 HOURS - ZERO DAY +376

Carl stood atop the hastily-erected rubble wall that blocked the bridge to Harrisburg. Liz Town had lined the road that led to the bridge with wooden Xs, and strung many of the Harrisburg dead to those as a warning to others who might seek to cross with less-than-golden motives. Lizzies were tough and pragmatic, but they had ensured everyone they strung up was already dead—Liz Towners were tough, not sadistic.

The Harrisburgers who continued to resist after the town fell were killed quickly. Those who didn't resist were kept alive if they had skills or a good story about how they had been forced to abide the town's raider government. Those who didn't resist but weren't useful, and had no compelling stories about their unfortunate circumstances, had been shoved across the bridge to survive or die on their own.

Yesterday, a horde of Free Republic refugees had arrived at the far side of the bridge. A battle between them and the Harrisburg exiles had taken place, but it was short and bloody.

Now Carl looked across the bridge at a sea of Free Republic citizens, people who were allies of the Confederation and in desperate need.

And there was nothing he could do for them.

Sunshine stood next to him. She and her Sewer Rats Band had volunteered to take over most of the Harrisburg defenses and looting, and Mary Ann approved. Carl didn't really like it, but the other Bands were happy to put distance between themselves and the Sewer Rats. Sunshine seemed happy to put distance between herself and Carl. Win-win for everyone but Carl himself.

"You called for reinforcements," Carl said curtly. "You seem to have them under control." His tone was all business.

In a tone mirroring his down to the inflections, she replied, "Not if they come across all at once. They'd overrun us without Liz Town reinforcements. Thank you for sending them. You needn't have come, yourself, though."

"I needed to see for myself what is going on here. As the Speaker's right hand, it's my job whether I want to be here or not."

She paused, then said, "I'd rather you weren't here, Carl." Her voice had lost its edge a bit, sounding less stiff and formal.

Carl glanced at her and saw that she gazed across the bridge, not at him. Part of him longed to just sweep her into a kiss. So much time wasted, and now that they could be together—as equals—she wanted nothing to do with him. "I still don't understand why," he replied.

"We're not going over this again. It is what it is." Her voice became hard again as she added, "So what will we do about these people?"

"They're allies. We've sent all the food we could spare, without asking to barter. It's all we can do. Their problems are their own."

"When the Mountain and the Empire show up at our doorstep, it'll be all of our problem. We should arm them, take them in, and make use of them."

"You got enough guns and ammo? Your whole food allotment wouldn't be enough to keep this many people fed."

In the distance, two men began to walk across the bridge, heading toward them.

Sunshine replied, "No, but if we supplied them with a week's worth and stripped the armory, we could send them to fight. We'd probably be able to feed whoever survived."

Carl nodded. It wasn't a bad idea, but it had one fatal flaw. "Until they turn those guns on us to get more food and to get away from the enemy barking at their heels."

The figures were now halfway across the bridge, Carl saw. They didn't look like anything special, just two guys. They didn't carry rifles or other weapons that he could see.

Sunshine grunted. "Maybe. Or maybe they'd stand beside my Band and fight for the Confederation. The enemy is coming. Once Lawson Heights falls—which it will, eventually—there's little between there and here to slow the enemy down. If we fall here, there's nowhere any of us could run that's safe."

Carl shrugged. She was right about having nowhere else to run, but it didn't matter. Liz Town would fight to the end. He changed the subject a bit. "People are dumb. They panic. This crowd will do something stupid, mark my words."

The two figures approached the rubble wall just below Carl and Sunshine. Carl waited for them to say something. After a long, awkward span, the shorter of the two men said, "Greetings, Liz Town allies. We've been sent to make some requests."

Carl let out a sigh. Of course they wanted more. Everyone did, these days. "We've given you all we can spare, and more."

The short man replied, "I understand that, and we know things are rough all over, but—"

The taller man interrupted him. "Dammit, we need more food. We got kids here, hungry. You sit up there and I know you got food. You traded with us all the time, now you turn your backs?"

The shorter man shrugged. Apparently he had nothing to add.

Carl said, "I can't give you what I don't have, mister. I think the wagon loads of food we sent over were more than you'd get from anyone else, and you know it. We got hungry people here now, too."

Sunshine nudged him with her elbow. Almost whispering, she said, "This will turn ugly if you don't recruit them. Look at the tall one."

Carl did so, and saw the man's face was turning red. He held his hands in fists at his sides. Sunshine could be right...

"Listen," said the shorter one, "we got guns, of course. Everyone alive does. We'd like to join you. Be a Band, or whatever you call your divisions." He looked up at Carl. "We could be the Roadrunner Band. Better than watching us die out here. We could be useful."

The taller man was silent and stared at Carl on the wall. No doubt he was waiting to hear the response before doing something stupid. Carl could just tell... that man was *itching* to do something stupid.

Carl considered his words carefully. "Mister, we'd love that. You're our allies. But we don't have supplies enough to go around. We could put out the word and gather them, perhaps, but it'll take at least a week I'd guess. You want to be a Band? We can talk about that when supplies are here."

"A week is a long time for kids to go hungry, mister."

Carl nodded. "In the meantime, it would go a long way toward convincing our people that yours mean well if you sent your able bodied people back into the Free Republic to fight the Mountain."

The taller man said, "See? I told you they'd want us dead before they gave us more."

The shorter one nodded at his friend, then said up at the wall, "Mister, that's good except for the part where all my people die fighting them while you sit on your wall. I don't think I could convince my people you had their interests in mind."

The taller man spat, then muttered something Carl couldn't hear.

Sunshine whispered, "Carl, do it. Better more friends than more enemies."

Carl glanced at the big cargo trailer that now protected the only break in the wall that blocked the bridge. The mob could climb over it pretty easily, given a little time, but the wall itself formed an arc from riverbank to riverbank, curving around the end of the bridge. He decided that he'd have to concentrate fire from the wall down onto these people if the mob approached.

To the men below, Carl said, "I do have their interests in mind. That's why we sent you what we could. If you don't appreciate that, feel free to send the food back. But although I care what happens to your people, I have my own people's interests in mind even more. I'm sure you understand. We'll do what we—"

"Bullshit," shouted the taller man, "you'll leave us out here to soak up the Mountain King's bullets and slow them down. You think we're stupid? Let us in, take us in. Do it or we'll let ourselves in, mister."

Sunshine spoke up unexpectedly. "That would be stupid, sir. That only puts you between two enemies—"

"Fuck you, lady. You don't want to help us, fine. What happens next will be on *your hands*." He spun on his heels and stormed back toward the far end of the bridge.

The shorter man looked at his associate go, then turned toward Carl and shrugged. "Sorry, mister, but he's right. I don't know how this will look tomorrow, but I do know we'll both be worse off for it. I tried to get this done peacefully, but I'm sure I just lost control of this situation."

He then turned, shoulders slumped, and trudged away toward his own people.

With a heavy heart, Carl watched him go. "Sorry, Sunshine. We just can't let everyone starve to keep these strangers alive for a while. I thought you'd have learned that by now, seeing as how you survived the Dying Times."

Sunshine let out a long, frustrated breath. "It looks like those times aren't yet over, Carl. I'll go spread the word, I guess. I need to get more Rats up on this wall, set them up for a battle."

Carl nodded. "I hope it doesn't come to that, but once they want to *take* what we won't *give*, they stop being our friends. Let's get ready for the suck. It's coming soon..."

# - **11** -

1500 HOURS - ZERO DAY +376

ETHAN WENT THROUGH the data he had gathered, scrolling slowly down the screen to get an overall sense, the Big Picture. Over the past two days, he had waited patiently while his bloodhound program, which was really a worm—a program that installed itself at each waypoint—sifted piles of log file data as it slowly spread from node to node.

It would usually have taken months to track Watcher One, because there would have been thousands or even millions of other servers online. Since the EMPs, very few remained, and those weren't monitored as well as they once had been. Some of his worms had been discovered and removed, but his program just went back in and kept reinstalling them when it could. A few were tough and well defended, but proliferation had gone by quickly and most of the servers left online with outside access had been infected. He had enough nodes to get the job done.

Ethan not only had Watcher One's presumed location now, he had found a number of new servers he wasn't aware of before. Some were only online at specific times each day. He had all that data, now.

And Watcher One really was in Virginia, just as he had guessed from their earliest post-EMP contacts. It showed up as being some dink town outside of Fredericksburg, deep in 'vader territory under General Yi.

Ethan had been tempted to try to break in and burn down Watcher One's systems, but he resisted the urge. It was better, he decided, to know where his enemy was and to have that knowledge as a hidden Ace up his sleeve.

Grinning like a fool, Ethan closed one laptop and went to the other, next to his HAM radio. It was that time of day when he had to prepare for communications from other survivor groups around the country. Work before pleasure. He had all the time in the world to gloat later.

\* \* \*

Cassy stood next to Dean Jepson looking at a battlecar's toasted wreckage. "So, how long do you figure it'll take?"

Dean spat into the dirt. "Bah. Y'all want miracles. I ain't an engineer, you know, I'm just good with my hands. All yer children ought to be learning this stuff. I ain't gonna be around forever, you know."

Dean was a grumpy old man, but a wiz with his hands. And the kids loved him, even if he did mostly yell at them to stay out of his way. In between yelling, he snuck them candy and other treats that were hard to come by. They must have cost him a fortune in trade, so everyone politely pretended not to notice, and they tolerated his gruff-old-man routine.

"True. You really are old, Dean," Cassy said, trying hard not to grin.

"That's what I said, ain't it? You want to hear about them cars or not?"

"Absolutely. No one could fix these up the way you do. So what have you figured out?"

Dean grumbled and took a step toward the wreck. He took a deep breath. Then, in the same voice one might use to explain to a child why you shouldn't stick a knife in a power outlet, he said, "Okay. First, the gasfrier got breached. I got to cut and weld with some scraps if we're gonna fix it. Worse, the copper pipes are all bent up like Ma's spaghetti. I need new pipes, so you send out some of them worthless teenagers to strip another house. Be good for 'em to do something besides looking at plants all day."

Cassy nodded. Dean didn't understand permaculture, and didn't want to. "Done. New pipes for the gasifier. What else?"

"Both cars, the radiator we put between the gasfrier and the pipes to the engine are messed up worse than your face. We need new ones. That ought to be easy, even for you."

Cassy sighed. "Yes, Dean. My face has scars. Thanks for pointing that out." Well, turnabout was fair play, she figured. She continued, "I'll make sure you get the radiators."

Dean ignored her jab. "The rest of it's easy enough. Patch up the truck bed, weld on some new horse-wire fencing over the back window. Repairing my gasfriers is gonna take a couple weeks for the two of 'em, though. These aren't the amateur rigs you paid too much for from Falconry, you know. These are works of art. I won't be bolting crap onto them like Frankenstein."

Frankenstein's monster, Cassy mentally corrected him, but left it alone. "Of course, Dean. No one does work like you do. Thanks for the update, and I'll get the things you need. But, I need them done in a week, not two."

Dean grunted and leaned into the open engine compartment with a socket wrench. She heard the *tzzk, tzzk* noise of the wrench turning, and smiled. He was probably just making noise with it to get her to go away. He didn't care much for small talk with anyone but Frank and sometimes the kids.

As she walked away, she smiled again at the thought of how lucky they were to have Dean in the Clan even if most of the adults couldn't stand him. But she knew he liked it that way.

\* \* \*

Carl wiped his tired eyes with his palms. "Ugh. Sunshine, this can't go on forever. We're tired, and there's just more and more of them every day. It's like fending off Harrisburg and Hershey right after the EMPs, all over again."

Sunshine smirked, but he noted her eyes were as red-rimmed as his felt. She said, "I told you we should have recruited that first group."

"*If* they would have fired on their fellow refugees who arrived later, and *if* they wouldn't have turned on us anyway. If, if, if. Things are what they are. How many do you figure we've killed?" Carl's expression fell as he said it. He'd have nightmares for years to come, he was certain.

"At least a couple hundred. They'd have been better off standing and fighting against the Mountain instead of us."

"Yes. But they didn't know that when they fled from Houle."

"You trying to get me to sympathize with them? We're *killing* them, Carl. I prefer not to feel sympathy for them, thanks."

"Roger that. I got word this morning that Liz Town is beginning to take fire. A few rounds here and there, for now. But it means some of the refugees found another crossing point."

Sunshine nodded. "Of course they have. They're flowing like water, hitting one obstacle and going around. But Liz Town can hold its own."

"Yeah. But here we are wasting time, ammo, food... We

need to solve this."

"Good luck, mighty Alpha of the Timber Wolf Band." She said it like it was an insult.

Carl took a deep breath and let it out slowly. "I think maybe you were right. It's time for Plan B—your Plan A."

Sunshines eyes widened slightly. "Recruit them? After we just spent two days shooting at them?"

"Yeah. What else is there? We had already sent word throughout the Confederation anyway. Supplies are coming, and a lot of them. We can do this. They can do this. Fight for their homes, in exchange for promises of their families' welfare."

"About time. We can't fight off the entire population of the Free Republic, not forever. And even then, we'd still have to face the Mountain and the Empire. Best to send these people to die against our mutual enemy than by wasting our own 'friendly' bullets."

"I'll send an envoy to talk at them. If they don't skin him alive, we may be in business." Carl frowned. That was a real possibility, he realized.

"Big 'if' considering how many of them we've killed."

Carl knew she was right, but they just had to make this work. Otherwise, he would win here, but then they'd all lose at the hands of the Mountain King and his Empire goons in the coming days or weeks.

"Better pray we make it work, Sunshine. It's the only hope for all of us, in the long run."

* * *

0700 HOURS - ZERO DAY +377

Frank waited at the Clanholme entry in the north food forest. Behind him was an array of people ranging from paramedics to stablehands, ready to take in Michael's exhausted mounts and his wounded. He had called in twenty minutes ago via radio, and now Clanholme was buzzing with workers and rumors.

Michael and his unit streamed around the corner, horses walking slowly, panting. Of the twenty men and five women he had left with, Frank counted only twelve men and Michael, now. They hadn't returned with any wounded, or even bodies. The lost were Clanners, and now there would be yet another mass memorial.

"Welcome home, Michael. Sitrep?"

Michael dismounted, and took a long swig from his water bottle, emptying the last of it. "Mission accomplished. Heavy losses. I'll tell you more when my people are taken care of."

Frank nodded, and for the next fifteen minutes, he mostly stayed out of the way. Few of the returning Clanners were uninjured, and a couple of the horses had nasty wounds that would probably be terminal. He let the paramedics do their jobs. Finally, Michael finished going from man to man, talking to them briefly, then moving to the next.

He walked up to Frank, and it was terrible how exhausted the man looked. Mentally as well as physically, he looked tired to the core. "So, we found our guys on day one, but they had intel that led us to a second group. There was a hell ride, their last stand, our people died. But so did theirs, to the last one. They all had that military look. Probably some variety of special forces. In the end, my battle plan was better than theirs. They were *good*, Frank. Trained almost as well as me. Almost."

Frank frowned. If the Mountain was sending SpecOps into the Confederation, it meant they thought they'd be attacking a lot sooner than the Clan had imagined. "At least you got them before they did any more damage."

Michael stared at Frank, but finally he nodded, ever so slightly. "It seems that way. But we don't know what else they were up to before they announced their presence with explosions. We don't know if there's more of them out there. I had twenty-five people. We killed about that many of them. Where's the other dozen? We need to be on high alert from now on, Frank."

"Of course, you got it. We'll do that. What other dozen?"

"A big op like that would use more troops, that's all."

"Oh. We can't do anything about that right now. How are our people?"

Michael glanced over his shoulder at the impromptu aid station buzzing behind him. "Of the twelve who made it back, two won't last the night. Two more are probably dead within a few days. Can't treat abdominal gunshot wounds out here, not in these conditions. We'll give them antibiotics and morphine, though, to give them their best shot at life. If they don't make it, at least the morphine will make their passing easier."

Frank reached out with his left hand and grabbed Michael's shoulder. "You did good, Michael. Those people were truly dangerous. We lost good people, but how many of us will live because of their sacrifice?"

Michael nodded. He rubbed his eyes again with grimy hands. "All of us. All of us will live, if I have anything to say about it."

"Of course. We're in the best hands possible with you. Now go get cleaned up, fed, and get some rack time. You need sleep or you're no good to anyone. I'll fill Cassy in on what you told me, and your official report can wait."

Michael grunted, nodding. But instead of heading into the Complex to get rest, he returned to the people he had come home with, sat next to a man with a chest wound, and began talking to him with an easy smile on his face.

Frank hobbled up beside Michael and bent down to whisper, "Michael, you need sleep, man. You don't do anyone any good if you drop out from exhaustion."

Michael waved his hand toward Frank as though waving off a mosquito, and kept talking to the wounded fighter.

Frank frowned, but turned away to go find Cassy. He'd leave Michael alone with his men, doing what a good officer did. He wouldn't rest until the wounded did, no matter what Frank told him to do.

\* \* \*

General Ree knelt on silken pillows, on a hardwood floor dominated by a thick Persian rug that would once have cost a fortune even in Iran. He and Major Pak Kim, now his most trusted right-hand man, sipped at the finest tea in New York City, completely irreplaceable. That tea was Ree's one vice, his one true luxury. Soft living made for soft soldiers, he mused, but what harm could come of drinking tea that few others could even fully appreciate?

"How do you find the tea?" Ree asked, and knew he was wrong for owning something that belonged to all. The Great Leader would have said so, but this was America, not North Korea. The Great Leader here was Ree.

"Excellent, my leader," Major Kim replied. He held the cup to his nose, breathing in the tea's aroma, with his eyes closed to fully enjoy it.

Ree understood the sentiment well. This was the finest tea he had ever had, certainly. "So tell me, little brother, what progress has been made to deal with the disruptions to our operations?"

He had been careful not to say "have you made," which separated Kim from the answer. Ree hoped this would encourage Kim to be more open and honest.

The corners of Kim's lips twitched upward when Ree called him "little brother," a term of endearment that also maintained the power structure—not equals, but not purely professional—yet his expression went carefully neutral when Ree asked the question. Ree braced himself for bad news.

Kim replied, "Big brother, I am pleased to tell you that we have reduced absences due to illness by withholding food from those too 'sick' to work. This encourages the lazy Americans to align their will with your own, and get the work done."

Ree wasn't fooled. This was good news, but there was more to it. He waited in silence for Kim to let the other shoe drop. Kim finally began to look anxious under that gaze, then shifted his weight to get more comfortable. Or rather, to fidget...

Kim continued, "My leader, that was excellent news of course, but I regret to inform you that our agents have found nothing regarding the subtle sabotage that is so rife in the work zones. Nor have your inquisitors."

Ree watched Kim's expression carefully. The man avoided Ree's gaze, of course. By calling them "our" agents and "your" inquisitors, he had dodged any responsibility. Ree allowed himself to frown ever so slightly, and he delighted to see Kim's face turn a paler shade.

Kim hurriedly added, "But I assure you that we are working diligently. We are making inroads into the People's Worker Army units, and hope to find what we seek very soon."

Ree nodded. "I see. Thank you. It is important that we get this problem under control. Worker resistance to the will of the People is like a cancer. It spreads and grows, out of sight until one day, we find the condition has become suddenly terminal. We have already been effectively imprisoned here on this island. We have nowhere left to maneuver, and so we must deal with this problem as clearly and effectively as we can."

Kim nodded. "Yes, General. Would you favor this old soldier with your wisdom on the matter, so that I can align my will with yours?"

Ah, what a splendid response! Ree favored Kim with a smile, then said, "Of course. Although you should already be in alignment, no? But let us forget that for a moment. I would never tell you how to carry out my orders, Major—you have your rank, and I have mine—but a thought occurs to me."

"I'm eager to hear your thoughts, of course."

"Indeed. Perhaps if we selected several of the slowest workers and subjected them to the ministries of the inquisitors, then an admission of guilt would soon be given."

"Whether there is guilt or not, my leader."

"True. But that's not important. It will cause fear and doubt among the saboteurs and especially their potential recruits. It will encourage those who do know something to step forward, both through fear of a similar punishment and because of the existing promises of rewards for their loyalty to the People. I believe the Americans call this a 'carrot and stick' approach."

"Of course, my leader," Kim exclaimed, "I've seen that technique used to good effect back home. We will begin at once."

Ree nodded, but said nothing more. Nothing else needed saying. He sipped at his tea, enjoying the shared silence with Kim. When his cup was nearly empty, he flicked his right hand up from where it rested on his knee.

A worker, bent as low as he could go without falling over, scurried forward to pour another cup. Ree kept his eyes half-closed, relaxed. There was a blur of movement, however, and Ree's half-shut eyes snapped open. The servant, a young

American man, flung the pot at Kim and then turned toward Ree. He drew a knife from the wide, draping sleeves of his Korean-styled tunic and crouched low. Ree only had enough time to wonder how the knife got through security before the American lunged forward, knife point out.

It was a clumsy attack, Ree saw. No finesse. But Ree was at the disadvantage, being on his knees and without leverage. He had only one move, one chance to live. He grabbed the man's knife hand into a lock at the wrist with both his hands, thrust himself backward while bringing his knees up into his attacker's stomach, and managed to fling the American back over his head. His attacker landed hard in a heap behind him, but this left Ree on his back, head toward the attacker. Vulnerable.

Ree rolled onto his stomach with his hands underneath him. Pushing up with his arms, he got his feet underneath him, but was still off-balance as the American, now on his feet, scrambled toward Ree with the knife.

Two deafening booms resounded throughout the room, and the American crumbled to the floor, skidding to a halt next to Ree. He stared down at the dying man, who lay still, mouth opening and closing like a fish out of water.

Ree kicked the knife away and stepped away from the American. Looking to Kim, he saw his right-hand man still kneeling, but holding a pistol in both hands. Kim's face showed outrage, the same outrage Ree himself felt.

Alarms went off throughout the compound. Four uniformed soldiers burst into the room, rifles ready. "My general! Are you injured?" said one in a flurry of words that strung together.

Ree said, "I'm fine. The American got a knife through security. Go and detain those who checked and cleared this scum, then send them to the inquisitors." Ree turned to Kim and said, "And go now, little brother. Begin what we discussed, and do it immediately."

Kim bowed halfway and then stormed out of the room. Two guards followed Kim, going to follow Ree's orders. The last two guards approached the fallen American.

One said, "He is now dead, my leader."

Ree frowned. Had Kim killed him intentionally in order to hide the attacker's masters? No, of course not. Kim had saved his life by killing the American. If Kim were a traitor, then he would have killed the American *after* the viper had killed Ree, not before. But what of the men who had checked the American for any danger? How far had the cancer spread? He would have to find out, and soon. Either way, those men's lives were gruesomely forfeit, an example to the rest...

Ree glanced at the guard who had ruined the fine Persian rug with his spilled blood. "Remove this filth. Make an example of his corpse. I want what's left of him put on display when you're done with him."

# - **12** -

"CHECK FIRE, CHECK fire," Nestor shouted as the enemy retreated again, leaving behind yet another handful of dead or wounded. His infantry stopped firing and his mortar went silent.

Nestor rubbed his eyes, which were blood-red from lack of sleep. He had been up until the wee hours of the morning to prepare the defenses in Lawson Heights, both where his own two-hundred fifty fighters were stationed at the small private airport and at the town's other two main strongholds, the high school and the strip mall.

He had been asleep only three hours when the enemy attacked with a mix of Empire and the Mountain's troops, who had hit them all across the defensive lines. So far, Nestor's forces still held the airport. The last he had heard, the shopping center and high school were also holding, but that was an hour ago. Things could have changed dramatically in that time.

Thankfully, everything around the airport was flat, without any cover except in one direction, so the enemy had been halted easily. Then the attackers had swung their approach from the southwest's open fields to the southeast. There, a few houses and landscaping had been overrun, allowing the attackers to get within two-hundred feet of the southern hangars. The fighting was intense. The bastards still had to charge uphill into Nestor's defensive fire, but would only lack concealment when they crossed a narrow uphill clearing.

Nestor evaluated the scene, and caught movement through his binoculars. "Mortars, send two rounds into the tree line," he ordered. He hoped the exploding trees would send hellish shrapnel into the rallying attackers there, but couldn't be sure it would work. He had seen it in a movie, but it made sense. It was worth a try.

*Thump, thump,* the two rounds arced up and over, then plummeted down into the trees. They exploded in the canopy, and the result was quite satisfying. Huge fireballs in the canopies tore the trees to shreds, leaving stumps of their trunks, and he heard agonized screams from the tree line. "I guess the movies were right."

Ratbone ran up to him, skidding to a halt. "Boss, we got problems. They're shifting that light armor from the high school, heading this way. ETA is one minute."

"Shit. Get our RPGs over there." Then he called to the mortar crew, "Adjust fire, zone Echo Three. That's where they'll come through. Ratbone, get spotters over there."

"Yes, sir. We only got two rounds for the RPGs, boss." Then Ratbone sprinted away.

Nestor followed behind, then waited with his soldiers for the coming attack. He only had to wait a few seconds before three Humvees and two scout tanks—Bradleys? He couldn't remember—burst from the tree line and accelerated across the field. "RPGs on the tanks," he shouted.

One round streaked out, smashing into the tank's front armor like a wrecking ball, but the little tank came through the smoke and fire unharmed. "Dammit. RPG, save your last round for a shot at the treads, got it?"

Then the mortar fire came in, landing among the vehicles and doing little to them, but shredding half a dozen Mountain soldiers.

The tank fired its main gun as the other vehicles opened up with .50-caliber machine guns, pouring fire into Nestor's emplacements. The man with the RPG was torn in half by two of the massive bullets.

Nestor grabbed the long tube and the man's last round, then ran south. He slid into cover and ducked down as a hail of bullets tore up the cement all around him. When the firing paused, he readied the RPG, popped up and snap-fired it at the tank, which now had its side facing him as it continued west toward the defensive line.

The round streaked toward the tank and smashed into its side. It stopped moving, but its gun didn't stop firing. "Sonovabitch." He dropped the tube and sprinted from cover to cover back toward his fighters, shouting, "Fall back, get out of range from that tank!"

The light vehicles were laughing off the small arms fire, although one stood ablaze in the field where a lucky mortar round had wrecked it. The other two hummers and the second surviving light tank were tearing up his troops. His people behind sandbags did okay against the heavy machine guns, but then the tank sent a high-explosive round into them, one after the other, ravaging the lines.

Nestor saw one of his troops, a Uniontown man if he remembered correctly, running toward the immobile tank. It couldn't move and the other vehicles had left it behind. He approached from the side and they either didn't see him or couldn't turn to deal with him. He jumped onto the front "fender," whatever that piece was called, and shoved something into the short barrel, then jumped down.

The resulting explosions were awesome. The first one peeled the barrel like a banana, but it must have set off something inside the tank because that was followed immediately by a second, larger explosion, and then a third explosion so large that Nestor felt the concussion all the way back where he was. Ammo bay, Nestor thought.

Seeing this, nearly a dozen of his troops from the line near the operational tank sprinted forward, ready to try the same thing, but the enemy infantry accompanying the tank mowed them down. Crap—that must have cost him half a dozen grenades. Those weren't so easy to replace.

The remaining tank kept advancing, and rolled over the smoking ruins of one sandbagged emplacement. The two Humvees followed its example. Once through the line, they opened up with their machine guns on Nestor's troops as they fell back, with devastating effect. His people were being slaughtered.

He heard shouts to the east and glanced; from the same tree line from which the vehicles had emerged, another infantry company now moved forward by leaps and bounds, making it hard to see one long enough to get a good shot off. They had waited for the vehicles and supporting infantry to punch a hole in the defensive lines, and now were coming like army ants to sting him to death. Nestor spat.

"Ratbone," he shouted. A second later, his sidekick slid into cover with him like he was going for home plate.

"Not good, boss," Ratbone shouted over the din. "Flee or fall?"

Nestor grit his teeth. "Flee. Fall back to the next line, see if we got RPGs or even propane tanks, anything we can use on that tank."

"Roger, boss." Ratbone seemed to vanish. That man was scary sneaky.

Nestor made his way as best he could toward the fallback

positions. He only hoped they were still standing when he got there. If he got there, he corrected.

*Bang,* he put a round into a Mountain soldier's back, grabbed the woman's grenades and ammo pouch, and fled. If the fallback positions fell, he'd have to gather whoever he could and try to head east to Confed territory. The Free Republic didn't have much left to hide in if Lawson Heights and Latrobe fell.

* * *

Ree nodded with evident approval at the inquisitors' handiwork. Four civilian workers and two ISNA troops who had let that American into his tea room with a knife, all were brutalized bloody messes and barely still breathing for the moment. Probably not for long, from the looks of them.

Ree turned to his nearby platoon commander who had overseen guarding the victims during their questioning. "Take these six and tie them to telephone poles outside our west gate. A warning to the rest. Try to keep them alive if you can, but you needn't try too hard."

The ISNA man saluted in his stupid, sand-eater way, palm out. Their uniforms were disheveled and filthy. Pah. Barbarians, but useful ones. Ree watched until they were out of sight, then returned to his office.

Ten minutes later, there was a knock. "Enter."

Major Kim stepped through, then bowed low. Too low... Ree frowned.

Kim reddened, then said, "My leader, news."

"Out with it, Kim."

"Yes, sir. The platoon you commanded to stake out our inquisitor victims was overrun right outside our very gates. There were dozens of civilians with pipes and even stones. All ten guards are dead or missing. They and our gate guards killed at least a dozen, yet the mob continued to attack until they had killed or taken both the detail and the traitors."

"You said that already. Quit babbling, Kim. Radio my Colonels and tell them to beware their own workers. I didn't survive in Korea by ignoring the signs of brewing storms. I sense that a massive storm now comes our way, little brother. Double the guards on the walls and gates, and double my personal guard. And yours. Dismissed."

Ree then went to his paperwork again as Kim bowed and backed out of the room. Then Ree let out a long, frustrated sigh. These damned Americans! They didn't have the decency to know when they were defeated, nor did they have any natural ability to work for the good of the People. Only for themselves. Every one of them had their *own ideas* and refused to bring their wills into alignment with their Great Leader's. He could only conclude that his Great Leader, safe at home in Korea, was wrong about the American temperament and the source of their obstinacy. Obviously, his advisors had given the Great Leader wrong information, but whatever the cause, this invasion had been a terrible mistake, and Ree was left to deal with the repercussions.

He resisted the urge to shout out in rage. That would be undisciplined. But inside, he seethed. Ancestors help whoever else crossed Ree today. He was in no mood for leniency.

* * *

Taggart grinned as Eagan gave his report. "...and that ought to make him feel the pucker, sir."

Taggart nodded. "Yes, it ought to. Out of the quarter-million veterans in New York City, it wasn't hard to find a few Green Berets."

Eagan grinned right back. "Yup. They may not be as

badass as Deltas or SEALs when it comes to a straight combat op, but *no one* does insurgency like Green Berets."

"Well, that's the focus of their training. Go in behind enemy lines and raise the level of suck for them. I never thought they'd be doing it here, to invaders, using Americans! But they've managed to get civilians working in small bands all over the city, both in Ree's turf and in his colonel territories. And those NoK colonels don't like to cooperate with one another. They get their stupid honor up in arms, and fall back on policies and procedures."

"Yes, sir. And we're learning to take advantage of it. Now we don't have to attack directly to ruin Ree's day."

"Don't get cocky, shitbird," Taggart replied with his own cocky grin. Then he grew more somber. "The enemy's domestic intelligence force is among the best in the world, and there's enough Koreans to make life hairy for our operatives and the assets they've recruited."

"There's not enough of them. Our operatives have hit a sort of critical mass. There's no way the gooks can find all of them now. The rebellion is spreading faster than they can catch up. Hell, they didn't even know there was a rebellion until we got within inches of assassinating Ree himself."

"That mission failed, I remind you. The volunteer died gruesomely, as did his wife and two children. But Ree hasn't yet figured out how we tick. Every time he puts corpses on display, it makes Americans *pissed*, not submissive."

"Well, sir, I figure he'll learn that lesson soon, according to our agents' reports. I doubt Ree will survive the lesson."

Taggart nodded and took another bite of his late lunch—veggies and rice—then dug into the dozens of various reports on his table. Eagan let himself out without bothering Taggart further.

Once he was gone, Taggart gazed out into space, lost in thought. If the rebels in the City won, they'd be faced with still more mass starvation. Reports said Ree was trying to farm Central Park, though. He realized he'd have to send some of his newly trained farming advisors into that mess just on humanitarian grounds, if and when the enemy threat was gone.

He made a note to get a few more people into Cassy's training workshops. Then he doubled the number, thinking that he might have to do the same with other survivor communities he ran across.

Maybe it was time to just hand recruiting power over to Cassy. He just had too much useless crap to do for him to be micro-managing this sort of thing anymore. "I miss being a sergeant," he grumbled, then went back to studying reports.

\* \* \*

Cassy got out of the truck and pulled down her goggles. They were necessary because the windshield glass had been removed, but she thought they looked "cool," intimidating even. She glanced around and saw the two other battlecars to either side of hers were properly arrayed in a V-formation, grilles pointed slightly outward. Visually, they were intimidating.

Up ahead, hundreds of refugees huddled together on both sides of the road that led west from Harrisburg, all staring at her. She saw desperation and even hopelessness in their eyes.

Behind her, the two supply trucks were pulling to a halt, having waited until the battlecars were in position.

Cassy picked up the megaphone from the battlecar's dashboard and clicked it on. "People of the Free Republic," she said, her voice amplified to the point of hurting her own ears, "I am Cassandra Shores, Chancellor of the Confederation. I come to help you as best as the

Confederation can. Who speaks for you?"

After a few seconds, she saw two men approaching through the crowd, one noticeably taller than the other. Both looked ragged and exhausted as they approached, but the taller had glaring eyes and a jaw set in stone. She'd be wary of that one...

The taller said, "I speak for the majority. What do you want? You've killed enough of us."

Behind him, the crowd shouted in support, but it was half-hearted. They were tired and beaten, these people. She could blame Liz Town for that.

Cassy set the megaphone down and waved the two men over. Whey they got close, the shorter said, "I speak for the minority, who wanted peace. At least, they are the minority now that you people murdered so many of us."

Cassy nodded slowly, finger on her chin, making a show of carefully considering his words. Then she said, "Majority Speaker, Minority Speaker, thank you for your time and for speaking with me. I hope to resolve these issues, and help however we can."

"Empty words. Can you resolve our dead?" the taller man said.

Cassy laughed, and both envoys looked shocked. Good. Cassy said, "No, but can you resolve ours? Perhaps the Free Republic has forgotten that the Confederation is independent and not their servants. Certainly the old republic forgot that, until we reminded them."

The short man's face turned red. "We're not the Midwest Republic—"

Cassy interrupted him. "No, but you came with guns, demanding what's ours, just as they did. You expected Liz Town to just give you all they had and then starve along with you? No, you did this wrong."

The tall one clenched his fists at his sides. "We were

*starving*, not coming for what we didn't need or deserve."

"Ah, but you were," Cassy replied. "You don't deserve to take our food by force if we say no. And at the barrel of a gun, we reinforced that much-needed lesson in manners and ownership. Yet I'm still here, trying to help you. Would the Empire do as much? So stop with the self-righteous indignation and ridiculous bad analogies."

Mr. Tall said nothing, and even took a step backward in shock. Mr. Short said, "So we both have lost people. And you come with promises of help, now that we're being good little doggies."

"Now that you're being *good little guests,* yes." Cassy's gaze didn't flinch. "We do understand your predicament, your motives. You aren't our enemy, and we aren't yours, unless you continue to wish it so."

Tall said, "Not our enemies now that you aren't shooting at us."

"Yes, that's right. Now that you aren't storming our gates with guns and knives, we can go back to being allies. I suggest to you that your real enemy is out *there*," Cassy said, pointing west.

The two men stared at her in silence.

Cassy continued, "In the trucks behind me are sacks of rice, quinoa, wheat. Barrels of vinegar and apple cider. As many nuts as we could gather. And more. You should know that, because of this help we *freely offer*, our coming winter will be a hungry one, but we'll survive. If you take our gift, then you will too."

"What's the catch," Mr. Tall said, his eyes narrowing. "Nothing's free in this new world."

"Nor in the last one," Cassy said with a faint smile. "The catch is, the Mountain King is coming with what's left of his Empire lapdogs. The simple truth is that if we don't kill you, they will. What, may I ask, do you two leaders intend to do about that?"

Tall said, "We'll fight to the last. We'll die free people, if we can't live that way. As Americans."

Mr. Short nodded, then shrugged. "We have few other options."

Cassy looked up at the sky. She put her right hand on the back of her neck and rubbed it, then looked Tall and Short in the eyes, each in turn. "You have one other option."

Mr. Short shook his head. "It's too late to talk of—"

Tall Guy interrupted him, cutting through the air with the edge of his hand, saying, "What option? I speak for the majority here." He shot a glowering look at the shorter man. "I'll hear you out before we decide who we'd rather have killing us, Empire or Confederation."

Cassy nodded. "Fair enough. My idea is simple. You leave everyone who can't fight in our care. The rest take up guns and wander out west in groups of fifty, or a hundred, and harass the Mountain King's supply lines. Raid the Empire's loyalists. Slash and burn. When it's over, whoever survives comes back for your loved ones and either settles in the Confederation or goes back to their Free Republic homes and starts over."

The tall man frowned. "Long odds on seeing them again when this is over."

Cassy nodded. "Yes. But shorter odds than trying to run roughshod over us again, or facing the Mountain alone."

Short let out a long breath and his shoulders slumped. "So you'd have us join the Night Ghosts to earn our loved ones' keep."

A jolt ran up Cassy's spine. Had she heard that right? "I'm sorry, join who?"

Tall replied, "Night Ghosts. The guerrilla army who fought the Midwest Republic, and now fighting them and the Mountain's troops both. I don't reckon the Free Republic would have been born without their help. The leader is a legend. They say he's two people in one. One leads, the other fights."

Cassy fought the urge to leap with excitement. Nestor lived! After all that time, how was it possible? She kept her voice even. "Yes, I know the Night Ghost leader. His name is Nestor. Join him in spirit, if not in person. Your kids and anyone else who can't or shouldn't manage months in the wild as a guerrilla... they may stay with us, under our supply and protection. Fighting the Mountain... That's the deal, and it's a good one."

Mr. Tall nodded, and Cassy saw that he ignored the shorter man, who glared at him. "Best deal we're likely to get. And I would rather fight those bastards than y'all, if I must pick one. We'll need guns and ammo and the like. I figure we can spend the next couple days getting all our ducks lined up straight, while you get us the guns we'll need."

Cassy nodded. Then she held out her hand, and he shook it. She smiled, since people were watching and must have seen it. Good. Now it was time to put the cherry on top and seal the deal.

She raised the megaphone toward the trucks in the rear. "Break out the food, people. Hungry people want to eat."

She spent the next several hours helping to pass out food allotments and water bottles, smiling at the refugees as they came up, shaking as many hands as she could. She hated doing this to these people, but when survival was on the line, it was time to get cold-hearted, and quickly. Most of these people would be dead come spring, but at least they'd die fighting the Mountain instead of the Confederation.

# - **13** -

0715 HOURS - ZERO DAY +380

CHOONY WIPED SWEAT from his brow and handed Jaz a loaded rifle, taking the empty one from her to reload. She had started with just her own rifle, but when the chaos started yesterday, spare rifles and ammo became easy to find. A chance to sleep for even twenty minutes, on the other hand, was nowhere to be found.

"Dammit, Choony, I can't see straight to shoot straight. I'm doing the one-eye thing, I'm so tanked."

Choony nodded. He knew she meant that she was exhausted, not drunk. Right now, he'd have rather enjoyed getting drunk... being anywhere but here would be an improvement. "Let it go. Your body is tired because it is tired. You are awake because you choose that over death."

Jaz handed another rifle back to him, retrieving the one he had just reloaded. "My shoulder is killing me. It wasn't healed all the way. This shit," she said over the din of firing her rifle, "is totally not fair."

Choony shrugged. She was right, of course. "The world has no fairness in it. Accept this or suffer in resistance, but nothing changes either way. You remain tired and hurt, or dead. To your right!"

Jaz swung the barrel right and fired just as a man stepped from behind a car with a grenade in hand. He fell, and a second later the grenade went off. Another man flew from behind the car as well, propelled by the blast.

"I wonder how Nestor is doing," Jaz shouted over her rifle fire. "You see where he went after the airport got overrun?"

"No. He may still live but either way, we'll have to pull back soon. His Night Ghosts killed the tanks, but there are still infantry."

There was a lull in the shooting just as Jaz exchanged weapons once again, and in the sudden quiet, Choony heard the unmistakable sound of heavy gunfire coming from the distant auditorium. "Jaz, our left flank's about to get overrun. We must fall back." His voice was calm and even, a counterpoint to Jaz's adrenaline-filled ragged voice.

"Shit. It's not fair, Choony. We lost too many people to walk away from this school."

"I recommend running, not walking. I'm sure the dead will not mind."

Jaz shouted an angry, wordless bark toward the invaders. They answered with renewed gunfire.

"If we stay here, we'll get flanked next."

Jaz's face flashed with anger. "Goddammit, Choony. Fine, grab the damn ammo pouches and let's pull back."

Choony understood her reckless anger. Wild thunderstorm that she was, of course pulling back made her angry. She resisted the idea, so it caused her great pain. "Let it go, Jaz. And let us go. Now!"

She and Choony sprinted toward the classroom's back wall, where the door promised life for a little longer. Bullets peppered the walls randomly around them, knocking more bits of cement away, but they made it through the door and turned left, away from the flanking attack. They followed the wall into an open hallway intersection, then bolted right. They only had to cross one hundred yards to reach the final remaining fallback point near the strip mall, the last defensive lines. At least that put the school between them and their attackers, Choony realized, and thanked Buddha for the small grace.

If Nestor lived, they'd find him at the strip mall lines. There wasn't anywhere else for him to be. As they made it to the first cover in the last remaining defensive line, they heard gunfire far behind them, but then they were safe for the moment. "Safety is relative," Choony muttered. It wouldn't be safe for long, he knew.

\* \* \*

Cassy stood on the Liz Town walls with Carl, having returned there several hours ago well before dawn. Carl was agitated, but she couldn't blame him. There had been no right answer to the Harrisburg refugee situation, but then Cassy came along with resources Carl hadn't had and saved the day. A man like Carl, she knew, didn't like to be showed up by anyone, much less someone who wasn't even a Liz Towner. "Stupid pride is stupid," she muttered.

Carl had been trying not to let his irritation show. "Yeah, ain't life a bitch? So what did you ask me up here for?"

"Well, you have a problem with the wildlanders falling back toward Liz Town. They're afraid Harrisburg will fall."

"Don't forget the bike raiders who crossed elsewhere. Your guy Ethan says they're wreaking havoc right now along the Confed's western edge. They could easily raid into Elizabethtown."

"Right," Cassy said. "My point exactly. What will you do when the wildlanders get unruly and desperately want to get inside, where it's supposedly safe?"

"Shoot 'em, same as anyone else who tries to get in."

Cassy nodded. The Liz Town answer to most problems. "But your Sewer Rats band has loyalty to them, and friends still out there in the wildlands. Do you think they'll be happy about that? Or do you think they'll sneak in as many as they can, right under your nose? Then you'll have a hell of a conflict, internally. You don't need that."

Carl let out a long breath and pinched the bridge of his nose. "What choice do I have? I can't just let them in. The other bands would take things into their own hands then, no matter what I say. Even some Timber Wolves would go along with them. Wildlanders didn't build Liz Town, and they didn't cement the rubble with their blood like we have."

"True. They just bled and starved the whole time you were behind these walls. That is why you snuck them provisions, isn't it? Yes, I heard about that. The Sewer Rats will be forever loyal because of it, if you don't abuse that loyalty."

Carl nodded slowly, his shoulders slumping as he dropped his arms to his sides. "So what do you suggest I do?"

"Bring them in."

The words hung between them for a long moment.

Finally, Carl said, "What, like we did with Sunshine's people? It isn't that simple."

"How so?"

"First, convincing the other Bands to take in refugees, when the whole confederation has been drained to supply the guerrilla Free Republic people. Of course, talking the refugees into coming in will be an issue as well—they don't much trust Liz Town."

Cassy nodded, but remained silent.

Carl continued, "Also, finding a band willing to house, defend, and police all those strangers would be a problem.

Letting Sewer Rats sneak them in might solve some of those problems, but then the other bands will go apeshit."

Cassy was quiet for a minute. Carl seemed content to just stand up there with her in silence, no doubt politely waiting for her to reply. At last, she said, "I have one solution that fixes your three problems and raises one more."

"Fire away."

"Put a call out for all their able-bodied adults armed with at least a knife or bat. They can come inside, but only with their immediate family members. They will form another band, or two if there are enough, but they start at a deficit and must work that debt off."

"Makes sense."

"And the Confederation will put out another call for supplies, both from the Confederation and New America. When this war ends, the newcomers will either be dead or they will have earned their stay in Liz Town as a new Band. To sweeten the deal, the Clan will accept any wildlanders who later want to come, and we'll set them up among our Clanholds."

Cassy saw Carl slowly nodding, probably against his better judgment. "That might work, but I can't give the new Bands voting power until after the debt is paid off."

"Understandable."

Carl wiped his face and said, "Yeah. I know the existing bands will worry about losing influence in our system if they add another group. But in the long run, they'll be thankful to me and the Speaker."

"Gratitude breeds loyalty, if that gratitude isn't taken for granted and abused."

"So true."

Cassy nodded. "And we can make another Confed run on the armory that you, me, and a couple other people know about. Arm the new Band for defense of Liz Town. This would be a debt to the Confederation that Liz Town would be responsible for, but I'm sure we can work out those details later. I trust both you and Mary Ann to honor your word, once given."

"I'm not sure the Confederation can come up with enough supplies for all of them, but they'll be better off than they were before. I'll talk to Mary Ann about it, but I think I can convince her."

"She's a good Speaker. Smart, reasonable. Not to mention pragmatic."

Carl chuckled. "She's all of that and more."

Cassy looked out over the slowly decaying ruins of Elizabethtown outside the Lizzie walls and let out a long, slow breath. "It's beautiful, isn't it? These cityscapes, I mean."

"In a macabre sort of way. In a hundred years, what will be left? If aliens came to visit, what would they find?"

"Humanity will go on, but nothing will ever be the same, no matter how far we come in recovering our old way of life, our old tools and technologies."

"But maybe that's not so bad. I like many things about this new world. What did you once call it?"

"This dark new world," she replied. She smiled briefly at the memory of her first conversation with Carl, when he was a new envoy to Clanholme and she had first used that term with him. "No power, no civilization. Kind of a double entendre."

"Yeah, well, not all of it is dark. Yes, billions died or are still dying—humanity's worst tragedy ever, I think—but we who remain are the smart and the lucky. The strong and the loyal. Because everyone who doesn't have those traits is gone, burned away like deadwood."

"It's like a reset button on humanity. But there's still evil in the world. That much hasn't changed."

"Yeah, that's for sure," Carl said. "Anyway, time's up. I have meetings, but I'll talk to Mary Ann tonight."

They shook hands and Carl left Cassy on the wall with her thoughts. Then a new idea struck her. What if she looked elsewhere for those much-needed supplies she promised Carl? The northern invader cantonment... They couldn't possibly want the Mountain King and the Empire to win this war with New America and the Confederation. If the Mountain won, the invaders would have an aggressive new neighbor. Maybe they'd be willing to help provision the new Bands. The enemy of my enemy is my friend, the old saying went.

She wished Choony were there to talk to. He'd talk in riddles, mostly asking more questions until Cassy found her right answer by herself. She missed her confidante and counsellor. "Wherever you are this morning, Choony," Cassy muttered, "I hope you and Jaz are well."

Cassy let out a sigh, and then heard her stomach rumble. It was past time to get breakfast, she decided, and hurried down from the wall.

\* \* \*

After lunch, Ethan sat at his desk, opened up his laptop, then cracked his knuckles as he stretched. Time for business. Right after breakfast, his bloodhound programs and the zombie army of computers it had created alerted him that penetration was complete. Every computer they could find through the network had either been infected and tracked or their data line was grayed out in his logs—after ten attempts, his program stopped trying to infect that computer and deleted the logfiles of its attempts from whichever server it attacked from.

Amber sat next to him, reclining in the other office chair

with her pretty little feet up on his desk. "Whatcha doin'?" she asked.

"I'm about to hack into Watcher One's intranet through a back door I installed. I want to see what he's up to, and what connections he has that I don't."

Amber leaned her head back, staring up at the bunker's red, corrugated metal ceiling. "Sounds like tons of fun. Well, I'll leave you to your games, then."

As Amber began to get up, Ethan groaned and said, "But who will I share my upcoming victory with?"

Amber grabbed her shoes from beside the desk. "Me, later. If you win, that is. But I have a ton of work to do. I'm on kitchen duty from nine o'clock until evening chow. Man, I hope they put me on pies instead of canning. It's too damn hot to be standing next to the stoves for eight hours."

"Oh no," Ethan said with a smirk, "it's so terrible that you have to work on all that food. I feel your pain."

"You ever want to get laid again?" she said, and punched him in his arm. Hard.

"Ouch! Brat. That hurt." Ethan grinned as they went through what had become their morning routine.

She struggled to get her shoes on while standing up. Shoes finally on, she put her hands on his shoulders, leaned down, and kissed him quickly on his lips as he looked up at her from his chair. "See ya tonight."

Ethan nodded and waved goodbye. When she was gone, he turned back to his computer. What she ever saw in him, he'd never know, but he sure wasn't going to ask.

Okay, now it really was time to get down to business...

He spent the next hour setting up another Virtual Machine on his main computer, and loaded it with the programs he figured he'd need. Which was most of them, so it took a while to get that done, too. Then he connected through his old backdoor on a satellite, the one he didn't normally use. If he was tracked, that bird wouldn't have miles of logfiles with him on them. He was pretty good about clearing his tracks, but he could never be certain he got them all. From there, he connected through a series of VPNs that led around the world and back again.

Then he homed in on his target. Watcher One's gateway was marked in red on his monitor, just a line of data that looked like gibberish to most people. Not to a hacker, though. He connected to his friendly little worm-bot...

...and he was in! Watcher One's intranet revealed itself to him in all its glory. Three terminals, or computers, were visible. He set his bloodhound-slash-worm to work on infecting those, then activated a packetsniffer. It was complicated and involved spending an hour installing a couple utilities onto Watcher One's system, disguising them as system files. This activated an alert, but because he had slaved Watcher's box, he alone saw the query pop up asking to authorize the file changes. He clicked "Approve."

His packetsniffer would begin to filter and record everything Watcher One did, every password he used, every VPN he accessed. All of it. And once per week, it would spit that data back to a temp logfile on an enslaved computer in Germany, just waiting for "Dark Ryder" to come and collect it.

Ethan stood and stretched his back. Looking at the clock, he saw he had been hunched over his computer for two hours. The extra time and precautions were necessary, though, because Watcher One was almost as good as Dark Ryder himself.

Ethan sat back down once the knot in his left lower back relaxed a bit. He went into Watcher One's files throughout his little network. Of course, he wouldn't see anything kept on a computer that was currently not connected to that intranet or stored on a USB drive, but nothing could hack that. Not directly—he'd have to wait for his packetsniffer and logfile snooper to relay information about any of those. Even that wouldn't be very useful, though, as they wouldn't be the actual files themselves.

He found one oddity. It was labeled as an image file, but it was exactly 7.0 gigabytes in size. "There's no way that's a simple JPEG," he muttered. More likely, it was a disguised virtual drive. He set up a download manager he had programmed himself, which would copy that file byte by byte and piggyback tiny fragments to his German slaved system. It was essentially a peer-to-peer utility, much like a Torrent. It could take days or weeks to get all the data collected, and even then he'd still have to decrypt and decipher it, but it had to contain something juicy or Watcher One wouldn't have bothered to encrypt and hide it like that.

Hours later, Ethan decided that was enough for one day. He had set up a grand hack, but it would take time for everything to come to fruition. He was about to back out of Watcher One's intranet when a fourth terminal appeared, blinking faint and red. Ethan almost let out an excited victory yell. Someone else just connected to Watcher One's network, bringing their intranet into connection with his own. And it had Admin permissions! Ethan laughed. Who on Earth would have permissions to openly connect to Watcher One's intranet through a remote connection? "I'll give you one guess," Ethan said aloud without realizing it.

He quickly set up a mirror of Watcher One's system, allowing him to see whatever Watcher One saw, go wherever Watcher One could go on this new arrival, and anyone on the other side wouldn't even see it. It was just part of their existing data stream unless they were carefully monitoring it, which he highly doubted. That would be too resource-intensive to use on what was clearly a trusted connection.

He entered the new addition to Watcher's network, but

did nothing beyond looking around. He didn't want to raise alarms, just snoop around the unsecured accessible portion.

It immediately became clear to Ethan that the new connection was exactly who he had thought it was. He was looking around the honest-to-goodness network at freakin' NORAD itself. Hot damn... NORAD... He was inside the Mountain's network.

Okay, he mused, it was probably just a brief connection to sync files or something equally mundane. That meant the connection wouldn't last long. Ethan took a deep breath and loaded a utility on his computer, adjusted the settings, and then his finger hovered over the Enter key. If this worked, he was about to install a worm into NORAD itself. Had that ever been done before? He didn't know, but he did know this was a golden, once-in-a-lifetime opportunity.

On the other hand, if someone noticed it, the connection would be severed and NORAD would begin aggressively backtracking through the fake maze of connections behind which Ethan hid. He'd have to immediately begin wiping every trace of himself from each system he had connected to, beginning with the earliest one and moving on in order, so that they couldn't follow him all the way back home. And they'd definitely install software to look for him in the future. Every connection he made from then onward would be a deadly risk.

But this was NORAD. The risk was worth it. He clicked Enter and watched as his worm tried to install itself. The popup on Watcher One's end came up asking for authorization, which Ethan approved. But had someone on NORAD's end received the popup, as well?

Ethan felt himself sweating, heart beating fast, as his worm continued to install. But then it was done! Ethan raised his face toward the ceiling and screamed, a primitive victory roar. A geeky one. He took two deep, slow breaths to steady himself, then started the process of backing out of Watcher One's network. One node at a time... delete only the logfile lines that related to his own activity... and he was out of NORAD.

Another deep breath, then Ethan began clearing his activity out of Watcher One's intranet network.

> *<<Connection terminated>>*
> *<<Session terminated>>*

Ethan stared at his screen, dumbfounded. What had just happened? He ran through possibilities in his mind. Only one fit everything, he knew, which was that Watcher One had rebooted his computer or turned it off. Otherwise, the mirror would have shown him disconnecting.

Okay, Ethan frantically thought, how dangerous was this? What was the worst-case scenario, and what was the most likely one? Worst case, he had been seen, hacked, then cut off, and now his own network was compromised. But by far the most likely scenario was that he hadn't been hacked, or that only his VM was compromised. Ethan cursed in frustration. He hadn't finished clearing his tracks from Watcher One's network. He might stumble across them, and though Ethan had deleted some, it was still possible Watcher One would find the programs Ethan had installed.

Would his torrent-like transfer of that JPEG finish before then? He couldn't be sure. He'd just have to wait and see. All he could do now was to try to meticulously remove every trace of himself from the computers between Watcher One's and the German slaved computer that would hold that JPEG file and the packet data, so that his nemesis couldn't track through them before Ethan could collect the file.

As he began to relax, Ethan abruptly grew a sloppy, happy grin. He, Dark Ryder, had hacked frikkin' *NORAD itself.* That was a damn fine feather in any hacker's cap. And who knew what dividends it would pay down the road?

* * *

As the sun made its way toward the hilly horizon, Carl motioned his people to open the main gate. As it slowly slid open, he saw a growing crack of space between gate and wall, which showed what lay on the other side. There was a huge crowd...

As it continued to open, however, he could see that the teeming throng of people wasn't just a chaotic mob. They were lined up in a long, snaking line of people that wove back and forth as it extended away from the gate, like amusement parks used to have. When the gate clanged to a stop, fully open, the whole vista lay exposed before him. In addition to the orderly snake of people that must number in the hundreds, he saw a dozen Liz Town people holding tall poles that had the Liz Town banner hanging from each. Those people stood to the sides of the crowd, spaced evenly and well apart. They acted as a boundary rope for the crowd. None in the crowd violated the invisible line that stretched between the Lizzies on either side of the crowd. Everything was well ordered.

The scene was also eerily quiet as the people stood patiently waiting in line. The faces Carl could see bore determined expressions. They were all between their late teens and late twenties. Fit. Healthy, without a crutch in sight.

Carl's heart sped up with excitement. Cassy had been right—the wildlanders rallied at the chance to join Liz Town, even at the cost of leaving family and friends behind while they went off to fight the Mountain's troops. The cowards would already have found reasons not to be here today.

Carl's unannounced "take a meal and go home" offer would weed out the other cowards who had merely been chastised by friends and family into coming here. That had been his own idea.

He stepped through the gateway onto the narrow strip of empty land between the wall and the crowd, and raised a megaphone to his mouth. He pulled the trigger, and for a couple of seconds it made a terrible screeching noise that faded out only slowly. When it stopped, he announced, "Wildlanders, welcome to Liz Town. You are here because we need each other, and because you aren't afraid to do what you must to take care of those you love. We all have that in common, and for that you have the respect of Liz Town."

He paused a moment to let it sink in. All heads were turned toward him, it seemed, and the crowd stayed quiet as they listened. That was a good sign. He had feared they would be hostile due to having been walled out early in Liz Town's history. Maybe they were, but that was then and today was today.

"Tonight, you will step forward when told to. Keep the line orderly. Disruptions will result in dismissal. When it is your turn to approach the gate, come to the nearest recruiter with his or her hand raised. Sit in the chair before them. Answer their questions. I expect this to take all night. We will be handing out water bottles throughout the night. That is all."

Carl clicked off the megaphone, then turned back to the gate and waved. A couple dozen Lizzies rushed out with a bunch of folding card tables and folding chairs, then set up in a row just outside the gate. The gate slowly closed, leaving only a crack for people to get through.

Six Lizzies went to sit behind the tables. All six raised their hands and held them up. The other workers moved to a huge pile of water bottles at one side of the gate, gathered up armfuls and then headed toward the crowd to pass them out.

Carl put the megaphone to his mouth again. "If you are ready, then begin. The first six, move forward. The rest, move up and keep the line in order. Carry on."

He turned his back to the crowd and walked through the gate, returning to Liz Town. Behind him, the gate clanged fully closed. The many guards on the wall stood with weapons at the low ready, not threatening but also not making any attempt to disguise their purpose. Carl didn't think they'd be needed.

Mary Ann approached after the gate was fully closed, having been waiting just inside "Well done, Carl," she said.

"Thanks for agreeing to this."

"It seems like the smart thing to do."

Carl nodded and said, "I knew you'd agree. And you're a good person—hell, you overlook the food and supplies someone sneaks out to the wildlanders. I knew you'd hear me out on this."

"Yeah, well I truly hope it works."

"I'm surprised at the turnout."

Mary Ann winked at him. "I think that has less to do with the offer itself than it does with the trust those people have for *whoever* it is who keeps stealing supplies and smuggling them out. That built the groundwork for this to happen."

"Kismet," Carl replied. "If I find out who did the smuggling, I'll let them know you forgive them and send your regards."

She laughed and looked into Carl's eyes. "Do that, but let them know it's still stealing and I'll take it out of the coffers of whatever Band is responsible."

Ha. Like hell she would. But it was a warning to keep it quiet.

"In the meantime," she continued, "I'll leave you to your circus. Oh, and Carl? Thanks for everything."

Carl watched Mary Ann leave, then turned his attention back toward the gate. Maybe he could still make himself useful somehow, and he didn't have anything else to do.

Out of the corner of his eye, he saw Sunshine behind a cluster of other Liz Towners. Carl wished she'd talk to him, but lately she had found reasons to be too busy to accept his meeting invitations. She stared at him, jaw set tightly, then clearly turned her head to look at Mary Ann's back. Her eyes narrowed.

# - **14** -

0900 HOURS - ZERO DAY +381

JAZ DUCKED BELOW the bigbox store's shattered bay window as the Mountain's troops returned fire. Right now, there were only a squad of them, backed up by a ragged company of Empire goons, but that Mountain squad was deadlier than anything she had seen. They totally looked like alien bugs with all those scopes or whatever over their faces. She had shot one dead-center with a burst from her M4; he fell, only to get back up and keep coming.

"They're not superman," Jaz said to the Free Republic fighter beside her. "You gotta hit them in the legs or the face. Legs only immobilize, but the face is harder to hit. Once you take out those optics, though, they're just normal soldiers. If they don't die, they're blinded."

The trooper popped up and fired a burst, then return fire made him duck back. "We ain't getting out of here alive, miss," he said, "but I'm damn sure gonna take some with me."

Choony handed her a loaded rifle. "One can only make one's best effort," he said.

"Forget that," said the fighter as he fired another burst.

Jaz kind of agreed with the guy. Choony's was the way of inner peace, but Jaz had none of that right now. She was totally amped up and jonesing for more kills. The bastards had to die. She rose up to fire, and just then one of the Empire goons darted between two bits of cove, carrying him smack dab into her crosshairs. *Bang, bang.* He dropped, sliding to a stop on his face. "Eat it, goon," she shouted as she ducked again.

To her left, a woman from the Night Ghosts shouted, "Jaz, time to go! They're coming."

Jaz was amazed Nestor not only lived, but had raised another unit to fight the Empire. This woman was in one of his squads that got separated, but she didn't know where her squadmates were. They had scattered, and she had cliqued up with Jaz's peeps.

Jaz rose high enough to peer over the window ledge. The Mountain's soldiers were popping up and down like groundhogs, each closer than the last. None stayed up long enough for Jaz to draw a bead on them. The unit was in a scattered wedge formation, coming on fast.

"Final assault. Fall back," Jaz shouted. She and Choony got to their feet and bolted. Bullets flew all around here, and to her left, another running man screamed and fell, his blood splattering a display of moldy bread. She kept running.

"Run faster, Jaz," Choony shouted from right behind her. "Move it!"

They made it to the end of the aisle and doglegged right into a new aisle, which then headed straight toward the warehouse area in the back of the store. Freedom... Bits of shattered something-or-other flew off the shelves to Jaz's left, pelting her, but she didn't think any of it cut her. The sounds of autofire from behind her reached her ears...

...and then she was through the swinging double

doors, sprinting into the warehouse area itself. "Left or right," she shouted.

"Right," Choony replied, shoving her in that direction.

Screw it. Jaz figured he had a fifty-fifty shot at being right, so she ran with him. Then she saw the emergency exit ahead of her, leading into the back parking lot. She put her head down and redoubled her efforts, ignoring the pain of burning thighs, heedless of her shoulder-slung rifle repeatedly smacking into her elbow on every other step. When she hit the door, she didn't slow down. Please, God, don't let it be locked. That would totally hurt...

But it wasn't locked. As she plowed into the door's activation bar, it crashed open. She lost her footing as she flew through the doorway, and ate pavement. Hard.

Choony appeared at her side immediately, and roughly wrenched her to her feet. "Rest later," he said hoarsely as she found her balance. Then they were off running again.

* * *

Nestor slapped the back of each fighter as they ran by, cutting through the mammoth store in single file. He had found a few FreeRep fighters dead on the ground as his forces secured the huge store. He had hit that store damn hard with over one-hundred fighters in three platoons, and the Mountain King had only held it for only a few minutes, Nestor recalled with a savage grin. He had trapped and slaughtered an entire squad of the supposed super-soldiers, and a boatload of Empire goons. Bye, bye. It was unfortunate the dozen FreeRep defenders had been killed during the brief time the Mountain held the store.

Ratbone, panting, held the bandage over a larger cut in his left bicep. It still oozed, but Ratbone was all business.

"Building clear. Battalion of goons inbound behind us, you know. We can't stay here."

"I know. We gotta run. But it was nice to get this last 'screw you' in on them, yeah?"

"Where we headed?"

"Thirty miles east to Johnstown. I have a feeling it's going to be a rough day."

No more fighters came filing through the doorway, and Nestor popped his head out to be sure. No more friendlies, and their pursuers weren't yet close enough to see. "Looks like the squad of wounded did rear-guard well. Now let's go."

Ratbone nodded. "Rest their souls." He ran toward the back of the building.

They went through the winding warehouse area at the rear of the store, out the back door. A small parking lot lay between them and cover, and Nestor ran toward those trees as fast as he could, at the tail end of the stream of fighters. The trees loomed, then they were through the tree line. Nestor stopped, panting, and looked around.

His troops were clustered up, catching their breath. They were reloading, checking bags, tying boots. The usual. What wasn't usual was the three new faces standing with one of his newer recruits. Nestor knew two of them, and his eyes bugged out. What were the odds?

"Holy crap," he said. "Jaz? Choony? I thought you were south of Confed."

The stunningly beautiful woman—attractive despite looking like a ragged little street urchin at the moment—grinned. "Nestor lives. Long time no see. We were in the store, got overran. We fled here, then heard your assault and stayed to catch a peek on what was going down."

Nestor laughed. "Well, glad you're alive. We got real problems, though."

"Yes," Choony said, stepping up to stand beside Jaz.

"So here's the situation as I know it. Lawson Heights is falling. It was a hard fight, but those Mountain troops are scary rugged and they got vehicle support. Can't beat that. They even got drones for eyes, but most of those should be out of juice by now. We can move without being seen from the air, I think."

Choony said, "Lawson Heights is important to us, but just a small theater to our enemies."

"Well, they won this small theater," Nestor said, nodding. "You need to head east. About thirty miles, head to Johnstown. We have units rallying there from all over the damn place. Tomorrow, those troops are striking out to the east. The Appalachians are their bug-out destination, so if you miss them, head there. FreeRep is going guerrilla, it seems. Or, more guerrilla."

"Sounds like they'll be playing your song, Nestor. But what about you?" Jaz asked. "How many peeps you got, and what's your party plan?"

Ratbone stepped up and said, "We got about a battalion of guerrillas left. We're going to harry the enemy with small-unit actions to buy time for the FreeRep fighters to get up into the mountains."

Jaz paused, her eyes clicking to Nestor. She looked pensive. "You sure?"

Nestor nodded. "Yep. We'll be fine, or we won't. I might let my other half out to play for a while. Either way, it seems to be what I was born for."

Ratbone glanced at Nestor, like he had something to say but decided not to. Nestor had noted a lot of that from his people lately, whenever he mentioned finally letting the Other out to run the show for a while. Those looks made Nestor nervous, but dammit, he didn't have time to play games.

Choony nodded, a faint smile on his face. Of all of the

Clanners, Choony would be the one to best understand…

Choony said, "Things are as they are. I wish you the protections and blessings of Buddha, the Dharma, and the Sangha."

Nestor grinned. "Thanks, I'll take his blessings, too. Any help I can get is fine with me. Okay, kids, recess is over." He turned to Ratbone and said, "Make sure we send a squad with these two, but send them light on gear. They can forage on the way and up in the mountains. Stock 'em up on ammo, though."

Ratbone nodded curtly and walked away.

Nestor said, "Okay, you two. In five minutes, head northeast for a couple miles, then bee-line east to Johnstown. If you can handle it, keep moving all damn day. You want to get there in time to rest up before they move out, or they'll leave you behind, so push hard. I'll see you later, maybe."

Jaz gave him a hug—which was awesome, of course—and Choony shook his hand. They said their farewells, and Nestor watched as Jaz, Choony, and some of his own fighters double-timed it out of there. He let out a long breath. He didn't expect to see them again in this life, but hopefully he could buy them time to get to safety. Lawson Heights was lost, and there wasn't much else around to hide in. Ah, well. He'd had a good run, lately, and never had expected that to last forever.

He turned and shouted, "Alright, gather up! Take a knee, and standby for orders. We're the rear guard this time, and here's the game plan, boys and girls…"

\* \* \*

Frank looked up and saw the sun high overhead. The sundial said it was around noon. He glanced at the digital clock Ethan had set up, which was synchronized with the prior day's noon. Local time was always accurate by the sun, timezones long forgotten. The clock said 12:46 p.m.

Most of his morning had been spent in meetings. First up had been Liz Town, their envoy and Frank talking to the chancellor about the supplies situation. It would be a lean winter, but they'd have just enough, and Frank agreed with her plan to arm and supply an army of refugees and wildlanders to throw at occupied Free Republic. It wasn't all occupied, but the signs indicated the Free Republic forces were collapsing on every front. It was only a matter of days, he thought, before the formerly Free Republic territories were all green on Ethan's map. Or whatever color showed General Houle's territory.

Then Cassy had told him of her idea about requesting supplies from the 'vaders in northern Pennsylvania. He had agreed it was worth a shot, but insisted that whoever went to them were volunteers. Too bad Choony wasn't around, because he would have been a perfect choice.

Then he had met with two Clanhold envoys embroiled in a dispute. A young man from one hold had knocked up his girlfriend from the other, and then he had bailed out on the relationship. Her Clanhold leader wanted him to marry her, or at least cover every resource she and her baby would require. The young man's Clanhold wanted to either pay nothing or take custody of the child when it was born.

Frank had ruled that the young man's Clanhold must cover half the supplies needed to raise the child to age thirteen. He could raise the child every other year, *if* he wanted to, but they would pay regardless. Frank figured the man's Clanhold would insist on taking the child on their years, since they were paying for it anyway, and so the baby would have some kind of relationship with both parents and hopefully bond the two holds more tightly together.

It was messy, but apparently, life went on even in the

middle of a war for survival.

Then the guard tower air horn sounded. Non-hostiles coming in from the south. Frank hobbled in that direction. A couple minutes later, two riders came trotting up. They dismounted and saluted Frank, who awkwardly saluted back.

Frank decided they had to be from the Gap. No one else saluted higher-ranking people from other settlements, if they saluted anyone at all.

"The Clan welcomes you," Frank said when they were close enough. "What brings you here today?" He smiled, and patted one of the horses on its neck.

"Nothing good," one man said. "The Gap fell, and now the Mountain King holds it. Only some of us escaped. The majority are still back there, though whether they're dead or enslaved, I couldn't tell you."

Frank stood stunned. His mind raced. He blurted, "Why didn't we hear of it on the radio?"

The man shrugged and frowned. "The Mountain had special forces or something. A small unit infiltrated our HQ and wiped everyone out, right before they began their attack. We hadn't even heard they were coming, so we were caught with our pants down. Complete surprise. Houle's soldiers must have killed or captured anyone they saw on their approach so they couldn't flee and warn us."

A worm of fear began to wiggle in his mind. SpecOps. Michael must be told. The Clan would have to take precautions to avoid either Frank or Cassy getting taken out by surprise. At least the Bunker was safe, as few people knew where it was or how to get into it.

A few Clanners, including a woman on guard duty, had joined them by now. Visitors always drew curious onlookers. Frank told her, "Find Cassy. Tell her, 'Bravo Oscar Bravo.' She'll know what that means. Tell her I'll fill her in later, but that this is no drill."

The guard nodded once and she ran toward the Clan's HQ.

Frank said, "Alright, Gappers. You are both welcome here with open arms. Where are the survivors who escaped? You said most remained behind. What of the others?"

The poor guy, who looked like he could fall asleep standing up right now, said, "They're coming, but they're on foot. Men, women, children. Two hundred in all. An hour behind us."

"Shit. That's too many for us to handle without preparations. Alright, go back and split them into four even groups. Send one group here, another to each of Ephrata, Lititz, and Brickerville. We'll get them taken care of, friend."

Frank gave instructions to several Clanners to make the arrangements for their fifty or so guests. Now Cassy's supply commitments to the FreeRep refugees were looking less and less like a good idea. It would be a hungry winter, if they survived that long, unless the 'vaders miraculously agreed to give them supplies.

Frank saw Michael jogging toward them. When he arrived, he wasn't even breathing hard. Frank saluted back to the outgoing Gappers returning to their horde of survivors, then turned to Michael.

"No estimates on enemy size, I imagine?" When Frank shook his head, Michael said, "Give me authorization to talk to the chancellor about diverting Taggart's two battalions back to Clan territory. We're next in line from the Gap, if Houle's troops are going to keep rolling forward northward, maintaining the offensive."

"Yes, good idea. Cassy will be confined to the bunker for her safety, by the way. Apparently, Houle's troops that hit the Gap included some special forces, and they took out the Gap HQ and radio before anyone in town knew they were under attack."

"I'll put our people on alert until we know more," Michael said, "and send out scouts to screen our southern borders."

Frank nodded, and Michael walked back toward Clanholme while talking quietly into his walkie-talkie.

\* \* \*

Taggart looked up at the scorching afternoon sun and wiped his brow with his sleeve. Part of him wished he was back in his headquarters, where they had rigged up a simple old generator and bypassed the central A/C's fried controller unit. They had finagled the A/C into working, despite the fact that temperature control had been reduced to manually turning the unit on and off with a switch that interrupted the power supply. Crude, but it worked.

Another part of him hated that place, however. Not because the HQ's original owners had been found in the cellar, decomposed almost to skeletons, but because he wasn't used to being a general. Much less, the president! The opulence that showed in that house's every detail was alien to him, and discomforting. He had grown up in a two-bedroom house with five kids and three adults, where "luxury" had been to take a dump without people banging on the one bathroom's door the whole time.

It was time to stop letting himself get distracted. He'd think about the "palace" later. Right now, he was being flooded with reports from his resistance cells all over western New York City and adjacent New Jersey. Ree's territory, or rather his underlings—he had implemented honest-to-god feudalism, and still called it communism with a straight face. Taggart grinned to think of the verbal acrobatics it must have taken to justify *that* little decision.

Eagan cursed as he almost knocked over his coffee cup.

Then he said, "So, have we figured out what the hell is happening, yet?"

Taggart looked at the huge wall map of Ree's territory, which had been laminated and spray-glued to plywood, then into a table. He had little wooden blocks of many kinds and colors all over the map, and notes written in grease pen. Many of the largest blocks, green, had showed rebel cells' operational areas but were now swapped for red blocks. "Yes, some info. It appears that most of our friendly neighborhood resistance cells have activated."

Eagan snorted. "No shit, sir. I mean, do we know why? Do we even know what their operational objectives are? We can't support them effectively if we don't know what the darn heck they're doing."

"Why would you say shit and then darn heck? That's a buck in the jar, by the way."

"Because I only have one buck on me, sir."

Taggart shook his head. "But no, we don't know what our resistance friends are up to. We're getting lots of reports and the desk-jockey spooks are putting together projections."

"I'm sure they will be one-hundred percent accurate and factual, sir. Intel is an exact science."

"Shut up, shitbird. Those people put their carpal tunnels on the line every day in the fight for freedom."

Eagan smiled and said, "Do you got enough data for a gut check on it, though? You're usually right, and I'd like to start coordinating supporting efforts as quickly as we can, even if we need to make adjustments when Intel finishes massaging the data."

Taggart nodded. Eagan had a good point. "Fine. Anyway, the info we're getting from the few with radios suggests that this is a response to Ree cutting everyone's rations. There is plenty of food for his civilian survivors, now, between planting in every bit of dirt they could find and a fleet of fishing boats. And yet, Ree still cut their rations. We don't know if that was a punitive measure or some other cause."

"So we can expect them to focus on securing the harvest substations, I imagine."

"Yes... But if you look at the map closely, you'll see that most of the cells' activity isn't actually in Ree's personal territory, but that of his vassals. Which is—"

"Brilliant," Eagan interrupted. Taggart nodded, and Eagan continued, "By focusing in his lackey turf, they pretty much ensure Ree won't make more than a token effort to help them unless it looks like those territories will actually fall. It cuts the forces they have to fight in half."

"Divide and conquer," Taggart muttered.

"If they intend to take over, which is a big damn if, then they wouldn't have to face Ree's reinforcements until later."

"That's how I read the situation," Taggart said. "Alright. Activate our own SpecOps people and send them in to coordinate intel and support. Remember the rough plan we had outlined for such a scenario?"

"Yes, sir. We load them up with as much supply as they want to carry, and then insert them into the situation. For this mission, are we using that contingency plan's HQ and fallback?"

Taggart looked at the map to double check that he was right about the insurgents focusing primarily on Ree's vassals. Nothing else made much sense of the intel he had received so far, though it could change quickly as more data got evaluated by the spooks. He didn't really think it would change, though. Going after the vassals first just made sense.

"Affirm. Use the listed insurgent cell for that. Now get going."

Taggart watched Eagan leave. This was an unexpected development, and it was happening prematurely, but things were what they were. Sometimes, events didn't give him the luxury of following The Plan. He'd have to make the best of it. Despite the problems created by the premature uprising, however, Taggart still felt a perverse glee at the thought of those invading bastards waking up to a popular uprising.

"Hope you hate it," he said to his far-away enemy.

\* \* \*

Ethan nibbled at a late-night snack of ice cream and berries. The ice cream was a super-rare treat, pretty much restricted to Cassy, Frank, and the Council because it used the limited ice from Cassy's small refrigerator/freezer. There was no way to make enough to go around, certainly not with the hand-cranked ice cream maker.

Abruptly, an alert popped up on his laptop. Ethan leaned forward and clicked the alert window. One of his firewall applications opened and he saw a known I.P. entering his VM's artificial intranet. It was an older I.P. address that he had associated with Watcher One a long time ago, but it was almost never used.

Ethan observed as Watcher One attempted to install a small program, which he guessed to be a combination of worm and data packet sniffer. He enveloped it in a fake, static environment; it would never find any useful data.

Then he saw that his main firewall—again, the Virtual Machine's mirror image of it—came down hard and fast. Watcher One must have had programs loading, waiting to strike, because as soon as the firewall crashed, half a dozen installation alerts popped up along with another half-dozen file alteration alerts. This was no infiltration, Ethan realized. It was an assault.

Then his satellite connection froze up, causing his system to buffer. An application installed itself in the brief time it took his system resume letting him click anything.

Ethan cursed when he realized that the install had been an autonomous packet sniffer. As Ethan's system attempted to re-connect to the weather satellite he had used to connect to a server in France, and from there out to other servers, that data went through the enemy packet sniffer. In two seconds, his system caught up to what was going on and became responsive again, but at just that point, the attack stopped. No new installs or file changes popped up, and the connection from Watcher One's I.P. address terminated.

Ethan spat another curse, then shut down his VM. He wouldn't be able to back-track Watcher One because this had left the laptop completely isolated, not connected even to his intranet—he was paranoid beyond belief about his computer security, but it would be a lifesaver if his network were ever fully compromised.

Ethan rolled his chair to his other active laptop, feet pawing at the ground for traction. He moved his USB-attached mouse and the screen lit up. He opened several monitoring and defensive tools, admin tools, system monitors, and others. When they had loaded, he clicked his internet connection and told it to connect to Bird2, his weather satellite. He wanted to grab its log files, if they were still there, and install some other defensive software on the bird's controlling computers. The connection listing was grayed out on his screen. He clicked it anyway, but again, nothing happened.

Then another app popped up. It listed a different satellite—ostensibly a weather satellite, but actually a military bird for monitoring missile launches—with an alert. He clicked it to open the alert window.

"Possible launch detected," it said, the words blinking in red.

Several clicks later, he had visual on the supposed launch. He froze in his seat and watched helplessly as, with a five-second delay, something in mid-orbit glowed red as it re-entered over the Atlantic Ocean. Ethan felt like a ship with the wind knocked out of its sails. His stomach sunk. There, in full color, he watched as one of his precious few controlled satellites cremated itself in Earth's upper atmosphere.

And because of that, Ethan would now be without internet connection for a couple hours every evening while other birds drifted into useful positions during their orbit cycles. He clenched his fists and imagined himself with his fingers around the bastard's throat. Watcher One had retaliated, alright, and had killed a priceless satellite to do so.

Ethan swore aloud, "I promise you, Watcher One, I'm going to burn you down for this." He didn't yet know how, but one way or another, this game was going to end, and soon.

# - **15** -

0600 HOURS - ZERO DAY +382

"SHIT." FRANK LEFT the outhouse and crutched carefully down the two steps. Oh man, someone's head was going to roll for this one. All the worms must have died, because the outlet pipe was clogged and that just didn't happen with the worms doing their thing.

He crutched out behind the outhouse and saw that nothing flowed out through the perforated pipes into the constructed wetlands, either.

"Sonovabitch," Frank muttered to himself. The "wetlands" was made of trenches behind the outhouses, in which swampy plants had been growing. They filtered the drainage, cleaning it to the point of looking crystal clear before it flowed out into the two retainer ponds.

Frank went to the closest guard he could find and said, "Go find Amber. She's on shit detail today. Someone dumped something into the damn toilet that killed the worms. Now it has to be dug out, the material burned, and the pipe diverted so we can flush it clear."

"Yes, sir. Maybe bleach? One of the idiot teens could have dumped a mop bucket in there after cleaning up the outdoor kitchen."

"No way to tell which shift crew did this. It might have taken awhile for all the worms to die off. Amber manages maintenance, so tell her I want it managed. Make sure none of that crap gets into our ponds, either. The pit has to be burned out, and that outhouse has to be taped off so no one else uses it."

The guard nodded and left.

Frank let out a long frustrated breath. Even in the middle of a war, someone still had to take care of the damn toilets. At least they had put in a bunch of new outhouses that spring.

He went to the guard tower to get the night's report, and found that a scout team had radioed in on a short range hand-held. They'd be riding up in a few minutes, and had a report to make.

He crutched off in the direction they'd be coming in from, but then his metal-and-wood foot got caught in some grass. After yanking on it a few times, he had to unsnap the straps, take his stump out, and then yank back and forth on the fake foot until it tore free.

This morning was not going well, and he hoped it wouldn't turn into "one of those days."

Just as he got the prosthetic back on and the straps snapped, the scout team rode up. One dismounted and walked up to Frank.

"Good morning, boss. I figured you'd be here waiting for us and I'm glad you are, because we found something you need to know." He had to swallow hard a few times to get that out.

"Go ahead," Frank said and braced himself for bad news. On a morning like this, it could only be bad. Maybe he had done something to piss off Karma...

The scout took a swig of water from his canteen. Putting

that away, he said, "It's the Gap—we knew it fell, but there's more. There's new construction going on there."

"Construction, already? What are they building?"

"Hard to say. We could see that they're using the captured survivors to do the labor. They were feeding the workers but no one else, so it's probably a food-for-work program."

"Anything else?" Frank ran his fingers through his hair. So far, it was bad news but not anything he could fix immediately. Just more intel for Cassy and Michael.

"Yeah." The scout shifted his weight from one foot to the other and scratched his neck. "Frank, they got stacks and stacks of supplies. The whole market area was fenced off with chainlink, and inside are pallets stuffed with boxes and crates. They had flatbed cargo trucks. No gasifiers. Soldiers in camouflage. Two real live tanks, but small ones. A bulldozer and a backhoe. They're building up the town wall, and putting some wall up on our side of the bridge, too."

Frank frowned. Castellation in action, it just had to be. "Alright, thanks. Go write up your report and then get some chow." Frank patted him on the arm and waved to the other, and watched them walk their horses into Clanholme proper.

Frank was left alone with his thoughts. It was a good thing he had already put the word out to gather Taggart's two battalions. The Gap's occupiers couldn't be allowed to finish building their defenses. Having a Mountain fortification and supply point on the Confederation's southern flank was like having a knife poised at one's exposed throat. They could hit the Clan from two directions, west and south, splitting Confederation defenses and creating an exponential number of possible threats to deal with. Of course, he'd need to tell Cassy. She had to know about the enemy activity and plan accordingly for the Confederation as a whole...

Yes, it was definitely turning into one of those days.

* * *

Jaz wandered among the wounded outside of Johnstown while the sun rose higher in the morning sky. Those Johnstown peeps had no walls built, and she didn't get why they didn't just let the Free Republic fighters take some buildings in the empty parts of town, but they had been adamant about keeping the fighters outside of town. She understood why they worried about disease and all, but how they treated the fighters was totally uncool. At least they had coughed up their first aid supplies, once someone explained to them that it was give them or have them seized. A lot of the units she and Choony had retreated with were shot up pretty good.

Walking beside her, Choony said, "We should sleep. You are exhausted, just as I am. You can help no one if you're asleep on your feet, and the Mountain will probably be here in a day or two, if not sooner. However long it takes them to mop up Nestor's rear guard, they'll be here right afterward."

He was right, of course. Jaz could only see out of one eye at a time. She was so tired that if she tried to keep both peepers open at once, one eye wandered off, so she totally had to one-eye it as she walked. She was staggering like she was smashed, too, from sheer exhaustion. "Fine. Let's get some sleep. I'm totes wiped out, and my shoulder kills."

"Yes, I'm sure it aches terribly."

Right again... "Let's head into town and squat a vacant. I can't sleep out here with all these peeps around, and the wounded moaning and stuff. Plus, the sun will be up real soon."

"They can't help it, you know," Choony said. "They're injured. Many of these fighters probably won't survive until morning."

"Another reason to get out of here. I've seen enough

people die."

Choony slid his arm into hers, and they walked arm-in-arm into Johnstown. "Funny," he said, looking at the town's antique construction in the neighborhood through which they walked. "Parts of this town are older than America is. Johnstown saw America's birth, and was still around to witness its death."

"Well, that's just morbid. Way to cheer a chick up, Choon."

He laughed, which brought a smile to her weary face. He had an amazing laugh, rich and full of life, and it sounded kind and decent. Or maybe that was her feelings affecting how she saw him. She didn't care, though.

Choony said, "Did you know that over half this town was vacant even before the war? It got flooded for the third time in the '70s, and never really recovered. People gave up on it."

Jaz only nodded. She was too exhausted for small talk or history lessons.

"Unemployment here was over ten percent before the war. The Dying Times hit this place hard, since the people had so little. They say only about a thousand people live here now. Over ninety percent had died off before it joined the Empire."

"Fantastic. Let's get some sleep. This pad looks cushy," Jaz said, pointing at a nice single-story home. It was relatively newer construction than the others in that neighborhood, even among those that weren't historical buildings. The house had been boarded up, but there was no indication that it had been broken into.

She said, "It looks like they secured it as best they could and then headed out of town, probably early in the war. I'm sure they won't mind if we crash."

"Coolness," said Choony.

Jaz giggled. He sounded so *stupid* when he tried to talk

like normal peeps. It was cute, though, not like, embarrassing or anything.

They tested the windows and doors, but all the windows were securely boarded and the doors were locked. They went around back, and Choony checked under the doormat. A key. "I could have kicked it in, but better not to damage the things we borrow, right?"

She didn't care, but nodded. It was his way, and the key was easier anyway. They stepped inside as the sun crested the horizon, and found everything inside was covered in sheets. The air smelled stale, but there was remarkably little dust on the counters. It must have had good weatherproofing. "Nice. Let's head upstairs and find a bed to sleep on."

They walked up the stairs, Choony in the lead, and checked the first door. It was a bathroom. He closed the door, and they checked the next one. It was a small room with a single bed. The next room, however, was the big one. Inside was a Queen-sized mattress, thick and comfy-looking, which had been stood in one corner.

"Bingo." First night in a bed in a long-ass time, she was going to enjoy it. She grinned as Choony yawned and practically dove into the bed to get under the covers. Jaz took her time and stopped to stretch before climbing in; Choony looked like a cute little deer in headlights, unable to look away as she stretched out.

She grinned at him. "Don't worry, Choony. You're safe with me. I won't take advantage of you."

He chuckled, but it sounded awkward, which made her laugh again. For a minute, they just teased one another and laughed, at each other and at themselves.

It was nice to just relax like that, she mused. No fear of someone stumbling across their camp as they slept, no worries about the war rolling over them before they could pull up stakes and bail. And the house was cozy, as was lying in bed together and having a laugh. She wondered if that was how normal people felt all the time.

"Ever wonder what your life would have been like without the war? Do you think you'd be happy? Married?"

Choony stuffed a pillow under his head.

"No, contemplating such things would be pointless. There is the war, and pretending otherwise—wishing for the world to be different—would help no one. Anyway, I doubt I'd be married. My parents wanted me to marry a nice girl from Korea, and even had one picked out for me like some off-the-rack jacket, but I didn't want to marry her. I never saw the point of maintaining old traditions."

Jaz nodded. In a way, she understood. It was like when her dad wanted her to sleep with his best friend when she was fourteen, because he was going to pay her dad enough money to get their rent caught up. She had bailed with a quickness—she had enough of his friends' attentions and took off before the dude got there. Boy was her dad pissed! But that was totally his problem. Even if her dad never saw beyond the messed up way he had been raised, she wanted more out of life. She wanted the life the other kids at school had, where they didn't worry about eating and didn't have to get on their knees to pay the rent for their parents.

"Besides," Choony added, interrupting her thoughts, "I wouldn't have met you. I'd trade the world to be here with you right here, right now."

She loved the things he said. She knew deep down that he meant every word. This man saw her how she wanted to see herself, not how she and the world actually did see her. It made her want to be a better, stronger person so she didn't disappoint him. For some reason, when he was disappointed in her, it felt like her world was coming apart. She hated it. "I know you would. I don't know why, but I do know you're honest. It's why I feel the way I do about you, too. Wherever I go, whatever I do, I know I'll be okay if you're with me. Plus, you keep me honest."

"Ha. I'm glad for that. You're a hurricane on your own. A force of nature. All this wonderful energy, but lacking focus. It's beautiful like a lightning storm, but it would burn you out so fast... You'd roll on by, leaving wreckage behind you, until you had spent all your force and just faded."

"I'm not that bad," she said, laughing, and lightly hit his arm. She never hit him hard, because she knew he wouldn't play-fight with her and that would just make her feel like a bully.

"Not bad. Just like Nature, neither good nor bad, but you would leave a trail of wreckage behind you without even realizing it. Broken hearts, broken trusts. But you're better than that. I feel like I might help you focus all that power. You have a mighty aura, Jaz."

"You believe in auras? Like, witchcraft and stuff?" She raised an eyebrow. Of course he didn't, but she didn't know what he meant.

"No. It's just that... You know how when some people enter a room, you just *know* they're there, even if you haven't seen them yet? They come in and the attention shifts to them. The very air seems to change, and they own the room just by being there. That's you, Jaz. That's your aura."

She flopped from her elbow onto her back and looked up at the ceiling. Someone had once painted it a beautiful, peaceful cerulean blue, like an ocean sky. Or how she imagined an ocean sky looking. "You know, it makes me feel weird when you say stuff like that. I like it, though. And I like that you think about this stuff. Most guys aren't thinking about that when they're with me. They got other ideas."

"I've thought of that, certainly," Choony said, and she could hear the smile in his voice.

She was surprisingly glad. Everyone seemed to think of her in *that way,* so it would have thrown her off balance if he hadn't—and it would have broken her heart. She quickly grabbed that last thought and stuffed it deep inside, though. That was her vulnerability showing, and she didn't need that. Not now, not ever again.

Choony continued, "You are beautiful, and you know it. Like the most beautiful flower I've ever seen. When other people are around, looking at you is like seeing a rose centerpiece at a bouquet. The other garnish in the vase may be present, but all I see is the rose."

Jaz felt her heart racing, and a weird feeling in her stomach. It was desire, she knew, but not the kind she had grown used to feeling. It wasn't that raw, animal thing. If lust was a plain sheet of paper, then her feelings around Choony were more like origami, she thought, trying to make sense of her feelings. They were complicated, with many folds and turns, but in the end that plain sheet of paper had become something much greater.

"You're a good man," she blurted. "You see something in me I don't. I want it to be there, this girl you see, but I don't see it. I just try to live up to it. I don't even know why I care, but I do."

There was a long pause, and Jaz was content to merely lay in bed feeling his closeness, his warmth. It would be so easy to just give in, too. She was almost naked. He was almost naked. Why couldn't she just... Do something? Jump on him. Anything. Usually, sex was easy. It was just a thing people did, nothing more. But with Choony, she just couldn't treat it that way. And, she realized, she didn't want to. Not because she wasn't attracted to him—the warmth she felt at the moment was proof of that—but because it wouldn't be the right way. It would be like stepping on that origami swan, destroying the beautiful and leaving only a mangled sheet of paper. She let out a long breath, feeling frustrated, happy, confused, content. She was a jumble of all those things. Thankfully, Choony never pressured her.

Choony finally responded, thankfully taking her mind off those alien thoughts. "Often, when we look at ourselves, we see only the reflection we believe will be there. The one people have told us is there. We don't see that which is truly there under the disguises, the scars, the masks we wear. Like when you read something with a typo but don't notice it, because you know the word that is supposedly there."

Dude, that was deep. She found herself nodding, though. He made sense. She did see the broken street kid even now, not whatever she really was. The things she had done in the past were things she had been forced to do for survival, not who she truly was. Her reflection in the mirror was really just an adjective, not a noun...

That thought made her laugh. "It's like the masks we wear. What I see in the mirror, it's just a description, right? Like, it's not who I am inside, just what I did. That's what I mean though, you make me feel like I can be more than what I see. I can be the person I want to be, when I'm with you. Not the chick my dad said I was, not the girl his friends saw when they looked at me."

"That person is dead, Jaz. You are blessed to have been reincarnated while you still live, transformed into this girl, beautiful inside and out. I am pretty sure I'd choose to follow you to the ends of the Earth, just to be with you."

Jaz smiled to herself. "The fact is, I'm just not willing to be a victim anymore, or to see myself that way. I'm stronger, or I took some inner strength I already had and decided, screw all this. I was tired of being *weak*. How many battles have I been in?"

"You spend your days being hard outside, because the world is hard. It's always been hard, but in this new version of the world, you get to be who you are truly meant to be. You're the Warrior. But when we're alone like this, with the world out there and us in here, you can let your walls down even if just for a little while."

Jaz felt her flesh goosebump. Despite the chaos around them, she fell asleep draped across his chest, and for the first time in a long time, she had happy, pleasant dreams instead of nightmares.

* * *

1400 HOURS - ZERO DAY +382

Ethan logged on again and allowed his many slave computers to upload to his computer the data his worms had diligently acquired. From there, he compiled it with his existing data, then transferred the new, larger file to a USB drive. That was the only way to get the file out of his virtual machine safely, since he wasn't willing to connect the VM to the real system.

He was about to terminate his connection when his "DRyder" email dinged. He saw from the popup alert that it was from Watcher One. He also noticed that it was an hour old, but had only just finished downloading... The internet wasn't what it used to be. It was a bit odd, though, because Watcher usually used the chat box to talk to Ethan, using email only for delivering files. That could only mean it was important enough that he didn't want to wait until they were both online at the same time. The beauty of email was that it would be received whenever the other party logged on, even if it had been sent in the middle of the night.

Ethan clicked the email icon to open the message, and read it aloud.

From: WatcherOne
To: DRyder
Subject: Retirement Notice

Hello "Dark Ryder",

I spoke with HR about the early retirement option you suggested. I am both pleased and sad to inform you that HR has approved your early retirement, effective only within 72 hours of receipt of this email. You will need to get your affairs in order and depart the office premises within that time. Should you decide not to vacate said premises by then, your employment will be terminated immediately after the 72-hour window. Assuming you choose the retirement option, please remember that your non-compete and nondisclosure agreements remain binding.

On a personal note, I will miss our sparring at the office. Being your supervisor has been both a challenge and a pleasant diversion from my other responsibilities in these turbulent times. I hope you understand that anything that happened between us at the office was purely business, and not personal. I for one wish you well. Perhaps I'll see you online sometime and say hello. I'd like that.

From all of us, and especially from me personally, we wish you success in your future endeavors.

Sincerely,

Watcher One

Ethan was stunned. He actually hadn't expected to get permission to walk away from all this. Granted, they might just Predator his ass on the way out of town, but regardless, their agreement would spare the Clan from getting bombed by planes or drones, right? His mind raced, trying to look several steps ahead. How would this play out, his leaving?

First and foremost, he'd have to leave Amber, and his farewell could only be via a note. If he told her in person, she'd either beg him to stay or she'd insist on coming with him. Neither option was workable. He couldn't take her away from the Clan, because she had a daughter and life on the road would probably be both brutal and short. He wouldn't subject a child to that. And he couldn't stay, or it invited retaliation on the Clan itself.

But... would Houle really leave the Clan alone if he left? The Mountain had intervened in the Empire's secessionist troubles, but then again, the Empire was their client state. But the Mountain had also conquered the Gap and was busy building a fort there. That was a direct act of war against the Confederation, and by extension, against Taggart's New America. Would that aggression stop when Ethan "retired"?

He was doubtful. Houle wouldn't just walk away from that fort. He was too invested, had spent too many resources on the conquest and the construction. Ethan's discussions with the 20s couldn't be the reason for Houle's invasion at the Gap. The more he thought about it, the more he decided that Houle wasn't going to let up on the Confederation if he left. Had the Mountain not occupied the Gap, Ethan's course would have been clear, but with that new development, the lie was even more clear.

And that must be the reason they finally replied to his retirement offer... It would remove Dark Ryder from the situation with no expenditure of resources or effort on their part, yet it would change nothing in the long run.

Goddamn it all, he was being played. The Gap was proof. Ethan shouted obscenities and threw his coffee mug, the sharp *clang* hurting his ears as the metallic cup bounced away, splashing hot liquid all over the floor. He clenched his jaw and his fists, took a deep breath, and then went to pick up his cup. Throwing it had been way less satisfying than he thought it would be. Metal cups didn't shatter.

He settled his thoughts and went back to considering his next move. He had three days to come up with something, and if he failed at that, he would have to leave anyway on the off-chance it would actually help the Clan. They were his family. Even if he died out there in the wilderness, the Clan would go on, right? That was the point of leaving. If it wouldn't accomplish that, then he needed to figure something else out.

Alright, he decided, it was time to go talk to the Clan leader directly and work this out with another sharp mind to offer input. It was time to find Frank.

* * *

For evening chow, Carl went to his favorite food truck. Ever since Sunshine had more or less completely retreated from him, the place reminded him of her, which only added to the joint's charm. He wasn't yet done beating himself up over how badly he had handled what could have been an awesome relationship.

Beef cost more than he cared to spend on a meal. He ordered a simple meal that was made with perfectly seasoned rat meat. The food truck people raised their own rats in a warehouse, and added rats the neighborhood kids caught after quarantining them. The owners guaranteed the rats' health, making it one of the safest places to eat besides his own kitchen—and he was a terrible cook.

He polished off half of his meal when a shadow fell over his shoulder. He turned his head, hand sliding toward his pistol by reflex, but then saw that it was two Sewer Rats who approached him. "Good to see you."

"You too, Alpha. Do you have a minute?" asked the taller of the two.

"Sure. What's up? Take a seat."

"Thanks," the tall one said, and they both sat opposite Carl. "There's a problem, and we figured you'd want to know about it. Our Alpha has disappeared."

Carl was stunned. Sunshine... He felt a moment of near-panic, but squashed that quickly. "When was she last seen, where was she going, and what happened?"

"We don't know. She went to lunch and never came back. We went to her quarters at Rat headquarters and found her room all busted up. There was a little blood, but we think she was alive when she left. Or when she was taken. It looked like a hell of a fight happened there."

"What of her guards? I know your HQ has guards." Carl frowned. This was bad, even if the Sewer Rats Band would go on without her. He didn't want them to have to.

"They don't go into her quarters, you see, so they were posted at the front and rear exits. They say they saw and heard nothing, and didn't see anyone enter or leave the building or her quarters. The whole Band is scouring our territory for her, but nothing so far."

Carl's lips pursed and his jaw clenched. "Thank you for telling me. I promise you, the Timber Wolves will do everything we can to help look for her. Do you have any idea where she might have been taken?"

The question was met with silence. So, that would be a no... "I didn't think so, or you'd have gone and got her. Alright. Thanks for telling me. I swear to you that if she's alive, we'll find her one way or another. You have my word that I won't rest until then."

The two Rats nodded. "I expected as much. The Sewer Rats are grateful, Alpha."

They left hastily and Carl stared after them, food forgotten. Sunshine was gone and definitely in danger, if she still lived. She was his friend, one of the few true ones, and she was more than just a friend to him. Also, she was an Alpha and for her to get seized right now, while war loomed all around, couldn't be just a coincidence.

Well, someone had just kicked over a damned hornet's nest, he fumed. Whoever had taken her, they were about to learn what it meant to be hunted by the Wolf pack... He'd lean on every one of the Timber Wolf contacts in other Bands and among the refugees, and he'd turn over Heaven and Earth to find Sunshine.

# - **16** -

0330 HOURS - ZERO DAY +383

CHOONY AWOKE SUDDENLY, and a sense of dread flooded through him, his heart hammering in his ears. He opened his eyes wide, like saucers, but it was pitch black inside and he could see nothing. Jaz was still curled up next to him, but he felt her stiffen and her breathing change. She was waking up, too, he realized. Neither said anything, frozen in place until he heard the faint *skrit* sound of Jaz's hand sliding under her pillow. She always slept with a pistol there.

Abruptly, there was an explosion of noise and activity, and Choony was so startled that his chest hurt. Immediately, rough hands grabbed him by both arms and wrenched him to his feet. He heard Jaz try to shout, but her voice was muffled mid-shout, as though someone had clamped their hand over her mouth.

Choony saw two faint, green lights from tiny LEDs bobbing around near Jaz at about the height of a person's head. He felt something move around his wrists and there was a zipping noise as they zip-tied him. No doubt they had secured Jaz, as well.

The green lights vanished, and Choony was shoved face first onto the bed. He felt Jaz beside him. There was a flood of light that half-blinded him, and he squinted against it. He could see four men in the room, all wearing tight-fitting black clothing. They had NVGs pushed up onto their heads— he had been right about that. Their faces were painted in dark green and black camouflage paint. They appeared to be unarmed, but he assumed they had pistols or knives on them.

The shortest of the four men wasn't the smallest. He was muscular, and moved like a bodybuilder, not gracefully. He said, "Would you look at that. The clanmark, just like they said. The rumors are true." He grabbed Choony's chin and pulled his face toward him, painfully, and said, "What is the Clan doing in Johnstown?"

Choony felt a moment of irritation that they automatically addressed him, not Jaz, but sexism from his captors was the least of his problems. "Running home," he said, not bothering to deny his Clan origins, which were inked onto his arm for anyone to see. "We came out to make trade deals, but then you attacked this Free Republic."

The man laughed. "We're not invaders. This is our home. We had it good under the Midwest Republic, and you damn Confederation people fucked it all up. You gave the traitors guns and food, then set them loose on us. You should see what they did to my neighbors."

Jaz, lying on the bed, looked at the man with eyes wide in fear. Voice pleading, she said, "Not us. We didn't supply anyone. We're just travelers."

"Well, I feel bad for you two. We're going to kill you traitors and then impale you at the east gate, a warning for the rest of you Confederation fuckers."

Choony nodded. Tied up, there was little he could do. He felt his heart beating faster, but he was more calm now than when he had been awoken so abruptly. "I face my fate, then. May the Buddha, the Dharma, and the Sangwa protect us, and may you find forgiveness in your soul for the Karma you bring on yourself."

"Shut the fuck up, zipperhead," the man said. "I'm fine with this. We do what we gotta do, that's all." He turned to face another man, who stood beside the bed and Choony. "Blue, take Red and get these traitors to their feet. We got about a two-minute window to get the hell out of here."

Choony was yanked to his feet, as was Jaz. The burly leader and the man beside him went to the bedroom door, then the leader poked his head into the hallway. He looked both ways and said, "Clear. Move out."

He and the fourth man left the room. Choony saw they both moved like oxen, not smoothly at all. These weren't soldiers, he realized—soldiers would have cut their throats while they slept. Even so, if he and Jaz were taken from the room, they'd be killed in minutes. He felt calm at the thought of dying, but Jaz's eyes were wide with fear and rage. She was most definitely *not* okay with the situation.

Fine—he would try to save them, though he knew they'd most likely die in the attempt anyway. "Now!" Choony cried as he thrust his right foot back and upwards. It landed hard in his captor's gut, and he heard the satisfying *oomf* of the wind being knocked out of the man.

Jaz's captor was close behind her, left hand on her left elbow, right hand on her other hip, one finger under the hem of her panties. She threw her head back hard, connecting with the lecher's nose. It shattered, and blood sprayed over his face.

Choony turned around and put his bound hands on the back of his doubled-over captor's head, then raised his knee as hard as he could into the man's face. He felt a crunch, and the man cried out in pain.

From the corner of his eye, he saw Jaz raise her bound hands over her head, then she brought them down hard into her stomach, elbows slightly spread like chicken wings. Her ziptie broke with an audible snap from the force and flew off as though it was a mere toy. She spun and planted her knee in her bleeding captor's crotch, then slammed her clasped hands over the back of his head, and he fell to the floor face down.

Choony swung his elbow, smashing it into the side of his now-bloody captor's head. The man collapsed to the floor with a cry of pain.

Jaz dove onto the bed and pulled her pistol from under the pillow. She rolled over and sat up, holding her gun before her, pointed toward the door. Their leader and the fourth man tried to come back in through the doorway at a run, but they were big men and crunched together in the doorway. Jaz fired four rapid shots in just over a second, and both men fell in the doorway.

Choony's man scrambled into a crouching position and launched forward, colliding hard with Choony's midsection. It knocked the wind out of him, and the two flew backward across the small room until Choony struck the wall behind him.

Jaz turned her pistol on her own former captor, and while he struggled up to his hands and knees, she fired two rounds into his back. He collapsed to the floor again. She swung her pistol toward Choony's attacker.

It was too late, though. With the wind knocked out of him, Choony's captor had easily gotten him into an arm-lock, then pulled him hard to get him between himself and Jaz. He deftly slid a small Mora knife from its sheath on a lanyard around his neck and held the blade to Choony's throat.

Choony felt his left arm burn like fire, like a red-hot poker had been jammed into his shoulder, and the arm lock kept a tortuous pressure on the joint. He wondered if it was dislocated, but otherwise his mind was blank. Events were happening, and he registered them, but his mind just spun uselessly. Everything he thought of wouldn't work. So this was it...

Things were what they were, he reminded himself, and prepared to leave this lifetime. He'd miss Jaz, though.

"Put the gun down, woman, or I'll slit your boyfriend's throat." Choony felt the man's breath on the back of his neck, hot and humid.

Jaz's face was expressionless, and her pistol didn't waver. "You were going to kill him anyway. There's no way you leave this room alive." She sidestepped to place herself more fully between him and the door.

"Don't fuck with me," he snapped, and Choony heard panic rising in his voice. "I'll cut him, bitch. Believe it."

There was a groan from the bulky man who had been their leader, lying in the doorway. Jaz kept her eyes locked on Choony's captor while her barrel glided toward their leader. Two shots, bang bang. Jaz didn't even blink at the pistol's deafening roar inside room's enclosed space. She swung the barrel back toward Choony's man, and her expression never changed.

Jaz said, "I'm giving you one chance to live through this, then. Let that man go and walk out of here, or—"

"Or what?" he shouted. "I'm going to kill him!"

"Mister, you only leave here feet first unless you let him go. Your choice."

Choony saw an opportunity. "You're companions are gone. There is no one who can say what happened here—no one but you. You get to live. You can leave with your Karma increased."

"Fuck Karma, dude. Fine, lady, but we do this my way. Step aside, and when I'm at the doorway, I'll release him."

"Nope. I told you. Unless you release him, you leave here feet first. That's it. That's the offer."

There was silence for two seconds, three heartbeats, and an infinity of moments. Choony made his peace with dying, mentally thanking Buddha for a fine life. Jaz would live, even if he died, and he accepted that trade-off.

Surprisingly, his captor said, "Fine. I walk, you both live. I don't know who you are, but I'm only in this so my family can eat. We had to run to live, when the traitors took over. It ain't personal."

Jaz locked eyes with Choony, and he nodded at her. He saw that she kept her finger tight on the trigger, and the barrel didn't shake or waver. She was now calm and cool, in battle mode, which might just keep him alive. Part of him rejoiced, and part of him decided he had a lot of meditating to do if he survived this encounter.

The man gave Choony a rough shove toward the bed. Choony tried to use his arms to break his fall, but his left arm refused to hold his weight and he collapsed onto the mattress, groaning and gripping his useless shoulder.

The lone surviving attacker's voice trembled as he said, "I'm leaving now."

As Choony rolled over, he was startled by two deafening reports—Jaz fired twice into the man's chest. He collapsed to his knees with a look of surprise on his face, then toppled forward to the floor and moved no more.

"You said he could live," Choony said, keeping his tone even. He concentrated on bringing his heartbeat down.

"Sorry, Choony. I can't have him running off and getting reinforcements for payback. We gotta leave, like right now, before someone else makes a try for us. Pack up."

Choony grabbed his backpack and began stuffing his things into it, while Jaz slid into her day clothes. He felt a bit dizzy.

"Let's go." Choony forced himself to smile. As he stepped over the doorway corpses, he said a prayer for the dead, but chose not to burden Jaz with that knowledge by praying aloud.

In minutes, they were on the road, fleeing again. It was good to feel the comfortable, well-worn wagon's seat cushions under him.

Jaz said, "This whole place feels like death. Like, they know death is coming for them, but instead of facing it, they're falling apart and turning on each other."

Choony nodded and guided their wagon onto the road heading northeast out of Johnstown. Jaz was right—the rebel army was indeed falling apart as it fled, surrendering to fear and hopelessness, as though such emotions changed their fate. It was chaos, and he was glad to leave the town behind.

\* \* \*

Ethan looked around Cassy's living room as he ate standing at the kitchen island. Her house was pretty shabby now, more than a year after the end of the world. It was packed with people daily, and the wear and tear showed. Plus, all the decorations were long gone, replaced by useful stuff and more stuff, and maps, and shelves with stuff. Ethan remembered an old TV commercial—too much good stuff—then couldn't get that damn word out of his head. Stuff... Blah.

Cassy mercifully interrupted his little OCD cycle by coming downstairs again, this time more fully dressed. "Well, good morning *again*. Sorry, I didn't mean to freak you out. I wasn't awake enough."

"I have something pretty significant to talk to you about. I already hit Frank up with this, and he said to talk to you, too. He'd support whatever I decide, but only after I talk to you."

Cassy's eyes narrowed a bit and she said cautiously, "Me? He's the Clan leader."

"It affects more than just the Clan."

Cassy handed Ethan a cup of coffee, with fresh cream and crystallized tree sap for sugar.

Ethan said, "You know that I talk to the 20s, and you know they turned out to be Houle's personal, off-the-books intel people."

Cassy nodded. "I guess I better sit down," she said with a sigh, and hopped onto one of the two stools on the island's living room side, facing him. "So what's going on now?"

Ethan frowned, and slid his coffee cup around on the counter, eyes locked on the cup. He was having a hard time looking at her. After a long pause, he steeled himself and decided it was best to just rip off the bandage. "So, the 20s want me to leave Clanholme, never to return. I haven't been as dedicated and loyal to them as they would like, so they want me out. But instead of just killing me, and probably anyone near me at the time, they will *allow* me to go into exile."

Cassy stared at Ethan intently for a long moment. It made him uncomfortable, and he redoubled his attentions to his coffee cup, unable to meet her gaze.

Finally, she said, "So what you want to know is whether the Clan and the Confederation are willing to fight over you, knowing it'll lead to conflict with Houle and the Mountain?"

Ethan nodded. "More or less. Things can get a lot worse than they are now, you know. They have Predator drones. They have some fighters out of Camp Pendleton. They aren't sending their full strength against the Free Republic right now, and look at how effective their support to the Empire has been... The Republic is falling, and we all know it."

"True, but they aren't the Confederation. We aren't putting our weight behind them the way Houle is with the

Empire. We're only arming the FreeRep people who still have any fight left in 'em, then sending them back into the lion's den to get slaughtered. Every Mountain soldier they take out is one less for us to eventually deal with."

Ethan looked up at her, nodding. So far, she was right. "But the Mountain will get real serious about us, real fast, if I don't leave. Hell, they have the ability to simply bomb Clanholme itself. And who knows if they still have Tomahawk missiles, or how many jet fighters they really have. We've only had to deal with light armored vehicles, so far. I don't know how we'd take out an Abrams tank."

"With C-4, of which we have a lot. And with pit traps. I'm not supposed to tell anyone this, but we looted a less well-known military armory. The Clan has cached a stockpile of mines, both claymore and anti-tank. We scrounged cases of those shoulder-fired, single-use bazooka things. We're good."

"They aren't bazookas."

"Seriously, look at me." She waited until he looked up at her again, then said, "We're already at war with the Mountain. They took the Gap. You think if we appease them, they'll go away? When has appeasement ever worked? Soon they'll have a shiny new base that can strike anywhere in the Confederation quickly, and the military folks do always seem to want a chance to use their shiny toys. You staying or going isn't going to change a damn thing in the long run."

Ethan nodded slowly. He had often had similar thoughts. "So, we have two options as I see it. First, we can flip them the bird. Or B, we can give them the illusion that I left, and I never leave the bunker again until this is all over."

Cassy shrugged. "Eh. Not really. You couldn't go online or they'd know you were here, and if you aren't doing your Dark Ryder thing, I know you'd be bored to tears down there. That only leaves us with giving them the bird. Got something in mind?"

"Sort of. It would definitely turn this thing into climax-mode and get it over with one way or the other."

Cassy wrinkled her eyebrows. "If we can stretch the conflict out, though, that works in our favor. Fighting their whole, fresh strength all at once doesn't sound like the best strategy."

"Actually, it might be just what we need. What they don't know is that I've already hacked NORAD, before the exile thing came down. I put in a backdoor so I can get back in easily, but I'll only get one shot to do anything inside their systems. Once they realize there's been a breach, they'll find my backdoor and close it."

"So, you figure you can do something useful, but only once, and if they're all coming at us at once, hacking NORAD will help us on the ground here? Do I have that right?"

"Yeah... more or less. I'm not sure what I'll do once I'm in, but I'm still studying the huge mounds of system and configuration data I liberated from their network. All of this assumes you want me to stay, though. If you want me to leave, hoping it'll keep the conflict at a low intensity as long as possible, I understand. I might even agree with you. Either way, I'd do as you say."

"Of course you would, Ethan. Otherwise why would you have even told anyone about this? You could have just stayed, and we'd have been none the wiser. But you didn't."

Ethan felt his heartbeat spike a little with anxiety. Staying would bring risk into the Clan, but it was possible that leaving would expose the Clan to even more risk. "I'll have to hold off on using that backdoor until the last possible moment. We may face increased pressure before that climactic, critical moment."

Cassy gave him a faint smile and said, "So finish your coffee with me, then get back into your cave and do your thing. Just a day like any other."

Ethan nodded. "Alright."

"And, Ethan...we never had this conversation."

* * *

General Ree stood in the newly constructed tower and stared out to the west. A stream of troops and officers trudged toward his fortified gate. An hour ago, he had received first word of his colonels' defeats at the hands of the American peasants. He was angry enough to spit, but to his troops he showed only steel, hard and cold. A good officer never showed emotion accidentally.

To Major Kim, he said, "It is a pity I must execute the officers—they may still be of use."

"Of course, sir. But failure of this magnitude cannot be left unaddressed."

Ree nodded. "Some might also say the failure was mine, for making them vassals. For giving them responsibility beyond their capabilities."

"Yes, sir. Some might. But not in public, not if they know what is best for them. The fault is theirs, not yours, unless they wish to admit they presented to you a false confidence— at which point the fault is again theirs for the deceit. If they weren't certain of their ability, they could have turned down the assignment as I did."

Ree nodded at him. He had made a good point. "Very well. How many can we admit? I know we cannot feed them all without their civilians and their lands, two things they lost. They left with only their guns."

"And their lives, sir."

"Which is something they will lose soon, too." Ree struggled to keep his anger contained.

Kim had the good sense to pretend not to notice. "We can support them all only if we can hold Central Park, my leader. If we lose that, then we can support very few extra mouths."

"We should plan on losing Central Park. It's exposed on every side, vulnerable to a riotous population. My vassal who holds this side of the New Jersey route has reported that he too is under siege. He is holding it, but suspects he can keep it only long enough to allow the others to cross from New Jersey into the City on their way to safety here. He will follow them shortly thereafter."

"A calamity, my leader. I imagine that your plan is to admit them all, and then use them recklessly. Those who survive your missions will have earned their food and their place."

"And if I were to issue such orders, what does my little brother think are the risks, and possible ways to control those risks?" Ree looked at Kim calmly. On these matters, he gave great weight to Kim's advice, though the final decision would be his own.

"Sir, the core of any resistance will come from your vassals' popular senior enlisted and experienced lower-ranking officers. It will come from those who had experience before this war, and who have done well for their own small units in these hard times. Only they have the personal relationship with their soldiers to command loyalty enough for treason."

"I see. And how would you resolve this issue?"

Major Kim was stone faced, and Ree appreciated his discipline. Kim said, "We have such ranking soldiers in your personal forces who are not so effective. Some have created questions about their loyalty to you, their Great Leader, because they have not aligned their will to yours. Send those men out on a mission and bring your vassals' possibly troublesome men in. Also allow them to bring in the troops and underlings for whom they wish to take responsibility."

Ree nodded. Such a decision would have many implications, some far-reaching. But making them responsible for the acts of those they bring would ensure they chose only those soldiers they trusted completely. "Very well. If we are to lose New Jersey and the western City, we should not resist that, but embrace it and turn it to my own advantage, so that it makes us stronger rather than bleeding us to death."

Kim placed a deliberate smile on his face, and Ree nodded in approval. Kim said, "I will make the necessary arrangements, and create a list of missions on which to spend your men's lives."

Ree said, "Yes. Focus on securing Central Park. If we can hold it until harvests, we will be fine for winter. Redouble the fishing fleets in spring."

"I will make it so. Your wisdom will carry us through, sir."

Ree dismissed Kim and focused on properly experiencing his tea, noting in his journal the flavor characteristics, the aroma, the aftertaste. He had analyzed dozens of teas, and had many more left to go, but it was important for that knowledge not to be lost when the tea was gone. His notes would be his legacy to culture and civilization. Compared to that knowledge, the lives of a few soldiers and even the loss of half his territory meant little to Ree.

* * *

Nestor moved freely among the horde of refugees heading west. His had been a suicide mission, playing rear guard to the Free Republic people fleeing east, but he had succeeded in buying them the time they needed to get to Johnstown. When the enemy threw troop battalions at Johnstown from the south—fresh Mountain troops, tired from marching but unbloodied—he and his newly reinforced Night Ghosts had been cut off, but as a result most of the Free Republic troops escaped and continued to flee eastward, toward the Confederation.

The Night Ghosts, however, had only one direction in which to flee. They had moved at double-time to the north. But then, they had been hit from the north, first by more refugees on bikes and then by the bike and cavalry troops who chased them. Together, the refugees and Night Ghosts had broken their attackers, but more were coming. Nestor had been forced to turn west.

He had spent the day riding as fast as he could in the Night Ghost vanguard of four hundred people on bikes. Only those with bikes had escaped... Now, he was exhausted and his legs burned like they were on fire as he made his way up yet another hill. Once past the summit, the whole pack rested their legs as gravity took over. Nestor drew deep, grateful breaths.

Two riders rode toward the pack on the road, some of his outriding scouts. He made no effort to go meet them, and just kept enjoying his ride downhill until they reached him. One pulled up beside him, keeping pace, sweating profusely. The man panted as he reported, "Nestor, we got news. An enemy train is coming, but it's moving slow. Four rail cars, being pulled by like twenty damn horses. There is a U.S. flag on the lead car."

"General Houle's. Where?"

"A mile south of us, and the train is coming from the west. If we hurry, you can intercept it."

Nestor nodded. It would be worth the effort. Four rail cars potentially held a crap-ton of supplies, all probably heading toward the quickly shifting front line. It moved inexorably toward the Confederation. "Lead the way."

"Yes, sir," the man said. The poor guy was exhausted, but he obeyed and swerved off the road, heading south.

They rode for fifteen minutes across the rough terrain before Nestor saw the train in the distance, with the tracks downhill below. He called his unit and the refugees to a halt. Of the four hundred people with him, only a hundred were even armed, his Night Ghosts survivors. The refugees may have been Free Republic fighters, but they had mostly ditched their empty rifles to lighten their load when they had routed.

He called out, "Ratbone, take twenty rifles half a mile east, in case the train gets past us. Have the rest of our armed fighters lined up along the crest of this hill. When the train approaches, we'll ride down and board it. Make sure no one shoots those damn horses, either."

Minutes later, as the train pulled even with them, eighty or so armed men and women on bikes swept down from the hill crest, whooping and hollering. Atop the cars were maybe a dozen defenders, along with a man and woman up front to guide the team of horses. Horse-drawn trains moved slower than Nestor had expected.

At the sight of so many attackers, the people on the train's roof dropped their rifles and held up their hands. The train took a quarter mile to slow to a stop, even going so slowly. Nestor hoped to hell that meant it was stuffed to the brim with something heavy and useful. He barked orders to secure the guards, and they were quickly zip-tied on their knees off to one side, along with the teamsters who had driven the team of horses. None had resisted, so they hadn't been roughed up yet, but they looked plenty frightened.

*Let's scalp them. Mount their heads like antenna balls.*

"Shut up, Other," muttered Nestor.

*You put on the most boring shows. Let me out to play.*

"No," Nestor shouted, grabbing his head. The Other

struggled to get free, to take over the meatsuit, but Nestor grit his teeth, tuned everything out, and beat back the chaos, the evil. Eventually, Nestor felt firmly in control again.

When he looked up, his troops were standing around looking anywhere but at him, while the dozen prisoners stared at him with eyes wide in fear. Nestor forced himself to show them a feeble smile while the color returning to his face. "Sorry, folks," he gasped. "Don't mind that guy. He wants me to use your heads as antenna balls for the train, but he's not in charge of us. I am."

They didn't look any less frightened, which made him want to chuckle.

*See, you do enjoy scaring people.*

Nestor ignored the Other's voice in his head. He walked up to the teamsters and eyed the man for a moment. "Where were you going, where did you come from, and what's on board?"

The woman shook her head and looked at the ground. The man glanced at her, then looked up at Nestor. "Mister, we're coming from a depot in Morgantown, West Virginia, which is loyal to the leader of the United States, General Houle. We're going to Johnstown, recently liberated. The cargo is to resupply the troops there, who must have used up most of their supplies by now."

Nestor nodded. "Well, this train isn't getting to its destination."

The woman finally looked up at him, anger in her eyes. "If this train doesn't make it, my family is their hostage. My daughter. My son. And my sister. You understand what you're doing to them, right?"

Nestor nodded, and his brow furrowed as he bit his lip. "That's unfortunate, and I feel for you, but things are what they are. The Mountain King has cost my friends a lot more lives than that, and you support him. I can't help you."

Ratbone turned to some of the Night Ghosts and ordered the cargo containers be opened, and Nestor walked behind them to see their contents for himself. He left the prisoners on their knees, under guard.

When he saw what was inside, however, he shouted out a loud victory whoop. The first car contained crate upon crate labeled as M4s, ammo, boxes of grenades—stacked end to end, floor to ceiling. "Damn," he said with excitement. "Get a count on these."

He went to the next car and was equally impressed. The entire boxcar was filled with MREs and boxes of various canned goods. He couldn't begin to guess how many there were, but easily a week's worth of full rations, for his whole force and the fleeing fighters he had linked up with alike.

He slid the heavy metal door shut and went to the final car. Inside were cardboard boxes with all sorts of labels. First-aid kits. Backpacks with water-container inserts. Those amazing Lifestraw water filters that weighed damn near nothing. Aluminum mess kits. Night-vision goggles. Boots. Myriad supplies of all sorts. He closed that door, too, and turned to Ratbone.

Ratbone stared at him, eyes wide, with a silly grin on his face. "Boss, we got an army's worth of supplies here. And lo and behold, we got an army that needs supplies. You're back in business."

Nestor felt himself smiling back. "Yes indeed. Find out who wants to join the Night Ghosts, and dole out supplies to everyone who joins us. Those who want to leave can go, but they leave their supplies with us."

Ratbone said, "For sure. What do you want to do with the prisoners? We can kill them and leave their bodies in the rail cars, if you want."

Nestor shrugged. "See who wants to join us. The rest, send them off with their own gear, but no weapons. Let's get the cargo unloaded and distributed. I want to be done with all this by dawn. We got a fight to get back into."

As Ratbone strode away to follow the orders, Nestor thought about what this stroke of luck meant for him. For one, their pursuers would be in for a terrible surprise when they caught up to him near dawn, if they were still tracking him. For another, he'd now have a full battalion of armed guerrillas to throw into the war to the east. The enemy didn't know where he was or how many fighters were under his command, now, which made him once again the thing he most loved being—a wildcard.

*About time you got your balls back.*

Nestor grinned. Not even that psycho in his head could bring down his mood that night. "It's time to get wild again," he replied. "So many targets, so little time."

# - **17** -

0400 HOURS - ZERO DAY +385

CARL WOKE UP to the sound of tapping on his door. He rubbed one eye with the heel of his hand. "What is it?"

The door opened a crack, then wider. His assistant for the early morning shift poked his head in. That meant it must be after 2:00 a.m. He said, "Alpha, scouts have returned with a report on Sunshine's location. I thought you'd want to know immediately."

Even before he had finished his sentence, Carl had staggered out of bed, searching for clothes. He got on a pair of sweatpants and a tee shirt, but didn't bother with shoes. "Let's go."

His assistant led him downstairs. Two women stood near the door, talking quietly, but they stopped when Carl came down. Both put their clenched right hands over their hearts for a second. One said, "Alpha, we found her."

"Where is she?"

The two women exchanged a glance. "She was seized by a small force of Mountain troops. SpecOps, we think, but can't be sure. They took her, then holed up just outside of Harrisburg across the river. Now they're just camping, like they're waiting for something. She's bound, but she's alive."

Carl felt his pulse spike, and the room suddenly felt hot. Sunshine was alive, for now. Why the hell would the Mountain kidnap Sunshine, of all the Band leaders they might have targeted? He realized it must have just been because her Band's territory was the one closest to the west wall, least defended area through which to infiltrate. Nothing else made sense.

"How far from here?"

"An hour. Maybe two. There are twelve soldiers, seemingly divided into groups of four."

The assistant returned, and Carl gladly accepted a cup of coffee. "Very well. Gather our fighters and our battlecars. That whole area is a moshpit right now, with Empire, FreeRep, guerrillas, and Mountain all duking it out. We may have to fight our way through. Horses for my Guards Company. Bikes for as many others as possible. Move out in one hour."

His assistant left, and Carl gave cups of coffee to the two scouts while they waited for word the fighters were mobilized. They accepted with wide, amazed eyes—what better way to ensure loyalty than the occasional undeserved gift? Coffee was like gold, now. Then he went upstairs to get dressed and ready for a fight.

While he was upstairs, the scouts left to muster with the other Timber Wolf fighters, and Carl spent the rest of the time going over maps and intel reports. Johnstown had fallen, and the entire area between there and Harrisburg was a mess. The Mountain's well-equipped soldiers were turning the tide against the Free Republic and their Confederation allies.

In fact, there was a report that at one key moment in the battle for Johnstown, two fighter jets had basically incinerated the west edge of town, clearing the way for enemy soldiers to advance into town. That report was unconfirmed, and there hadn't been other such reports, but it was cause for concern. He decided to treat it as truth even without corroboration. That meant that any battle he hoped to win would have to be an all-or-nothing assault en masse to avoid giving jets a good target. Air power now was more of a game-changer than ever before, yet assaults like that meant high casualties on both sides. It sucked.

"It is what it is," he said, and ignored his assistant's curious look.

He grabbed his gear and headed toward the mustering point. When he arrived, he saw not only a battalion of Timber Wolf troops, but about the same number of Sewer Rats—they had mustered en masse in support of their Alpha.

He found that Kodiak Band had assembled a mortar company and a cavalry company, along with their Band's battlecars. No Diamondbacks were there—which he'd deal with later, and not to their liking—but Puma and Wolverine had each sent a company, too.

Carl grinned. That gave him a light regiment to work with, along with a company of armed and armored vehicles and a mortar company. Not bad for short notice. He gathered the officers and spelled out the plan.

"Battlecars will run interference, hitting targets of opportunity and any artillery or mortar squads that decide to join the fight. The rest of our troops will fan out northwest of Harrisburg, keeping a heavy screen ahead of the main body. Engage any enemy that wants a fight. Radios are being issued to each of you, out of Timber Wolf stocks. We've been accumulating them through trade with the Falconry, and I'm glad we did despite the cost. My Guards Company and I will be on a separate mission. If you find guerrillas, whether Night Ghosts or Free Republic units, bring them in or support them if they're engaged. Ideally, we will push the battle momentum away from the Mountain in this region, crippling them and then fading away. Any questions?"

There were a few questions about minor things such as who would provide the battlecar fuel, radio frequencies to use, and so on. Within an hour, though, the commanders had been briefed on their individual goals and operational areas, shown the maps with the known data, and everyone was as ready as they could be. The rescue team-turned-army headed for Harrisburg and the chaos beyond. Carl and his company would be the last to leave, with the other units sweeping aside any obstacles between him and where Sunshine was being held, but they'd avoid that area themselves entirely.

By 8:00 a.m., Carl and his company were within a half mile of Sunshine's reported location, and he called for the unit to dismount. She was held on the reverse slope of a small hill, their rear blocked by a larger, steeper hill. He gathered his three platoon commanders.

"First platoon, sweep west and approach through the glen. Second platoon, to the east, coming up through the copse of trees. Third platoon and I will first engage up the forward slope. We may surprise them, but we'll probably just get pinned down. That's when your two platoons will sweep in on them from either side. Make sure your troops know that if Sunshine is harmed, the one who did it is going to regret it."

Soon after, he and Third platoon moved up until they reached the forward slope, then began the uphill advance as quietly as they could. They were halfway up when shots rang out, and a cry from one of his troops told him the enemy fire was accurate. Carl and his unit dove prone. "Advance by pairs," he shouted. "Fire at will. Keep their heads down."

The next several minutes were harrowing. Fire, duck. Jump up, run, dive into the dirt. Repeat again and again. They weren't too far below the crest, now, and the enemy fire became withering. Dammit, he was pinned tight. If it weren't for the other platoons, he knew, it was very possible he'd lose this battle. Then again, he did have the other platoons, and he grinned savagely. Any minute now, they'd pour into the enemy from either side, and that would be that.

Carl heard a riot of noise as the two flanking units engaged the hapless enemy, and Carl leaped to his feet. "Charge," he cried, and Third platoon followed him up the hill. Scattered fire came at him from the crest, but it was almost random, as the defenders were beset from three sides.

Then he reached the top and hit the dirt. His unit dropped down to either side of him, and from the cover of the hill's crest they fired down the reverse slope into the knot of surviving enemy soldiers below. It was all over in another minute.

When the shooting petered out, Carl rose to his feet and snarled at the corpses below. Those bastards had found out they weren't invincible just because they had better gear.

The search for Sunshine didn't take long. After checking the obvious places, a fighter had stumbled across her in a shallow depression, which the Mountain soldiers had dug. They had gathered wooden poles and bound them together to form a lid, and rocks sat on the lid's four corners.

Carl looked down into the shallow pit and his jaw dropped. Sunshine was pale and covered in a sheen of sweat. She looked half-dead. Then he saw why such a feeble prison had been enough to keep her there. Her right leg had been cut off below her knee, and although the stump was wrapped, the bandage was filthy. Flies buzzed all over it.

"Good Lord, save her," he shouted, shocked. He turned to his fighters. "Get her the hell out of there. Where's the damn medic?"

"Right here, sir," a woman said. She stepped forward and helped the others remove the poles and pull Sunshine out.

They set her down next to the pit, and the medic removed the bandage slowly. Underneath the filthy layer of fabric, the wound was covered in dirt and dried blood. A simple tourniquet above the knee had kept her from bleeding out, but below that point her leg was a grayish-blue, tissue dead from the lack of blood.

"Shit. Okay, get on the radio. Divert one battlecar here to pick her up. She and I will go back to Harrisburg. Notify Kodiak's commander that she has overall command of the battle."

Carl's fighters exchanged glances, but said nothing. It was out of character for Carl to leave in the middle of a battle, but apparently no one felt like it was a good idea to challenge him on it, which was just fine with him.

When the car arrived, his troops carried Sunshine down to it as gently as they could and set her in the back seat. That required the top gunner to step out, but too goddamn bad. Carl hopped in the front passenger seat. "Harrisburg, as fast as you can without bouncing her around. Move out."

The car pulled away. Carl, looking back at Sunshine's unconscious form in the back seat, saw his troops staring after the car, but he didn't care. Let them be confused about his leaving mid-battle. Sunshine was an Alpha, he told himself, and her safety was a Liz Town priority. Plus, he had left the warband in good hands with Kodiak's commanding officer. They'd be fine.

The drive back to Harrisburg, which had better medical care than Liz Town, felt like the longest quarter hour of his life. The gates were open already as the car approached across the bridge, and a small crowd awaited him on the far side. They directed him to a nearby building that had once been a medical clinic, and now would again. When the car pulled up in front of the clinic, another crowd was waiting, this time with a gurney and a bunch of wheeled supply trays.

Carl was gently shoved aside as they got her on the gurney and wheeled her into the clinic.

Carl was ordered to wait in the lobby, and he had wanted to argue but realized every second spent fighting with him was another second they weren't treating Sunshine, so he had reluctantly stayed where he had been told.

He waited, and waited, but no one had come out yet. He was just about to force his way through the double doors that led to the medical rooms when a woman in scrubs came out and motioned to him. He practically jumped to his feet. His pulse pounded as he awaited her news.

"Alpha. Good news and bad. The good news first—she's alive and stable. The bad news is that she has sepsis in her leg above the point of removal. Much of her leg above the amputation point has become necrotic due to lack of blood flow."

"How bad is it?"

The doctor coughed once into her hand, awkwardly. "To put it simply, Carl, it's the poisons from her leg decaying that have made her ill, and the shock had already weakened her. I don't believe there was anesthesia used during the procedure. I should tell you, people often die from the shock of a severed leg."

Carl clenched his fists at his sides. "So what are you doing?"

She nodded and put one hand on his arm, reassuringly, ignoring his evident anger. "We've given her morphine to ease the pain. She's regaining consciousness, but she's in an altered mental state... She's high."

"So she'll be okay?" Carl could hear the desperate hope in his own voice.

The doctor shook her head. "No. To save her life, we must remove the necrotic portion of her leg, about mid-thigh. Otherwise, I guarantee you that she'll die within a few days at most without surgery, due to sepsis and gangrene. In the old days, we could have done more, but those days are gone."

Carl clenched his jaw. "Take the leg off, but make sure she doesn't feel any pain."

"Once we give her the chloroform, she won't. Do you want to talk to her, first?"

"Of course." He pushed past the doctor and through the double doors into the hallway beyond. Sunshine's room was obvious from the noise within, the only activity in the building, and he stormed in without knocking.

Startled, one of the nurses tried to get in his way, but he put his hands on her shoulders and deliberately moved her aside, his eyes boring holes into hers as he did. She didn't make any further effort to stop him.

Carl stepped up to Sunshine's bed and put his hands on the railing. She looked like shit. He forced a smile anyway. "Hey, Sunny. How you doing?"

"Been better," Sunshine said, her voice ragged. "Asked for a larger dose of morphine." She took a shallow breath, and closed her eyes. "I'm sorry I was so angry at you. Can you forgive me?"

Carl took a deep breath, mind racing. This was not the way he had envisioned this going. "Of course I forgive you. You weren't wrong to feel pushed aside. I did put you second. But I'm not going to let them give you that dose you asked for, Sunny."

"Carl, please don't stop me. I can't lead the Rats like this. They won't follow a cripple, and it's not right to ask them to support me when I can't contribute. There's not enough food or supplies to go around."

Carl closed his eyes tightly and thought of the supplies he gave to the Free Republic refugees. That's some shitty irony right there. Opening his eyes, he said, "I swear I'll make sure you're taken care of. You'll be okay."

Sunshine's eyes welled up and a tear streaked down her dirty cheek, carving a path through the grime, and Carl felt his heart break at the sight. She said, "I can't be a burden, Carl. I'm the Rats' responsibility, and you know that. You'll have grief from every other Band if you take care of me when so many others had to be left to die. There isn't enough to go around, and you can't abuse your rank to take care of me. It's either the wildlands or the morphine, for me."

Carl was silent for a long moment, staring at her. She was right, of course, and he hated it. He studied every feature of her face, beautiful despite the dirt and blood and bruises. She was a light in a dark world. He knew what he had to do. It was what he had really wanted to do for a long time now, anyway. "It doesn't have to be the Long Walk or the big sleep. There's another way. So what, you can't be a Sewer Rat anymore... but you can be a Timber Wolf."

Sunshine's eyes widened a little bit and she struggled to lift her head to get a better look at him, but failed. She looked him in the eyes as best she could and said, "You'd do that for me? You know that's forever, right? And I'm not sure I want to be a Timber Wolf who never sees her packmate."

Carl nodded. "Yes, I would do that for you. Forever sounds damn good to me. Sunshine, I love you. I can't lose you again. I always thought we'd have more time to work it out, but I was wrong. We don't. Sunshine, say you'll be a Timber Wolf and when the war against the Mountain is over, I'll step down as SecState."

Sunshine kept her eyes on him, her gaze roving over every feature of his face, and Carl felt like he was being interrogated. Of course, he realized, that was because he was.

After staring at him for ten eternal seconds, she raised one eyebrow—an expression that was comfortingly familiar to him. "You'd stop being the Speaker's right hand?"

Carl nodded, and put his hand on Sunshine's. It was clammy to the touch, but he didn't care. "Absolutely. The war won't last forever, they never do, and I am in love with you, Sunshine. I was a fool before. I didn't know how much of a fool I'd been until you turned your back on me. I thought it would kill me, when you did that."

She smiled at him, took a deep breath, and closed her eyes. "I did it because it would have killed me not to. I had to move on, Carl. But if you'll step down as Mary Ann's right hand... Then yes, I'll be a Timber Wolf."

Carl nodded. As the nurse injected something into her IV bag, he said, "They're going to knock you out, soon. When you wake up, you'll begin a long, hard road to recover. You'll stay at my Harrisburg house while you heal, and I'll make sure you get the best help still available. When you're well enough..."

She smiled and nodded slightly, eyes still closed.

A moment later, her breathing became regular and slow. She had fallen asleep again. Carl turned and saw the doctor standing behind him. "Make sure she lives."

She nodded, then shuffled him out of the medical room out into the lobby.

He watched the doctor go back inside. The helpless feeling that washed over him then was entirely unfamiliar, and he hated every second of it. The next few hours took an eternity.

* * *

1045 HOURS - ZERO DAY +385

Frank stared in awe at the troops arrayed outside of Clanholme. A battalion of Clan fighters from various Clanholds, one from Clanholme itself, and one of Taggart's loaned battalions. The regiment was supported by half the medically trained people in the Clan... and there were two dozen wagons loaded to set up a field hospital. Cassy's call for help from the 'vaders of northern Pennsylvania had borne unexpected fruit, and they had sent twice that number of wagons heavy-laden with jarred and dried foods. A dozen battlecars were lined up in the rear.

But what grabbed Frank's attention the most was four freaking cannons. Artillery looked even more impressive up close, he mused. Each piece needed a team of horses to pull it, and two more wagons for each were loaded with shells. They had all been rummaged from the same depot they had used to resupply their ammo and rifles, but he hadn't actually seen the artillery before. He let out a long, low whistle.

Michael chuckled. "Yes, sir, those are impressive field guns. They're more than adequate for taking out emplaced armor units, unless they have M1s—and maybe even then. Recon says we're going to face only Humvees and Oshkoshes, and a scattering of other LFVs. Light fighting vehicles. Not even a dozen in total, although they're all Strykers and Bradleys, which sucks. Those are emplaced behind barricades facing north."

Frank nodded. "Until those vehicles are taken out, it'll be hard to assault the target. These things," he said, nodding his head at the lethal artillery, "ought to help with that."

Michael said, "We have the GPS data on each emplaced unit, thankfully. We'll demolish those before going in. It'll create a smoke screen, as well."

"What of the civilians?" Frank turned to look Michael directly in his eyes.

Michael shook his head and said nothing. Frank nodded, frowning. Damn—that would be terrible, but it was unavoidable. The Mountain couldn't be allowed to finish fortifying the Gap. It had been the Confederation's southern strong point, before being conquered, and it controlled the best river crossing for miles in either direction.

Frank decided to change the subject. "How are the electronics on these artillery things still operational?"

"Ethan said most of the components are modular, and units for field repairs had been stored in mylar bags. He said the warehouse structures themselves also shielded a lot of the EMP energy, though not enough to prevent the onboard electronics from frying. We've swapped them out for some of the spares."

"Interesting. And very fortunate. Alright then, let's move out. Michael, you have command."

"Aye, aye, sir." Michael turned, then shouted, "Move out!" His voice carried crystal-clear across the field, and the various officers repeated the call. Slowly, the force lumbered forward.

It took half an hour for Frank and the other rumbling battlecars, last in the huge line, to finally move out. The troop column stretched out in front of him as far as he could see. It was kind of strange how long it took a unit to assemble, or to move out, or to get ready for a battle. Yet the battle itself always seemed to blur by at the speed of light.

"Nine parts boredom, one part terror," he muttered. He couldn't remember the actual quote, but that covered it just fine.

He had spent that time reviewing the strategy for the upcoming battle. Frank and the other drivers were more or less on standby, since a town was a deadly place for vehicles, if the buildings were infested with well-equipped infantry, and the area outside of town was threatened by the few light armored vehicles the enemy had brought with them. A battlecar made a nice, juicy target to both those forces, Michael had said.

Instead, Frank's main role would be to contain any breakthroughs the enemy made, protecting the artillery and field hospital from such thrusts.

At Intercourse—now mere wreckage after the Clan destroyed the Empire garrison there long ago—Michael ordered the artillery to stop and set up. The M777 had a range of fourteen miles, Michael had told him, so leaving them so far behind was safe enough that only a small force of guards would be left with them. The rest of the regiment moved on.

The river came into view and, as expected, it was defended. Two light tanks—Strykers, Michael had called them—were barricaded on the far side of the river. The Stryker had probably already seen them with its advanced day-night thermal vision, which Michael had said was effective for over a mile. He had also said some Strykers had deadly 30mm cannons, but these were probably the standard .50-caliber or Mk-19 grenade launcher models, as though that was any better. Worst of all, however, was that the Stryker had advanced command, control, and communications abilities. C3, Michael called it. Compared to anything the Clan could field, it was practically on the level of magic.

The radio squawked and Frank heard Michael order two rounds fired, along with coordinates. The way Michael had explained it, the artillery pieces had automatic fire systems. They figured out where the titanium guns themselves were, via GPS, and the target coordinates were just typed in or transmitted to the gun. It would then adjusted itself to fire with accuracy.

After the order went out, Frank counted seconds, just out of curiosity. Eleven seconds later, two gigantic fireballs erupted where the Strykers had been, raising small mushroom clouds of dirt, smoke, and flame. Frank was stunned. *That* was what artillery did? He felt a chill of raw fear, and his scrotum tightened in primate reflex. Did the enemy have these damn things? He prayed they didn't. Whatever the case, he was *not going to stop moving* once the battle began. Clearly, a stationary target was a freaking *dead* target. And he decided he hated artillery, even if it was on his side. Those things freaked out the primordial lizard-part of his brain...

Michael came through the radio once again, bringing Frank back to reality. "Second battalion, secure the bridge. India company will provide vehicle support."

Frank was grateful that Michael wasn't talking like a Marine. Although most of the units present were Taggart's loaned Army battalions, not everyone understood the lingo even among them. Most weren't regular army, having been discharged, and Frank and his people had no military experience. He keyed his radio. "India One Actual, roger that," he replied, and gunned his engine.

Second battalion, composed of fighters from other Clanholds, advanced.

Frank led the dozen battlecars in a broad sweep to the southwest, to the right of the bridge. He hoped to sweep back toward it and arrive just as the infantry did. He was damn eager to see what his car's newly mounted Mk-19 grenade launcher could do. When he finally got close to the river, he turned left to drive back north toward the bridge. He arrived about thirty seconds before his infantry did, so he pulled to a halt before he got in their way. A peppering of enemy small arms rounds hit his unit, but nothing intense, and it was pretty far away. Nothing the battlecar armor couldn't handle, at least, not yet.

Frank shouted up to his gunner, "Hey, what's the range on that?"

"Michael said to try to hold fire until they were at least

within a mile."

"A mile? Well, damn, I think this qualifies," Frank replied. "Let's have some fun before the real battle starts."

"I hear and I obey, oh master," the gunner said, laughing. A moment later, there was a loud *thud-thud-thud* from the Mk-19, each about a second apart. Not much of a "grenade machinegun," he thought to himself. That was what Michael had called it.

Frank could see the rounds arc high through the air; the big grenades struck a couple seconds later. *Boom-boom-boom*, came a string of explosions, and he could feel the concussion thumping in his chest even at this range. Where they had struck, at least a dozen of Houle's soldiers had simply disappeared from view in clouds of smoke, dirt, and fire. As that cleared, blowing away, Frank could see nothing moving within a dozen yards of the impact points.

"That's... also frightening," he said, stunned. "*This* is what soldiers train to face off against? Holy shit, man."

Above, the gunner grunted in agreement. Frank glanced at him and saw the man stood staring at the carnage, mouth wide open in shock.

The Clanhold fighters then streamed across the bridge, pouring heavy fire at anything that moved. In a minute, the shooting petered out and silence swept the field.

On the radio, Michael said, "India company, cross the objective and secure the AOI. Second battalion, provide defensive cover for the cars. Stay spread out! All other units, advance in order."

Frank acknowledged and then drove to the bridge. As he crossed over it, he saw the mangled, shredded meatbags that had once been human beings. The "mark nineteen" scared him almost as much as the artillery—at least until he drew close to where the emplaced enemy Strykers had been. Now there were only two shallow, broad craters, inside of which stood twisted metal that looked a lot like abstract sculptures, burning. Thick plumes of black smoke rose from the unrecognizable wreckage. Frank changed his mind about how scary the Mk-19 was compared to those M777 artillery pieces.

Twenty minutes later, the entire unit was across the bridge and marching onward toward the Gap.

\* \* \*

Jaz grinned and wrapped Nestor in a hug. "I can't believe you made it out," she said. The last time she had seen him, he was pedaling his way toward the enemy, buying her, Choony, and the refugees time to escape Johnstown. Once she and Choony had rejoined the refugee group after fleeing the Mountain troops, their journey had been slow-going. Apparently, Nestor's guerrilla force, after untangling from the rear guard action, had headed east to catch up with them. "And you survived with so many people? That's amazing."

Nestor grinned back and released her from the embrace. "We lost a lot of people, but we took a bunch of fleeing Free Republic fighters under our wing. They had ditched their gear to get away alive, earlier, but then we intercepted a train that was loaded like Santa's sled with goodies. Enough to rearm almost the whole group, and resupply quite nicely."

Choony stepped up to shake Nestor's hand. Jaz noted that he showed none of the jealousy signs she would have seen from damn near any other man if "his woman" had hugged some other dude. Choony said, "Fantastic news. That means the Mountain's soldiers must be running low on ammo and supplies? I would imagine."

Nestor nodded. "Every small Mountain group we've attacked since then was almost out of ammo. Good for fighting against, not so good for looting afterward. They gave us little in the way of salvage."

Jaz ran her hands through her hair—which, she assumed, must look like a rat's nest by now—and thought about the implications of that. "Nestor, we might have a window of opportunity to drive the Mountain out of this region. Free the Free Republic... again."

Nestor shrugged. "That's the plan. Almost their whole force has been hedged up between us and Harrisburg. Can't go north due to the 'vader cantonment, can't go south because my Night Ghosts are stomping around out there, and can't go west because FreeRep is rising up against them. Johnstown might have been decimated, but they caused heavy casualties to the Mountain's regiment rallying there. I hear it was total chaos, the worst kind of fighting you can imagine, but that when the smoke cleared, the Mountain wasn't the one left standing. Johnstown might be punch-drunk from that fight, but they're gathering up survivors and arming them with salvaged U.S. Army gear and weapons."

Choony said, "Then our personal reality is that an enemy army stands between us and home, and threatens Harrisburg directly. If they take that city again, they can resupply by river and divide the Confederation from our Free Republic allies. Or flee unmolested downriver."

Nestor clenched his jaw, nodding. "It's a desperate situation. Harrisburg is holding on for now, but half of Liz Town's forces are on *this* side of the river. They can't reinforce Harrisburg."

That wasn't exactly news to Jaz, but it bore careful thought. Tentatively, she said, "I suppose we'll have to hit the Mountain's army from behind. Go all-in to smash them between us and Harrisburg. If we're lucky we can wipe them out."

Nestor laughed, and his eyes seemed to sparkle with excitement. "That or they'll defeat us piecemeal. Well then, I suppose we should get started. Care to join the Night Ghosts for the fight? I'll make you honorary members, and even teach you our secret handshake and stuff."

"Damn straight. Fighting alone is stupid. We'd totally like to join your peeps for a minute. As long as Choony can come with me, I'm good. But you owe me a secret handshake."

Nestor shrugged. "Absolutely. I know that you two are a package deal. Besides, though he may not be the one shooting people, Choony is fearless and you fight better with him at your side."

Jaz smirked. Nestor didn't know about Choony saving her life *twice* now, but she wasn't going to tell anyone. That was up to Choony to say something, if he wanted to. "Okay. Time for the shooting and the stabby stuff. When do we leave?"

"Twenty minutes, if you're ready. I only need time to get things organized, then we'll go."

Choony nodded. "Certainly. Take twenty-five minutes, if you need it." He kept a straight face, but Nestor laughed, catching the joke. Jaz was surprised—usually she was the only one who could say for sure when Choon Choon was joking.

Jaz jumped up and down once. "Okay, dude. Second Harrisburg begins in twenty mikes, and then we totally bounce out," she said, thinking that if they won, she'd be able to go home again. Man, she missed Clanholme right now... The open road no longer held the appeal it used to.

* * *

The Gap rose up before him, and Frank eyed the wall nervously. It wasn't merely the simple-but-effective rubble walls that most settlements were building these days. It was bound by sturdy horse-wire fencing and strengthened with rebar throughout. Near the gates, the walls were faced with sheet metal, some of it corrugated from cut-up cargo containers. The wall was incomplete, but large parts were almost finished. Worse, scouts had reported four more vehicles positioned somewhere in all that mass of defenses. From the descriptions, Michael had said they were probably Oshkosh "M-ATVs," which were replacements for the older Humvee. They had more armor, great against the Afghanistan IEDs they were designed to deal with. The Oshkosh had a machine gun and some sort of anti-tank missile system that one of the soldiers had called a "toe-two."

As the Second battalion infantry approached the wall, scattered small arms fire began, sounding like faint popcorn noises from Frank's distant position. Then mortar rounds from within the Gap arced over the wall and began to land among the attackers. Thankfully, Michael had ordered them to deploy widely scattered—Houle's troops couldn't kill a lot of their infantry at once that way, but it also meant that the Clanners couldn't concentrate much fire on any one point.

Michael's voice came over the radio, sounding much clearer than before. Frank glanced at the radio unit and saw it was coming through on his direct command channel. "All unit leaders, keep the op tempo slow and steady. I want as few casualties as possible. Get our mortar company to pour rounds down on those M-ATVs. We probably won't knock them out, but we might mess up their weapons systems, and we can keep them blind."

Soon, Clan mortars were returning fire. Frank shook his head at the scene. It was like the infantry on both sides were only there to keep the other infantry from advancing while the bigger guns did the killing. He imagined the terror his people must be feeling. Houle's too, though.

After ten minutes of continual barrage, Michael came

over the radio again. "First battalion, deploy our drones. Find the damn mortar batteries in there, and get me some coordinates."

Frank saw small white things flying just above ground level, zooming toward town—the drones the Clan had in storage ever since crushing the 'vaders in a massive battle in a rock quarry long ago.

The drones flew up to the wall and then rose vertically, popping up and over. Soon, he knew, they'd be taking pictures of the targets and transmitting them, and the pictures would have GPS coordinates.

The radio chattered chaotically for several minutes, and then Frank saw the drones returning to their pilot squads in the field ahead of him. Fewer came out than had gone in, but that didn't matter...

*Boom...* The whole damn town was lit up with blindingly bright flashes of light, each of which was soon followed by small mushroom clouds. Frank grinned as Clan artillery did its thing. Enemy mortar fire petered out to virtually nothing.

Michael ordered the infantry to charge, and they did. A dozen fell right away, but the rest kept pushing forward. Frank double-checked his woodgas canister, as this would be the right time to change it out if needed, but it was still smoking away merrily.

"India company, advance zero-seven-two and engage. Let's get those Mk-19s into the mix, Frank."

"Roger," Frank said into his mic and gunned the engine. His truck dug its rear wheels into the soft dirt for a second before it gained any speed; the thing was a pig to get moving, but once going, it had the momentum and the cattle prow to smash aside most anything in its path.

The battlecars kept in a lopsided V formation, swerving left when they were close enough to the wall to get accurate direct fire. All through the vehicle company, the large 40mm grenades flew, streaking into the wall—the Mk-19 was a grenade machinegun, its raw power showed clearly all along the wall's crest as he drove parallel. To Frank, it looked as though the ugly wall had grown a beautiful hedge of orange and yellow fire-blossoms all along its length, and the gate fortifications were hammered hard.

He glanced to the rear and saw that Clan infantry had charged toward the resulting smoke and dust; it blocked the enemy's view, and the first Clanners had reached the wall without heavy losses. Like ants, they went up and over, more and more piling onto the wall as the battlecar company veered away. Frank circled away from the action again to await further orders.

Those orders never came, however. Once the Clan and Taggart's loaned troops were over the wall, there was little use for Frank and his cars, and there was little for him to do but wait for the inevitable end.

The Gap fell shortly after.

* * *

In the bunker, Ethan received information throughout the day about the progress of fighting, both at the Gap to the south and in the Free Republic to the west. The Gap fell after hours of fighting, though the Clan took heavy losses in intense, house-to-house action. The town was a wreck, but the Mountain's units there had been overwhelmed and destroyed.

To the west, meanwhile, the combined Mountain-Empire forces had been shattered by the Liz Town troops in Harrisburg and the Night Ghosts and other forces behind them. As a result of that action, the Confederation now had a small supply of real, working vehicles, ranging from M2 and M3 Bradleys—light tanks, basically—to a dozen Strykers and a couple dozen humvees. They also salvaged a dozen Oshkoshes, which apparently were bigger, badder humvees with armor and TOW-2 missile launchers. Not many, but enough to threaten the Mountain's real tanks if they actually sent some into battle.

The army's survivors fled in all directions, scattered in small groups that were being hunted down without mercy. The Free Republic was currently celebrating their regained freedom by slaughtering those Empire and Mountain troops, often gruesomely.

Ethan, however, celebrated the victory by hacking into one of his remaining satellites and looking over recent image files, in between receiving and passing on various reports coming in by radio. Searching those images was how he killed time, usually, and had often had productive results.

His celebration was short-lived. On the images, he saw a large body of troops gathered within a broad area just southwest of Pennsylvania, flying American flags on some of the vehicles. In one of the images, he caught sight of what could only be jet fighters... That made those Houle's forces. The Confederation had defeated a force much smaller than what he was looking at, and Ethan realized that what they had faced so far were advance units, not the vanguard. There was even an entire company of M1 Abrams, judging by their silhouettes. A boatload of Strykers. A ton of Bradleys, Oshkoshes, and other light vehicles. A force that size must have drained every fuel resource between Colorado Springs and Pennsylvania just to get there. That meant Houle's troops were on a one-way trip. They were coming to Confederation territory to stay, and they'd either win or they'd die...

Ethan closed the depressing image window and turned in his swivel chair to put his elbows on the desk. He rested his chin in his hands, and decided it was time to consider his hack into NORAD. How could he use that to his advantage? He'd only have one shot at making it matter because as soon as he hacked in, they'd quickly learn that Dark Ryder hadn't "retired" after all, and then all bets would definitely be off. He smirked, realizing that he had been right—leaving to "retire" would have had zero effect on an invasion this size, which must have been in the planning stages for quite a while.

No brilliant plan came to mind, however, so he refocused on the tedious radio comms.

Later that night, as the rest of the Confederation celebrated their victory, Ethan tossed and turned with doubt and fear twisting in his guts like snakes. Let them celebrate for tonight, he decided—he'd tell Cassy and Frank the terrible truth in the morning.

# - **18** -

FRANK STEPPED UP to the makeshift podium atop Harrisburg's rubble walls, facing the bridge. He was dirty and tired, but when word of an impending riot reached him, he had to divert. Otherwise it would have been Carl up there, and he remembered the body count the last time Carl had talked to these people. They probably remembered, too. And Cassy couldn't be the one to do it, because she had promised them land and safety if they defeated the Mountain. As far as the mob was concerned, they had done their part.

On the bridgehead below stood the mob's three self-elected spokespeople. The tall and short man from before, and a woman who looked plenty capable of handling herself. Frank was lowered down on a loop of rope, since he couldn't use a ladder very well. He eyed them carefully for a moment, evaluating the trio. He decided that being direct would be the best approach with this trio. "Thanks for coming over to talk to us. It's important that we work this out to everyone's satisfaction. We're on the same side, after all."

The two men nodded, Frank noticed, but the woman stood with arms crossed and eyes narrowed. The short man said, "Agreed. I tried to resolve it peacefully last time, but it didn't work out that way. This time, my friend here has agreed to try it my way. I don't know who whats-her-name is, but she decided she's important enough to be here."

Frank shrugged. Their internal politics weren't his concern. "The more the merrier." He looked at the woman and said, "I'm Frank, speaking for the Confederation today."

She turned her head and spat. "I don't care who you are, as long as you give us what's ours."

The two men took a step away from her, physically distancing themselves, and looked at Frank for his reaction.

Frank chuckled, and smiled. "Very well. I give you all the territory you can claim within the Free Republic." Then he turned to the two men and said, "So let's—"

The woman interrupted. "Fuck you. I said what's ours, not theirs. You promised us land and support in the Clan." Her face was reddening.

Frank let out a sigh. Yes, it was definitely time to be direct with this one. "Nothing of ours is yours until it's given to you, and I'll back out of that deal so fast your damn head will spin if you don't shut the hell up. I'm not your bitch."

She inflated and opened her mouth. Frank figured a tantrum was about to happen. It was weird to be talking to someone like her, because most of her brand of self-entitled shits were dead already. It seemed natural selection had missed one, unfortunately.

"Now you listen here—"

Frank cut her off and said loudly to the two men, "Get her out of here or I'll just walk away."

The woman screamed at him and drew a large, fixed-blade knife. A shot rang out, and she flopped over backward, missing the top half of her head.

"Shit," Frank said. He looked at the crowd, gathered a ways back on the bridge, and saw them surge forward. Frank stepped into the rope loop, but didn't yank on it. "Back 'em off or we figure this out like we did last time."

The taller one said, "I got this," and ran toward the mob. Both he and the mob stopped mid-bridge, facing one another.

Frank turned back to the short man. "You tell them what happened. What the hell is wrong with you people?"

The short man held his hands up, palms toward Frank, and shook his head. "I'll tell them. I should have mentioned that she's new among us. She speaks for the cowards and leeches, though they don't see it that way of course. But now that Felicia is out of the picture, let's get down to business."

Frank took a deep breath. He kept his gaze moving between the crowd and Mr. Short. "Okay then, let's get back to business. Here's our deal, and it's non-negotiable. Your people will get land, support, friendship, and protection as part of the Clan, just as we promised. But you might recall that the deal was you'd get all that *after* the Mountain King's troops were gone."

Mr. Short nodded. "Yep. And they are gone, so let us through. Simple enough, I should think."

Shaking his head, Frank said, "They aren't defeated. Those were only the advance units they had scrounged up from among their remote forward bases. The main body is coming now."

"My people will see this as a betrayal, and that fighting another round with the Mountain should be a separate deal. *Is a second deal.*"

Frank shrugged. "Well, we don't. Defeated means defeated. The war, not the battle. Moreover, even if you fought your way in, then what? The whole of the Confederation would view you as invaders and respond appropriately. Forget about helping you with seeds and tools and food and land. Same problem as last time—you want to take what isn't yours, and we don't figure that's the way we want to go with it."

"I get that. I guess my people would want to just take those things, once they were into their promised territory."

Frank felt a wave of disappointment. He had thought such short-sighted planning had died with the idiots of the old world. Maybe short-sightedness was human nature, he thought, but hopefully so was self-preservation. He said, "If that's your final answer, I guess that puts us at war, and we had better kill off this mob now instead of fighting them later. Meanwhile, winter is coming and... good luck."

Mr. Short grinned. That wasn't what Frank had expected... "I see you aren't much into renegotiating."

"Old-school zero-sum politics died with politicians. And good riddance. You can't have 'renegotiation' without 'reneg,' and if you do that, all bets are off. This is simple—fight against the Mountain King *with* us, or fight against him *and* us."

Mr. Short nodded. "He's coming, whether you and I go to war with each other or not. But these days, we're not inclined to roll over to threats. If we must fight you and him both, we will. It would be a tragedy, but things are what they are."

Frank shrugged. "The thing is, we're not inclined to roll over, either. But you don't have to fight us both. You could just fight on our side now until the Mountain retreats, as we all agreed, and then get the land and support we promised. We'll meet our end, but only if you do."

Just then, Mr. Tall came walking back and Frank saw that the crowd had backed off again. When Tall got close, he said, "I explained it. Her faction wanted to fight, but they weren't with us the last time and they weren't here to fight Houle, either. The rest of us told them to go ahead and attack, but without us. We didn't like her anyway. She made a lot of enemies, as you can imagine. Not a recipe for long life these days."

"Well," Frank said, "we were just at the point where the cards are on the table and a choice must be made. I bear none of you ill will. Join us to fight the Mountain until the war is done, and we give you land, seeds, all of that. Or, you attack us, probably die, and even if you win, then you'd face the entire Confederation *and still have to fight* against the Mountain King when his vanguard arrives. Either way, you fight Houle. One choice gives you allies, the other gives you more enemies."

"I remember how the last fight went. More important is the fact that you're right. We can fight the Mountain with or without allies, but we are going to have to fight them. Frankly, we didn't know more were coming. I thought the army we fought was his main force. So did everyone else."

Frank shook his head. "I truly wish that were the case. We wouldn't even be having this conversation, since you'd be on your way to your new homes. But it's not the case, and we have completely reliable reports that his main force is coming. What we fought were just the units he could scrape up from his far-away bases. Basically, his colonies, if you're familiar with Greek history. And like the Greeks did in the past, recall that we have most of your fighters' families with us, safe and sound."

The two men stiffened, and Frank continued speaking as though he didn't notice. "We wouldn't harm them even if you attack us today, you have my word. But you'll see them much faster if we work this out together so we can all go home."

Tall nodded. He held up one hand and, when he had Frank's attention, said, "Your integrity with that helps make this an easy choice. So... what is our next step?"

\* \* \*

Choony and Jaz made their way carefully through the crowd. Tensions were high, but so far there had been no violence.

He hoped it stayed that way, as becoming violent would not change their situation, wouldn't get them what they wanted. It would only make it impossible for them to get what they wanted later, after the fighting was truly finished.

Nonetheless, Choony wanted to be through the crowd as quickly as possible. If they did become violent, Nestor's liberated vehicles had grenade launchers that apparently were like machine guns, and he didn't want to be in the crowd when those landed. He shuddered at the thought, but Nestor and the Confederation would have no choice. There were hundreds and hundreds of people here, many armed with a few M4s taken from the Mountain and a horde of civilian rifles from the Empire. "Let's hurry, Jaz."

Jaz didn't answer, only sped up her pace to keep up with Choony. They made their way through the crowd for several minutes, then saw its leading edge up ahead.

A man stepped in front of Choony and shoved him in the chest, hard. Choony staggered backward but didn't lose his balance. He looked at the man passively.

The man growled, "Tattoo monkey. The Clan isn't welcome here. Best turn around."

Choony saw that he had a knife in his hand, held low by his side as though to hide it. He looked nervous. The people around them didn't cheer or join in, instead stepping away from the man as if to say they weren't involved with the guy.

Choony said, "Funny, then, that you are asking permission to join the Clan. Perhaps you and your friends should stay here, while everyone else enjoys a brighter future."

"Fuck you," the man said.

"How eloquent."

"The Clan made a promise they aren't keeping. I think we'd rather take what's ours than beg for scraps."

Jaz stepped between Choony and the man. Oh man!

Choony prayed Jaz would play this one easy, but that was unlikely. He said, "Go easy, Jaz..."

Jaz ignored him. "It isn't yours until the Mountain packs up and goes home, mister. But I'll remember you, jerkwad. You and your family? I'll make sure you don't ever get in."

The man snarled and charged toward Jaz, who crouched low to receive the attack, but he was grabbed from behind by the other refugees, who disarmed him roughly. One said, grunting with the effort of holding the angry man back, "Best get moving."

Choony needed no encouragement. He stepped forward, grabbed Jaz's sleeve in his fist, and strode through the parting crowd toward the bridge. They crossed the bridge together, and Choony felt safe enough to let her go when they were halfway across. On the far side, he saw Frank talking to two men, with a corpse lying nearby.

Once they got close, Frank saw them and his eyes went wide. "Hey, Frank. Buddha blesses you."

Frank smiled, a warm and genuine expression, then looked up at the wall and waved. A ladder was lowered down to them. Frank said, "Glad you made it, Jazoony. You two need to get home, okay?"

Choony said, "We'll meet you back home, then."

Jaz climbed first, and Choony came up the ladder right behind her. Once they were up and over the wall, Jaz said, "Let's go get a couple horses and skee-daddle, yo."

Choony grinned. "Yes. Yo. Let us bounce."

Jaz rolled her eyes and playfully tapped him in the shoulder with her fist. "You're such an idiot."

Choony was happy to see her in a good mood, but how could she not be? They had survived the chaos out there, and they'd soon be home again. Maybe they'd even get to stay home for a few days before being sent on another mission. Wouldn't that be fantastic...

* * *

Carl stepped into his shower and pulled the chain with one hand, releasing a flow of piping hot water from the attic water tank. It was heated through black tubing that ran from the tank to the roof, where it was arranged in a large spiral, then back down into the tank. The sun heated the water in the spiral, sometimes to almost boiling, but the day had been overcast so it was merely "hot tub temperature."

He hadn't had a shower in days, and his whole body ached from rumbling around in his battlecar, so he indulged himself and let at least five whole gallons wash over him before he let go of the chain to stop the water. He lathered up from head to toe with strawberry VO-5, Sunshine's favorite-smelling 3-in-1, then wasted at least another five gallons rinsing off and just unwinding. It was a privilege of rank, though not one that could be abused even by an Alpha.

He opened the frosted glass shower door and stepped out onto the bathmat. It was thick, foam-filled, and comfortable as hell. He liked to wiggle his toes into it while he dried off, even though he looked damn silly doing it. Who would see him, anyway? He smiled at the bathmat. Before the war, he had bought the cheap ones. Now, with most people dead or gone, there were more than enough luxury items for every survivor to live like a king or queen—so long as they didn't need electricity.

Then he went to the sink and shaved, using cold water to make his disposable razor last longer and shave closer. It also gave him fewer razor bumps that way, and anything one could do to lower the chance of an infection was worth doing, these days. He looked into the mirror and decided he needed a haircut.

He sighed... Getting his hair cut sucked. Before the EMPs, he had worn his hair long and shaggy, and people said he looked like "The Dude" from *The Big Lebowski*, which he'd enjoyed hearing. Oh well. Easy come, easy go.

Towel wrapped around him, he stepped out of the bathroom and into the bedroom. Sunshine lay on his bed, half awake. He glanced to the nightstand and saw her water glass was full enough for her to take a couple more Percocet. Thankfully, she had agreed to let him keep her high as a kite until she healed a bit from having her leg sawed off. The bandage, he saw, had only a pink haze to it, rather than bleeding through. It was a good sign.

"Morning, Sunshine," he said with a grin.

She frowned and looked away, avoiding eye contact. "Good morning, Carl. For you, anyway." Her voice had a weird pitch to it, a side effect of being blasted out of her mind on painkillers. "I need more percs."

Carl tucked his towel in so it would stay up without being held, walked to the nightstand and shook four tiny white, round pills out of a small bottle. These were the good ones, Percocets without any of that stupid acetaminophen in them. Whoever had thought of putting that liver-killer in with the otherwise harmless opiates should be shot. On the doses Sunshine needed, she'd have suffered permanent liver damage if he had traded for the ones with that garbage.

"You're lucky I found these pills. Three of these should work until morning. They're ten milligrams each."

Sunshine tried to nod but could only barely move her head. She was pale and clammy, and Carl cursed himself for letting her sleep instead of waking her two hours ago for more painkillers. Now she was half in shock from pain. He'd get used to the routine and wouldn't make that mistake again.

Sunshine didn't whimper though, and Carl was impressed at how tough she was. After he gave her the pills and made sure she took them, he made her drink the rest of the water in her cup. She drifted to sleep again, and he got dressed.

His day was far from over, despite being well after dinner. Several envoys from the Free Republic, each representing different areas, had come to Harrisburg to meet with him to renew their agreements with Liz Town and the Confederation. Also, Carl had agreed to be their mediator as they negotiated reuniting their regions into the Free Republic again, in the aftermath of kicking the Mountain King's dogs out of Pennsylvania. It was important to do so, and quickly, because Clanholme had passed word that General Houle had a new army coming together to make another try.

At that thought, Carl frowned. His eyebrows furrowed and he clenched his jaw, and for a moment, he zoned out into his own little world, one where he slaughtered an endless field of Houle's vile soldiers in increasingly painful and creative ways. Sons-a-bitches deserved worse than he could think up. What the hell did they need *more* land for? They could barely control the land they already claimed.

Carl spent a moment thinking about whether they could exploit the Mountain King being spread so thin, and an idea struck him. He'd need the Free Republic's help, though. He finished dressing in khaki pants and a black Polo shirt, sturdy black boots that he kept shined up for these dog-and-pony shows, and a light black windbreaker. Then he headed downstairs to await the envoy arrival.

At a quarter to ten, Carl heard a knock at the door. He stood in the living room off the foyer, and one of his guards showed them in. A man and two women came in together, and Carl noted that their body language was relaxed and they walked close together, smiling at each other. It was a good sign.

"Hello. My name is Carl, the Timber Wolf Alpha and

right hand to the Speaker of Liz Town. Won't you have a seat?" He motioned toward the two couches that were arrayed around a single table.

As they came in, Carl shook their hands. When they were seated, he sat in the recliner. It was a cozy, informal environment, and perfect for these discussions. The three introduced themselves as Heath, Marge, and Reba. Carl's briefing had said they led the three largest groups of former Free Republic people, and each spoke for a number of smaller groups that had given them their individual support, authorizing them to negotiate on their behalf.

Heath was short with close-trimmed brown hair, and looked to be in his late twenties. He said, "Thanks for meeting with us. I don't expect any problems, but a neutral third-party mediator seemed like a good idea just in case."

Marge nodded. She was the taller of the two women, a muscular brunette who wore a purple-and-brown dress. "I appreciate your time," she said, her voice soft and soothing.

Carl sat in a relaxed position, hands on his recliner arms, leaning back slightly. He smiled at each in turn. "I'm happy to help friends of Liz Town, which you are despite some disagreements in the past. Let's start with what each of you needs to get in order to make reuniting worthwhile."

The next hour went by quickly. The envoys were mostly in agreement about the big things, with only a few minor territorial disagreements and a bit of conflict about their leaders' roles in the restored government. In his head, Carl made a grid with each of their demands. On the few disagreements, he helped them trade out something they didn't need for the thing they really wanted. It was, overall, an easy meeting. They'd walk away from this with the Free Republic restored, working together.

Then Carl said, "Now that I have all of you here, I do have something that the Confederation would like to discuss with the Free Republic. Do you have time to handle that now, or would you prefer to wait until tomorrow?"

Heath said, "Now is good. I want to leave in the morning. There's a lot to do at home, as you can imagine."

Marge and Reba nodded in agreement.

"Then it's my turn to thank you all for your time. So, the situation is simple. Right now, the forces that the Mountain King used to keep control of unruly populations in the Midwest and the South were partly squandered fighting all of us. They still have control of those areas from their forts, but only barely. Reinforcements aren't coming soon, but the reason is that Houle's army is now gathering to our south. The real war has yet to come."

The envoys shifted uncomfortably in their seats. It was something everyone now knew, but no one enjoyed facing the facts.

Carl continued, "It's my belief that if we shotgunned small forces throughout Houle's eastern territories, spreading weapons and supplies to the locals, we might be able to encourage them to take advantage of their current opportunity. It won't last forever, this chance at freedom, and fighting now means Houle's supply chain has to go all the way to Colorado instead of close by. Supply will have to go through unruly territories the whole way, requiring more troops to guard them en route. It means fewer supplies for them here, during the coming fighting, and so the Mountain would be greatly weakened."

Reba said, "It sounds like a solid plan. Why are you telling us this, exactly?"

The other two envoys nodded their agreement, and Carl found all three envoys staring at him as they expectantly awaited his reply. It was disconcerting. He cleared his throat, buying himself a couple precious seconds to regain his focus. "The simple answer is that we want you to supply those small units we'll shotgun throughout Houle's colonized territories."

"Colonized?" Heath asked.

"Yes," Carl replied. "Houle doesn't control most of his territory directly. He built fast and cheap forts, or built up existing buildings to use as castles. They hold troops and not much else. The locals can't get at them, but they can ride out at any moment to raise havoc if the locals don't give them what they want."

Reba said, "I see. What do you provide?"

Carl shrugged, raised his eyebrows, and pushed his lips out for a moment, trying to appear nonchalant. "The Confederation will supply your remaining troops with what they need, rifles and food."

"What do you get out of it?" Heath asked. "We supply the raiders out of our army, and you supply our army out of yours. It's musical chairs with your own people left standing at the end."

"What do I get out of it? It's what *we all* get out of it. As I said, it'll hinder Houle's troops and his plans, slow the operational tempo—which can only help us—and give him another threat he has to split his focus on. We have supplies coming in that will replace what we give you. By shuffling them down the line like this, we can all supply our units much faster than if we wait for outside help before we do anything."

Reba said, "Very well. I'm game." Heath and Marge nodded also.

They talked for a couple more hours, looking at a marked-up map of America and making plans, figuring out how many groups they'd need, how many people for each group, how many wagons, what to put in those wagons. The meeting didn't end until the early hours of the morning, but Carl thought the resulting grand plan was solid. It would go into effect within the next three or four days.

* * *

Ree stood on the wall and faced south, looking down at the troops below. Ungrateful barbarians, those ISNA fighters. After all Ree had done for them, they turned on him with surprising quickness once Central Park fell. Sure, Ree's hunter-killer teams had slaughtered thousands from the mobs and created fear among the Americans stuck in that terrible city, but Ree had miscalculated. Instead of cringing and submitting to his will, the Americans had struck back hard, using everything from guns to baseball bats as weapons. Sure, thousands more had been slaughtered, but they forced Ree's troops who weren't behind the wall to fall back again and again.

Now they were huddled right outside his gate, and they wanted in. Ree had enough food for his loyal people within his fortress, and enough seeds and land to grow for them in the spring, but he had nowhere near enough seeds or land to take in the forces sitting below. He had promised to let them in if only they'd go on a terror spree, which they had done, and it should have worked. Dammit, no one could maraud through a civilian population like ISNA fighters.

Now he faced those same troops, once loyal to him, and watched as their fear rose and their loyalty waned. Ree had the strong feeling that this situation would go from bad to disastrous at any moment. Any spark could ignite the firestorm, and then "all bets were off," as the Americans would say.

Three majors, loyal to his three rebellious colonels, stood outside looking up at the wall. Ree had positioned himself where he could speak to them, but dared not reveal himself openly. He hid behind cover and loyal soldiers, avoiding anyone below who might take the initiative and shoot him.

Being so loathed by his fellow Koreans and many of his

ISNA former lapdogs was an odd feeling, and new in his experience. Ree shouted down, "No, I will not open these gates. I have given you direct orders to go forth and ravage the civilians—mere civilians!—yet they ousted you from the territories I gave you. You failed to hold your land against lazy, fat American civilians, and you failed in the mission I gave you afterward. Shall I reward your failure?"

From below, he heard, "Great Leader, we obeyed your orders, but you then left us to face the situation out here alone. Without support, and without even coordinating between your colonels, how could we succeed?"

Ree felt his face flush, and struggled to calm himself. This was not the time to lose his famed composure. And they were right in that he really had set them up for failure. Intentionally. "Perhaps that is so, but when I gave you the solution, you failed even there."

"We went among the Americans with an iron fist, at your orders, but they didn't cower. Instead, they rose up even more. Your leadership has failed, and we only ask that you meet your responsibility to your troops. We aligned our will to yours, and you must in turn provide for your people. That is how this works."

Ree growled. Impudent, insolent little bastards... How dare they tell *him* what he must do? "When you succeed at the mission I have given you, those who remain will be welcomed with open arms. Until then," he said, his voice rising into a shout, "I do not reward failure and stupidity. I do not bow to the insolent, the undisciplined."

From below, he heard, "General, you will soon find that your words are prophetic, for nor do we bow to such. You must step down as leader. Since you refuse to hear us, we now will say it with more emphasis. Prepare yourself, Ree. You will soon meet your ancestors, to their eternal shame."

Ree's fingers turned white as he gripped the galvanized

steel railing stretching along the catwalk. The arrogance...
But he could not let that insult go unchecked if he wanted to
keep his own troops loyal. If the mob outside intended to
turn on him, he decided, it was best to do something about it
now, while he still could. He looked at Major Kim and said
softly, "All men, throw grenades and then open fire.
Everything we've got. Kill them all, if we can."

Kim nodded and strode the catwalk, spreading the word.

Ree pulled out his little compressed-air horn and began
to count to thirty in his mind. He needed to keep the mob
from dispersing early, though. He shouted down, "What
gives the servant the right to question the master? You speak
of 'our way' even as you desecrate it. Very well, send forward
those who can negotiate for you, and we will talk. We must
stand together if we are to stand at all, here in this barbaric
place."

Five soldiers stepped forward, three Korean and two
sand-eaters. So now the ISNA barbarians wanted to have a
say in things, too, Ree noted. Delightful. He pushed on the
air horn's rubber button, and an ear-piercing shriek blasted
his ears.

The men below looked amusingly confused for a
moment, until a dozen grenades flew from the wall into the
crowd below. The series of explosions was most rewarding,
and signaled the gunners on the wall. Dozens of troops with
AK-47s and half a dozen light machine guns opened fire, as
did grenade launchers on either side of the gate. It was a
sudden, brutal onslaught. The rebellious troops below had
been lulled into lowering their guard, crowding together to
hear the exchange, and that curiosity was their doom.

Ree stood smiling atop the wall and risked a look over
the ledge. He wanted to see for himself what the results were.
It warmed his old soldier's blood to see such a carnage. As
those who could flee ran away, at least half of the mob lay on

the pavement below him, writhing amidst a growing sea of blood.

Ree shouted to Kim, "Order a general cease fire, then begin shooting anyone out there still moving. When you feel it safe, send a squad out with bayonets to finish off the survivors. There should be none left, when they finish."

Kim saluted and went to put Ree's orders into effect.

Ree took a deep breath, inhaling the coppery scent of hundreds of gallons of blood and the acrid smoke from thousands of rounds fired. It was the smell of war, and lifted his spirits greatly. Hopefully, the American workers would pick off the scattered, weakened survivors and be killed in return, reducing both his enemies at once. "Two birds with one stone," he said aloud. It was an American phrase, but it seemed the perfect comment to encapsulate that moment. He smiled. Those traitors might remain a vague danger, but they were no longer a direct threat to his own survival.

As the killing continued outside the walls, Ree headed down and walked toward his office. A bottle of American whiskey was waiting for him there, and it was time to celebrate. The deadwood had been trimmed, and Ree now had the core of loyal troops he needed to bring about a new, resurgent Korean epoch.

# - **19** -

FRANK SQUINTED IN the bunker's relatively low lighting as he examined Ethan's map. It was made of a few dozen printed pages that were taped up to cover most of one wall, showing a topographical view of the whole region. Ethan had added to the map, tons of points of interest, prior battles, troop movements, and so on. Over that had been placed a taped-together lamination made of cut-up sheet protectors, which allowed them to mark it up with grease pens.

Frank saw that battles involving any member of the Confederation and many battles of the Free Republic were marked by simple Xs. Harrisburg and the Gap were among them. Lost battles had circles around the X marks; of the several dozen marks, well over half were circled.

All in all, the map system was both simple and effective. Where Ethan had found the maps to print out, Frank didn't know.

The war so far had been frustrating. The Clan had lost several important people, though none of the Council had died... yet. After so many "traditional" Clan memorials, the Food Forest was full and could hold no more graves. They had begun to bury Clan losses in the plains beyond it, extending the forest by a fraction with each new ceremonial tree planting. If this war continued, the forest would double in size rather soon...

Ethan entered the room from the bedding area and nodded a greeting. "Pretty dark picture, isn't it?"

Frank let out a tense breath, making a hissing noise from his nose. More sharply than he intended, Frank snapped back, "Yes. It's fucking grim."

"Whoa. You can take it out on me if you want, boss, but I'm not General Houle."

Frank nodded. Ethan was right, of course. "It's just getting to me. Houle has more areas of operation than we can keep up with. His units are smaller than ours but a lot more effective. Our lost battles tend to be devastating, while his tend to mean he just ran away to fight another day."

"It's their vehicles," Ethan said. "They have lots, we have few. They have tanks, we have none. Those M1s are unstoppable. The best we can do is temporarily immobilize them with a tread hit or knock out their cannon barrel. Those get fixed if they win the battle."

"Yeah. And when we win, we have to just scuttle their lost vehicles. We can't tow those monsters with horses, and the battlecars aren't powerful enough to drag a tank overland, either."

Ethan shook his head slowly and clicked his tongue on his teeth. "Amazing how powerful vehicles are. Not to mention how fast they move around. They mostly fight only when they want to. They pick the time and place, and we can only react."

"It is what it is. Wrapping C4 around a propane tank and tossing it under a tank's treads worked once. We might try more of that." Frank eyed Ethan to gauge his reaction.

Ethan shrugged. "It's dangerous, but no more dangerous than facing a tank *without* a propane bomb. Problem is, they're damn heavy to be lugging around a battlefield and you can't put it on a road. Pretty much everyone who serves Houle was in Iraq and Afghanistan and they know what to look for. Maybe we can build up a few of those bombs at settlements and bases. If they get attacked, they can use the bombs without first lugging them all over the state."

"I wish there was a way to level the playing field." Frank let out a long breath. "With all those vehicles, never mind the tanks, it's hard to fight them even with cavalry or bikes. Our artillery helps, but not against moving armor. If only the armor at that depot wasn't fried."

Ethan froze and his eyes grew wide.

Frank suddenly remembered that it was Ethan who had punished the world by putting them in the same dark boat as America. He had EMP'd the globe for the 20s and General Houle. "Sorry, Ethan. But I still wish we could level the field against the Mountain like we did the 'vaders."

Ethan's face scrunched up for a moment as though he were in pain. After a long moment, he said, "It may be possible to do just what you were wishing. The problem is that it would destroy all those nice radios and Raspberry Pi computers we've been salvaging and sending out to our allies."

"So it would hurt us a lot, too. Not Clanholme itself, since we can weather the EMPs just like the last two times, but our allies and friends can't be forewarned in case they have Houle's spies among them. Best to save that idea as a last resort, but be truthful... Is that something you really could do?"

Ethan shrugged. "I think so. I have a backdoor into NORAD, and still have my connections to the missile systems, which Houle doesn't. Those connections are static, they don't change, but the clock starts ticking as soon as I use my hack. As far as Houle is concerned, I 'retired,' if you'll recall. Once they spotted the connection, they would know it was me, and they'd know just how dangerous that is for them. I'll have only limited time."

"Fair enough. We'll table that for now, but I want you to get a plan as ready as you can, so that you'll have time to do use that hack if needed. Compile coordinate kernels, or whatever it is you hackers do."

Ethan put on a faint smile, which Frank realized was mostly for his benefit, and said, "You got it, bossman. But first I need to show you something. If you look at the map..."

Ethan moved to the wall. With both index fingers, he pointed at two large red circles on the map. "So, see these? They're Houle's main army, split into Army Group East and Army Group South. Based on the patterns of their movement and that of the smaller scout units they've been sending out, it's my belief Harrisburg is their intended target. That's their Omaha Beach."

Frank nodded. It was what they had always expected. "Army Group East is in Pittsburgh—they walked right in, since the Empire retook it—and South is in Martinsburg, West Virginia. Remember, they had a huge supply depot there? They retook it last week. I think both army groups will get their act together and sweep aside everything in their way, then slam into Harrisburg together."

Ethan said, "The only other option is for South to go through York and Lancaster, crossing the river south of us. If that happens, then either we or Liz Town get hit before they move on to attack Harrisburg from both sides."

"I don't think that's likely, though. York burned down and Lancaster got sprayed early on, so both are barren of any supplies or fuel. There's a huge stretch of almost empty land with no supplies and very little fuel. It'll be Harrisburg from the west, I think."

"I agree. I don't even know how they're using that old

gas. It shouldn't really be working anymore. Gas goes bad. Diesel, too. We do know they have some sort of additive, stockpiled before the war, but they can't have enough of it to run those damn vehicles forever."

Ethan grimaced. "With any luck, we can drag this war on long enough for them to run out of either gas or additives. They're on a short window of opportunity with an operation this size. It's why they're being so aggressive and taking risks."

"Those risks are probably the only reason why we have the wins we do, so thank God for that. Let's assume they aren't going to go through Lancaster. They'll hit Harrisburg together, both groups. What can we do between their current staging areas and Harrisburg to slow them down or blunt their attack? If we could disrupt their two army groups somehow, we could deal with them piecemeal."

"Don't count on that," Ethan said. "Their swarms of vehicles make it more likely that they would outmaneuver us, not the other way around. We're stuck on defense as long as they have that advantage."

"Then let's think defensively. That depot where we got all those rifles and restocked ammo had crates of mines, both antipersonnel and antitank. Let's put up assloads of those things randomly, everywhere between them and us. Mark their locations with GPS so we can find them again when this is all over with."

"It won't stop them, Frank."

"No, but it will slow them down and start chipping away at their numbers. Those vehicles can't be replaced, and they have fewer infantry than we do—just a lot better equipped."

Ethan frowned. "Attrition warfare is ugly. I agree that we should do what you said, and so will Michael, but I'd just rather have one big battle and win it all."

"Or lose it all. Attrition warfare is the ugliest kind,

Michael says, but it's a kind of warfare we can stand up to better than Houle can, in the long run."

"Then the next logical step is to take the attrition to them. Disposable units to ambush or snipe at them, and maybe even knock out a few vehicles with rockets."

Frank shook his head. "You aren't thinking it through. We can't do that. Remember that they have drones, night vision, thermal scopes that see over a mile out. They have command tools in those Strykers, so they'll respond quickly to any threat they detect, and they'll see us before we are anywhere near in range."

Ethan looked down, as frustrated as Frank. "You're wrong. We should do this, and that's what I'm going to tell Michael. I'd rather lose one guy taking out an Oshkosh than lose ten in a skirmish."

Frank clenched his teeth. Ethan could be so damn defiant sometimes. He was like that before the war, too, from what he had said. But Ethan was right about one thing—it was up to Michael, their General, to decide. In the Confederation, civilian leaders stayed the hell out of the way and let the general do his thing, with their full support.

"Michael will see it my way, Ethan. But why go through that trouble? Why not just send teams out with laser spotters and arty the hell out of the target? They'd have ten to fifteen seconds to get out of the way, so we'd have to hit them when encamped, but what's the range on a laser targeter thing?"

"Michael said about four klicks on something as large as an M1 Abrams, two klicks on a Humvee or Oshkosh."

"Huh. He also said the max useful range on the optics in a Stryker was just over a mile. Maybe we can laser them when they aren't moving, and not be seen."

"Cutting it close, but we have little to lose. I like that better than my first idea."

Frank grinned. That little shit could be amusing

sometimes, even if he was a headache to manage. He was opinionated, but willing to change his mind if another idea came along that he thought was better. Frank said, "I don't mind saying that I like this idea better than your first one, too, but only because it was a shitty plan to begin with. Of course."

Ethan snorted. "Har har. Alright, let's get Michael on the radio and see what he thinks."

Frank watched as Ethan took his seat at the desk with all the radios and checked to see which channel Michael was on.

Frank thought about the plan while he waited. It wasn't a great plan, and it wouldn't do more than scratch the surface of their bigger problem, but in attrition warfare that's how it was done—one scratch at a time. Death by a thousand paper cuts. Besides, he figured, every time they blew up an enemy Humvee or whatever, they could shout about it all over the Confederation. Propaganda was important, especially when it looked like the lines were going to collapse soon. Once Harrisburg fell, Houle's forces could blitz all through the Confederation's heartland. It would take a lot of propaganda to make that one look like a win...

* * *

1300 HOURS - ZERO DAY +415

General Ree awoke to the sounds of shouting in the hallway outside his suite. He leaped out of bed and grabbed his pistol even before his mind caught up enough to identify what had jolted him awake. Armed, he stood still and rubbed sleep from his eyes with one hand and pointed his pistol at the door with the other. The door was locked and made of steel, so it'd take quite a while to bash it down. If that happened, he'd duck out through his emergency escape long before the door fell. Dynamite, however, would make short work of the masonry around the door and blow it inward like a missile, so its strength would be irrelevant.

Once he could see clearly, he threw on his brown uniform trousers and jacket, ignoring the uniform shirt for the moment, and buttoned the coat up quickly.

The alarm siren began in the distance, first a low, mournful wail. The volume rocketed to become an angry roar, impossible to ignore. That meant it was serious. Ree paused and considered his options. If he stayed in the room, he was ultimately trusting that his forces would be victorious, but if he was wrong then staying could well be fatal.

Or he could slide through a hidden hatch to the tunnel below, which ran west under the base and exited in the docks area on the island's west coast. There was a set of clothes and other gear in the hallway, waiting for him. His "bugout bag," as some Americans called it. He had heard the idea and liked it, and now he was very glad that he had done it.

Lastly, he could leave the room and go command his troops in defense of his last remaining, most important fortification. That would be betting on victory, too, but with the added risk of getting shot by his own men either by accident or on purpose, or by a lucky sniper. It could, however, improve the odds his troops would win.

There was a banging on the door and Major Pak Kim's voice bellowed through. "My leader, let me in."

Ree heard panic in the man's voice. Kim led Ree's Logistics department and wasn't a warrior, so it could mean nothing. Or it could mean he was being held by their enemies to fool Ree.

Ree walked silently to the wall left of the door and peered through an off-center peephole—anyone who saw him looking out could not hit him by shooting through the heavy steel door somehow. Outside, he saw only Kim. Ree wrenched the lever aside to unlock the door and pulled it open enough for Kim to slide inside before slamming it closed and locking it once again.

"Situation report, Major," Ree ordered. He kept his voice level, and fought to hide the stress he felt. "Just tell me honestly and directly what is happening."

Kim snapped to attention and saluted, which told Ree a lot about how panicked the man was. He was almost on autopilot right now.

Kim replied, "Hordes of Americans are storming the walls and coming up inside through the sewers, along with many troops of your colonels. I had previously blasted the tunnels people could fit through, but the traitor Worker's Army must know of others."

Ree nodded. There was no time to shout or be angry. Not yet. "Will this base fall?" It was a simple, direct question, and his expression was intended to show that he wanted the same kind of answer.

"Yes, Great Leader. Within the hour, all will be lost. This wing will likely be the last to fall, as your loyal soldiers fall back to protect you."

"Very well. Go, gather ten troops and full gear loads for all of them. Also for yourself. Then meet me back here in one half hour or less. I know what to do."

Ree watched his aide practically run to the door, open it, and disappear down the hall. Ree locked it behind Kim, then began to pace while his thoughts raced. His only option now was to make it through his secret tunnel to the western docks, commandeer a sailing boat, and sail with Kim and a few soldiers to the northwest. There was a deserted island out there that was not actually so deserted. It had been hollowed out prior to the invasion as an observation post and command center for the pre-invasion preparations, and though it was probably now deserted, it still remained intact. He could hide there and buy time to figure out what to do next.

He thought of Kim, out there running around. Damn you, Kim, hurry up...

* * *

Frank steered right and swerved away from the oncoming Stryker, passing to its left. Four holes appeared in his battlecar's right rear armor where someone else's fifty-cal had torn into it, but the Stryker had provided timely cover as he passed it. In the distance behind him lay the bridge to Harrisburg, smoke rising thick and black on both sides of the river.

He had lost a third of the Confederation's battlecars already. They were no match for Strykers, Bradleys, or even the TOW-2 missiles of Oshkoshes. The remaining two-dozen battlecars had destroyed quite a few of those Oshkoshes, but couldn't touch the other enemy vehicles. Houle's M1 Abrams, all eight of them, were untouchable goliaths striding the battlefield like kings, destroying anything that was unlucky enough to come into view for more than a few seconds.

Thirty seconds later, the *tink, tink* of small arms fire disappeared and he saw no more enemy vehicles. He whooped with a fierce joy and screamed at the top of his lungs. They had made it through the gauntlet! Or rather, most of them had. Now they would scour the enemy's rear looking for supply trucks, especially the fuel tankers. Without those, Houle's indestructible tanks would be immobilized, useless. It would give the Confeds a chance to hold Houle off. He smiled at the thought. If God was on their side, as Mandy said He surely must be, then Taggart's reinforcements would arrive in a few hours on the rail lines, fully equipped. That was a long damn time in battle, though.

Ahead, one of the battlecars veered left, and Frank looked to where they were headed. Trucks... a line of trucks in the distance. They wouldn't be undefended, but that didn't really matter anymore. Frank knew that he either won here today, buying the Confederation time, or everything would collapse.

"All units," he shouted on his little handheld radio, "turn south-southwest. The *Lizzy Borden* found us a target."

\* \* \*

Jaz galloped into Harrisburg with Choony close behind, and when she got to the HQ, they dismounted and handed the reins to one of Michael's men outside. She glanced at Choony to make sure he was ready, then the two of them entered the tent. Inside, it was all like, dingy and poorly lit. Jaz wrinkled her nose.

Michael's voice came from her right, startling her. He said, "Sorry my new home isn't up to your standards."

Jaz looked at him, but she couldn't tell if he was kidding or not. She decided it was best to pretend he was. Dudes lightened up when she smiled at them, so she did. She was rewarded with a smile back from Michael. It always worked. "Hi, Michael. Where do you need us?"

Michael shook Choony's hand, then gave her a brief hug. He said, "We couldn't send you out on mission with this mess brewing, but now we got a new mission. I hope you two enjoyed your vacation..."

Jaz said, "So, like, where do you need us? We're fresh and ready to do whatever you need, boss."

Michael's face lost its cheer. He said, "Yes. It's time to turn-to on defense, I'm afraid. Head to the gate and then man the wall sector just north of it. Your marksmanship will be a valuable asset there."

Jaz saluted, then she and Choony said their goodbyes and left for their assignment.

Before they were halfway there, the faint popping noise she had heard near the HQ had become loud and continual in the distance ahead of them. She felt her adrenaline rising. "Let's go kick some Mountain butt, Choon. Give me a good-luck kiss before we go get ourselves killed?"

Jaz grabbed his shirt and pulled his face toward hers. She was quickly reminded of what she was fighting for. Her grin was half for Choony, who always lit her fireworks when they kissed, and half for the thought of joining the battle. She was addicted to both feelings, she decided, and that was just fine. One could be a lover and a warrior at the same time.

They walked toward the wall hand-in-hand, each in their own thoughts as they headed back into battle yet again. Somehow, she always felt stronger with him at her side.

\* \* \*

Carl decided that the tempo of battle really had slowed. It wasn't only his imagination or wishful thinking. The enemy vehicles still moved, but not as much, not as aggressively. The Confed raiders must have had some success severing Houle's lines of fuel supply. Those M1s, and even the Strykers, required fuel in vast quantities to be effective. Without mobility, the Confed's larger numbers would allow them to dictate the battle's flow. God bless Frank and the other battlecar crews!

"Mortars," he shouted into his handheld radio, "I need barrage at seven-five meters from my position, bearing one-eight-zero. Danger close."

His aide shouted to the unit, "Incoming mortar fire, take cover. Down, down, down."

Carl watched as his platoon dove face-first into the dirt. They weren't highly trained like some of Michael's units were, but they had enough battle experience to know they should follow an order like that and *then* ask questions, not the other way around.

*Boom, boom, boom.* In a few seconds, the advancing platoon of Mountain infantry, along with a couple Oshkoshes, were torn apart by heavy mortar fire. Not the homemade stuff from Lebanon and Brickerville, but the good stuff that had come from Taggart back east, and from the armory the Confed had raided.

"Charge by squads," he shouted as soon as the thirty-second barrage ended. "Go get those bastards." He rose to his hands and knees and then to his feet, and sprinted forward. He ran ten meters and hit the dirt again. Then he took aim, looking for any enemies, as the other half of his unit bolted past him. Ten meters ahead, they hit the dirt. Meter by meter, Carl's unit advanced in leaps and bounds. Normally the leader of a Band wouldn't be on the front lines, but with the enemy's mobility, it was unavoidable. Now the bastards would regret this penetration to the Timber Wolves' rear areas.

*Bang, bang.* He fired two rounds into a camouflaged soldier, striking his chest and neck. Carl grinned; no trauma plates to protect the soldier's neck. He glanced to the rear toward Harrisburg. The smoke and explosions back there showed how tenacious the Mountain's soldiers were. When the two Army Groups had approached, the Confederation forces drove a wedge between the two. Yes, it meant the friendly forces had attackers on both sides, but the enemy units were now widely separated from one another, unable to concentrate their efforts.

Meanwhile, the Confederation forces were all together, able to respond quickly to major thrusts as they occurred.

The Confed troops outnumbered the attackers, so this was a plan that had worked so far. Mostly.

An hour ago, Right Flank North broke ranks to chase retreating Mountain forces, but it was a trap. Michael had shifted the whole line to shore up RFL, but as Houle's forces followed up, that now left them in control of this end of the bridge. Some of the Army group units were attacking Harrisburg haphazardly, but the city wasn't mobile and Houle's advantage in quality and equipment made his forces frighteningly effective at attacking fixed defenses.

So far, the city held. Michael had spent the last hour trying to dislodge Army Group South from the bridgehead. Then fifteen minutes ago, several Mountain units had broken through into the middle area between Right Flank North and South, threatening to cut the Confed line in half lengthwise, but both flanks had pushed in toward the enemy and now the Mountain unit ahead should be the last of that breakthrough to survive his bloody counterattack. When his troops up ahead began to cheer, so did he. The threat had been repulsed. Carl gave them five seconds to celebrate, then ordered his units back into position.

They had not yet had any luck dislodging Army Group South to retake the bridgehead, despite terrible losses on both sides. He had the ominous feeling that they were losing this battle. Cassy better come up with something quickly, or this would not end in their favor.

* * *

1600 HOURS - ZERO DAY +415

Ree hastily opened the door and waved Kim and the others inside. He clanged the door shut behind them and turned to evaluate what Kim had brought. Ten soldiers, with full standard field packs for them and Kim alike. Ree nodded in approval. "All right, we have little time. Explosions are getting closer now and I doubt we will hold the fort for another half-hour."

Kim walked to one wall, which appeared to be nothing but bare cement with contraction lines running from floor to ceiling every four feet. He bent down and did something at the floor, then shifted four feet to his right and repeated the process. Ree watched as Kim stood and stepped back. A second later, a segment of the cement wall slid inward and to the right. The new opening revealed a tunnel, six feet wide. Kim said, "Two with me in front, the rest behind our Great Leader. Last man, flip the switch to the left of the door."

Ree followed Kim and the two front guards down the tunnel, and a few seconds later he heard a faint grinding noise as the cement wall closed up again. Along the tunnel, bright 12-watt lights had been mounted in the ceiling every ten feet, lighting the way. The tunnel would go over four hundred feet to the west, then turn northwest. Ree smiled. They were out of danger, for now.

The tunnel shook and, even down there, Ree imagined he could hear the explosions going on above. Or maybe he actually could. He estimated that he was beneath the infirmary at that point, but he had no idea what could explode in there to make such a tremor.

A few minutes later, the tunnel turned right. They passed six foot tall stacks of crates lining one wall, stretching half the distance to the exit. Then the tunnel's smooth cement ended at a brick wall, and the troops came to a halt. Everyone was silent for some reason, but even to Ree, the silence just felt appropriate to the moment. An ominous feeling permeated the very air he breathed.

When Kim glanced at him, Ree nodded. He then turned to the wall and pressed on a pattern of three bricks. There was an audible click. Kim put both hands on the brick wall and pushed. It slid out about six inches, then slid to the left. Beyond was a small office.

Kim motioned to the soldiers, who walked in a line into the office, the first man stopping at a door on the opposite wall. The man turned the handle and pushed the door open as he stepped aside, and those behind him bolted through the doorway. They arrayed themselves in a semicircle outside the office, weapons at the ready, allowing them to cover every direction.

Only then did Ree leave the secret tunnel to enter the office. He turned and closed the brick "door" behind him, then strode forward out of the office to stand in the middle of the troops within the warehouse proper. He looked around the place and saw that it was only a very small warehouse. He had never been beyond the brick wall before, but he had the local map memorized. To his left would be a steel rolling bay door and a regular personnel door, both leading outside and facing the marina.

The rest of the building was essentially barren, with only trash scraps here and there to give the illusion of being just another abandoned building. Ree knew that in reality, this warehouse was ideal as a hideout. It had been abandoned for a couple of years before the invasion, but was small enough that no one had been too eager to lease it. It had no windows and only those two doors to the outside. In other words, it was hidden in plain sight and no one could see inside.

Ree said, "Ears!" The soldiers turned their heads to listen, and Ree continued, "We have six hours until it's dark enough outside for us to move out. Get some sleep, half on and half off. Sleep on a two hour cycle, so that everyone gets a chance. I want you all wide awake by the time we must scurry to the American marina like wharf rats. From among those not sleeping, two men will cover the doors at all times."

The ten soldiers responded in unison, quietly acknowledging the order. Then Ree and Kim went back into the small office, closed the door behind them, and each sat in one of the three office chairs inside.

Kim took a deep breath, closed his eyes for a moment, then looked at Ree and said, "Great Leader, I thank you for giving me the opportunity to continue to protect you and serve your needs."

Kim closed his eyes and, leaning back, interlaced his hands behind his head. "You are most welcome, my loyal soldier. We began this together, and your faithfulness has not wavered, so we will also end it together."

Ree heard Kim ask, "When we leave here and arrive at the island in safety, where then will we go? Or do you intend to stay on the island?"

"I don't yet know, Major. There are radios on the island that must have withstood the EMPs. There may even still be soldiers there, for all we know. And it has a very modern closed-loop food production system, so if we can get that running again, staying is an option. We will know more when we listen to whatever radio chatter exists."

"Yes, sir."

Ree thought Kim sounded exhausted. It was still early, but Kim's sleep cycle was odd and always had been. He said, "Try to rest up, Major. It will be awhile before we can sleep again, so we might as well take advantage of the next four hours."

Ree leaned forward, crossed his arms on top of the desk, and rested his head on his arms. In minutes, he drifted to sleep. He dreamed of home, and slept with a faint smile on his face.

# - **20** -

1815 HOURS - ZERO DAY +415

REE WAS JOLTED awake by a single, faint metallic clank. He glanced at his watch and saw that only two hours had passed. He rubbed his eyes, then looked around in confusion as he listened. He couldn't hear the noise again, however, but he wasn't sure it had been real and not some dream.

Then he heard the sounds of birds outside, coming faintly through the corrugated metal siding. One bird, then two, and then more than he could easily count since they chirped over one another. Some part of his mind realized that the chirping was not the screeching call of seagulls.

Ree got to his feet and shook Major Kim. "Get up. Something is wrong. Get up, dammit."

Kim raised his head and stared groggily at Ree, but nodded. He got unsteadily to his feet and picked up his rifle. Clearly confused, he asked, "What is it, sir?"

Ree shook his head. He wasn't sure what it was, but his gut said to pay attention, so he damn sure would. "I hear birds. Listen, they are all around us."

Kim cocked his head to listen, and when he tuned in on the bird chirping sounds, he frowned. "Nothing odd about birds, sir. Although those aren't seagulls, nor are they on the roof or overhead wires."

Ree hadn't realized that. He nodded, taking the observation in and considering it. Birds would be up above, too, wouldn't they? Not merely all around them. "Major, alert the men. Form defense around this office."

Kim didn't waste time bowing or saluting, instead bolting from the office without another word. Ree heard him quietly waking those who slept outside the office, and a faint murmur from the guards who had been awake and on sentry. If they were attacked, Ree decided, he would flee back into the tunnel, closing it behind him. Kim would do his duty and fight off any attacker as long as he could.

And he still wasn't sure it was an attack, so he didn't panic yet. Calmly, he walked to the concealed door to the tunnel and activated it, allowing it to open just a crack, just in case. He could wait out half the war by himself in that hidden corridor, after all.

After what seemed like ten minutes, the bird sounds stopped abruptly. Ree called out, "Major Kim, report. What is going on out there?"

There was no response for a moment. Then one of the soldiers—not Kim— said through the door, "The major has gone outside with two men, sir. They are chasing away the bothersome birds."

Ignoring the hint of insolence, Ree told the man to carry on and waited. And waited. At last, he sat down in the chair again and struggled to keep his attention where it needed to be. He glanced at his watch and saw that Kim had been gone twenty minutes. "Soldier, report. What is the status out there?"

There was no reply. Ree tried again, louder, but still got no response. His fear had waned in that twenty minutes, and now boredom shifted into anger. How dare a mere soldier ignore him. Him! General Ree, Great Leader of New York! It was unforgivable. He waited a few more minutes, then decided he'd had enough. If you wanted something done right, you had to do it yourself. That was an American saying, but it certain rang true at the moment. He stormed to the office door and flung it open, then stomped into the warehouse area looking for the nearest soldier. Whoever it was, that man would suffer greatly for ignoring him, he decided. The thought warmed his liver as he crossed the threshold into the warehouse.

Ree stopped abruptly. His mind tried to make sense of what was going on. There were twice as many people as there should be. He realized most were American, and one of those traitorous Yankee dogs sat in a folding chair, facing the office door. He wore a white tee shirt, khaki pants, capitalist branded sneakers, and had the ridiculous fedora-style hat on his head, covering his face. Americans and their gangster fedoras. Pah.

"What is the meaning of this," Ree demanded, and began to raise his rifle at the American in the chair. The sounds of a dozen or more rifles being racked stopped Ree mid-movement. His eyes went wide as he saw so many barrels pointed at him. "Damn you, answer me," he raged, but self-preservation had introduced a seed of doubt. He tried to calm himself, both to avoid being shot and to clear his mind. "How dare you point weapons at General Ree!"

The man in the chair chuckled, the stupid fedora still hiding his cowardly American monkey-face, no doubt covered with monkey hair. The disrespectful little shit then finally looked up, grinning.

Ree froze and his eyes went wide. Rage and outrage competed in his mind, but they both lost out to disbelief, because there before him—clearly alive—sat Spyder, the treacherous Latino gang leader whom the Americans had killed, strung up, and burned. He was once Ree's henchman, but he had never been anything but a headache. All thoughts for Kim's safety left his mind. A bubble formed, rising into his brain. Shock, outrage, fear and hate boiled together and mixed with panic.

The man snorted, and Ree felt the cold derision behind that one simple gesture. Spyder's eyes were unwavering and cold as ice when, smiling, he said, "General Ree. I had no idea I'd ever see you again."

Ree felt himself losing control, the bubble in his mind bursting. He tried to stop himself, but screamed, "This is not possible. You are not possible. Dog!"

Spyder ignored the insult. "When my little birdies told me you was all holed up here, *puto*, they didn't say it was you, just some fucking slant-eyes. Imagine my surprise when I recognized your little goddamn toady. Guess what I did to him?"

Ree's eyes narrowed. No one should talk to him that way. His rank had earned him respect even from his enemies, but this piece of garbage knew nothing of respect. "If you've harmed him, I'll see to it that you burn for it, Spyder."

The gangbanger laughed at Ree's threat. "Empty, yo. You ain't so good at bargaining when you isn't in charge, kimchi. Don't worry, though. I didn't hurt him. Instead, I told him I'd let him live if he could cough up an officer higher ranked than his own *pinche* ass. *Te dejaron arollao*, my old friend. Sucks to be you, today, eh?"

Ree grit his teeth and remembered that he still had a rifle in his hands. He hissed, "That is impossible, American pig dog. You are not even smart enough to spell your own name correctly. Tell me how you could outsmart my loyal aide? You could not."

Spyder laughed loudly at that. It was a full belly-laugh, and Ree almost thought the American would have tears from his pathetic, undisciplined display of emotion. He felt his anger grow at being mocked by one such as this... this *Spyder*. The gangster's ancestors must be so ashamed of him. Ree's rage burned hotter, brighter, threatening to consume him. Only with the greatest of effort did he stop himself from trading his own life for that fool's.

When he could breath again, Spyder choked out, "Oh, dear old friend! I don't got to be smart, *esse*. I only got to be quick. Spyder is quick like ninjas, fool. A gun in his mouth changed his mind pretty quick, yo. He walked us right in here, and we took over without a shot. Your soldiers, they are not as brave and loyal as mine, *acho*. I told you long ago, when you were the king and talkin' down to me like a dog, I told you. I said I'd get you, one day."

"And so you have, but not through your own skill. Only because of a traitor. Like yourself. You have not earned that pride, foolish American."

But instead of being angry at that mortal insult, Spyder only smiled. "I ain't a traitor. Maybe to America, but not to you. Know why?"

"Because you are too stupid to understand the meaning of the word."

"Ha. No, it's because I was never your dog, *puto*. I had to lay low all this time, buildin' my esses up again, but I'm the real king. Not you."

"I came and demolished you and your army of comic book gangsters. You were nothing until I gave it to you."

"No, *esse*. I was here 'fore you, and I'll be here when you're gone. That's why your man betrayed you. He saw how worthless you is without an army behind you. Shit, you screwed up the whole beautiful setup even with an army."

"That is a lie! It was people like you who destroyed the glorious plan. And Kim would never betray me. He must be dead."

Spyder stopped, and a smile crept across his face. "You're an idiot. I built my army because of who I am, not my rank. You be just a poser with a rank. Your little pet monkey, Kim? He knew it. He handed you to me on a silver platter, gook."

One of Spyder's gangbanger thugs came forward then, dragging Major Kim with him. Kim's hands were bound in front of him with a zip tie. As he was roughly shoved to a spot next to Spyder, Kim looked at the ground, not at Ree.

Of course. The traitor Kim had proven himself a coward now, so now he would not look to see the judgment on Ree's face. Very well, Ree thought, but if he was going to die, there was no way that traitor could live. Kim's crime was worse than Spyder's, because the gangster never pretended to be anything but the worthless scum he was. Kim had pretended to be a soldier of Korea—a high and noble creature—but he did not deserve the title. He was lower than the gangster who refused to die.

Ree allowed his body to relax. "Little brother, you disappoint me and your ancestors alike." Then Ree's body coiled and sprang into one fluid movement, shifting his rifle's barrel from pointing at the floor to Kim. He pulled the trigger, snap-firing a three-round burst. Two bullets struck the miserable traitor in the stomach and chest, and Ree grinned savagely.

The next moment, everything sounded like the New Year celebration in Pyongyang, full of pops and snaps and flashes and smoke. The room tilted crazily, then Ree found himself lying on his side with his face on the floor. He stared at Kim with open hatred, and the bastard finally looked Ree in the eyes. Kim's mouth opened and closed wordlessly, like a fish out of water, and he toppled over like a tree falling. Ree felt the rage in him fade away.

As the lights began to dim, Ree saw Spyder's legs—the

rest was out of view and he lacked the energy to look up— walk up to Ree. Spyder said something, but it came out sounding only like a confusing series of noises.

There was one last, loud bang and then all was black.

* * *

0400 HOURS - ZERO DAY +416

Carl grimaced as the doctor sutured the gash over his left eyebrow, and counted the stitches as they went in. Twelve, in the end. "It could be worse," he said.

"Seen worse," the doctor said. She stepped back and eyed her work. "It'll hold. Now get the hell back out there and save us."

Carl gave her a faint smile and nodded. "You take care of my boys and girls back here. The rest of us out there will do what we can, and I'll try not to send any more back your way. Good luck."

The doctor nodded and turned to the next patient without another word. There were more wounded than the doctors could take care of, and Carl knew someone had probably died while they were busy taking care of him. The idea of it pissed him off, but he knew that without him, the lines would crumble. Sometimes, it was just the presence of their leader that kept troops fighting to victory in the face of impending defeat.

He grabbed the nearest bicycle and pedaled furiously toward the front. He passed out of Harrisburg through the gate, across the bridge while keeping as low as possible, and entered into Hell. The Confed troops had retaken a quarter-mile space around the bridgehead, but the enemy's two army groups had finally met up and had begun to hammer at his troops in unison. Thankfully, the M1 tanks had become less effective, since this was no longer "maneuver warfare." The only good news was that his Confederation army had just been reinforced by a battalion of fresh fighters from Lebanon, albeit poorly equipped. That was fine—there was plenty of gear lying around for them to upgrade.

Michael's special forces troops, the ones he had gathered and been training with when all this started, had taken out a few of the M1s and over half the enemy Strykers during the night's fighting. The once-shifting lines that had put the Confederation back in control of the bridgehead now meant the end of maneuver warfare, slowing the Mountain's units down further. That had made them easier targets for Michael, though most were still banging away at Harrisburg merrily.

The silver lining was that with those losses, the Mountain's "C3" capacity—command, control, communications—had degraded significantly. It still beat the hell out of the Confed's own feeble capacity, though, and the losses to Michael's special ops teams had been heavy. The loss of those irreplaceable special forces troops had been worth it, since they succeeded, which Carl decided was a damn morbid thought.

He made it to his command post, swept the canvas flap aside and went in. Lanterns within lit up the space brightly, making it hard to see for a moment. "SitRep," he said as his eyes adjusted.

A man with lieutenant's bars saluted him, and when Carl returned the gesture, the lieutenant said, "The lines are holding, sir. With only a few tanks and Strykers left, it has turned into basically an infantry battle and we have numerical superiority."

"Last night, they had artillery fire on our positions. What's the situation there?"

"Our counter-battery fire was effective. Unfortunately,

theirs was just as effective. Essentially, we destroyed each other's artillery. If they have any left, they aren't firing. Neither are we."

Carl frowned. He didn't like the idea of his artillery sitting silent, but Michael knew what he was doing, so he couldn't really complain. Not to this junior officer. "So how many guns do we have left sitting around?"

"Three, sir. Michael reports the enemy may have two still operational. If we need to fire ours, we can—"

"But they'll take our guns out and then fire without fear," Carl said, interrupting. "Very well, keep them on counter-fire duty. Have we heard from the battlecars?"

The man nodded. They are still wreaking havoc on the enemy's fuel convoys. They report the convoy defenses are getting weaker, not stronger."

Carl raised an eyebrow and relaxed slightly. "That's good news. I guess they're running out of forces to spare on guard duty."

"Yes. Michael's last briefing report said he believes Houle sent everything he could at us, but hadn't counted on how much we've grown in the last few months, nor on Taggart's units supporting us. He says that's just a guess, but a good one."

Carl paused. What would the enemy do now? A shiver ran up his spine. At the lieutenant's confused look, Carl said, "This was all-or-nothing warfare, right? Well, these are *not* all that Houle has. Have you seen one aircraft since this started?"

The lieutenant shook his head. "Of course not. I mean, our crop duster fleet, but they can't hurt even the Oshkoshes with those little bombs of theirs. They're mostly good for getting a good strategic view of the battle, and harassing the enemy a little."

"Funny," Carl said without a trace of humor, "when we

fought the Empire, those same crop dusters were a game changer. Against the Mountain, they're mosquitos."

"Yes, sir."

Carl let out a long, slow breath, then said, "Very well. Keep the supplies going up to the front lines and the wounded coming down. I've got something to do."

He spun on his heels, heedless of the junior officer's salute, and headed toward his HQ. Its comm room was a haphazard bunker, dug in and covered over with lumber and dirt. Such a position was safe from mortars, but not from modern air-to-ground missiles, and that was what had been tickling the back of his mind. He sat down at a station and turned the radio unit to Ethan's reserve channel. "Charlie Two, this is Carl. You there?"

A moment later, the radio crackled. "Yeah, how are things? We were worried about you after that artillery duel."

"I'm fine. Listen, where the hell are Houle's jets? He has to have a few, right?"

"He must have some out at Pendleton, if nothing else."

"Right. So either Houle didn't have access to those planes, which implies Camp Pendleton isn't on board with the Houle dictatorship, or he does have access but hasn't used them. Yet."

Ethan's voice crackled, coming through garbled. Then he repeated himself. "Maybe they're a last-ditch thing. They aren't exactly making anymore jet fuel, you know. Nor jets, for that matter."

Carl nodded. His thought exactly. "They blew their wad trying to break through here, and we've managed to grind them to a halt even though it was touch and go for a while. We got real lucky, yeah? So maybe now would be the time for any last-ditch efforts."

There was a pause. After about fifteen seconds, the radio crackled to life again. "Copy that. It's possible. We can't check, though. We won't know until they're shoving Hellfire missiles up our butts."

"Can't you check your little birdies?"

The reply was immediate. "Negative. We get one chance at that. The one bird that could tell us is unfriendly. We can't connect twice."

So. If Ethan hacked a satellite, they'd see it and take steps to deny it to him. He would have only a short window to work in. But what good was it to have a connection to a satellite, then? Damned if he used it, damned if he didn't. Crap. "Copy that. Put your thinking hat on and figure out a way to at least find out if we're about to get hit from the air."

"Um... Ten-four, Carl. You too, eh? Meanwhile, an aerial recon report just in. The Mountain is shifting troops to strengthen Army Group North. You may want to keep up with that."

Carl thanked Ethan and terminated comms. He turned to his staff and barked orders to strengthen the bridgehead's north perimeter. That situation, unlike his worries about airplanes, was real and immediate. He'd worry about hypothetical air strikes later.

\* \* \*

0700 HOURS - ZERO DAY +416

Nestor grabbed the prisoner by the scruff of the neck, his fingers turning white from the force of his grip, and shoved him face down into the dirt. Nestor felt the urge to wash his hand where he had touched the bastard. The Mountain soldier looked to be maybe twenty years old, but he was clean shaven, his hair trimmed, and he had some actual fat on him. Lazy, overprivileged pig... And he was pale. No one was pale these days, and it marked the man more clearly than any uniform could.

Nestor imagined himself slicing the man's throat open. His voice tight from the effort of controlling himself, he said, "You will operate this fucking radio, or Ratbone here will skin you alive."

The soldier, who wore sergeant stripes, spat blood from his torn lip and climbed to his hands and knees. "You'll kill me anyway," he said, voice cracking.

Nestor reviled the panic in the man's voice, but killing him wouldn't accomplish the goal. "To the contrary. I don't give a fuck about you. If you cooperate, we'll take your weapons but not your life. I'll give you three MREs and send you on your way. That's my promise, and it's the best deal you're going to get. After that, it'll be Ratbone making the offers, and he's a sick fuck...so choose wisely."

Nestor stared into the man's eyes, unwavering. He had meant it when he said Ratbone would be the next to question the prisoner, but intellectually, he preferred getting his way more quickly.

The sergeant stared back for five seconds, then blinked and looked away. A tear formed at the corner of his eye. "Fine. I'll do it."

"Good," Nestor said. Smart guy. This particular message he was trying to get out was important enough to spare a prisoner's life if it would help him send it where it needed to go. "Turn on the radio in that Stryker and tune into the non-military bands. Show me how to change the frequency, and I'll do the rest."

The sergeant nodded, and Nestor led him back into the cramped interior of the immobilized Stryker. He watched as the sergeant turned on first one system, then another. The radio's faceplate lit up with a bunch of function symbols he didn't understand. The sergeant said, "Now what?"

"Civilian bands. Show me how to change frequencies."

The man pressed a few buttons. Nothing came out of the speakers, but he said, "Alright. This pad lets you type in a direct frequency, while these two buttons shift frequency up and down manually. This other button will encrypt your transmission, but unless the other end has the same gear, they won't be able to decrypt it."

Nestor nodded and had the sergeant removed, leaving him alone inside the Stryker. From the inside, the damn thing looked cramped as hell, and stuffed with technology. It didn't have the menacing, deadly appearance it did on the outside.

He pressed a series of numbers. A second later, static came through, then broken voices. "Fall back... the wall... before the bastards..."

Nestor thought it sounded like Ethan's voice. He pressed the up and down buttons a few times until he found the exact channel, removing the static, then put on the headphones. Into the microphone, he said, "Night Ghost One Actual to Charlie Two Actual. Come in."

There was a short pause before the reply came through. "Charlie Two here."

"Charlie Two, listen up," Nestor replied. "Whatever you're doing out there pissed Houle off enough to send in the big dogs. We observed about a dozen jet fighters heading east, going your way."

"Shit. Really? What's your location and what was their bearing?"

"My twenty is western Pennsylvania, and they were flying east, high up. That's all I know. Where else would they be going, though?"

"Copy that. Thanks."

"Ten-four. Let us know if you need anything."

"Copy that. Night Ghost One out." Nestor clicked the radio off. He had lost half a dozen men and women during the ambush that secured this Stryker, but there had been no time to play it safe. The Confederation, and especially the Clan, had to know what was coming their way. One pass from a dozen fighters could possibly shatter their forces.

He climbed out of the Stryker and looked around. "Give the sergeant three MREs and some water, then set him loose. Ratbone, get a couple sticks of dynamite so we can make sure they don't salvage this beast. Toss the corpses inside, too."

Ratbone mounted a horse and headed south, toward their encampment and supplies, and Nestor watched the crazy little monster ride away. He hoped his warning had come in time.

* * *

0700 HOURS - ZERO DAY +416

Cassy stood in the HQ pavilion with Michael, who was examining the map on the table and comparing it to a digital one Ethan had sent via HAMnet. The two chatted back and forth on the radio, updating each other on new developments. It was vital at this point because the Mountain King had finally sent in real aircraft, according to Ethan.

To Carl, she said, "I guess we put up a stiffer fight than they'd imagined."

Carl grinned at her. He was shifting from foot to foot, but Cassy understood his anxiety. When were those damn planes going to hit? She almost just wanted to get it over with. He said, "With Michael and Ethan now moving our units around like this, I'm hoping we take minimal damage. But if they bring in bombers, we're screwed."

"Don't fighters have bombs?" Cassy raised an eyebrow at him.

"Yeah, little ones. And missiles. But they're a scalpel, used to hit specific targets. Bombers, well, they're like Gallagher, spraying watermelon everywhere."

"So where are those planes?"

A moment later, her question was answered when the mobile air raid siren they had rigged to a wagon, taken from the Clanholme watchtower, began its low and lonely wail. The sound quickly grew louder by the second until it had become a terrible scream that echoed all across Harrisburg.

Michael shouted at Cassy and Carl over the din, "Take cover, dammit." He turned back to the table and began alerting the larger units' commanders about the threat.

Cassy grabbed Carl's shirt sleeve. "Come on, man! The Army will push hard at us as soon as those planes strike."

Carl nodded and followed her. They darted out of the tent and raced toward the wall, two blocks away. When they were halfway there, Cassy saw the jets in the distance. They were coming in fast, and seemed to grow larger just in the time it took her to glance. Smoke streaked away from them, leading toward the wall, seeming to spreading farther apart as they approached. She guessed there were about twelve smoke trails, though she didn't count them. That was consistent with what Nestor had said. Thank God for Nestor's alert or they'd have been caught with their pants down. Even with the alert, she knew, they'd suffer under those planes but at least they had been able to spread out and take cover.

To either end of the bridge, massive fireballs rose and the shockwave was deafening. Cassy felt like she had been struck with a huge hammer, but she kept to her feet despite staggering. Ahead, she saw that the wall had been blown out like it had been thin as paper. Any enemy troops who crossed the bridge wouldn't be funneled through the narrow gate that had once been there. No more choke point...

Not all the missiles struck the wall, though. Half had actually peppered the area behind the wall, striking buildings that now burned even as their rubble and shrapnel still rained down over a huge area. But the jets weren't done; they came in low, strafing the Confed positions. She saw one house collapse in on itself under the strafing.

Once the planes were over the city's edge, they veered sharply and hit their afterburners, screaming off in the same direction from which they had come, and she knew they'd be back in minutes. As she ran, she looked to the horizon and saw two more groups of planes, though at this range they were merely dots on the horizon. Little puffs of smoke announced more missiles incoming.

Cassy stopped and snatched Carl by his jacket to halt him. "More missiles," she shouted, then moved toward a culvert. If those missiles struck farther into the city than the last wave, she and Carl were at risk themselves. "Take cover."

Carl nodded, and glanced around. He saw the culvert, used to divert overflow rainwater. It was only a few feet deep, but he didn't hesitate to follow her as she dove in. They lay face down in the ditch, soaking up a light trickle of cold water that flowed through it.

She pulled out her radio and clicked it on. "Charlie One Actual to Charlie Two," she shouted.

"Mike One Actual, go for Charlie Two." It was Michael's voice.

Cassy cursed herself for a fool. Of *course* her little handheld wouldn't reach all the way to Clanholme. But Michael's radio would. "A dozen jets just hit the wall. Two more groups on the horizon, missiles incoming," she blurted, the words racing out.

"Affirmative. Expect more. Take cover, Charlie One Actual. It's time for Omega. Mike One out."

Cassy's mind spun trying to recall what Omega was.

She'd heard it, she had been briefed, but she was in a near-panic and the words weren't coming to her. "Shit."

Carl looked at her from his prone position. "Cover your head with your arms," he said, his voice calm and firm.

Cassy found herself reflexively following his instructions, and she was actually glad to have someone give her a specific action to take. She covered her head with her arms and began counting seconds in her mind. When she got to three, there were more explosions all around her, louder, shaking the ground itself like an earthquake. A jet streaked overhead, and she heard its guns chewing up buildings, dirt, derelict cars and anything else in its path.

"Shit," she cried out reflexively, and curled into a ball. After a moment, she looked up and saw Carl doing the same. They sat up together and looked around. The neighborhood burned, like a scene from one of those war reports back in the day, or like something out of a World War II video. There was no way Harrisburg could withstand this assault for long.

\* \* \*

Ethan finished with Michael and, on the heels of new reports coming in about jets and missiles, he looked at Amber. She had been furiously scribbling notes as he talked to various field commanders, and now looked at him expectantly. He said, "This is it, isn't it? They couldn't crack us, so they're going to vaporize us."

Amber stared him in the eyes. "Dammit. I heard what Michael said about it being time for Omega. What are you waiting for?"

"It'll cripple them, but it'll cripple us too. And not just us, but almost everyone who has made any progress rebuilding. Can I do that *again*? Even if not doing it costs us our freedom, or even our lives?"

Amber's eyes narrowed. "What the hell is Omega?"

Ethan saw her eyes ablaze, her brow furrowed, lips pursed, jaw clenched...

"Now Ethan." She was pumping adrenaline and ready to pounce on him if he dicked around with the fate of the Clan.

He took a deep breath and let it out slowly, trying to get rid of some tension. He eyed her nervously, then said, "Omega is the last resort. The final option. I launch a ballistic missile into high orbit and detonate it there. It does no real nuclear damage, but the EMP covers however much territory I decide it must, based on altitude. Any EMP wide enough to take out all of Houle's assets not hidden inside NORAD. It will also take out everything we've built with the radios and the Raspberry Pi modules and so on."

Amber listened carefully throughout his explanation, and her eyes never left his. He could almost feel her boring into his skull to ferret out the truth behind his words. She was silent for a dozen heartbeats before she replied. "Did you have something to do with the first EMPs? Goddammit, Ethan, you tell me the truth right now, or so help me—"

"Whoa," Ethan said and held up his hands, cutting her off. "No. Those were launched by our enemies, as far as I know. I had nothing to do with with it in any way that I'm aware of."

Amber's face was flushed, and Ethan noticed a sheen to her forehead. Sweat. She was livid, he could plainly see.

"If you launch another EMP, what happens to the tanks and planes out there?" Her voice was abruptly monotone and emotionless. Or rather, he decided, overly full of emotion and only barely under self-control.

"They die. Cannons and guns still work, but without the ability to move or aim, they do little good. The planes stop flying and start falling."

"And our own artillery?"

"Dead too, although with time we can replace the control modules with fresh ones from the depot. They're stored in mylar bags inside metal crates that act as Faraday cages."

Amber nodded curtly. "Then what... What the fuck are you waiting for, Ethan? Do it."

He frowned. He felt his pulse begin to race at the thought of doing it. Again. Flashes of dreams came flitting through his mind, the nightmares he'd had after sentencing the rest of the world to die as they had done to America. He opened his mouth to reply, but couldn't think of what to say. How could he do this again? But how could he not?

He took another deep breath and felt shivers down his spine. His scalp tingled, as did his cheeks. Hyperventilating and adrenaline crash, he realized. "Very well. I don't know for sure that I can do it, but let's find out."

It was time to put on Dark Ryder's finest performance.

\* \* \*

Cassy and Carl darted from building to building, using the still-standing ones for cover. Once, they had to run between two burning homes to escape a cul-de-sac of flames. Her ponytail was terribly singed, while Carl lost half an eyebrow. Both had minor burns on their faces and hands.

But they had made it out alive, and now ran through the brisk morning air toward the wall. The wind felt good on her burns. "Left or right?" she asked as the street ended in a "T" intersection.

"Left, then right," Carl panted. "Then straight on."

She ignored the burning in her thighs and lungs, and put her head down to run faster. She made the second turn, then the street did indeed run all the way to the wall. It loomed ahead larger and larger as she ran. They got to the end and Carl broke right, so she followed him wordlessly. After a couple of minutes, they came to an area where a missile had blown out the wall.

The *rat-tat-tat* of a jet fighter's guns sounded, tearing large chunks of asphalt up about twenty feet ahead of them. Cassy didn't slow down, just stepped around the holes. Two Confed fighters stepped out from behind the burning carcass of a minivan, their weapons aimed at the two of them, but one recognized Carl immediately.

"Alpha! Thank God you're alive. You saw the planes? We're getting hit hard on the bridgehead." The two men lowered their weapons.

Cassy nodded and looked at Carl. "Go, get up there. And try not to get a missile up your tailpipe." She waved him toward the wall furiously.

Carl took one step, then stopped. He looked at Cassy and said, "Will you be okay? What will you do?"

"Don't worry about me, dammit. Get your ass moving. I'll see you when we win, Carl."

He nodded and sprinted away, followed by the two Liz Town fighters, leaving Cassy standing alone in the roadway.

She turned right, moving away from the wall as she ran toward Michael's HQ. She wound her way between the burning buildings scattered throughout the neighborhood, giving the flames as wide a berth as possible. When she arrived at the HQ, people were running in and out of the pavilion tent. She waited until there was a clear moment to duck in. It was dark in the tent, but with the sun's ambient light, she had no problem spotting Michael. She stepped aside to clear the doorway and called to him, while her eyes adjusted to the lower light.

Michael looked up, and when he saw her, he looked relieved. "You made it. Good," he said, and set his radio down long enough to step up to Cassy and hug her. "I feared the air strikes got you. You smell like Aunt Margo's cooking, though."

"Ran through a fire," she said. "Nothing that won't grow back."

Michael said, "We're getting pushed back. We've lost the bridge, and we're losing the bridgehead on this side. With no more wall there, once they clear a path those M1s are going to barrel across the bridge and shatter our line. Then we'll probably be evacuating the HQ to go to a fallback being set up right—"

The back half of the pavilion seemed to disintegrate. The two officers on that end of the map table and half of the table itself exploded into pink mist and shrapnel. Cassy felt a sliver of something slice the side of her neck. She put her hand to her neck, stunned, and then pulled it away, only to find it red with blood. It didn't look like enough to worry about at the moment. Her mind raced to make sense of it all, until she heard the whine of jet engines pass overhead. They had been strafed.

Cassy looked up at Michael and saw him pointing and shouting orders, but she didn't hear anything except a ringing in her ears. She understood that she was in "white space," as Michael had trained everyone to called it, a stunned state where sensory input was disrupted due to the sudden shock of an unprepared mind. Why had that thought crossed her mind? She found herself focusing on how strange it was to think of it at that moment. Slowly, the sounds around her penetrated her fog, and she became aware of voices.

"...and get the radios moved, dammit," Michael was shouting.

Cassy shook her head to clear it.

"...Cassy! Cassy, dammit, *move*. We have to get you out of here. We may have been compromised."

"How?" she asked, dumbfounded.

"Signal monitoring. Probably got a missile incoming.

Now go! Get to the wall and lead the fight while I get HQ relocated. That's an order, boss," Michael shouted.

Cassy staggered east toward the wall without thinking, just mindlessly obeying his steady, stern voice. In the fog of battle, Michael's voice was like an anchor that held people steady amidst the storm. She found her coordination returning, and ran.

* * *

Jaz shook her head to clear the daze. She remembered standing on the wall and the jets launching missiles, but she couldn't remember the impact. She wasn't on the wall anymore, though, but on street pavement. She found herself on her hands and knees, and looked around in confusion. Her rifle lay nearby, so she crawled to it. It looked undamaged. Then she looked for Choony, but didn't see him. There were bodies scattered all around her, some with clothes burning, others merely smoldering. She frantically checked several, and felt her stomach drop every time she flipped one over, but felt relief when the body wasn't Choony's.

From the nearby wall remnants came sounds of heavy, continuous shooting, and a woman's cry of pain that was cut short.

Then she felt someone's hands under her arms, lifting her up. She hadn't heard the footsteps over the din of battle. Startled, she glanced up and saw Cassy's face. For a moment, Jaz thought she had lost her mind.

"Are you okay? God, Jaz, you look like shit. Are you injured?" Cassy looked Jaz up and down.

Jaz took a moment to think about that. Was she hurt? She felt her head, then concentrated on her arms, hands, fingers. She wiggled her toes. Then she got her feet under her and cautiously stood, arms out for balance, but without Cassy's help.

"No, I think I'm okay. Where's Choony?" she cried, feeling a growing desperation.

Cassy shook her head. "I don't know. We've got to get to the wall, Jaz. After those air strikes, the ground troops will hit the wall hard. I'm sure Choony is fine, and he'll find you. But we gotta go now, dammit. We don't have time."

Jaz nodded and let Cassy pull her back toward the wall. In several places the wall had vanished, leaving only a low ridge of smoking rubble in between sections that were damaged but still stood. The gate itself had been obliterated. They climbed the few feet to the ridge of the rubble mound and went prone. Jaz looked out toward the bridge and heard herself gasp, just as Cassy did...

The scene on the bridge was a nightmare turned real. Bodies lay heavy on the ground around the bridgehead on this side, as well as on the bridge itself, but there were dozens and dozens of infantry crossing toward them. Behind the soldiers rumbled metal giants, the M1 Abrams. Their cannons were firing as fast as the crews could reload and pick a target. Left and right of Jaz, the upright segments of wall were billowing smoke and fire blossoms, seemingly at random.

Jaz felt a growing rage. Those bastards were killing innocent people for no reason but to enslave them. They had separated her from Choony, and God only knew if he was still alive. And they were coming on hard, right here and now. She tilted her head to crack her neck, took a deep breath, and settled into a battle mindset—calm and almost blank, yet tracking every movement, deciding on targets at blinding speed. She fired six rounds in six seconds, and saw five of her targets fall. Beside her, Cassy fired an M4 on single-fire mode, almost as fast. Jaz didn't waste time seeing if her targets still moved, instead just moving to the next one. Then she reloaded, and got ready to repeat the process.

\* \* \*

Cassy took three seconds to aim. The helmet sticking up over the bridge railing presented a pretty small target, but every time that bastard popped up, she heard someone nearby scream.

On one, she drew a bead on it. On two, she inhaled and then slowly exhaled. On three, she stopped exhaling and held it, squeezed the trigger, and the shot felt right. She knew it would hit, even before a spray of blood and a flying helmet announced her bullet's arrival. She was proud of that shot, even though she had heard Jaz fire three times in those three seconds. She swung her rifle to another soldier. Bang, he dropped.

Cassy took a second to thank Michael for showing her the whole "scout-mounted scope" idea. Her rifle scope was mounted far out toward the barrel, rather than up by her eye, which helped her to stay far more alert and aware of her surroundings. She could even snap-fire at targets that were up really close, which a normal scope mount would have made difficult. It had taken practice to get used to, but now she wouldn't have it any other way in this environment.

Next to her, Jaz said between shots, "Why are you... here instead of... leading the Confed?"

As Cassy reloaded, too, she replied, "Frank's the Clan leader. Michael's the war leader. Screw sitting back home to wait it out." Then she flipped her M4 to burstfire mode. She heard Jaz grunt acknowledgement, then they both returned to firing. She quickly got into a rhythm. Bang, bang. Bang, bang. Reload when empty. Repeat.

She had just finished reloading with her third 30-round

magazine when she felt Jaz punch her arm. She turned to snarl at the girl, but when she saw the look of fear on Jaz's face, she stopped. Jaz was pointing toward the enemy, but... over them.

Cassy followed where she was pointing and felt the blood drain from her face. Far away, beyond the oncoming ground troops and tanks and Strykers, she saw a line of fighters. They were arranged in three groups, and the one group she counted had twelve fighters in a V-formation. This must be every fighter that had been randomly strafing Harrisburg. If they fired missiles all at once, the Confederation line hemming in the bridge would be decimated.

Oh shit. She was in that line. "God... Jaz, *run*," she shouted, and scrambled to her feet while sliding down the rubble hill's back slope. They had only seconds to get the hell out of there, yet she knew that even if they avoided being blown up, thirty-six or so fighter planes strafing in tight formation would pulverize just about everything along their path. Well, she'd try to run anyway. She wouldn't just lay down and die.

All around her, other Confed warriors had the same idea. Not all of them ran, but enough did that some got in her way. She felt a twinge of guilt for running when so many stayed behind to man the wall, and a bit of irritation at the other ones who did run. The thought struck her that she was being a coward, but the more experienced fighter in her told her that dying pointlessly helped no one.

Behind her, she heard the rising chaos as more troops spotted what was coming and attempted to get the hell out of the area, screaming, but she knew they'd be too late. Cassy was probably too late, too, she realized, but she would run anyway. God save them all...

Ahead, a low thumping sound grew in volume and pitch, and then abruptly she saw a helicopter rise up in front of her.

It was green and looked like the incarnation of Death. Spinning chain-guns were only the cherry on top of its missile pods. The animal part of her brain knew that the strange flying creature meant death if it saw her.

The helicopter suddenly slid away sideways, leaving the area, but it fired guns and missiles as it moved. A man running just a little behind Cassy and to one side let out a weird noise, and she looked behind her in time to see most of his torso disintegrate—a parting gift from the helicopter as it fled the area. One cannon round had done that to him...

Behind her, a missile exploded close enough that she could feel some of the heat on her back. She was surprised to find herself still alive, after the helicopter had gone, but she expected to explode at any moment.

*** 

Carl stared in awe at the long line of fighters approaching. Death from above was coming fast. "Fall back," he shouted, and began grabbing men and women who were too caught up in the firefight to hear him, sending them running to the rear. He clicked his radio on and alerted Michael, as quickly as he could, that the situation changed. Then he, too, began to run. He heard on his radio as Michael openly broadcast to unit commanders with directions and fall-back locations, but it was going to be too late for many of them, Carl knew.

He was half a block away when the first missiles struck. He turned in horror to witness the devastation, but his horror only grew when he realized that only half the missiles struck the bridgehead and staging area. The other half streaked overhead and peppered dozens of buildings throughout Harrisburg. He cursed the rat bastards for that— those would slaughter civilians and soldiers alike, and half the town would probably burn down. As the concussions passed by and the noise faded, he heard Michael on the radio giving orders to Carl's unit, and he heard his second-in-command confirm the order. Dozens of jet fighters passed overhead, strafing, and one came within feet of hitting him. He looked out over Harrisburg and truly saw devastation clearly for the first time. It was a disaster.

Sunshine's name sped through his mind. He felt a sudden twinge of panic pulling at his thoughts. Was she okay? If there was a fire nearby, she wouldn't be able to flee, he realized with shock. Screw it. His unit was in good hands, so he turned right and ran hard. His Harrisburg home was only six blocks away. He put his head down and focused on his breathing and his pace, and quickly ate up the meters between him and Sunshine.

Only three minutes later, he rounded the corner and finally saw his house. His heart sank like a lead weight—the house was a wreck. It looked like old pictures of Dresden after Allied bombing, with the rear wall upright and half of a sidewall leaning inward crazily. All else had collapsed, and now burned.

Carl screamed and ran at the short brick wall that encased the property, hopping up to wedge an elbow over the top and using his momentum to get one leg swung up and over, then leverage got the rest of his bulk up and over. He landed without slowing down and ran across the huge front yard, heedless of anything around him. He passed a half-burnt body that lay in a heap, arms and legs all at unnatural angles, but it had been a man, so he didn't stop.

Seconds later, as the heat from the burning ruins blasted him, he had to stop. As the heat built up on him, he was soon forced back. He held his arms up to try to shield his face, but simply couldn't get closer. He stared at the fire, tears coursing down his face. The entire upper floor was gone, having collapsed inward. Then, like the final curtain at the theatre, the lone remaining wall slowly crumbled downward. The impact kicked up coals and flames, forcing him to back up farther still.

Carl sank to his knees, his clenched fists on his thighs, and looked up to scream at the sky.

\* \* \*

Jaz picked herself up and brushed shards of wood and plaster off herself. She looked around, trying to get a sense of her situation, when some nearby rubble seemed to moan as it shifted. She rushed over to it and began to pull off chunks of rubble, throwing them aside one after the other until she came to a large section of plywood lying flat. She grabbed the edges and pulled hard, her muscles straining, and felt it shift loose. She shoved it aside. Where the plywood had been, she saw the source of the moaning.

Cassy coughed severely when the fresher air hit her lungs, and Jaz saw a puff of dust come out. Jaz wrapped her arm around Cassy's shoulders and helped her to her feet.

"Are you hurt?" Jaz asked.

"I don't think so." Cassy gave in to a long coughing fit before continuing, "What happened?"

Well, damn if Cassy didn't look just totally confused. Jaz hoped she didn't have a concussion. "The jets fired missiles, remember? Half the city is burning. I think the lines must have collapsed, so Houle's soldiers will be coming right up our ass in a minute. And the jets are circling around again. We gotta move, Cassy."

Cassy staggered, but Jaz kept a tight grip on her. A few seconds later, Jaz felt Cassy's pace steady as she got her balance back, so she relaxed her grip.

They headed south, trying to put as much distance as they could between them and the wall's remnants. In the distance, Jaz heard a sudden increase in the faint popping noises of small arms fire. "The Mountain is pushing across the bridge. Now that they can get their tanks across, nothing can stop them. We gotta get out of here. Fall back to Renfar, maybe. Those old Renaissance Fair grounds are a maze, so we can disappear there."

Cassy grunted her agreement, and they turned to head southeast. That would allow them to skirt the flaming neighborhoods and have some chance at survival.

Jaz glanced over her shoulder and saw the entire line of jets coming again, flying in several tightly packed V formations. Whatever resistance to Houle's troops remained would vanish once those jets unleashed. And if she and Cassy didn't hurry, they would surely get blown to bits.

Out of the corner of her eye, she caught a glimpse of movement in the sky, off to her left. She tilted her head to look, forgetting the chaos around her for a moment. High above and far, far away, a brilliant dot appeared. In the span of a second, the dot grew several times larger, but without knowing the distance Jaz had no way to tell how big it truly was. What was it?

Abruptly, it flared and became far brighter than even the sun itself, and Jaz had to look away. She saw spots everywhere she looked, and suspected that if she had kept looking at it, the bright flash might have damaged her eyes.

She heard Cassy gasp, glanced at her, then looked to where Cassy stared back the way they had come. Jaz blinked rapidly to try to clear the spots, and her view cleared enough to reveal what Cassy had seen. The long line of jets was approaching from the west for another run, but something was clearly going wrong. Two veered into each other and exploded midair. The others began to bank randomly left or right, quickly turning into nosedives or flat spins. They had fired the missiles just before that, and Jaz watched in utter amazement while they too spun crazily out of control, landing in harmless fireballs far from the bridge.

In a few more seconds, the jets struck the earth one after the other. One landed on the bridgehead on the Harrisburg side, immolating tanks and a huge mass of infantry. The ground beyond the bridge, too, blossomed into a hellish peppering of fireballs.

Jaz screamed at the top of her lungs, a wordless cry of hate and victory.

Cassy stood next to her, grinning like crazy. As Jaz's cry petered out, Cassy shouted at her, "Ethan did it!"

Jaz nodded and let her rifle fall from her shoulder where she had slung it, steeling herself for what would come next. She stood silent, barely hearing Cassy's voice over the roar of the flames.

"Now let's get back to the bridge and kill some Houlites!"

# - **21** -

0500 HOURS - ZERO DAY +417

CHOONY RAISED HIS head and opened his eyes, but saw only blackness. He had a dawning realization of something heavy on his legs and chest. He let his head rest a moment as he gathered himself and collected his wits. What had happened? The last thing he remembered was jets firing missiles. He considered that for a minute, and as he woke more fully, he had a remembrance of fire, and something striking him like a massive hammer.

"Concussion," he said aloud. No one answered. He turned his head to look around, but he struck his temple on something hard and jagged. He tried to move his hand, by reflex, to his head but found he couldn't. It too was pinned. He breathed in and out deeply, biting his lip until the pain subsided. Damn, that hurt.

Dust rained down onto his face, and he spat and sputtered. Then he realized why he couldn't move, and why it was so dark. He was buried beneath rubble. "The house…"

He cautiously tried to move his right arm, and found he could. Not much, but if he kept his elbow on the ground—or whatever was beneath him—he could bring it up to his face.

An air pocket. He was alive because his top half was in some sort of bubble. He moved his hand away from his face and reached out to his right. When his arm was almost fully extended, he felt something smooth, hard, and cold. It was metallic. A washing machine, maybe.

The appliance, whatever it was, had created the 'triangle of life' he'd heard about from his mother. As a kid, she'd always told him the best place to take cover from a quake or bombings—the latter being more common in those days back in Korea—was near appliances because rubble would form a pocket next to those. This one must have fallen next to him. Which was far better than landing *on* him. Clearly, his Karma had saved him.

"Thank you, Buddha, Dharma, and Sangha," he muttered. Then he felt a faint breeze tickle his sweat-soaked neck. Somehow, he was getting at least a little fresh air. And that meant he was close to the surface. He paused to listen, breathing as quietly as he could.

Muted voices reached his ears, as though he were underwater. He felt his heart beat faster as hope surged through him. "Here! Down here!"

The voices grew louder, and Choony shouted again. He heard someone call out from above, and seconds later, the sounds of people frantically moving the rubble over him. He shouted again, every few seconds, so they could hear him.

He had no idea how long it took, but eventually, the blackness over his face moved out of the way, and he could see faces. Happy faces.

One shouted, "Survivor! Medic!" then looked at Choony again in the faint light of dawning day. "Are you hurt? We'll have you free in a minute. Damn, you're one lucky S-O-B."

Choony didn't have a chance to reply before even more of the rubble was removed, and he could feel the weight on his chest lift. His heart soared.

Two rescuers threw aside final bits of debris and then pulled him up by his arms, patting him on the shoulder and grinning like mad. "Thank God you're okay, man," said one, as the others moved off to continue the search for survivors. He pointed east. "There's an aid station set up half a block that way. Can you make it?"

Choony paused for a moment and tried to feel any terrible pain that might show injuries. He couldn't see out of his right eye, he realized. "My eye?"

The man said, "Dried blood. Maybe a scalp cut."

"I can make it," Choony said, shook the man's hand, and staggered east. It didn't take long to find the aid station. It consisted of a few pavilion tents and a lot of beds lined up on the sidewalk, no doubt taken from the nearby houses and rubble. It was overloaded with wounded. Just farther east, a small pile of person-sized black bags was stacked.

"Jaz..." he said, his voice choking. Where was Jaz? She would have looked for him. A growing sense of dread nestled in his chest, and he walked up to the nearest nurse. He was about to say something, when she spotted him.

Her jaw dropped. "Sir, come with me," the nurse said and grabbed his arm lightly, pulling him toward a tent.

"What of other survivors," Choony said, and heard the desperation in his own voice. "Did you treat a woman named Jasmine?"

The nurse shook her head. "I don't know, we're seeing too many to keep track of."

She led him into the tent and toward a vacant chair, one of the hard plastic kinds found in school rooms, and asked him to sit. She methodically took his vitals, the whole time asking questions about broken bones, nausea, difficulty breathing.

She waved at a man in scrubs, and he came over. "Probable scalp laceration, no known broken bones or

internal injuries. Possible concussion, but vitals are steady."
And then she was gone, off to the next patient.

The man nodded in greeting. "I'm Nurse Powers," he
said. Choony could see one heck of a bruise covering half his
face. "Let's see what we have here."

Choony sat patiently as the nurse used a squirt bottle to
clean off masses of blood, the water running down his face
onto his gray, dusty shirt and turning it pink. Then he felt a
sharp pain as the suturing began. The nurse kept up a steady
monologue, ignoring Choony's questions about other
survivors. Choony counted twelve stitches running from his
hairline toward the back of his head.

Finally, the nurse said, "All done. Stop by the table out
front for antibiotics. And there's a station posting names of
survivors who have been rescued from the rubble, another
block east from here."

Choony thanked him, but Powers had already turned
away for the next patient. Total time elapsed: ten minutes,
Choony figured. He made his way out of the tent, got a bottle
of antibiotics from the front table, then headed east again.
He practically ran the whole way, two blocks, ignoring the
pounding headache that struck with every jarring step.

There was a small mob arrayed in front of the one table.
To either side of it, sturdy room dividers of the sort found in
schools had been lined up, with handwritten pages posted
haphazardly on them.

Choony let out a frustrated sigh, then strode toward the
crowd, intent on sliding through the mob to get to those
pages of hope—

"Choony! Oh thank God," a woman's voice shouted from
off to his right. Jaz's voice!

His head whipped around to find her, but when he
stopped moving his head the view seemed to continue
shifting to the right, and he staggered. Through double

vision, he saw the most beautiful sight in the world rushing toward him.

Jaz grabbed him by his arms and steadied him, then wrapped her arms around him in a crushing hug. She buried her face in his neck, and he enveloped her in his arms, his cheek welded to her hair.

"Don't you ever scare me like that again, Choony," she said, and he heard her voice crack with emotion. She grabbed fistfuls of the back of his shirt, as though he might be whisked away at any moment.

Choony felt tears come to his eyes, but didn't bother to hide it or wipe them away. "I thought I'd lost you," he said, and had to sniff hard as his eyes welled over. "What happened to you?"

Still clinging to him, she didn't answer for a long moment. At last, she took one step back and wiped her eyes with her sleeve. "I was thrown clear in the blast." Then her expression grew angry. "I couldn't find you," she said. "I just prayed and prayed that you were okay. I've never been so helpless." Then Jaz charged into him again, another desperate hug.

Choony took a deep breath, eyes closed, and simply kissed her hair. For once, he had no words of wisdom, no Buddhist sayings to make the moment easier. He just clung to her like a drowning man grabbing a thrown life preserver. Without her, in truth, he knew that he *would* drown in a way.

At last they separated, from one person again into two.

Jaz said, "I got us a couple horses. Let's get the hell out of this place. And Choony? Don't you ever leave me like that again, okay? Promise me."

Choony smiled down at her. As long as he lived, he decided, that would never be a problem. "I promise."

\* \* \*

0600 HOURS - ZERO DAY +417

Cassy yawned, squinting tired eyes. The dawning light revealed the carnage that had occurred overnight in the battle against General Houle's forces. Harrisburg was in tatters everywhere, with several fires still raging out of control. The wall between town and bridge had been reduced to piles of rubble and craters.

"The bridgehead on both sides, and the bridge itself, looks like a carpet of bodies," she said to Frank. His battlecar had been destroyed a few hours ago, but he had not been injured and another car had driven him to Harrisburg. She had been with him since.

"Look how it seethes," he said, shaking his head. "Lots of wounded crawling around."

Cassy shrugged. Honestly, who gave a rat's ass? Frank, maybe. She did not. "Let them suffer or put them out of their misery. I don't care either way, but fortunately, that's Carl's problem, not ours."

"Where is Carl?"

"I think Carl's wandering Harrisburg looking for his friend, Sunshine."

"I haven't seen him since Houle's last assaults collapsed."

"Once their trucks and planes went down, they sure went banzai, didn't they?" Cassy wondered if her admiration for their bravery showed in her voice. It was the only thing she admired about them, but she'd never make the mistake of underestimating such an enemy.

"Yes, but what else could they do? Without a supply chain, their situation became win-or-die."

Cassy took a deep breath and let the rising sunlight wash over her upturned face, heedless of the dirt and blood that covered her. Eyes closed, she said, "So what do you think happens now?"

Frank put his arm around Cassy's shoulders as they stared out at the carnage together. "The Free Republic wants to join the Confederation. Didn't you say you'd grant them no vote until they've gotten themselves stable and have spent a year or two learning permaculture and so on?"

"Yeah, but I still need to think on it. They're more devastated than we are, so we may not want to take on that burden just yet. We'll see what they bring to the table, I guess. Even if we don't let them join, I think we'll do what we can to help them. They'll be good allies."

Frank only nodded. Cassy rather liked the feel of his arm around her, though, and she was content to just stand with him for a few minutes. God only knew how many sleepless nights she now faced as the Confederation recovered from this latest war.

Eventually, Frank said, "Not looking forward to all the work there is to do."

Cassy rested her head on his shoulder and felt her exhaustion grow. It was comfortable, standing together like that. Her vision swam. "Yeah. I'll be riding home soon with the wounded who can be moved. I can't wait to get back home."

Frank rested his cheek on her head for a moment. "Me too."

\* \* \*

0900 HOURS - ZERO DAY +417

Frank took his aviator goggles from the rearview mirror and put them on, adjusting the bungee strap so it didn't press so much against his ears. He glanced to his passenger and said, "Ready to go home?"

"Yeah," Ethan said. "This place is a total dump."

Frank nodded. He figured Ethan regretted his decision to volunteer driving one of the cargo trucks out to Harrisburg, though he could tell he was grateful for the ride back.

The battlecar started up with a cough, but then the engine caught and it rumbled nicely. Frank threw the column shifter into Drive. A little pressure on the gas pedal and the beast crept forward. He increased the gas as the car gained momentum, and soon they were going a respectable twenty miles per hour while off-roading. They'd be home quickly enough at that rate, and the slower speed conserved wood.

Besides, as much as he needed a shower and sleep, he needed to decompress from the battle and its aftermath before the inevitable hyperactive love-fest from his son, Hunter, when he got home. He looked forward to that with all his heart, but dreaded it as well. A leisurely drive would clear his head from all the chaos and killing.

After a few minutes of silence, Frank began to feel better, his mind less jumbled. Finally, he said, "You and Amber seem to be doing great. When are you going to make an honest woman of her?"

Ethan laughed and said, "We don't need a contract for that. But the truth is, we've been talking about it. I think she's leaning toward a Winter Solstice wedding."

"I think it's been long enough," Frank said. "I miss Jed still, but he'd want her to be happy."

Ethan nodded but remained silent, obviously lost in thought.

Frank veered the battlecar around a depression that appeared suddenly before them. The car handled the turn fine, but did kick up a bunch of dirt that make them both cough for a moment.

"Listen, if Amber and I do get married on the solstice, how would you feel about being my best man? You're my best friend in the Clan, you know? It'd mean a lot."

Frank answered without hesitating, "I'd be honored."

The rest of the drive home, Frank thought about all the changes and challenges they had gone through since the EMPs first hit, and he realized with total clarity that it was Cassy's insistence on making friends with everyone they could that had kept them alive. She fed people he would have turned away, and for that she got Taj Mahal. She negotiated trade with Brickerville when conflict was just as easy an outcome, and earned their loyalty. She sent supplies to Liz Town to help them fight off Harrisburg and Hershey, making diehard friends out of the most combative of their close neighbors.

Step after step, when Frank would have hunkered down and circled the wagons, she opened them to help others, but she did it wisely. Never when she thought it would cost more than it was worth, never when the other side wasn't going to be useful in return. She said it was all in keeping with her "permaculture principles." He had learned a lot from her example that he went ahead and applied to managing the Clanholds, and they were working out great.

And all their many blessings, even his and his family's survival, happened because he had been nice to Cassy when she had just been a strange woman who came across them in a bad situation. His wife, Mary—God rest her soul—would have turned Cassy away simply out of fear. There had been plenty of fear in those early days, and plenty since.

He smiled, wondering what the old Marketing Executive Cassy would have thought of this new version of herself.

\* \* \*

Cassy finished rubbing down her horse and giving her water, then led her into the lower stables. Once her mount was taken care of and secured after the long journey home, munching happily on hay, Cassy walked outside.

Tiffany came around the bend from the guard tower and waved her down. She smiled wanly, and when she got close, said, "Cassy, have you been to your house yet?"

"No. What's going on?"

Tiffany wouldn't meet her eyes, and looked down at the ground, at the stable, anywhere but at Cassy. "It's your mom. We've been up with her all night. She's waiting for you."

Cassy didn't ask another question. Instead, she sprinted home. The front door was ajar, as though the house itself had been waiting for her. Bright sunlight outside made the interior look pitch black on the inside, or what she could see of it through the doorway. She came to a stop at the door and took a deep breath, then opened it all the way and stepped inside.

On her living room couch, her mom lay with a pillow under her head on the armrest and a blanket draped over her. Frank and Ethan stood nearby, and looked up when Cassy entered. Their expressions were grim.

Cassy said, "Whats going on?" and could hear her voice rise in pitch.

Frank held his palm up to her, the motion for "stop," and started to hobble toward her, but she darted around him to get to her mom. She knelt beside the couch. "Mom?"

Mandy was ashen, her skin gray and moist from sweat, her eyes red-rimmed and only half open. When she saw Cassy, she smiled weakly. Cassy noticed a sick, sweet smell that was almost like when people were drunk, but Mandy didn't drink.

Mandy reached for Cassy's hand with her own, and it trembled. She looked almost too weak to do even that, and Cassy noticed how sunken Mandy's cheeks and eyes appeared. She looked as though a vacuum cleaner had sucked away half of her life, leaving only a baggy, sallow skin behind.

"Oh, sweetie, you're home," Mandy said. "I'm so glad to see you're okay."

"Why didn't you say something, Mom?"

Mandy patted her hand gently. "I stopped taking my insulin about a week ago. I didn't say anything because you were going into battle, and I didn't want you distracted."

"How could you do that? You should have told me. I'll just go get more—"

Mandy coughed, then tried to cry out her daughter's name, but she was already out the door, sprinting.

Cassy headed to the far bunker entry. She wanted to be alone and if she'd used the stairwell entry, that would defeat the purpose. She reached the shrub, saw no one around, and slid it aside. She punched in the mechanical lock code and was quickly down in the long tunnel that led to the bunker's escape hatch. Once inside, she headed for the storage segment. The lone small refrigerator sat there, taunting her, running merrily. Inside it lay life for her mom. Insulin.

Cassy reached for the refrigerator, when she heard scuffing noises behind her. Dammit, someone was there. She looked back and saw Frank. Why couldn't he just leave her alone? In her head, she screamed, and tears continued running their trail down her cheeks. Instead of screaming, she spun to face him. "How could you not tell me?" she shouted, face turning red.

Frank didn't flinch. "Your mother is sick, Cassy. She won't live much longer. They don't make insulin anymore, and we have young people who need it. When I talked to Grandma Mandy about the situation, she was the one who—"

"This was *your* idea, Frank? Goddammit, how could you do this?" she screamed. Now her eyelid began to twitch with anger.

Frank glowered at her, but his voice was even and calm as he replied, "This has to be done, Cassy. For the Clan."

Cassy's tears fell freely, now. "But that's my *mother*." In the next moment, she collapsed onto the concrete floor, feeling its coolness beneath her hot flesh.

"Can't you see, Cassy?" Frank said, his voice softer. "We lost so many people in this last battle. We only have so much insulin. There won't ever be more, not in your mother's lifetime. And if we take that away from the people we have left, *they* won't live to see that day, either. Every dose your mother takes is a chunk of life off someone else's tally."

Cassy stared up at him, sucking back tears, and the silence hung heavy between them.

"Your mother is doing a noble thing, Cassy. She's giving *life*. She's giving us a better chance to thrive. You have to know this isn't about you. I never wanted to hurt you, but this is important. It's how it has to be. *And it's her choice.*"

Cassy felt the rage slowly draining from her, leaving only... defeat? Sorrow, maybe. She was too jumbled and confused to know what she felt. His gaze met hers again, and after three heartbeats, she looked down at the ground and simply nodded. Even she had to realize the truth, when it struck her in the face like that. Her tears still fell, but she felt her heartbeat slow. She saw Frank relax his guard a bit.

"Come on," Frank said. "Mandy deserves to see her daughter before it's too late. And I'll go get Bri and Aidan."

He helped her up and wrapped one arm around her shoulders. They walked back to the tunnel that way, and she led him up the ladder to the house.

When she finally climbed up, she sat beside her mother, holding her hand. Mandy said weakly, "I'm glad you finally understand, honey. I knew you would."

Cassy nodded, forcing a smile with trembling lips.

Mandy patted her hand lightly. "There's never a good time to decide to die, my precious girl. But I lived long enough to see you rise to this challenge, and I know you and my grandkids will be all right, now. It's a good time for me to say goodbye."

Cassy struggled not to beg her mother to reconsider. She knew her mom of all people wouldn't change her mind, not about this. After a long moment, she whispered, "I've been able to spend more time with you since the war than in the ten years before that, Mom. I'm glad I got the chance to really know you. I love you."

"I love you too, sweetie."

As Cassy stayed and talked with her mother, Frank hobbled out the front door and out toward the fields where Brianna and Aidan were playing with the other kids and burning off tension. Many of those kids were still waiting for parents to come home from war, yet some never would.

Cassy sat near her mother, knowing her time was nearly up. She wanted to spend every last second with her until the very end. She held back her tears, focused on cherishing the present.

Life would go on, she knew, with all its ups and downs, triumphs and losses. The Clan would be ready to face whatever came, and maybe, just maybe, she and Frank would still be alive to deal with them together. But whatever happened between then and now, Cassy would be there for them, and so would Frank. Tonight, they'd celebrate victory and surviving. Tomorrow, they'd bury their dead. Because, in the end, life had to go on. And maybe now, they'd find it worth living in a way they never had before the war.

# # #

To be continued in Book 7...

## About the authors:

JJ Holden lives in a small cabin in the middle of nowhere. He spends his days studying the past, enjoying the present, and pondering the future.

Henry Gene Foster resides far away from the general population, waiting for the day his prepper skills will prove invaluable. In the meantime, he focuses on helping others discover that history does indeed repeat itself and that it's never too soon to prepare for the worst.

For updates, new release notifications, and more, please visit:

www.jjholdenbooks.com

Made in the USA
Columbia, SC
01 December 2020